The Spell Book of Listen Taylor

Jaclyn Moriarty

The Spell Book of Listen Taylor

YOUNG PICADOR

This edition first published in the UK 2008 by Young Picador
an imprint of Pan Macmillan Limited
20 New Wharf Road, London N1 9RR
Basingstoke and Oxford
Associated companies throughout the world
www.panmacmillan.com

ISBN 978-0-330-44636-5

Originally published in a different form 2004 as *I Have a Bed Made of
Buttermilk Pancakes* in Australia by Pan Macmillan Australia Pty Limited
St Martins Tower, 31 Market Street, Sydney

1 3 5 7 9 8 6 4 2

A CIP catalogue record for this book is available from
the British Library.

Typeset by Intype Libra Limited
Printed and bound in the UK by CPI Mackays, Chatham ME5 8TD

Acknowledgements

I would like to thank the extraordinary people at Macmillan Children's Books, especially Ruth Alltimes, for making the experience of publishing so delightful. Thanks also to Arthur Levine, Anna McFarlane and Cate Paterson, to my agents, Tara Wynne, Jonathan Lloyd and Jill Grinberg, and to my generous readers, Liane Moriarty, Nicola Moriarty, Corrie Stepan and Colin McAdam.

Extract from the Zing Garden Shed

Imagine if you did not have knees!

When you walk downhill your body's natural tendency is to fall forward. Unconsciously, you bend your knees, contracting the quadriceps muscles as you do. The knees prevent you from falling.

Now, imagine if your quadriceps muscles were so weak that they could not stop your knees from bending once they started! If the knees did not stop bending, you would fall flat on your face.

Falls Creek Institute for Arthroscopic Surgery

Part 1

Monday

1

After midnight the apartment waited, still in the moonlight and the heat. A moth touched its wing to the front porch light and the apartment cleared its throat sharply.

Inside was a sleepy confusion of boxes, paint tins, sandpaper, buckets and bananas. A wooden ladder, flat on its stomach, stretched the length of the hallway.

A young woman, perhaps twenty-eight years old, emerged from a bedroom at the end of the hall. She stepped over the rungs of the ladder, one careful rung at a time, and paused at the entrance to the living room. There was a crocus-shaped scar on her forehead.

The moonlight followed, intrigued, as the young woman drifted to the kitchen.

Next, a man stepped into the hallway. He wore boxer shorts and sleepy eyes. He too paused at the living room, but this was to yawn and stretch. The muscles in his arms and his chest seemed perfectly placed for this stretch. He disappeared into the kitchen.

When he emerged his arm was through the elbow of the woman and he was speaking to her gently. 'No, Marbie, there's no green turtle in the kitchen.'

The woman eyed him suspiciously.

'OK?' he said. 'Ready to go back to bed?' But she was looking past his face to the wall on the far side of the room.

'I can*not* believe it,' she murmured. 'Again! How many nights is this?'

'What?' The man looked around uneasily. 'Are you awake?'

'Watch your eyes, Nathaniel. I'll take care of this.' She

marched across the room muttering, 'Little alien starships! Putting your elevator shafts on *our* –' She stopped as she reached the wall and stared at its smooth surface.

'It was just here –' She turned back to Nathaniel, who was waiting patiently.

'Yes?' he prompted.

'Huh.'

'Are you awake now?'

'I was sleepwalking.'

'I know.'

They both stood still in the moonlight.

'It's hot, isn't it?' said the woman after a moment. 'I wonder if we should –'

'It depends on whether Listen is awake,' agreed the man, peering into the hallway.

'Yes.' The woman raised her voice slightly. 'I wonder if she *is* awake?'

'COULD SHE BE AWAKE?' boomed the man.

'I HOPE WE HAVEN'T WOKEN HER!' shouted the woman.

They both paused, hopefully.

A twelve-year-old girl appeared in the hallway, blinking into the darkness.

'Oh no!' cried the woman. 'We didn't wake you, did we, Listen?'

'Hot, isn't it?' said the girl.

'Exactly,' said the man.

A few moments later, all three walked out of the apartment, down the driveway and on to the street. They walked beneath the street lights and the charcoal starry sky, their bare feet silent on the asphalt. The man slapped a mosquito on the woman's shoulder. The girl stubbed her toe, hopped for a few steps and then recovered completely.

Eventually they passed a row of suburban houses, each

with a small front lawn. One particular inoffensive blond-brick house caused all three to crouch and scurry past.

Alongside this house was a hedge, a wrought-iron gate and a sign:

BELLBIRD HIGH SCHOOL
To strive itself is to succeed
Please Close the Gate

The woman looked up and down the street, then nodded to the others. All three climbed over the gate.

On the dark front lawn of the school they began to run. They ran through a courtyard and a car park. They ran across a basketball court and along the stone walls of school buildings. Occasional security lights flickered.

At the back of the school was a sloping lawn, which fell into patches of long grass and tangled bush. A narrow dirt path wound through this bush and ended at a gate which, once again, they climbed.

They stood at the edge of a swimming pool. Across the pool was a bank of wooden benches; alongside the benches, several piles of yellow boards, each stamped in fluorescent white: 'Training Device – Do Not Remove'.

On an easel beside them:

BELLBIRD HIGH SWIMMING POOL RULES
- NO RUNNING
- NO JUMPING
- NO BOMBING
- NO SPLASHING
- *NO SWIMMING* WITHOUT TEACHER SUPERVISION (MEMBERS OF SENIOR SWIM TEAM EXCEPTED)

Without a word, all three dived in.

The woman in the pool was Marbie Zing. The man was her boyfriend, Nathaniel. The twelve-year-old girl, floating on her back and gazing at the stars, was Nathaniel's daughter, Listen. The three of them had just moved in together.

Listen Taylor sat on the floorboards by her bed. Her nightie had dried in the breeze on the walk home, but her hair spilled occasional water drops down her neck.

It was 3 a.m., but she was wide awake and she was thinking about her name. 'Listen Taylor,' she said, and then in its place she tried: '*Listen Zing*'. Only that was a question: *Listen Zing?* Because she was considering: *Am I now a Zing?*

If you and your father move in with a Zing, go shopping with a Zing, paint the walls with a Zing, go swimming in the middle of the night with a Zing, go along with a Zing to Zing Family Secret Meetings each week – do you, eventually, become a Zing yourself?

Maybe.

To be fair, only her dad knew the Zing Family Secret – Marbie had told him a few months ago when they bought the apartment together. So only he went into the garden shed for the Zing Family Secret Meetings. Listen stayed in Grandma Zing's house and watched movies with little Cassie.

Also, and more importantly, the name *Listen* worked better with *Taylor*. The Taylor part relaxed the 'Listen', or gave it an approving tick. 'What's your name?' 'Listen Taylor.' 'Oh. OK. Well, hi.'

'What's your name?' 'Listen Zing.' The stranger, already skating on Listen, would whack her head hard against the Zing. 'It's *what?*'

You had to think about these things when you were about to begin Year 7.

Primary school would start the year today, Monday – the

Zings were excited about Cassie going into Year 2 – but Listen would go to an exclusive private secondary school and it began the year on an exclusive, private day: Wednesday.

In just three days, Listen thought, *it will all be different.*

Of course, it was already different: she and her dad had moved out of the camper van and into an apartment with a Zing.

She sat up to look around at the boxes. It was not possible to open the boxes because they were so well taped you needed scissors or a knife to get in. Meanwhile, the scissors and knives were packaged up inside the boxes.

Listen wondered which box had her new school uniform inside. If they hadn't figured out how to unpack by Wednesday, her dad would have to write a note:

> To *whom it may concern*,
> *We are very sorry but Listen Taylor will not be able to attend Year 7. Her uniform is stuck in a box.*
>
> *Fondly,*
> *Nathaniel Taylor*
> *XXX*

She was smiling sleepily at this idea when she noticed the book. It was sitting on top of a box.

It was a flimsy book, lime green with huge white letters on the cover: SPELL BOOK. It looked like one of those early school workbooks, in which you have to do things like draw diagonal lines between COLD and HOT, or BUSY and CALM. But when she opened the first page of the book, that's not what it was at all.

> *Congratulations! You have found this Spell Book!*
>
> *Hooray for you!*

Listen gave the book a sceptical look and noticed, when she did, way down at the bottom of the page, a disclaimer:

Disclaimer
This Spell Book will only work if you follow the instructions VERY CAREFULLY. For example, you may only turn a page when we say you can. If you skip ahead, it WILL NOT WORK. Right now, you have to put the book under your pillow. You can only turn the page on Wednesday at 5 p.m.

At that moment, Listen jumped because Marbie Zing was knocking on her window. 'Listen?' she called. 'I think I'm asleep. Can you let me in?'

2

Cath Murphy (teacher, Year 2B) stood on the Year 2 balcony, blinking and smiling in the morning sun, her hands in the pockets of her new jeans, her neck feeling warm beneath her short blonde hair.

It was the first day of term, and the children were gathering downstairs.

The new guy, Warren Woodford, was at the other end of the balcony, outside the 2A classroom. He leaned his chin towards the railing and gave Cath a firm little nod: *Yes, there they are, gathering.*

She responded with her own solemn nod.

The new guy was sure to be a hit with the kids. He was very tall, so he would be able to reach up to touch the ceiling, or to tack paintings high on the wall. Also, he could pull down one side of his mouth while raising the opposite eyebrow. Kids think that kind of face, especially when done to tease them, is the essence of grown-up humour.

Cath looked back at Warren and he was making that exact face at her.

It was actually funny, and she surprised herself by imitating him. He smiled softly, looked away and then called something that sounded like: 'From the highlands.'

'Pardon?'

'Aren't the highlands!'

'Yes,' she agreed, tentatively. Then she really wanted to know, so she ran a few steps along the balcony towards him. 'I'm sorry?'

He waved her back. 'I only asked if you were frightened! Are you scared?'

'Of course I am! Aren't you?'

Then she ran back to her spot to wait again, and felt awkward and foolish, but also she felt this: quirky, cocky, small, funny, wicked and extremely blonde.

In fact, she was not really frightened, more excited. But, as her mother liked to say, all meetings with new people, even locksmiths or seven-year-olds, can make you a little afraid.

Cath had been teaching for three years now, and had a reputation among the children as very nice and pretty, can be strict sometimes, but mostly nice.

She was known to be generous with gold stars and SUPER WORK! stamps.

Among teachers she had a reputation as *serene* and *conscientious,* perhaps a little shy, but prone to fits of giggling.

She ate a Granny Smith apple at lunchtime each day, and believed in smiles which continued for 5–3–2-clear! after corridor nods. She had a Mary Poppins glint in her eye, but not the Mary Poppins spots on the cheeks, or the carpetbag.

Now, as the children filed up the stairs, jostled and excited, chatting with each other and at her, she herself chatted back: 'Good morning!' and 'There you go!' and 'Just leave your bag on the bag-rack, that's a good girl!' and 'Oops! It's a bit early in the day to be tripping on your shoelace, isn't it? OK there?'

But she noticed, as she chatted, that the new guy, Warren, was welcoming his class in silence. He was holding one arm high in the air and using the other to wave them into his classroom. He was like a stately policeman. The children, she noticed, were obeying him in wide-eyed wonder.

Later, as she spent the morning playing educational welcoming games (Luke's name begins with the same letter as Lion! Scary!), Cath was conscious of long periods of silence in the classroom next door. The silence was interrupted now and then by storms of laughter.

3

The telephone rang like a rooster that was learning how to crow.

It was Grandma. She was on the walk-around phone. 'Why, it's my Cassie! How's my Cassie?'

She was fine.

'And how was your first day of *second grade* today? Was it exciting?'

A bit.

'And who will be your friends, do you think? Still friends with that Lucinda?'

Yeah.

'You're such a fast runner, aren't you? Will you win all the races at the carnival again this year?'

Probably.

'And what about your new teacher, Cassie? Ms Murphy! Was she nice? Was she nice to you today, sweetheart?'

Uh-huh.

'And were you nice to her?'

Uh-huh.

'And were the other children nice to her too?'

A bit.

'Well now, Cassie, can I talk to your mummy? Is she around?'

Cassie took Grandma down the hall, nestled in her arm like a soft baby duckling, and into her mother's study. Her mother wasn't there. She put the phone on the spare bed and sat at her mum's desk, to read some words from the computer screen.

Then she remembered, collected Grandma and flew her down the hall like a kite without a string. Grandma got bumped against the wall once, and then Cassie saw her mum at the kitchen sink and said: 'Grandma's on the phone.'

'All right,' said her mum, peeling off her washing-up gloves. 'Just put her over there for me.'

Cassie put Grandma down, gently, alongside the teapot and a saucepan lid.

4

Picking up the phone from the kitchen counter, Fancy Zing announced: 'Today, Mum, the sky was *very* blue.'

At which her mother cried, 'Yes! Wasn't it? A beautiful first day of term! Cassie seems excited about second grade, doesn't she? I can't wait to hear more! I bet you had trouble getting her up this morning. She likes her sleep, that Cassie, doesn't she? Now then, as madcap as it sounds, I'm thinking of making a strawberry risotto for dinner.'

They discussed the merits of strawberry risotto, but Fancy found herself drifting to a day at the seaside, years before, when she had scolded a pair of seagulls. The seagulls were stretching their necks to bully one another. 'You *stop* that!' she scolded. 'You be *nice* to each other.' The birds had glanced up at her, startled but also repentant, and she had longed to gather them into her arms and say, 'I'm so sorry for shouting, darlings, but you really *mustn't* fight.'

'And then,' said her mother, 'there's beef stroganoff. It's a good old standby, isn't it?'

'It *is*,' Fancy agreed, 'but I'd better go now, Mum – I think Radcliffe's at the door.'

Radcliffe was Fancy's husband, and just that moment he had called from the front porch: 'Fancy that! My Fancy is at home!' This was his standard greeting from the porch, before he even opened the front door.

'I'm in my study!' called Fancy, and she hurried down the hall from the kitchen to her study and sat down at her desk. She took a notebook from the drawer, and at the top of the page she wrote: *Irritating Things About My Husband*. Then she used a ruler to draw a box.

Her husband leaned through the study door and said, 'Mwah!' which was his way of kissing her hello.

'Hello!' she replied, ruling boxes furiously. He nodded calmly and wandered down the hallway, calling, 'What have you done with Cassie?'

Fancy ignored him and began to write inside the first box.

Irritating Things About My Husband # 1

Well, in the mornings, he has this routine where he shaves at the bathroom sink while I take my shower. He uses a Valerio Close-Shave! which he keeps on a toothpaste-stained holding tray, and every few moments he taps it on the side of the sink.

Tap, tap, tap, and then a little while later: tap, tap, tap. Through the rush of shower water and the snap of my shampoo-bottle cap, I can hear it, the regular tap, tap, tap. Even as I step into my towel (which he hands to me from our heated rack, without looking back from his reflection), even then he taps: tap, tap, tap. Then he turns the water loud to wash his face and to wash the little whiskers down the sink.

The whole thing drives me wild!

She closed that notebook, took up another and wrote the heading: 'Prize-Winning Novel'. It had occurred to her that she might write a prize-winning novel in italics. Italics, she thought, had both gumption and mystique. Also, a particular italicized sentence was floating around in her mind these days:

How is your ocean bream, my love?

She was not sure what she meant by this sentence, but

16

found it very moving. It would presumably be spoken in a restaurant.

She sent a text message to her sister, Marbie. 'HOW IS YOUR OCEAN BREAM, MY LOVE?' Just to see what Marbie would say.

Then she returned to the first notebook and ruled another box.

5

Marbie was taking the train home from work when her sister's text message arrived. 'A little overcooked,' she texted back. 'On the flaky side.'

Like her sister, Marbie had a sentence in italics floating in her head these days. Her sentence was this:

It was a decision she would regret for the rest of her life.

Because she was so excited by her good luck in meeting Nathaniel and his lovely daughter Listen, she feared she would take one tiny wrong step and lose them.

For example: let's say she opens her wardrobe and sees her short blue dress hanging alongside her long floral skirt. Which one should she wear? Hurriedly, she chooses the long skirt. *It was a decision she would regret for the rest of her life* – because later! On her way to work? The skirt gets tangled in her sandals and trips her up! And she breaks her ankle! And she has to go to hospital! And Nathaniel comes to visit with flowers, and the nurse says to Nathaniel, 'What lovely daffodils,' and he says, 'Actually, they're tulips,' and then their eyes meet, and they *fall in love, and Nathaniel and Listen leave Marbie for the nurse!!*

Part 2

Tuesday to Friday

6

Tuesday, Listen went to her friend Donna Turnbull's place for a strategy meeting.

'IMHO,' said Gabrielle, 'we don't need a strategy meeting. We just turn up at the school tomorrow and it happens. Twenty-seven, twenty-eight, do you want me to keep going?' She was counting the freckles on Joanne's back.

'Keep going,' Joanne commanded. 'I need to know the truth.'

'There's a lot,' Caro said. 'Do you need more truth than that?'

'You think you can go to Clareville College and just live?' Donna was withering. 'Power up your brain cells, I don't *think* so. Listen, would you stop dancing for one second in your life?'

Listen and Sia were sharing Sia's iPod, and they were both dancing. They stopped and looked at Donna. Listen hitched up her jeans. The jeans were too long and the right cuff had slipped into her sneaker and was caught under her foot.

'There's going to be a fundamental shift in the universe when we get to Clareville,' Donna explained. 'That's why we need to have a strategy.'

'Hey, Listen,' said Gabrielle, bored of counting freckles. 'Give me your jeans and I'll get my mum to take them up for you.'

'Yeah, you don't fold them like that,' Sia explained. She glanced at Gabrielle. 'We should have taken them up for her before we gave them to her for her birthday.'

'Shut up about Listen's stupid jeans,' pleaded Donna. 'My

cousin was, like, in meltdown the whole first year she was at Clareville. Why? Because of the shock of the things that transpired. We can*not* let that happen to us? OK? We cannot.'

The others stopped talking to each other and turned to Donna.

'What transpired?' Joanne said. 'For your cousin?'

'Well, for a start,' said Donna. But she couldn't really remember. Only, for instance, her cousin had said that you didn't play games at lunchtimes any more like you did at primary school. You sat in a circle and you talked.

'Oh my God,' said Gabrielle. 'We'd better practise that. Does anybody know what a circle is?'

'What is this other word you use?' Joanne sat up looking mystical. 'This word. How do you say it? "*Talk*." What can it mean?'

They all laughed until they saw that Donna was crying.

So they took turns comforting her, apologized for disrespect and agreed to an eternal pact. They would stay friends forever, no matter what transpired.

Wednesday was a strange, shiny, sharp-edged first day of school.

When she got home, Listen opened the fridge door but all she could see was the gap between the teeth of the Clareville College principal, a loose red thread in the seam of Sia's shoe and the jar of pickled snakes in Science Lab B11.

These images loomed up at her from a ketchup bottle in the refrigerator door, each one swimming straight towards her nose and bouncing back.

It was strangely exhausting. She sat down at the table to rest.

At assembly that morning, the Principal had welcomed them to Clareville by explaining that they would not see their next birthdays if they ever knocked on the upper staffroom door between 1 and 1.35.

At lunchtime, Gabrielle said she was going to sit the Principal down and talk her through the concept of 'welcome'. Joanne laughed about how strict the teachers were acting to make a first impression (it was so transparent). Caro could not *believe* they sold pecan pies in the tuck shop. Sia worried there was something wrong with the seams of her new school shoes. And Donna went through everybody's timetables to figure out which classes they had together, then lectured them all on the importance of eternal pacts.

In Science that afternoon the teacher breathed loudly through his nose and said, 'Let me give you the key to survival at Clareville. It's not in the mysteries of Science Lab B11, much as the beakers and Bunsen burners might intrigue you! No. It's doing two hours of homework *every single day*.'

'What say there's a day when we *get* no homework?' Caro asked, shrewdly.

'Wonderful point!' said the teacher. 'If there's ever such a day, give me a call and I'll let you take your pick of pickled snakes.'

Caro missed the point and said she didn't want a pickled snake.

Now Listen looked at her backpack and thought about doing some homework. Instead, she watched TV until her dad phoned from the Banana Bar to ask about her day. She watched TV again until Marbie phoned from the insurance company where she worked, also to ask about her day.

'Hey,' Listen said, after they had philosophized about fundamental shifts in the universe for a while, 'what time is it, Marbie?'

'It's five! It's the end of the day!'

'Gotta go,' said Listen. 'Gotta go do something.' And she hung up the phone.

Hooray for you! You waited until 5 p.m. on Wednesday! You can clearly follow rules, and that's just what you need to be able to do, because otherwise this Spell Book won't work!

Here are the rules:
1. You have to do *every single* Spell in the book, one at a time. You can't skip ahead!
2. Usually you won't even know if a Spell has worked or not! But *never mind*! Trust us! It *has*.

You can turn the page now.

OK!
Now put the Spell Book back underneath your pillow *and DON'T GET IT OUT AGAIN until 4 p.m. this FRIDAY.*
YOU WILL THEN BE ABLE TO DO THE FIRST SPELL!!!

(Note: take great care not to say the word 'walnut' from now until then.)

Thursday, Listen searched through her drawers until she found the postcard her mother had sent her from Istanbul. She sat on her bedroom floor curling the postcard in her fist.

She was thinking about her English teacher at Clareville. At first, Listen had liked him because he wore a Mayor McCheese T-shirt and faded jeans, but then the teacher had said: 'Look, girls, now that you're in high school, you're not big fish in a little pond any more, are you? No! You're *small* fish in a *big* pond!'

Immediately, Listen stopped liking him.

For a start, two other teachers had already said the same thing. An English teacher should be more original.

For another thing, the image made Listen think that last year she and her friends had been bumping around in shallow water, eating all the fish food, blocking out the sunlight, crowding out the pond and accidentally knocking little fish in all directions with their enormous, clumsy tails.

'Hey there, kid,' her mother's postcard said. 'Aren't you starting high school this year?!!! Watch out for all the big fish!!!!!!' The postcard had arrived two years before. Her mother had always been vague about things like Listen's age.

Listen flicked the postcard with her thumbnail a few times, then dropped it back into the drawer.

Friday, after school, Listen opened the Spell Book.

HELLO AGAIN! YOU DID IT! IT'S 4 p.m. ON FRIDAY!
You can go ahead and do the First Spell now. The First Spell is simple. You probably already know this one, but you still have to do it, I'm afraid. You know what I'm talking about?

The Spell To Make Someone Decide To Take A Taxi. Of course! That old favourite. You know the drill. Take two lemons and cut them in half. Take five bananas and peel them. Fill up the bathtub with lukewarm water, toss in your lemons and banana peels. WAIT UNTIL 5 O'CLOCK AND THEN say the magic words – 'Bob's your uncle' – and *Bob's your uncle*! The Spell is done.

Now put the Spell Book back under your pillow. Don't turn the page until the Thursday after next!

7

Tuesday, Cath got a chance to talk to her friends Lenny D'Souza (teacher, Year 6B and school counsellor) and Suzanne Barker (teacher, Year 1A). This was at recess.

Cath told them that, at the start of the summer holiday, she had broken up with her boyfriend from last year. Lenny and Suzanne said 'Oh' sadly, but Cath just laughed and said she couldn't even remember his name. Suzanne reminded her what the name was. 'Thanks,' said Cath.

'I never thought he was right for you,' Suzanne offered. 'You didn't have the aura of someone *truly loved*.'

'Thanks,' said Cath again.

Lenny told them she had been out to dinner with, guess who? And Cath said 'Who?' and Lenny said 'Guess,' etc. Then Lenny admitted it was *Frank Billson* (School Principal).

Cath and Suzanne shrieked and, when Lenny ran to get her sandwich, they lowered their heads and said 'Oh my *God,*' and raised their eyebrows: '*What is she thinking?*' Lenny came back and they straightened their faces and shoulders again.

Lenny asked Cath what the new guy, Warren Woodford, was like, and Cath was about to reply, but Suzanne interrupted to say she'd heard he studied *acting* before teaching.

And Cath found herself thinking: *Actually, Suzanne, the new guy belongs to ME.*

Because *she* was the other Year 2 teacher.

On Wednesday, arriving home late after a meeting, and tossing her keys on to the table, Cath caught a glimpse of her busy, thoughtful face reflected in the dining-room window. She paused to consider the face. 'You wouldn't know,' she said to the window, 'that my heart was broken not so long ago.'

The heart had been broken by last year's boyfriend, despite what she'd said to Lenny and Suzanne. He had left her for a job in New Orleans. He brought the job to her place one evening; it was in a small, white envelope, and was very enthusiastic about the boyfriend's environmental science degree. 'When do you leave?' she asked, making her voice as amazed as his was. 'Next week!' 'And how long is it for?' '*Indefinite!*'

He only seemed to remember her at the airport. By then, of course, it was too late. His luggage was checked in.

Could he really have broken your heart? said Cath's reflection, sceptically. But then she thought of the nights after he left, how she cried herself to sleep in her empty apartment, kicked the telephone across the room, mistreated the flowers that he sent from New Orleans (she left them to die in their wrapping), cut her hair short and enrolled in a part-time law degree. Whether or not he was worth it, he had certainly broken her heart. (He had added a '*Cheer up!*' note to his flowers from New Orleans.)

'But now,' she announced to her cat, Violin, as he twirled between her ankles, 'I am recovered!' The bell on Violin's collar tinkled faintly.

She gazed at herself in the window, thinking of how good it was to be single. Just last night, for example, she had made chocolate-chip cookies at midnight, to celebrate the start of the school year! And tonight, she planned to watch *MTV* for as long as she liked. (Most boyfriends get restless and want to try the cricket instead.)

Lovely!

And plus, said the tiny, secret voice at the back of her mind, *I am sure to get a new boyfriend now that I feel this way! Whenever I get to the stage of happy, independent singlehood, THAT'S when I meet a new boy! It makes me ATTRACTIVE, being happy with JUST ME. I'm about to –*

'HUSH,' she said firmly, and turned away from her reflection. Then she found that she was jittery and had to take a walk to the corner store.

On Thursday, Cath thought: *I like being single!* as she walked around the classroom, complimenting children on the pompoms they were making. *I'm going to study law part-time!* Some of the children smiled back at her. Then one of them said, 'Toilet brush, toilet brush, toilet brush.'

What was that child's name? Her name tag was on the floor.

'CASSIE KEEPS SAYING TOILET BRUSH!' shouted Marcus Ellison.

Cassie. That was it. Cassie Zing. She was that little sprinter who broke records at the athletics carnival last year. On the other hand, she had been five minutes late for school that morning. Her mother had written an apology note, which was polite of her. *In return,* thought Cath sternly, *I should remember her daughter's name!*

But, to be fair, Cassie Zing's name tag was rarely on display because she made dramatic speeches, waving her arms for emphasis and sweeping pencils and name tags to the floor.

'Toilet brush,' declared Cassie.

'That's enough, Cassie,' Cath said firmly.

Cassie looked up in surprise. 'But I have to say it five hundred times!'

'Who said you have to?'

'I did.'

'Well then, tell yourself you don't have to.'

'OK.' She nodded, and went back to her pompom.

Friday, Cath sat on a wooden bench, waiting for Warren Woodford. They were going to have a Year 2 curriculum meeting, but Cath had playground duty. So they would have it outside in the sun. She was swinging her leg to play her secret game in which she imagined she could lever herself up into the sky. She'd had a skiing accident as a teenager, and they used metal joints to reconstruct her knee. Since then, she had thought of the knee as a magical levering-hoist.

As she levered, she called 'Hey there!' crossly, to a boy who dumped a salad sandwich in the trash, 'Ho there!' sternly, to a girl who pinched another girl's nose, and 'Hey *now*,' lovingly, to a boy who approached to show a grazed elbow. Once she had dealt with the elbow, she leaned back to get the big picture (mainly games of elastics today and loud conversations about a new computer pet called *Mr Valerio*, which you fed by remote control), and to think. *It's great being single!* is what she thought. But something was bothering her, and she stopped swinging her leg to confront what it was.

That's what it was. The one thing she liked about having a boyfriend: *the relaxed atmosphere when you meet a new boy.* In conversations with boys who might become friends, Cath liked to joke around a bit, maybe even flirt, but she had found that boys grew wary and found a way to mention *my girlfriend*. This left Cath feeling irritated, put in her place, and wanting to explain: *I'm not making a move, I'm just making friends.*

It was much better when she had a boyfriend herself, so she could respond with *my boyfriend*, to redress the imbalance and get on with it. Or even better, say *my boyfriend* first.

'White, no sugar, yes?'

Warren Woodford's voice was behind her, and when she turned around it was not just his voice, it was him. His left arm was pinning a bundle of folders awkwardly to his side, and his right hand stretched to hold two mugs of coffee, long fingers looped around the handles. He was staring ferociously at the coffee mugs, as if that would keep them from spilling.

He has noticed how I take my coffee! Or maybe that's how people take their coffee, as a rule.

She helped him to sort out the papers and mugs, then he straddled the bench, and now it was strange, because she was facing forward, while *he* was looking at her shoulder. Like a set-up for a photo shoot. Or like he was riding a horse the regular way, and she was riding it side-saddle. His nose was quite long, and his mouth was a bit big for his chin.

'I hear you're studying law?' he said, as if he didn't care that his mouth was too big for his chin.

He has heard things about me!

'Not yet,' Cath explained. 'I only just enrolled. The classes start next week.'

'Huh.' He nodded to himself, as if this was just as he'd imagined. 'Why would you do that? Study law, I mean?'

'Something to do.' Cath shrugged.

'*Something to do,*' he repeated slowly. And then, in a chant: 'Something to do; someone to sue; somewhere to queue. Hmm. Queue. Forgive me.'

He put down the mug and said, 'This is terrible coffee. And another thing, I don't know if I'm going to be able to work with the Principal here. What's his name? Billson. He seems a bit, I don't know, slow?'

'I think,' said Cath, 'that he is brilliant.'

'Well, *brilliant,* yes, of course. Frank Billson, eh? A remarkable man.' He took a thoughtful sip from his coffee: 'And this is *excellent* coffee.'

So far, in five days of school, and three brief chats on the Year 2 balcony, Warren had not said *my girlfriend* once. Cath appreciated that. Either Warren did not have a girlfriend, or he did not see the need to mention her. Either way, it was respectful of him.

Cath liked being single, but she wanted to make friends with this man, this Warren Wishful Woodford. (His eyes had a wistful, wishful look.) She wanted to make friends and, to do that, she might have to flirt.

8

Tuesday morning, Fancy Zing dropped Cassie at school and came back to the smug, empty house. She sat at her desk with tea and honey-on-a-crumpet.

Irritating Things About My Husband # 2

When it's just the two of us, in bed, he talks in this low, husky voice, which is nothing like his own. More like somebody hiding in the pantry and phoning the police while a robbery takes place.

He uses the voice to say things like You've still got it, baby, which is acceptable, though not to my taste. But he also uses it for ordinary things, such as: Don't answer the phone, they'll leave a message. Gotta put the garbage out later. Remind me?

I am always clearing my throat at these times to indicate that he should clear his.

At fourteen, Fancy had worked part-time in a hardware store and she still remembered fondly the counting out of change.

'Twenty dollars? Thanks. So, that's eleven, that's thirteen, that's fifteen, and *that's* twenty. Would you like a bag with that?'

No thanks, the men always said. But sometimes she gave them no choice, putting their screwdrivers straight into plastic bags. They never used the handles when she did that, but grabbed the bag around the neck as if it was a hen.

Now she wrote wilderness romances: stories set in remote

locations such as the Guinean forests of Sierra Leone, or the shopping malls of South Dakota. The challenge was getting enough characters out there in the wilds to participate in the romance.

She was was making a start on a prize-winning novel, though she didn't know what about yet.

Wednesday night, Cassie found her parents in the TV room. She had just had a bath and was wearing her summer pyjamas.

'Here's trouble!' This is what her dad said whenever Cassie walked into the room. Or even if she'd just gone to the bathroom at a restaurant and was coming back to the table. 'Here's trouble!'

Where? Where was trouble?

What did her father mean?

Cassie sat on the carpet by the couch and crossed her legs so they'd forget that she was there.

Her mum had the remote control and was zipping through some recorded ads. Now she was zipping through the actual show. Did she mean to do that? She missed the end credits and zipped through a whole new programme. Cassie sat quietly, pretending that nothing strange was happening.

'Well!' said her mum, finally noticing Cassie and pressing STOP on the remote.

'No!' cried Cassie. 'Don't say "Well!" like that! I don't like it when you say it that way!'

'How would you like me to say it?' asked Mum. 'Well? Well? Well!!' She tried out different pronunciations. 'You choose, Cass.'

'I don't want you to say it at all. It means you want me to go to bed.'

'Oh ho!' Her dad leaned forward on the couch. 'Casso has clinophobia, has she?'

'What?'

He grinned at her. She stared back. Then she turned to her mum and explained: 'Just say "well" in a way that doesn't sound so happy, OK?'

'All right, darling, say goodnight to your father.'

'My little clinophobic!' Her dad held out his arms for a hug.

'It's a fear of going to bed,' Radcliffe confided later, leaning into Fancy's study. 'Clinophobia? A fear of going to bed.'

'I'm trying to work, Radcliffe,' Fancy said coldly.

Irritating Things About My Husband # 3

His family once owned a dog, a Rhodesian Ridgeback, whom they named Fancy, which is my name, and he cannot leave that coincidence alone.

Thursday morning, Fancy felt that there could be nothing wrong with driving your daughter to school in your pyjamas. Also, nothing wrong with jumping out of the car on the way in your pyjamas to dump two garbage bags of second-hand clothes into the St Vincent de Paul blue bin. Nothing wrong with that at all!

Except that the man next door was having breakfast on his porch as she emerged in her pyjamas, shouting, 'CASSIE! GET A MOVE ON! WE ARE *VERY, VERY* LATE,' spilling worn-out clothes from two garbage bags that were hopelessly clutched under her arms.

He was one of those dull Canadians, the man next door, the kind who speak slowly and with a mild, polite amusement about everything.

'Got your hands full there,' he declared from his porch, with his knife and fork poised over his bacon, and that little smirk of his. Their houses were very close.

'Yes!' Fancy agreed, and then she had to pause, for the sake of politeness, before shouting at Cassie again.

The neighbour returned to his bacon and pancakes and Cassie emerged from the hallway with a comb and scrunchie hanging from her mouth, the car keys looped around her finger, her hair falling into her face, dragging an enormous garbage bag behind her.

'What on *earth* are you – Cassie, darling, that's the bag of books! We're not bringing that one.'

Cassie took the comb and scrunchie from her mouth. 'Why not?'

'Darling, we're giving that one to the school fete, not to St Vincent de Paul. But *thank* you, that must have been *very* heavy on the stairs.'

Cassie raised her eyebrows and turned to drag the bag back inside.

'No!' Fancy panicked. 'Just leave it by the door there. No need to take it back upstairs.'

'OK.'

'Have you got your lunch?'

'What is it?'

'It's peanut butter. On the second shelf of the fridge; run back in and get it, quick.'

'*Peanut butter!*' shouted Cassie and stamped her foot. She had loved peanut butter yesterday, but sometimes her taste took an unexpected swerve.

'In Newfoundland,' said the Canadian from his porch, 'the kids swap lobster sandwiches for peanut butter.'

Cassie stared at him.

'Gosh!' Fancy said, politely.

'That's how common lobster is,' confirmed the Canadian, 'in Newfoundland.'

'Cassie,' Fancy said after an agonizing pause for politeness, 'quick, honey, go and get your lunch.'

*

The news was starting its triumphant drumbeat as they pulled into the bus zone at Cassie's school. 'Toilet brush, toilet brush, toilet brush,' said Cassie, counting on her fingers. She pointed at the radio. 'The news is on.'

'Here.' Fancy craned into the rear-view mirror and brushed Cassie's hair behind her ears. 'Pass me the pen from the glove box. I think I'd better write you a note.'

> Dear Ms Murphy,
> Please excuse my daughter, Cassie Zing-Mereweather (better known as Cassie Zing - her choice!), for being late today.
>   I had to take some second-hand clothes to St Vincent de Paul.
>
> Yours sincerely and VERY best wishes,
> Fancy Zing

Friday night, Radcliffe and Fancy drove to Fancy's parents' place for a Zing Family Secret Meeting. Cassie was in the back seat with the first week of Year 2 piled around her.

'They are going to be *amazed* about this, aren't they, Mum?'

She leaned forward in her middle seatbelt and waved a butterfly painting around in front of them, blocking Radcliffe's view of the road for a moment.

'They sure are!' agreed Fancy.

'For Christ's sakes!' snapped Radcliffe, at the same time. This threw Cassie back into her seatbelt for a moment. Then she recovered. 'First I'm going to show my Arithmetic book with the gold star, *then* my painting and – no, *wait* –'

'We must be just about due to have the Samsons and Bellamys for dinner, eh?' Radcliffe said to Fancy, tapping on the steering wheel. He had the habit of talking over Cassie when he found her boring.

'Yes,' she agreed. 'But Cassie's birthday's coming up in a few weeks.'

'Well then, sixth, I'm going to sing and – did you say something about my birthday, Mum?'

'Hey Cass-kid.' Radcliffe glanced in the rear-view mirror at Cassie. 'Let's hope you don't suffer from alektorophobia, eh?'

There was silence from the back seat for a moment. 'Pardon?'

'Alektorophobia.'

'Is it something for my birthday?'

Radcliffe chuckled. He pulled up at a red light, and Cassie sat quietly, waiting.

'It's a fear of chickens,' Radcliffe explained to Fancy, in a low voice. 'Alektorophobia. A fear of chickens. We'll probably have roast chicken for dinner tonight, eh?'

'Well, tell Cassie then! Cassie, don't worry about Dad, OK? He's being silly.'

'Leave it,' said Radcliffe, accelerating off as the light turned green. 'This is how she learns.'

'Learns what?'

'Electra,' murmured Cassie from the back seat. 'Alektro? Electro.'

Radcliffe turned on the radio.

9

Tuesday, running late for work, Marbie Zing chose her long floral skirt (*it was a decision she would regret for the rest of her life*) and then, with a shiver, replaced it and picked the blue dress.

'Nathaniel,' she said, waking him with a kiss on his bare shoulder, 'what would you think of a woman who didn't know the difference between daffodils and tulips?'

Nathaniel opened his eyes and said: '*There is no such woman.*'

Marbie worked in car insurance and, along with her colleagues, played car crash on the edge of her desk. Second party car enters roundabout *here*, third party car is reversing *here*, family of elephants distracts attention *here* (these doughnuts are the family of elephants), *our* car heads straight through the middle and boom!

Little plastic people went zipping through the air.

Wednesday, running late for work, Marbie tripped out of her high heel. A bicycle courier held the lift door open while she reached a stockinged foot back to collect it.

Marbie had always been a slippery kind of person. In restaurants, serviettes slid from her lap to the floor. Hairclips never stayed in her hair; they slipped to her shoulders where they perched like silver butterflies. And her shoes were always falling from her feet. (It was because of this that she was first (aged six and a quarter) stung, on her toe, by a bee. 'You ran right out of your sandals,' scolded her mother, who was always cranky when they hurt themselves.

Today, however, she was slippery because she was distracted: it was Listen's first day at Clareville College. 'She's too small for that school,' Marbie had said to Nathaniel last year. 'Send her somewhere nice and little like Bellbird High.'

Nathaniel had pointed out that Listen was an average size. Also, that her friends from primary, Donna Turnbull and the others, would take care of her at Clareville; also, that the only thing Listen's mother ever did for her, besides sending a postcard or two, was set up an education trust fund. It was important that he spend every cent.

But Nathaniel was older than Marbie and seemed to have forgotten school. She herself remembered high school as a cacophony of shrieking bells and thudding teachers' voices. All day she was distracted by images of Listen quietly dissolving in the noise. Papers drifted out of Marbie's hands, and ink slipped from pens and stained her fingers.

She phoned Listen at home as soon as she could, to ask about her first day, and was strangely relieved to hear that the girl still had a voice.

Thursday morning, running late for work, Marbie almost stepped into the path of a lorry. A passer-by shouted a warning just in time.

She phoned Nathaniel at the Banana Bar, to tell him about it. She liked to phone Nathaniel at work, especially when he was busy, surrounded by customers. It was then that his voice took on the edge that it had when she first met him.

Actually, when she first met him, his voice had been jocular, like someone playing tennis. They had met in a hotel lift in Melbourne and had spent the next few days drinking coffee together, while Listen danced around their table.

It was not until they were all back home in Sydney that he began to telephone.

He carved off an edge of his voice for the phone calls, making it cool and restrained, which caused her to press her forehead to the wall, hushing even her breath so she could hear.

'Are you there?' he would say, in his nonchalant voice.

'Uh-huh.' And then she would fall silent at once so that his voice would go on in that way.

Friday, Marbie met the aeronautical engineer.

Tabitha (Marbie's supervisor) had arranged for him to visit, to demonstrate the tendencies of airborne cars.

Everyone was buoyant that day, saying cheerful things with tilted heads. The aeronautical engineer arrived with a swinging paisley tie and purple shirt, and right away he recognized the mood. He put both hands to his head and said: 'To begin. The aeroplane!' Then he asked for a page from Marbie's notepad and showed them how to make a paper plane.

They spent the afternoon making paper planes, paper fans or paper swans, and drinking all the wine from the boardroom fridge, while the aeronautical engineer wandered around with his hands behind his back. Then he took out a handful of toy cars and they threw them at each other for a while.

At four o'clock, everyone decided they had done enough work, and they invited the aeronautical engineer to join them at the Night Owl Pub. He had a meeting, he said, and would only have time for a quick drink. But first he had to run and move his car.

Marbie phoned Nathaniel at the Banana Bar to tell him she was going for drinks but would be back in time for the Zing Family Secret Meeting.

'Don't get hit by a lorry on your way,' instructed Nathaniel.

'Where's Listen?'

'Well,' said Nathaniel, 'I suppose she'd be at home.'

At the Night Owl Pub they were depressed because the aeronautical engineer had not shown up. They had made aeroplanes out of beer-damp coasters and wanted to show him. And now Tabitha and Toni had to go to their step class, and Abi and Rhamie had their husbands waiting, so Marbie said goodbye, and she would just stay and finish her beer and take care of their coaster aeroplanes, and then she'd go home.

'You've all gone home!' It was the aeronautical engineer. Standing beside her in the Night Owl Pub.

'Have *I* gone home?' said Marbie, rhetorically.

'May I?'

He was carrying a beer and tilting his chin at the seat opposite.

'Of course.'

He sat down and nodded to himself, as if agreeing with a thought.

'My car got towed,' he said sadly. 'That's why I was late. So now I'll have to take the train to my meeting. And look at this, I've missed everybody.'

He looked around sadly at the empty beer glasses and soggy aeroplanes.

'Am I not *somebody*?' said Marbie.

'What time is it?' he asked.

'Five o'clock.'

'So late!' cried the aeronautical engineer. 'I've got to *run*!'

But he moved his chair closer, and smiled.

Part 3

Friday Night

10

Listen peered out of the kitchen window. She had turned off the light so she could see into the moon-splashed yard: a sagging trampoline, a tangled hose, crouching trees, a vegetable patch and, hulking down by the far back fence, the Zing Family Garden Shed.

Cassie was asleep on the couch in the living room, but the rest of the Zings were hidden in that shed, and Listen was trying to see through its walls.

Today, Listen had walked to the art rooms with Donna, where they separated for their different classes. 'See you,' Donna had said, and then stared at Listen hard. Listen had had the curious feeling that Donna wanted something from her. Maybe she was upset that they were in different groups for Visual Arts? Maybe she needed more reassurance about the eternal pact? To be honest, Listen was getting a bit tired of Donna's obsession with that pact. *Get over it,* she almost said. *Nobody's going to break the pact.* But she only smiled in a compassionate way and went to her own art group.

Then, after school, she had done the First Spell in the Spell Book: a *Spell To Make Somebody Decide To Take a Taxi.*

Exactly why she had done that spell (or why anyone would ever need such a spell) was a mystery to her. Somehow, the imperious tone of the book had made her do it. Or the fact that she had waited obediently before turning pages.

She'd only just cleared the remains of the spell (lemons and banana peels) from the bathtub when her dad arrived home and took her to Grandpa and Grandma Zing's for the

Friday-night dinner and meeting. Marbie met them there. She always came straight from work and that night she had arrived late.

They had started the night in the kitchen. Gravy simmered in a saucepan on the stove; the chicken glowed golden in the oven. Grandma Zing had leaned against the bench, drinking ginger ale through a curly straw. Grandpa Zing had shown Listen's dad how flexible his knees were, bending low and looking up in triumph. Listen's dad had been impressed. Marbie and her sister, Fancy, had been sitting side by side on the edge of the table, their legs swinging in time to their chat. Fancy's husband, Radcliffe, had been standing where Listen was now, gazing out into the backyard and shifting his jaw from side to side to make it click. Little Cassie Zing had tipped the contents of her school satchel on to the floor.

The Zings had asked Cassie a hailstorm of questions about her first week of Year 2: whether there were any new kids (three, but all boys), exactly what she had learned that week (alphabetical order and how to make a pompom), details about her teacher (Ms Murphy: she was nice). They had asked just as many questions about Listen's first week of Year 7. She wondered if they were good actors. Could they really be as interested in her as they were in Cassie? She was not a Zing, so how could they be? But they seemed enthusiastic about everything she told them and, when she mentioned her school's Walkathon next week, most of them offered to sponsor her.

Of course, she didn't tell the Zings about the beseeching look on Donna's face when they arrived at the art rooms today.

Eating dinner with the Zings that night, Listen had concentrated hard. She was very interested in how families worked. She had grown up with her dad in a camper van parked out the back of the Banana Bar, and they had spent their nights mopping the shop floor, or lying in their bunk beds reading books to each other, or sitting at the fold-out table outside, Listen doing her homework while her dad used an oversized calculator for his accounts. She knew that this was all irregular and had always watched carefully when visiting friends to find out the truth about families. But the Zings seemed like the *ultimate* family, and she got to see them every Friday night now so she could observe them closely over time.

Also, this was the first family ever to include her as one of them.

So she stared at the Zings in the same way you might stare at the stars on a clear, cold night in the country and think to yourself: 'Look at them all! Who knew there were so many and so bright? Now, at last, I'll see the constellations!' But you can't see the constellations because they're tangled in the excess of stars. (And you don't really know what they look like anyway.)

That night, the family had told stories about a tennis ball that fell on to the roof of a car; about a bird that landed on a fence, tipped backwards, then swivelled itself upright again, an embarrassed look (Fancy assured them) on its face; about how strong the coffee was at the Muffin Break these days; about the school kids at Bellbird High next door (Listen looked sideways at Marbie when they talked about Bellbird, but Marbie's face stayed engaged in general chat); about the value of marshmallows; about reality TV, macrobiotic food, lemon trees, ants and the future of photo albums.

Some of the stories were extremely dull. Grandma Zing tended to repeat the last phrases of these stories in a voice heavy with amazement, and Listen wondered if she did this to liven up the story or to emphasize just how dull it was.

Listen's eyes flew from Zing to Zing but there was an excess of conversation and no constellations became clear.

Then, at dessert time, while she was spooning cream on to her cherry pie, she heard Radcliffe say, quite distinctly, to Fancy, 'It's getting on a bit. Shouldn't we head out to the shed?'

She thought of all the secrets in the room. Her own small secret (a Spell Book underneath her pillow at home), the secret she shared with Marbie and her dad (midnight swims in the Bellbird High pool) and, like a great tarpaulin draped across the room, the Zing Family Secret itself.

Those were just the secrets she knew about too. She looked at Fancy Zing, who was ignoring her husband and murmuring with disbelief that her glasses were lost again. ('Look on the piano,' Marbie instructed. 'Whenever I lose anything here it turns up on top of the piano, and *I don't even play!*' Meanwhile, Cassie was crawling around under the table in search of the missing glasses.) Fancy, Listen noticed, had a long, elegant neck which made her seem calm and poised, but she also had flighty, nervous hands. She wore almost-invisible rimless glasses, which she was always losing. No wonder, since they were almost invisible. And she had a way of gazing at her daughter, an astonished expression on her face (especially when Cassie found her glasses for her), which Listen guessed must be the way mothers gaze at daughters.

Also, there were surprising dimples at the edges of Fancy's smile, and Listen suspected that the dimples were full of little secrets.

Maybe, she thought now in the darkened kitchen, leaning her forehead against the window glass, maybe family secrets were a sort of constellation? And now that she had a secret of her own, she herself was linked to the Zing Family Secret constellation?

Something occurred to her: maybe *all* regular families had family secrets? All these years, her friends' families might have been meeting in their garden sheds on Friday nights, and *Listen had never noticed*. Could she have missed something like that? It was possible. She had missed the fact that people got things dry-cleaned, and had once asked Sia what a dry-cleaner was. It could even be that her friends knew each *other's* family secrets, forming a separate constellation among themselves, to which she could never belong.

Maybe that's what Donna wanted from her? A secret.

She could tell her about the Spell Book, but wouldn't Donna say, 'Bring it in so we all get to do the spells'?

Or more likely: 'Yeah, like I really believe in *spell books*. Power up your brain cells, I don't *think so.*'

Well.

She could tell Donna about the Zing Family Secret.

But first she'd have to find out what it was.

The backyard was still and silent. The shed walls were dark and unblinking. A warm breath was touching her arm.

Cassie, in pyjamas, was beside her. 'You can't see into the shed,' Cassie told her through a yawn. 'I've tried, but there aren't any windows.'

Part 4

The First Few Weeks of Term

11

In the early light of a birthday once when she was small, Cath Murphy woke to the shapes of presents huddled by her bed. One was a short-fat-barrel-shaped present, wrapped in bright pink paper.

I know what that is. She sat up from her pillow with a whisk of excitement. *That's a pair of rollerblades!*

Only rollerblades would come in short-fat-barrel-shaped presents like that. Under the pink wrapping there would be a silver barrel. She would prise the lid open with her fingers and inside, wrapped in bubble-paper: sleek, black rollerblades.

Cath had never tried rollerblading before, so she lay in bed thinking about how she could learn.

Opening her presents on the veranda that morning, Cath saved the rollerblades until last. Her father ate his bran flakes, and her mother peeled an orange, wiping her sticky hands now and then on a roll of paper towel. They watched while Cath opened each present until there was nothing but the rollerblades left. All the time, she had been tempering her reactions, conserving energy for this particular gift. Now she regarded its pink wrapping. What would she do when she saw the rollerblades? She would let out a high-pitched squeal, shout: 'NO WAY!', jump to her feet and give both parents a high five. That should do it.

She felt intensely nervous as she opened the wrapping. Then the paper fell away.

It was not rollerblades. It was not even a silver barrel.

It was a waste-paper basket. There were plastic butterflies sewn into the straw.

Cath held the basket for a moment. It was shaped like a barrel.

'Butterflies,' she whispered. She had one of those moments of dissociation: *Can this be happening? Am I really here? Is it a dream?*

Then she rallied: 'Butterflies! Hey, Mummy, you know how I've got birds on my curtains? You know what's going to happen? The birds are going to fly off the curtains and play with the butterflies on my new basket!'

Her parents laughed happily.

Cath joined them at the table, feeling shaky at the knees. 'OK there?' said her father. 'You look kind of white.'

Her mother explained that it was just the excitement.

Cath sat quietly, feeling strange and wise. She had been tested. She had passed. For here was an important lesson in life, and one she had never suspected: *Sometimes you get a bad surprise, but you have to act calm and un-amazed.*

The first few weeks of the school year seemed to Cath to be stage-lit. She was always shading her eyes from the sun, blending her squint into a smile. Often she threw back her head in laughter, or tilted her chin as if struck by an inspired thought. She smiled warmly or ironically at children, and she told quick, quirky stories to Lenny and Suzanne, who obliged her by shrieking, 'Cath! Cut it *out!*'

While they hooted – or while she shaded her eyes or tilted her chin, opened her car door or adjusted her rear-vision mirror – Cath would glance around quickly and, sometimes, there he would be: Warren Woodford.

Watching her.

He often had a single eyebrow raised.

In the first few weeks of the school year, also, Cath and Warren became friends. This was only natural – they were the Year 2 teachers and had to hold curriculum meetings after school. When they held their meetings, one of them would run across the highway in the heat to bring back iced caffè lattes. Then they would have a break and Warren would ask Cath's advice about difficult children. This was his first year of teaching, whereas it was her third, so she had wisdom to share. He also liked to hear about her part-time law classes, and she would memorize the best cases to describe to him. As she talked, he would gasp slightly at surprising facts and ask innocent questions, and she would explain the law to him, feeling articulate and smart.

Meanwhile, Warren quickly gained the reputation, among teachers, as a charming and light-hearted young man, quick to give an inquisitive look whenever someone said something obtuse. 'He cuts through the crap,' Lenny declared to Cath, and she nodded, feeling proud to be his friend.

Among children, Warren had a reputation as VERY funny, and you never know what he's going to do next, and sometimes he doesn't make sense, but he's nice if you hurt yourself.

It was now acknowledged by Lenny and Suzanne that, as far as information was concerned, Warren Woodford belonged to Cath. 'Hey, did Warren do any acting work before he became a teacher?' Lenny might say. 'He's so funny with that face of his at staff meetings!' And Cath would explain: 'No, he only did two years of drama training – then he went straight to teachers' college.' 'How come?' Suzanne would ask, humbly.

'Well, one day,' Cath explained, 'he was doing this practical drama exercise with a bunch of kids, and he realized he loved working with them, and he thought: *What if I could do MORE than entertain them?*'

'Huh,' Lenny and Suzanne would say, impressed.

Sometimes Cath would watch their faces, waiting for some hint that they expected romance between Warren and herself.

Had they not noticed how he *watched* her? Did they not think she was *good enough* for him?

But there was never even a suggestion; instead, the three talked about the romance between Lenny and Frank Billson (School Principal). Sometimes Cath thought wistfully: *Shall I die of boredom?* But she was pleased for Lenny.

The late afternoons were sultry and hot and, once all the other teachers had gone, Cath and Warren would sigh in the heat of the staffroom, leaning forward over their work, elbows sliding out in either direction so their chins were low above the table.

Once Warren slid an ice cube along the back of Cath's neck to cool her down.

During school days, they held joint Singing or Arts-and-Crafts lessons, with all of Year 2 in a circle on the assembly-hall floor. Warren had a surprisingly deep voice when he sang, which made the children stare and sometimes giggle.

One brightly lit Thursday, Cath sat on the edge of her desk in her classroom, swinging her legs and looking around at the room full of small, fidgeting people. *I'm pretty happy, you know*, she thought. She was the Queen of Her Own Life! She had so many little kingdoms! Her classroom, the staffroom, her car, her apartment! And in between the kingdoms, she went to law classes, or had iced caffè lattes with friends.

'Let's talk about the *environment*,' she said to her class, happily. 'Anybody here know what the environment is?'

They all nodded, and many said, 'Yeah.' Anthony McMasters said contemptuously, 'The *enviroh-ment*?!' and put his fingers in his ears.

'Take your fingers out of your ears, Anthony.'

Lucinda Coulton said, 'I know, Ms Murphy, because do you know why? My dad's a biological engineer.'

'Hands up, Lucinda,' chided Cath. 'Is he *really*?'

Marcus Ellison said, 'My dad's an astronaut.'

'He is *not*.' Cassie Zing turned to Marcus in a fury.

'You don't have to put both hands in the air,' Cath explained to Lucinda.

'My dad *is* an astronaut. He already went to Venus, OK for now?'

Cassie Zing lifted the lid of her desk and slammed it down hard. The slam ruffled her hair and surprised her eyes.

'We'll do careers then, shall we?' Cath said smoothly, imagining her voice through the wall between the classrooms, imagining how gentle and sensible it might sound. 'We've had biological engineers and we've had astronauts. Anybody know another career?'

Cassie Zing announced: 'My mum is a writer of wilderness romance.'

'Anthony,' said Cath, 'take your fingers out of your nose.'

Driving home, Cath wondered again why Lenny and Suzanne never mentioned Warren as a potential boyfriend for her. Did they not realize how good-looking he was? Did they not see that he was sexy?

Or were they, like her, simply waiting? Perhaps they sensed that this would be romance of a different kind – romance so fine it was as fragile as crystal, romance unfurling delicately, like a silken bud, or a cygnet hatching. It had to be watched through binoculars with steadiest hands.

Cath changed gears, and her hand seemed to tremble on the gear stick. Perhaps, when she was not looking, Lenny and Suzanne glanced at one another, and held the glance a moment, silent and steady, glad for their young friend Cath.

At home that night, Cath phoned her mother across the country and her mother said, '*Darling!*' and wept a little. It was a recent habit, this weeping, and must have been hormonal. After all, it was not her but her parents who had moved interstate, leaving Cath with no home, no Mum, no Dad, no my-room-become-sewing-room, no Sunday baked dinner, no cappuccino-Sunday-afternoons.

After her mother had wept, she called: 'Dad! It's Cath! Pick up!'

Cath's parents were named 'Mum' and 'Dad', even when she was not around. She had paint-stripped their names, and now they existed only so long as she herself existed. *Too much power for one girl to have*, she sometimes decided grimly.

'I was just reading that the child you love best is the one who is far away,' said Mum. 'And aren't you far away, Cath, darling?'

'Yes,' agreed Cath. 'So you love me best.'

Cath was the only one. There were no siblings. But anyway.

'Cath, you all right, love? How goes the new school year? Any little monsters in your class?'

That was Dad on the extension, his voice a layer closer than Mum's.

'Breaking any hearts over there?' he said.

'Any young men on the horizon?' agreed Mum, changing abruptly to a businesslike voice.

Breaking any hearts was funny. Cath's own heart was broken so often it was just about a write-off. But she always considered the horizon, obediently, for her parents.

And there he was on the edge of a sunset sky: Warren Wishful Woodford, a little self-conscious, damp with drops of ocean mist.

'No,' she said. 'Not really.'

She shook the horizon gently, tipping him off the edge. Let him climb back up in his own time.

*

'Hey, Cath,' whispered Warren, sneaking into the assembly hall and sitting down beside her, late on Monday morning. Mr Billson was giving a lecture on punctuality, so a lot of kids pointed at Warren and said: 'WAH–HAH.'

'Hi,' she murmured. 'How was your weekend?'

'Oh, fine, fine. Kind of a strain, you know? Eh, cut it out,' sternly, to some kids who would not stop pointing and trying to get the Principal's attention.

'Kind of a strain?'

He nodded, distracted, and she raised her eyebrows, watching him. His shirt was already patched with sweat: he must have run from his car to the assembly hall. He must be in some kind of trouble – *kind of a strain* – and mentioning it like that, he must want to talk. She would find a gentle way to ask him later.

For now, she looked down at the folder of papers on her lap; at Monday assemblies, she always pretended to be making notes of what Billson was saying, but in fact she was catching up on class records. She was ticking through last week's lesson plan when she came across this word: *Environment*. She put a tick beside it.

Then she thought, hmm, and changed it to: ½ ✓, before writing at the end of the list: *Careers*: ½ ✓.

'Did you know,' she whispered to Warren softly, 'that Cassie Zing's mother writes wilderness romances?'

'As you do,' agreed Warren, nodding.

'And Marcus Ellison's dad is an astronaut.'

Now his nod became a slow, impressed tilt: 'An *astronaut*?' He looked at Cath admiringly, as if she was the astronaut.

She returned to her class plan, and flipped the page, but Warren was leaning into her shoulder and taking the pen from her hand. He turned a page in her notebook and wrote:

She leaned forward and circled 'yes' and 'yes'. Warren studied her answers, and then he put a ✓ alongside each 'yes'. Underneath, he wrote the word: *Excellent*.

The next day, Tuesday, wandering her classroom aisles like a queen, Cath remembered that she didn't actually know 'the Carotid Sticks'. She had them mixed up with 'the Clotted Creams'.

She felt strangely embarrassed, yet also excited, to realize this, as if she had cheated in an exam. Also, she had a heart-pumping moment of terror, remembering how close she had come to getting caught – she had almost mentioned to Warren how much she liked the goldfish in a small glass bowl that the drummer brought along to his shows. (She had seen the Clotted Creams a couple of years back.) She had almost *drawn* a *sketch* of the goldfish on her notes and shown this to Warren! Showing off her knowledge. Imagine if she had! Warren would have frowned in confusion, and she would have tried to explain, and realized her mistake as she did so, and then she would have tried to cover up and got flustered.

She must look up the Carotid Sticks in HMV and listen to

a CD so she could prepare for the Date. *Not a Date. You don't know it's a Date. Who said it was a Date?*

'Yeast infection, yeast infection, yeast infection.'

'Cassie?'

Cassie Zing coloured by numbers and murmured: '*Yeast infection.*'

'Cassie? You want to keep quiet for us? Or see if you can find some new words?'

Cassie looked up and blinked once. She leaned on to her elbow and spoke into her fist.

I really should mention this habit to her parents. It's been going on for weeks now. And her mother sends so many notes! Really, an amazing number of notes from that Mrs Zing. I wouldn't even notice that Cassie was late if she didn't bring notes from her mother. Maybe I shouldn't have written back that time? Now she thinks we're penfriends and she'll never stop. She may be a loony. Of course, the compliments are nice.

I hope I'm not late on Friday. I'll have to go straight from my law class to the Borrowed Cat. I'll wait until Friday night to ask him what he meant by that comment about his weekend being 'kind of a strain'. He will open up to me then after we've had a few drinks, and I will listen sympathetically and try to make him laugh. Perhaps he'll even cry on my shoulder!

OK, but it's not a Date.

What colour should I wear? What colour is the Borrowed Cat? I should try not to clash with the walls.

It was a strange week for Cath, waiting for Friday and the Clotted Creams. Then remembering that it was not the Clotted Creams but the *Carotid Sticks*. (She found them at HMV and they were kind of bluesy. She didn't like *blues*, but whatever.) She walked around under a spotlight, but a secret, private spotlight, because she didn't mention the invitation to anybody.

Not even Lenny and Suzanne, even when Suzanne suggested the two of them see a movie on Friday night. 'I'm busy Friday,' is all she said. 'How about Saturday?' Because here it was: the invitation. The first fragile step in the unfurling. She would not even *whisper* his name.

But you ARE allowed! He asked you out! He asked you to see a band! And you don't do that to just anyone: and who knows what will happen AFTER –

On Wednesday afternoon, Cath and Warren were working on a class plan.

'I am,' said Warren, '*extremely* hungry,' and he looked around the room.

Cath opened the fridge and found her cheese and pickles sandwich. She hadn't eaten it at lunch, on account of buying a cheeseburger instead. 'You can have it,' she offered generously.

Warren was pleased with her, opening up the sandwich from its greaseproof paper as if it was a birthday present. But then he paused and said, 'Imagine if this were toasted.' He held out the sandwich towards her.

'Are you saying you want me to toast it for you?' demanded Cath. 'Because I won't.'

'It's ten to five!' Warren slid back his chair and leaped to his feet. 'We will *buy a sandwich maker*. Quick! Let's go!'

They ran across Castle Hill Road together, among the lanes of traffic, skidded to the department store, scanned the directory for kitchen appliances, ran down the up escalators accidentally and got there just in time.

They went halves in a DeLonghi Sandwich Maker, and carried it back in its box. They were sweaty from the heat and the excitement, and the fading sun blinked in their eyes.

'We keep it here,' said Warren, showing Cath the second shelf of the corner cupboard. 'And it's for us, and us alone. We alone get toasted sandwiches for lunch. Is it a fact? Is it a pact? Is it a *tac*-tic?'

On Thursday night she felt jittery and had to go to the corner store. The corner-store girl had such long plaits they drew attention to her hips. 'Hello there, *you*!' she always said to Cath, who felt she could never live up to this greeting.

'You know what *I* dreamed last night?' declared the corner-store girl as she reached for Cath's sixty-watt light bulb. 'I dreamed I was in a bathtub, right? With a zebra! What did you dream?'

'Hmm,' said Cath. 'Can't remember.'

'Come on! You always have the *best* dreams! And it's been so hot lately! Doesn't that make you dream? It makes me dream. Look at the time! It's so late and it must be what? Thirty-six degrees? Any nightmares?'

'Well, OK, I had this great dream where Doctor Carter from *ER* wanted to cure me of this disease which made me pale and beautiful, and I was hoping I'd get to stay pale and beautiful even when I was cured. Also, I've been dreaming a lot about extra rooms for my apartment. In the dreams, I keep finding doors in my hallway which open out into things like sewing rooms or saunas. I'm so happy when that happens. Maybe I think my apartment's too small? So. Those aren't nightmares, I guess.'

'How *is* your health anyway, Cath? I notice you've picked up some lozenges there. Sore throat?'

'Just hay fever,' explained Cath. 'It makes my throat itchy. How about you?'

Sometimes the corner-store girl liked to chat, but often she became vague and glassy-eyed when asked about herself.

When she got home, Cath was still jittery, so she got out the bucket, the Windex and a roll of paper towel and washed all the windows in the apartment.

*

On Friday afternoon, she was supervising children whose penalty was to hunt down apple cores, orange peels, paper bags and popsicle wrappers after school. She would let them stop soon because she wanted to get home, shower, change into a summer dress, get to law class and *then* to the Borrowed Cat to meet Warren.

Warren, striding past, his arms and legs moving like the spokes of a wheel, slowed to a helicopter hover.

'Still on for tonight?' His eyes went straight into Cath's.

There was a whisk of excitement in her stomach. 'You bet,' she said.

'Breanna might be a little late,' explained Warren.

Cassie Zing, walking past at that moment, swinging her school bag in circles, said 'Ms Murphy?'

'Yes, Cassie?' said Cath. Also, to Warren: 'Breanna?'

'I wanted to tell you something important,' said Cassie.

'Breanna,' said Warren. 'My wife?'

'Did you, Cassie?' Cath turned smoothly. 'What did you want to tell me?'

'That it's my birthday tomorrow,' whispered Cassie.

'If she misses her train from the coast,' Warren explained, 'and she says that she might.'

Cath had bent forward so she could hear Cassie Zing. She kept her eyes on Cassie's face and said, 'Your *birthday* tomorrow! What are you going to do? Will you have a party? Happy birthday! That's *so* exciting.'

Cassie nodded. 'I know. And I'm having a party at my auntie's place tomorrow.'

'Wonderful!' said Cath, still leaning forward. 'We'll have to sing "Happy Birthday" on Monday, but you know, we could have sung today. Why didn't you tell me sooner?'

Then there was a HONK, and Cassie cried, 'My mum!' and skidded away.

Cath straightened up and looked at Warren. 'Your wife?' she said, with a friendly smile.

'She lives up the coast during the week,' he said, 'so we only get the weekends? Which is a strain. Which is a drain. Which is a *brain drain*.'

Cath considered him.

'You didn't like that one?' he said. 'Fair enough. But anyway, I hope *you're* not planning to be late?'

'No, Warren, that's not what I was planning.'

'Great!' he said. 'See you there!

12

In the afternoon light of a summer day, Fancy, a teenager then, sat on her beach towel and watched Radcliffe's toe.

The toe sprouted from his foot like a plump little table-tennis paddle. It also sprouted hairs, like an unkempt hedge. The toe was writing in the sand:

RADCLIFFE MEREWEATHER
LOVES
FANCY ZING

The toe took a long time to write this.

Next, Fancy was distracted by Radcliffe's hands. The hands were thin and knobbly and were clutching at her sunburned shoulders. *I should put some sun cream on those shoulders,* Fancy thought. But now was not the time.

Radcliffe's hands clutched tightly. He had a tear on the edge of each eye. 'I don't want to hurt you,' he was saying. 'I never meant to hurt you.' She stared at him. He was hurting her shoulders, but, apart from that, it didn't really hurt.

'I appreciate you telling me,' she said, pleased by her own maturity.

Radcliffe had kissed another girl. He had gone to the surf-club party the night before, leaving Fancy at home with an asthma attack.

'Did you meet a girl?' she teased the next day, side by side in the sun.

'Well, kind of,' he replied, alarmed.

'Did you kiss her?' She did not think for one moment that he had.

'Well . . .' and then he was silent, and the odd feeling started, her face stretched out, and she thought: *Perhaps he did!*

And he had.

Radcliffe! Her First True Love! Her long-lashed boy with the sneakers and guitar! Radcliffe, who bought her marzipan and chocolate, had kissed another girl! They had only been together for a month.

'I don't want to hurt you,' he said, fervently, and his toe had just proved it by etching in the sand: Radcliffe Mereweather LOVES Fancy Zing.

They sat solemnly, looking at the words, their legs stretched out to the sun. A man shouted, 'Turkey! Win a turkey in the raffle!' Nearby, Marbie shook her towel and Daddy growled, 'Marbie! The sand!' Mummy called, 'Look, everyone! There's a skywriter!' and an announcement warned about the dangers of the rip.

'If you will only forgive me –' Radcliffe was anxious – 'I will love you for ever and ever. Even, say, you get old and wrinkled? I will love you. Even, say, you get as fat as your mother?'

At that, Fancy pounced. '*Don't* call my mother fat!'

'Sorry.'

'I mean it. That's a stupid thing to say.'

'Sorry, I didn't know,' he explained. 'I didn't know you were sensitive about your mother's weight.'

'That's *not* the point! You don't know a *thing* about my mother.'

'What do you mean? What's to know?'

Strange. How she told the whole story, in a flood, right then. Radcliffe stared, the sun burned freckles on to Fancy's shoulders, and the Zing Family Secret ran straight into the letters of:

The first few weeks of the school year were hot and, as usual when the sun burned white, Fancy remembered the day at the seaside when Radcliffe revealed he had kissed another girl. Fancy had trumped him with the Zing Family Secret.

Also during the first few weeks of the school year, Fancy wrote seventeen notes to her daughter's Year 2 teacher. She was just finishing the third of these notes –

Dear Ms Murphy,
Thank you so much for teaching Cassie (and the rest of your class, I suppose) that lovely song about the sparrow and the iron bark tree etc. etc. She has been entertaining her father and me with the song (on and off) all week, and it is such an unusual tune!
Just thought I should let you know.

Best regards,
Fancy Zing

when her husband, Radcliffe, arrived home from work.

'FANCY THAT! MY FANCY IS AT HOME!'

Fancy sat up straight and waited patiently for the sound of his key in the front door, the scraping of his feet on the Welcome mat and the 'Huh!' of pleasure as he put his umbrella in the stand. He had given Fancy the stand for a birthday, and he used it assiduously, taking his umbrella back and forth to work each day, even during heatwaves.

The footsteps approached.

Radcliffe leaned into the room and smiled around at the

bookshelf, the scanner and the corkboard. He looked at the printer next and chuckled. 'What have you done with Cassie?' he said, wandering away down the hall.

'I haven't done anything with Cassie,' murmured Fancy. She opened her desk drawer and took out her Irritating Things notebook.

They had frozen quiche for dinner, and watched *Hot Auctions!* and the next day, the moment she woke up, Fancy remembered this: *It is possible to change a person.*

People went around warning you: *Never imagine you can change someone, for people NEVER CHANGE.* Then they talked about leopards and spots. Forgetting altogether about chameleons. Or that octopus which lives on the ocean floor and can change its shape to become a stingray, a sea anemone, or even an eel, depending upon its fancy.

Stepping out of the shower that morning, Fancy regarded her husband, shaving at the basin. *Tap, tap, tap,* said his razor.

'So, that's how you get the whiskers out of the razor, is it?'

He turned to her. He had a white towel around his waist, a white smear of shaving cream around his chin, and he was squinting in the steam from Fancy's shower.

'Is there another way you could get the whiskers out?' she suggested.

'We should change this routine,' he replied, turning back to the steamy mirror. 'Me shaving, you showering. Same time, eh? Look at the mirror here. Can't see a thing.'

She leaned around him and flicked the switch on the over-head fan, so the room was filled with its buzz.

'What's with that rash on your arm there?' he said, raising his voice over the buzz.

'I know.' She reached for her skin cream. 'I feel like a fish. It's just dry skin. I burned my skin too often as a teenager.'

'Wouldn't be that, would it? It's eczema. Or what? Psoriasis?'

'No,' said Fancy coldly. 'It is not.' But Radcliffe was picking up her arm, turning it this way and that to catch the light and whistling through his teeth.

'Here, Cassie, don't forget to take this note to your teacher, OK? Where are you going to put it so you don't forget?'

'In my pocket.'

Cassie stood on the footpath next to the open car door and showed her mother her open pocket.

'Good girl. Will you remember it there?'

'Yes, because I'll sneeze and then I'll have to get out my hanky, and then I'll find it there and I'll go: I HAVE TO REMEMBER TO GIVE THIS TO MS MURPHY.'

'That's my girl,' said Fancy.

'See over there.' Cassie pointed to a bench just inside the school gate. 'That's Lucinda.'

'So it is! We'll have to invite her over again one day soon. What do you think?'

'OK,' agreed Cassie, nodding. She walked through the school gate and, without turning back, raised one hand to farewell her mother.

'Eczema, eczema, eczema.'

Cassie had a new word. It was a disease which made your skin fall off and then your blood went everywhere, like a laundry flood. Then you turned into a fish. Then you died.

'Eczema, eczema, eczema.' Cassie sang her word, eating her sandwich before school had even started.

'Eczema?' Lucinda put her elbow in Cassie's side. 'I've got eczema.'

'No you haven't.' Cassie rolled her eyes at an imaginary person on the bench alongside Lucinda. She looked back from her imaginary person to Lucinda and saw that Lucinda was also eating her lunch before school. Lucinda's lunch was brown bread with soggy tomato. It was disgusting.

To change the subject, Cassie pointed to the ground and said, 'See that? That's a stick insect.'

'No,' said Lucinda. 'It's just a stick.'

It was a stick insect though.

Lucinda pointed to her wrist: 'See that? That's eczema.'

'There is no *point* in our having this discussion,' Cassie announced.

'Yes, there is.'

'Eczema's when you turn into a fish, actually, *Lucinda*.'

'Do I look like a fish? No. I don't think so.' Lucinda swung her legs and ate her tomato sandwich.

The word, Cassie realized, was spoiled now.

'Eczema, eczema, eczema,' she said listlessly. She had her eye on the stick insect, but so far it was just asleep.

When she got back from taking Cassie to school, Fancy knew that she ought to be working on her wilderness romance. She had promised thirty thousand words to her editor by tomorrow, and she had only written eleven. Specifically:

His rhinoceros smelled like a poppadom: sweaty, salty, strange and strong.

Her editor would cut that line.

She reached for the phone and selected the button for MARBIE AT HOME.

'Hello,' said Marbie's voice.

'You're at home! Why aren't you at work? I was just going to leave a message. Well, if you're home, let's go out for a coffee!'

Marbie agreed, explaining that she and Listen were taking a day off because they had ticklish throats, which could be the start of colds.

'Or hay fever,' suggested Fancy. 'I'll call Radcliffe and let him know in case he was thinking of coming home for lunch. And then I'll see you in Castle Hill.'

Marbie looked fine when Fancy saw her, although Listen appeared to be weary. Also, she was behaving strangely: wearing sunglasses inside the shopping centre, walking backwards wherever she went.

Marbie was excited about buying a tennis racquet, and wanted to talk about something that the tennis racquet had which was called the *sweet spot*.

After the coffee break, Fancy did not feel ready to go home so she shopped for Cassie's birthday. At home again, she stood before her computer and decided she ought to do some housework.

Luckily, by the time she had finished washing up, it was just about time to fetch Cassie from school.

Dear Ms Murphy,

This is just a note to thank you for keeping an eye on my daughter (Cassie) yesterday afternoon. I noticed that you were on 'bus duty', and I also noticed that you are very good at keeping all the children within your 'radar'. As I waited for Cassie, this is something I observed, and, as a mother, I was pleased.

I do hope our Cassie is behaving herself. I know she can be a little erratic, but she has a good heart.

Kind regards,
Fancy Zing

'You look tired,' remarked the Canadian from his porch next door. He was eating sliced mango and kiwi fruit this morning.

'It's funny you should say that,' said Fancy, 'about me looking tired. Because I just saw myself in the hallway mirror without my glasses on and I thought, "I look awful," and then I thought, "Isn't it lucky I wear glasses so that nobody can see my eyes?" I put my glasses on and felt safe. And now I come out here and you notice right away.'

The Canadian took a pensive sip of coffee.

'Cassie, honey!' Fancy called, as usual, through the screen door.

'Mum, I can't find my shoes, where are my shoes? What did you do with my shoes?' came a panicky little call from upstairs.

'I didn't do anything with your shoes. They're right here by the front door where you left them.'

'To be honest,' said the Canadian from his porch, 'I didn't notice that you look awful. If you look awful,' he continued, and peeled the foil lid from a boysenberry yoghurt, 'your glasses are hiding that well.'

Fancy looked at his wide white breakfast plate, with its elegant butterflies of fruit, and tried to think of something to say besides 'Isn't it hot?'

'Kiwi fruit is very good for you,' she declared. 'Vitamin C and zinc.'

'You don't say?'

Cassie clattered down on to the front-door mat to put on her shoes.

'I'll do one lace and you do the other,' offered Fancy.

'No, Mum. I'll do them both.'

'Bye now,' called Fancy to the neighbour as she tightened the straps on Cassie's satchel, her keys at the ready to open the car door.

'It is possible,' called the Canadian, his voice melting distantly against their car windows, 'to be both beautiful and tired. A sleeping beauty. You see?'

Fancy adjusted the rear-view mirror and reversed with the regular bump of the fender on the steeply graded drive. Cassie, meanwhile, wound the window down slightly and gave the Canadian a stare.

Dear Ms Murphy,
Please excuse Cassie for being late today.
It was all my fault! I was up late last night, working, and then overslept this morning.

Best regards,
Fancy Zing

Dear Ms Zing,
Thank you very much for your note!
I'm sure that Cassie was not more than a few minutes late – some of the children are much later than that and we seem to get along all right. It is very kind of you to write notes of explanation, but please do not trouble yourself.
I look forward to meeting you at the Parent–Teacher Night later this year, when we can discuss Cassie properly. She certainly does seem to have a good heart and is quite popular. (I often see other children gathered around her while she entertains them with funny stories – I wonder what she tells them!)

Best wishes,
Cath Murphy

Turning into her driveway one day, Fancy looked across at her neighbour's veranda and saw that there were two of them. Her neighbour had become two.

She got out of her car, and glanced over quickly. Yes, there were now two men sitting at the breakfast table, slicing up kiwi fruit, sipping from their coffee mugs. She kept her back straight, and hurried across the burning driveway to the soft, cool grass. She never wore shoes to drive.

'. . . so he ate his own arm,' she heard from the porch next door, just as she reached her front door. And then a chuckle.

She couldn't help it. She turned and stared.

'Fancy,' said her neighbour, 'hello there. This is my brother, Bill. He's out from Canada for a couple of days. Bill. Meet Fancy.'

'Did I startle you?' said Bill-the-brother with a friendly nod. 'You heard what I just said? He ate his own arm?'

How direct the Canadians were. 'Well . . .' she began.

'It's what happened to a guy I know,' he explained. Meanwhile, Fancy's neighbour looked down, slicing up another kiwi fruit. 'You want to hear the story? OK. My buddy's hiking in the Rockies up Jasper way, he stops to take a picture of some plant or other, somehow he crouches down by a cougar trap, he gets his *arm* caught in the cougar trap. I mean, seriously caught. Next thing, dumb effin luck, a big mother of a bear comes along and takes a bite out of his leg. Seriously, a bite out of his leg. He's screaming and punching it with his one unstuck arm, but nothing he can do. The bear goes off but he knows, he can just *tell*, that it's coming back later to finish him off. But he can't get out of the trap! I mean, his arm is *completely* stuck! You're in that predicament, what are you going to do?'

Fancy tilted her head to the side. 'What are you going to do?' she asked.

'You're going to chew through your own arm.' Bill-the-brother nodded to himself and picked up a slice of kiwi fruit. 'That's what my buddy did,' he said, green juice dripping down his chin. 'He ate through his arm and got away.'

Fancy stared.

Her neighbour offered her a cup of coffee.

'No, thank you. And thank you for the story, Bill. Nice to meet you.'

She opened the screen door to her house, and it let out a long, thin squeal.

Dear Ms Murphy,

How kind of you to write! I, also, look forward to meeting you at the Parent-Teacher Night.

I'm so pleased to hear that Cassie is popular! I hope she does not give you any trouble.

You know, I just thought I would let you know that I was talking to Barbara Coulton the other day - she is Lucinda's mother - and she told me that Lucinda is happier than she's ever been at school! Barbara is delighted with the standard and variety of work that Lucinda brings home and is especially pleased that you correct Lucinda's spelling mistakes - such a rare thing in modern teaching.

Take care, and
Best wishes!
Fancy Zing

'Write this down,' Fancy said to Radcliffe on Sunday afternoon: '*Toilet paper*.' Radcliffe wrote it down. 'Follow me down the hall,' she instructed, taking out the vacuum cleaner from the hall closet. Obediently, Radcliffe followed, writing the list.

'The vacuum cleaner's broken, you know.'

'I don't want the vacuum cleaner,' said Fancy patiently. 'I just want the bucket from behind it. *Kitchen towels*. I've decided to wash the glass doors. Or will Cassie just run through them? OK: *butter, self-raising flour, Valerio Pies*.'

'I think she'll run through them,' agreed Radcliffe, writing carefully. 'Don't wash them. Let's go for a walk instead. Anything else?' His pen at the ready.

'Yes. *Spaghetti*. OK. Let's go for a walk. Radcliffe, what do you mean it's broken?'

'What's broken?'

'The vacuum, you just said it was broken. Since when?'

'Oh,' he said vaguely, 'since the other day. I came home to surprise you at lunchtime and you weren't here, so I smashed a glass, then I tried to vacuum it up and the vacuum cleaner jammed, and now it's broken.'

'You smashed a glass? Because I wasn't here? Where was I?'

'That came out wrong. I think you were having coffee with your sister in Castle Hill. Remember that day? And Marbie brought Alissa along, you told me. They both had colds. Or at least Alissa did. That's how you put it.'

'She prefers to be called Listen, you know.'

'Anyhow, let's go for a walk and, tell you what, I'll take the vacuum into that new repair shop by the hardware store.'

Thursday already, and tomorrow she had to prepare for the Zing Family Secret Meeting, and Saturday was Cassie's birthday, and Sunday she never worked, so that only left today to write thirty thousand words. Fancy stared at her computer in wonder.

She decided to write to Cassie's teacher.

> Dear Ms Murphy,
> Just wanted to let you know that Cassie has a
> loose tooth –

But then there was a knock at the front door.

She opened the door and there in the sun-shadow stood a

handsome stranger. Tears sprang at once into Fancy's eyes. She blinked them away.

The stranger was carrying a plate covered in a tea towel. He was wearing a loose T-shirt and jeans, and sneakers without socks. His shoulders were broad, his face was tanned, and his eyes, behind small, wire-rimmed spectacles, were glinting.

'*Hello* there,' he said.

At that, he transformed into the Canadian-next-door.

She was so disconcerted, she did not open the screen door. She stood and simply stared.

'*Not* in any way intending to bother you,' he continued, in a slightly formal voice, 'but I've baked you an *apology* cake. My brother from Canada. The other day. I just wanted to apologize for him. He's a good guy, but not exactly – and I just about died when he told you that apocryphal story of his. I could tell it bothered you, and I just about died, and now I am here to apologize.'

'Oh!' cried Fancy, in a flutter. 'The man who ate his arm! I wasn't bothered by that story at all! I mean, I didn't believe a word of course. Ate his own arm! And what about the blood loss from the wound in his leg . . . Anyway, but I write wilderness romance. That's my occupation. So, see, bear and cougar stories are *fine*! My characters are always running from cougars and into the arms of handsome strangers. They don't usually eat their own limbs, of course, because then there'd be no arms to run into . . . But, anyway, it's my career! I know it must sound strange, me, a mother in the suburbs, writing wilderness romance, and the only person I ever slept with my whole life is my husband!'

There was silence for a moment.

Fancy opened the screen door, and it let out its usual squeal.

'I could fix that for you.' He was looking at the door.

'No! No! I can do that! All it needs is a bit of WD40!'

'I agree,' he said, with that odd little smile. 'I still think my brother bothered you, so please take this maple cake. OK?'

He used one foot to hold open the screen door as he passed the cake towards her. She took the cake, and he withdrew his hands, palms upwards. She saw that his palms were calloused. Then he saluted, with the same glint in his eye, and ran down the steps of her porch.

Rather than crossing directly to his own porch, he took the driveway, walked along the street, and then walked back up his own driveway. She found this extremely moving.

Driving to the Zing Family Meeting the next night, Fancy felt very happy. She was excited about dinner that night – it would be roast chicken, as usual – and about the meeting afterwards (she had prepared a slide show). She also felt relaxed about Cassie's birthday tomorrow. How wonderful that Marbie, Nathaniel and Listen were hosting it! She might go to the gym before the party. How thin she was these days now that she was going to the gym regularly. And she could always get an extension for her wilderness romance.

She leaned back into her seat, humming along with the tune that Cassie was singing in the back seat.

Then Radcliffe said what he said. 'You remember Gemma in the pay office?' he said, changing lanes.

'No,' said Fancy.

'Come on! You must remember Gemma. She's the one who spilled her drink everywhere at the office Christmas party? Remember?'

'No,' repeated Fancy.

'Well.' He shrugged. 'Well, trust me, there's a Gemma works in my pay office. She works afternoons only, lucky duck. Anyhow, turns out she had some kind of laser treatment done on her moles. You know, you'd call them freckles, but they're really moles. Anyhow. Extraordinary. She got about ten of them zapped.'

Fancy could not believe it. She lowered her chin to check the freckles on her bare shoulders: nicely spaced, attractive freckles. *Beauty spots*, really.

'What exactly do you mean by that?' she said coldly.

Radcliffe turned swiftly towards her, a hurt, confused expression on his face. Then he looked back to the road.

Tomorrow, it would be Cassie's birthday. It was a secret, almost scary, wonderful fact which she'd been carrying around the last few weeks, like a smile about to happen on her face.

But what Cassie was actually realizing today was that it used to be better than this, back when she was little. Maybe when she turned five or six, it was more than just a smile: it was like everything was whispering and just about to skip. Now, turning seven, her excitement felt a bit wrong.

It's because I know you can get disappointed, she realized to herself. One time she got too excited on her birthday and jumped on the table where the grown-ups were sitting and at first they laughed but then she knocked over their champagne and champagne spilled on to her dad's lap and she got in trouble.

She cried, and you should never cry on your birthday.

13

In the hot noon light of a summer day once, Marbie, nine years old at the time, was almost killed by an umbrella.

She was distracted at the time.

The day before, her sister Fancy had walked into the beach house at sunset and announced that she had done something incredible.

Marbie was supposed to be washing the sand off her feet but, hearing this, she ran inside. She made herself invisible by placing herself in the shadows just beyond the open sliding doors.

Fancy was standing in the centre of the main room, her hands on her hips, waiting for her parents. Mummy leaned in from the kitchen, where she was making a beetroot salad. Daddy leaned in from the bathroom, where he had just had a shower.

'What incredible thing did you do, sweetheart?' called Mummy.

'What's up, Fance?' said Daddy.

'I told Radcliffe the Secret,' said Fancy, defiantly. She looked up at her parents and folded her arms, but her mouth trembled. Marbie, in her door space, thought of the episode of *Charles in Charge,* when the good sister tries to be bad, but she can't pull it off because of her nature.

Now there was a stampede of parents – Mummy's purple hands flying, Daddy's bath towel flapping – and they gathered around Fancy.

'When?!' cried Daddy.

It turned out she had told her boyfriend *everything*. She did not know why.

'Oh, Fancy,' said Mummy, in a low, shivery voice.

'Tell us what you told him,' Daddy commanded. 'Tell us exactly.'

'Well, I told him about Ireland and about the cherry pies –'

'Oh never mind,' grumbled Daddy.

He looked at Mummy and she looked back.

It was quiet.

From the shadows, Marbie murmured to herself, 'Should I tell them that I never told anyone the Secret? Should I say that out loud?'

The others turned to her. 'GET OUT OF THAT WET SWIMSUIT!' Daddy shouted.

'OK,' agreed Marbie, looking down to the floor where there were little splatters of sea water from her bathing suit. Quietly, she walked into the room and sat down on the couch.

'Radcliffe's not going to tell anybody.' Fancy's voice collapsed into her arms, and her next words were tangled in a sob: 'He promerr ewerd terl *any* obee.'

Mummy and Daddy were quiet, figuring out what she had just said. After a moment they both breathed in an 'Ah' of comprehension.

'Well,' said Daddy, 'if he promised he wouldn't tell *any-*body, I suppose we have to trust him.'

'But heaven help us when the two of you break up!' fretted Mummy.

'We're not going to break up,' Fancy wept. 'He loves me! He said that he loves me forever!'

'There now,' said Mummy, apologetically. She put her arms around Fancy and said, 'Of course he does, hush now, of course he does, sweetheart.'

*

So the next day, in the high noon sun, Marbie was distracted.

Fancy was sitting on her beach towel under the umbrella, one arm curled around her knees. Her boyfriend, Radcliffe, was bodysurfing, pounding both fists in the air and grinning in Fancy's direction whenever he caught a wave. Fancy gazed moodily down at the sand.

Daddy was trying to tune in his transistor to hear the cricket. Mummy was on her fold-up chair, reading *New Idea*. The seaside noises and the radio fuzz and the magazine pages turning were only there to heighten the quiet of the family.

From her towel in the sun a few metres away, Marbie was able to observe her family and, in particular, Fancy. It seemed to Marbie that Fancy, who was usually smart, had now been stupid in two ways. First of all, it was stupid to tell her boyfriend the Secret. Second of all, it was stupid to tell her *parents* that she had told her boyfriend the Secret. In fact, and this was what interested Marbie, the second stupid thing was a whole new level of stupidity.

She stared out to sea, thinking hard about the two different levels of stupidity until an umbrella hit her smack in the forehead.

It was a beach umbrella, snatched out of the sand by a random gust of wind. It had streaked through the air like a javelin while men shouted 'Ho!' and leaped after it. The sharp end hit Marbie in the forehead and knocked her out cold.

While she was in the hospital, there was a lot of talk about how lucky it was that it hadn't hit her just over to the right. Or just up a bit. Or a tad lower. Or a smidgen to the left. And imagine if it had hit her in the eye! She was that close to death, but all she got was ten stitches, two black eyes and one night under observation.

Fancy was very emotional so Radcliffe held her hand and nuzzled his nose into her shoulder, for support.

That Friday, Radcliffe came along to his first Zing Family Secret Meeting and was quiet and polite, but couldn't stop looking at Marbie, who was on a couch surrounded by pillows and whose forehead was a thunderstorm of purple. The following week he had relaxed enough to point out that the circles of black around her eyes made her look like a raccoon. 'See you later, raccoon girl,' he called as he left the garden shed that night. Everybody laughed.

Afterwards, Marbie took over responsibility for putting up the family beach umbrella. She alone knew the full extent of the risk. And she was left with a crocus-shaped scar on her forehead and a lifelong fear that long sharp items (such as umbrellas or fence posts) would somehow end up in her eye.

Friday morning, the second week of the school term, Marbie stood on the porch of their new apartment, drinking a berry-and-banana shake and saying goodbye to Listen.

'Don't walk too fast,' she suggested. 'You'll need your energy for the Walkathon. Why don't you skate to school today? Or I could give you a lift.'

Listen laughed and strode off at her regular high speed.

'You look good,' called Marbie. 'You look great. Like a really *hip* walker is how you look.'

Listen laughed again and changed her walk to something hip and groovy for a few steps, then continued in her normal way. Because of the Charity Walkathon that day she was not wearing her school uniform, but hipster jeans and a tank top that showed off her stomach.

Marbie herself locked up and set off to her car, which was parked down the street. Halfway to the car, the neighbour's black cat crossed her path.

Every day since the day they had moved in, the neighbour's

black cat had crossed her path. Sometimes it made an elaborate effort to do so: a triple backflip from a tree followed by a high jump over Marbie's head, for example. But that Friday morning, it didn't even try, it just walked on across her path.

'Oh, for heaven's sake,' Marbie said aloud. 'You don't scare me, you know that, Gary?'

Gary was the name of the cat, and in fact his name alone scared her.

But it was a perfectly pleasant day at work: a lot of chatting, stamping documents, a plate of left-over sushi from a conference on another floor. Toni went to stationery and came back loaded with gifts, so, also, a lot of time setting up her new magnetic paper-clip holder.

She spilled some of the paper clips on to the carpet, and picked up a handful, deciding to leave the rest on the carpet there. *It was a decision she would regret for the rest of her life.* (Let's say, one day, Marbie knocks over a vase of flowers. The water seeps into the carpet, while flowers roll under the desk. She gets down on her hands and knees and crawls under the desk to retrieve a flower or two, and, *without her noticing*, a paper clip sticks to her knee. Unaware, she leaves work, travels home, meets Nathaniel, playfully knees him in the thigh, and *the paper clip somehow sticks into his skin, and he gets lead poisoning, and dies*!) (Her eyes filled with tears at the thought.)

So she crawled under the desk and picked up every single paper clip, afterwards brushing her knees carefully for remnants. Then she wrote replies to all the email in her 'FRIENDS – MUST REPLY' folder.

That evening, at the Night Owl Pub, the others had just left and Marbie was finishing her drink when the aeronautical engineer appeared.

'I have just enough time for one beer,' he informed her, sitting down opposite.

'What makes you think that I have time for one beer?'

'Sure you do! What's the rush?'

The Zing Family Secret Meeting was the rush.

'OK. Just one.'

The aeronautical engineer went to the bar and returned with a pitcher of beer, which they shared.

'Play a spot of tennis?'

On the train home, Marbie wondered why she had agreed to play tennis with a stranger. They had arranged to meet at courts close to her place the next day.

She drove from the station to her parents' place, imagining her arrival in time for dessert, hopefully some kind of cherry pie tonight, and also imagining excuses for her lateness.

By the time she got there, dinner was already over, and the Meeting had begun. Listen and Cassie were watching a movie, as usual, in the living room. 'Hello!' she called, running through on her way out to the garden shed. 'How was the Walkathon, Listen?'

'Fine,' said Listen, her eyes on the TV.

In the garden shed, Marbie sat next to Nathaniel and leaned over to whisper in his ear that she had just agreed to tennis with a stranger. Before she had a chance to whisper, Nathaniel kissed her. He quietly passed her an extra copy of her mother's handout, which she immediately made into a paper aeroplane. Nathaniel took the aeroplane from her hand, held it up, and said a dismissive *'Tch!'*, at which Marbie giggled, and her mother, at the front, said, 'SHH.'

She and Nathaniel were always getting into trouble at Meetings.

Then Nathaniel reached under his chair and he had a plate of cherry pie hidden there for her, with a spoon.

After the Meeting, they drove home in Nathaniel's car.

'Hey, Listen,' said Nathaniel, checking in the rear-view

mirror. 'How was the Walkathon today? We forgot to collect your sponsorship money from the Zings.'

'Fine,' said Listen. 'It was fine.' She didn't say any more than that.

The Walkathon was fifty-five times round the oval to raise money for an international mine-clearance charity. They got their purple sponsorship cards ticked each time around. Every five times they got a cup of orange juice, and every ten times they got to stop and have a Vita-Wheat, and the teachers laughed and said things like, 'Come on! Pick up the pace! Hup-two!'

They walked in groups with their friends, and Listen walked with Donna and the others.

After eight laps, Donna said, 'Raising money for mines, eh? What do you reckon we should do with the mines when we get them?'

'Depends on what kind of mines,' said Sia. 'If they're diamond mines, we should get out the diamonds. If they're gold mines, we should get out the gold. If they're silver mines . . .'

The others were laughing, so she stopped.

'We should plant them in the Science labs,' suggested Caro. 'So we wouldn't have to go to Science any more.'

'Yeah, you would,' said Gabrielle. 'It'd be cool, because Science'd be like a minefield. So you'd have to get someone to go into the lab first and, like, test out the path to your bench.'

'You'd get Caro to do it,' said Donna.

'You would NOT!' shouted Caro, and they all laughed again.

'Let's run now,' Donna said, when they'd stopped laughing. 'You wanna run for a while?'

Then she counted. 'One, two, three and four,' she pointed as she counted, Joanne, Caro, Gabrielle and Sia, and pointed at herself, 'and five.'

She didn't point at Listen.

'Just us five,' she said, without looking at Listen. 'Let's run.'

They had funny sparks in their eyes, and smirks, and they all began to run.

Listen was confused for a moment. She thought that Donna had just forgotten to point to her, and she started to run too, but they were running faster, and looking at each other as they ran, like: 'She's coming with us! What will we do?!'

She slowed down for a moment, to see if they would stop.

They didn't stop, they kept on running into the distance, and around the corner of the oval. They slowed to a jog, without looking back. Then they kept walking, fast.

OK, thought Listen, the idea is to catch up with me on the next round?

Listen walked alone then, forty-seven times around the oval, slowly, to give them a chance, but they never caught up with her once.

On Saturday morning, Marbie explained to Nathaniel through the bathroom door that she was going to her parents' place to look through decorating magazines and collect her car.

'Look at you,' said Nathaniel, coming out of the shower and seeing Marbie dressed up in her sports gear. He pretended to box with her, but Marbie did not have the time.

On the way to her parents' place, she stopped and bought a can of tennis balls. She stayed at her parents' place for ten minutes, and then she drove to the tennis courts. Her old racquet was hidden in the trunk.

The air was still under a low, hazy sky, with vague swarmings of pollen and specks of black bugs. Crossing to the courts, Marbie felt the dry grass crunch beneath her sneakers, and then, in the distance, she saw the aeronautical engineer. He was already at the court, unzipping his tennis racquet and staring at her. He was dressed all in white, including white ankle socks and bright white sandshoes. The only other colour on him was the black of the hair on his legs and arms.

From a distance, the aeronautical engineer looked troubled. But as soon as she arrived, he smiled his shiny smile and said: 'Warm up?'

'No,' said Marbie. 'Let's just play.' If they played, she could call, 'Good shot!' whenever she missed the ball, so it would seem to be his skill that made her miss, instead of her lack of skill.

'All right.' He seemed surprised. 'Here, I'll spin my racquet.'

'Ah!' *Why does he want to spin his racquet?!*

The aeronautical engineer spun the racquet, asking: 'Rough or smooth?'

'Rough!' panicked Marbie. She waved at a swarm of bugs, and sneezed: once, twice, three, four, five.

'Phew!' he said (about her sneezes) and the racquet hit the court with a low-level thud. 'Rough it is!'

Marbie served into the net, twice, and clicked her ticklish throat, annoyed. The bugs touched her tongue and the edges of her nose, and she scratched at her ears and her knees.

'Love-fifteen,' called the aeronautical engineer, helpfully.

'Thank you.' She stamped one foot at the itches and the bugs and agreed: 'Me too! Love it too!'

The aeronautical engineer said: 'What?' and then laughed once: 'Ha'.

Arriving home, sweaty, Marbie explained to Nathaniel that she had decided to go for a run around the oval after she visited her parents and that was why she was sweaty, and so now she would just have a shower.

'Listen's gone shopping,' Nathaniel said, following her down the hallway, 'but I just remembered I forgot to tell you something she suggested the other day. She had an idea. OK, let me remember the idea. The idea was, she thinks we should have a housewarming party. She'd invite Donna and the others from school. And she said we should combine it with Cassie's birthday – have Cassie's birthday here. She tells me it's Cassie's birthday in a few weeks.'

'Does she tell you that, does she?' said Marbie, taking off her sweaty sports clothes and stepping into the shower. 'I think it's a perfect idea, and I think Listen is beautiful, and I think that you are too.' The last part she gurgled through the shower water.

'Thank you,' said Nathaniel, pulling his shirt over his head, unbuttoning his jeans, pressing them down his legs and over his feet and stepping into the shower with her. Marbie stared at the fine, light brown hair on his chest, and at his muscular shoulders and arms. He was well built because he was always lifting boxes of bananas. As he kissed her in a warm, wet, shower-water way, Marbie began to draft a Letter to a Problem Page inside her head:

Help!
I'm a twenty-eight-year-old woman (Sagittarius) and I've just moved in with my boyfriend and his daughter. My boyfriend is wonderful and an excellent lover. I can confirm right now, even as I speak, that he really is a sensational – that he is –

Anyway, the problem. You won't believe it, but I seem to have had an affair this morning.

(Why?)

Well, it wasn't so much an affair. More a game of tennis.

The score was 6–0, 6–1. I lost. And that game I won in the second set was just because he hit four double faults. 'Hooroo,' he said (mysteriously) after

every double fault, and then he wiped the sweat from
his sideburns.

   So, that was strange enough. But then do you know
what I did? I arranged to have a SECOND AFFAIR.
Well, not so much a second affair as another game of
tennis. (Why?) I arranged it for next Wednesday,
during my lunch hour, at the Sydney University courts.
I've got to say though, because this is what's so
mystifying and the reason I'm asking for help – I've
got to say, and this is really ironic – but Nathaniel is
really an excellent – that he's a fantastic –

The Monday after the Walkathon, Listen watched Donna and
the others out of the corner of her eye, waiting to see what
would happen. At first she thought: *Well, if they don't want
me around, that's fine with me*, and she went to the library at
lunchtime. You weren't allowed to eat in the library so she
saved her lunch to eat walking home. In classes, she decided
to concentrate on what the teachers were saying. *It's pretty
interesting anyway*, she told herself, but actually it wasn't.

   Meanwhile, the others were getting on with life, talking to
each other about ordinary things.

   The same thing happened on Tuesday. But on Wednesday
morning Listen woke up and thought: *This is all a mistake!
They think that I'm the one who's ignoring them! It was just
a joke, that running away thing at the Walkathon, and now
they think I can't take a joke!* How terrible! But such a relief,
and she practically ran all the way to school to clear things up.

   Caro was arriving at the school gate at the same time as
her, so Listen called, 'Hi!'

   Caro looked around and said 'Hi-i-i,' sort of comical and
musical, like the 'Hi' you might say to a big blue beetle that
landed on your plate at a picnic. Everyone would laugh and
you'd shake the plate and the beetle would fly away.

'What's going on?' said Listen, walking in step with Caro.

'No-o-thing,' said Caro, quickening her pace. 'SIA!!!' she shouted suddenly, and she waved at Sia, who was down in the teachers' parking lot. Sia turned and stared, and Caro sprinted away from Listen, pounding down the driveway. Listen paused and watched as Caro reached Sia and seemed to hunch over, gasping and talking rapidly, until Sia hugged her as if she needed comforting.

Listen walked on quickly then, in a different direction.

Later that day, packing up to go home, Donna spoke to Listen in a kindly voice. 'Can I just explain something?' she said.

'If you want.'

'It's just that we all agreed on this, OK? It's no offence *at all*. See, the other day we had a strategy meeting at my place and we decided we have to kind of like make the tough decisions? If we're going to survive, because, you know, I realized that this place is even more of a fundamental shift in the universe than I thought it would be? And we have to shift away from you, if we're going to survive the shift. It makes sense if you think of it that way.'

Listen nodded, trying to figure out what Donna meant.

'And it was a good example at the Walkathon,' Donna continued, looking thoughtful. 'It was kind of like confirmation that we'd made the right decision? When we were all making jokes about mines and that, and you were *laughing* but you weren't making jokes yourself. You were kind of like *taking* because you were laughing, but you weren't giving anything to us. And this is really, really hard for us, OK?'

'O-K,' said Listen, trying to give her 'OK' a lilting, comical edge.

The next day, Listen stayed home from school. Marbie was taking a day off work because she had a ticklish throat, and she suggested Listen might need a break. After clearing her throat several times, Listen decided she had a tickle too.

'I'll write a note and say you've got pneumonia,' offered Marbie. So that was settled.

Marbie was reading a novel in the sunny part of the kitchen, and Listen went into her bedroom, stared around the room and remembered: *It's the Thursday after next! I'm allowed to do the next spell!*

It was a Spell To Make a Vacuum Cleaner Break.

'Well,' she said to herself, 'that's a pretty stupid spell.' But then she remembered that their new vacuum cleaner was already broken. It got broken in the move: Grandpa Zing dropped a wardrobe on top of it in the back of the truck. Maybe a Spell To Make a Vacuum Cleaner Break would have the reverse effect on a broken one? You never knew.

These were the instructions:

---

1. Wear sunglasses all day. From now on.
Quickly, go and get the sunglasses and put them on.
2. Walk backwards, but every few steps skip a bit and say 'Oh!', as if you've just remembered something.
3. Phone up a Tae Kwon Do class and sign yourself in, then phone again ten minutes later and cancel.
4. Peel fifteen potatoes and sticky-tape the peelings back together.

NOW YOU HAVE TO WAIT SIX WEEKS PLUS ONE DAY BEFORE YOU CAN TURN ANOTHER PAGE!
(You'd better put the date in your calendar.)

These were challenging things, but Listen did them all. Even when she and Marbie went out with Marbie's sister, Fancy, for a coffee in Castle Hill. It was difficult wearing sunglasses inside and walking backwards, but she explained that her theory about the flu was to disguise herself and run away from it so it wouldn't find her. Marbie and Fancy were impressed.

That night, Listen checked in the hall closet, but the vacuum cleaner was still crushed, as she had known it would be.

She instant-messaged Sia, but Sia didn't answer. She found Caro and Gabrielle in a chat room but they slid offline when she tried to join the chat. Finally, she phoned Joanne.

'OK,' said Joanne. 'You deserve the truth.' Then she explained in detail the strategy meeting that Listen had missed at Donna's place.

The next day Listen joined a new group.

She chose Angela Saville's group, and each day she asked them questions. For instance, she asked everyone what they did on the weekend, whether they watched the Valerio movie last night, whether they liked it, what subject they had after lunch, whether they liked that subject and so on. She listened to their answers.

One day, at lunchtime, the lawn was set with its garlands of girls. She saw Angela Saville's group and she walked the grass carefully towards them, ready with a smile. The circle felt funny. Angela and the others saw her coming; their heads bobbed down and their eyes giggled slyly at each other.

Listen, from not far away, saw that the circle was perfect, and tight. She stopped. She was not going over.

She stood on the lawn among the garlands of girls, and she felt, for a moment, like a Christmas tree. A fading Christmas tree, awkward and bulky in the centre of a room, when Christmas had finished weeks before. Stupidly conspicuous and perfectly invisible, both at once. Coloured lights were blinking down her legs, her arms were branches slung with rusting baubles, and strings of stale popcorn dangled from her hair.

Seriously! Help!
Well, it's continued, and I can't figure out exactly why.

In the last week or so, I've had three more affairs, well, three more games of tennis, with the aeronautical engineer. I bought a new tennis racquet, thinking it would improve my playing, but it didn't.

It's true that the A.E. is wild and weird and the world needs more of that sort of thing. He's kind of side-on to the universe. But so what? I really, really love Nathaniel.

Anyhow, this morning I played tennis again and three important things happened.

First, when he arrived at the tennis court, A.E. mentioned that he has read 'Madame Bovary', in the original French. 'Have you?' I said. 'Yes,' he replied.

Second, halfway through the first game,

A.E. stopped and took off his right tennis shoe and sock, to check on a blister. The blister was so bad that he had to PEEL the sock away from his foot. It was disgusting. I noticed that his toes are hairy.

Third, and I guess this is actually the only important thing, third, after he'd put a Band-Aid on the blister and replaced his sock and shoe, he stood up, turned to me, and said: 'You want to come to my place, and, you know, fool around?'

Fool around!!

I said: 'I have a boyfriend!'

He shrugged. I'm not sure whether his shrug meant 'So what?' about my having a boyfriend, or 'Oh well' about my not wanting to fool around.

Whatever, we played a set of tennis, I lost every point, and then, of course, I went back to work.

So my question is, why have I been playing tennis

'Have you noticed,' Marbie said to Nathaniel, 'that Listen isn't talking about school any more?'

'I know,' he said, serving up the soup. 'I've been thinking the same thing. I mean, she's always quiet, but then she usually has –'

'She has those sudden outbursts of talking,' agreed Marbie. 'And I keep waiting for one. I've been asking her questions about school but she –'

'Exactly. Me too. Every time I ask her a question, she says "Fine". The other day I asked her what they sold in the school tuck shop and she said "Fine".'

'Maybe she doesn't like us any more,' Marbie said, sadly. 'Maybe she's become one of those teenager people who only talk to their friends. She's got the volume on her music turned up pretty high right now, so that's a symptom, I guess.'

'Well, when your family's here for Cassie's birthday this weekend, they'll ask a lot of questions,' Nathaniel pointed out. 'They won't let her get away with "Fine".'

'Remember her first week of Year 7, how she didn't stop talking?' Marbie said, nostalgically. 'She told us about the Geography teacher who ran around the room pretending to be the monsoon wind, and about the Science teacher who said they had to dissect frogs and Caro said she would get a note

94

from her mum saying she didn't have to dissect frogs and the teacher said, "Notes don't count!" and Caro said, "Notes *always* count," and the teacher said, "Have you read –"

At that moment, Listen walked in and sat at the table, saying, 'Cool. Pumpkin soup.'

'Have you read *Madame Bovary?*' Marbie said, smoothly. 'In the original French? Oh, hi, Listen, I like the music you're playing down there.'

'No,' replied Nathaniel. 'I've only seen the movie.'

'I've read *Charlie and the Chocolate Factory*,' offered Listen. 'But I haven't seen the movie. The old one or the Johnny Depp one either.'

'You haven't seen the movies!' Marbie cried, and Nathaniel rain-danced around the table. The telephone rang and he incorporated the answering-of-the-phone into the dance, so that his head was upside down for most of the conversation.

'Yes . . . yes, there's a Listen Taylor here, shall I . . . OK, sure, you're from where? . . . From the Kenthurst School of – really! Uh huh. She did? Well no, I didn't . . . I mean, of course! Well, I'm sorry about that. You know what? I'm going to call you back in five minutes. OK. Can I get your number? OK, OK, I'll call you back.'

He wrote a number on the back of the electricity bill (which he swiped from under a magnet on the fridge), and then he turned his head right way up to hang up the phone.

'Hey, Listen,' he said, sitting back at the table. 'Why didn't you tell us you wanted to do Tae Kwon Do?'

'Because I don't want to do Tae Kwon Do.' Listen took a bite of her bread roll.

'Well, the guy on the phone says you joined his class and then you phoned back ten minutes later and cancelled.'

They both looked at Listen. She dipped her roll into her pumpkin soup, studying the soup to do this, and then she looked up from under her fringe, saw they were still staring and said, 'What?'

'Could it have been a different Listen Taylor?' suggested Marbie. 'There would be a lot of them around. *Listen* is a very common name.'

'OK, shut up. You can talk. *Marbie Zing*. I wanted to do Tae Kwon Do but then I didn't want to. I changed my mind.'

'In the space of ten minutes!'

'I decided it would be too expensive. Hey, should I sand the kitchen cupboards tonight, ready to repaint?'

'Don't try and change the subject. Nathaniel, call the man back and enrol Listen in his class.'

'What do you think I'm doing?' Nathaniel was reaching for the phone.

'Oh no, that's OK. I changed my mind. I *seriously* don't want to do Tae Kwon Do, guys. Do we have enough sandpaper?'

'Because it's too expensive!' cried Marbie. 'Listen! You must do *anything* you want. You should be learning Portuguese and auto-mechanics and candle-making, and *definitely* Tae Kwon Do! Fancy learned the drums when she was your age and she is now a more interesting person than I am! Because I don't play the drums! Money is no *object* where *interest* is concerned! Would you like to play the drums?'

'Well, but I'm not really *interested*—'

'Shh, Listen, it's ringing.'

'You don't need to be upside down this time, Nathaniel.'

'Is this the Kenthurst School of Tae Kwon Do? Yes, we just spoke. *I have a new student for you!* I know. I know! I know.'

What have I been thinking?!
Forget I said a word.
OK, it's after midnight and I'm lying awake staring at
Nathaniel, and thinking of how great he is with his

daughter, and how I've never even seen the movie of Madame Bovary, *let alone read the book.*

Plus, it's not an affair. I've just been playing tennis with a stranger. He did ask me back to his place to fool around but maybe he was talking about PlayStation?

The only reason I called it an 'affair' is that I haven't told Nathaniel about the tennis. Interestingly, the only reason I have NOT told him is that it's NOT an affair.

Tomorrow, Nathaniel and Listen will spend all day helping to prepare for Cassie's party. And I know Nathaniel thinks our Family Secret is dangerous and wrong, but he still accepts it's part of my life, and he comes along every Friday night, and he's much more punctual than I am.

He just woke up and asked if I'm OK and can I sleep? Should we go for a swim at Bellbird? he said, even though he has a cold and an early start.

I told him I was writing a letter to a magazine problem page, and he kissed my elbow.

I will cancel our meeting on Monday. I will never see the A.E. again.

Yours,
Temporarily Insane, but Now Recovered

Part 5

Cassie's Birthday Party

14

Neighbourhood children were playing a skipping game on the street. Occasionally, the game would pause as the sun-heated tarmac became too much for one or another of the children. A garden hose was turned on to burning soles. Then the game would continue.

Across the street, Marbie said, 'Hmm,' Nathaniel took a sip of beer, and Listen shook her head and murmured, 'Why no shoes?' They were sitting in a row on their front porch, waiting for their party guests.

'If this front driveway belonged to us,' said Marbie, 'instead of to the whole apartment block, what would we do with it?'

'I'd put in a duck pond,' said Listen. 'And gentle, grazing horses.'

'I'd build a university,' Nathaniel said. 'Educate the youth around these parts. Talking about education and the youth around these parts, what's happened to Donna and the others that they prefer to be researching at the library than coming to our party? That just doesn't sound like the Donna I remember.'

'I know,' agreed Listen. 'It's because they're all scared of the teachers at Clareville. And we got this assignment yesterday and it's due Monday, so, actually I should be with them at the library too. But they said they'd photocopy the research for me and I'll meet them tomorrow and collect it.'

'So it's worked out perfectly,' Marbie said.

'Exactly.' Listen nodded.

Two cars of party guests arrived, and the neighbourhood children had to clear off the road.

'Look at that!' cried Grandma Zing, bustling out of the first car. 'We all arrived at once!'

Grandpa Zing got out more slowly and saluted the hosts one at a time.

'We're here!' cried Fancy, climbing out of the second car. 'And we've got the birthday girl!'

The birthday girl opened the back door, twisting her mouth around to make her face casual. She stepped out and brushed down her dress.

'HAPPY BIRTHDAY, CASSIE!' Nathaniel, Marbie, Listen and Grandma Zing shouted, and Cassie looked up with a shining smile.

'I've got my friend Lucinda too,' she remembered, and everyone said, 'Oh!' as another little girl emerged from the car.

'What's Radcliffe doing?' said Grandma Zing, squinting through the window of Fancy's car. 'Why isn't he getting out? Radcliffe! What are you doing in there?'

'He's just trying to figure out the air conditioning,' explained Fancy. 'He couldn't get it to work.'

'Fancy, darling, tonight's good, between seven and ten. I've got the new code; it's in the mint.'

'All right,' agreed Fancy, but her mother had already turned away, and was rapping on the window with her keys, calling, 'Too late, Radcliffe! You're here now!'

In the living room, everyone exclaimed about the multi-coloured beanbags and the table covered with treats. There were banana fritters, chocolate bananas, banana tarts, banana bread, a pavlova covered in bananas and jugs of banana smoothie. Also, there was a large bowl of punch in which bananas and strawberries floated.

'Look at all the strawberries in the punch!' cried Grandma

Zing. 'Cassie, do you know, I almost forgot to bring your presents! Can you imagine?'

'Not really,' said Cassie.

'Your place is looking gorgeous,' said Fancy.

'A *garden apartment* is such a precious find!' declared Grandma Zing.

'What kind of a security system do you have?' said Radcliffe.

'Does it have a bathroom?' asked Cassie's friend Lucinda, politely.

'You got a pest inspection done, right?' said Radcliffe.

'That's not termite damage, what you're looking at there, Radcliffe,' said Grandpa Zing. 'That's just regular wear and tear.'

'Haven't they done it up nicely,' said Grandma Zing. 'They've put silver covers on all their electrical outlets. Isn't *that* a nice touch?'

'Nice painting job here,' said Radcliffe. 'Professional or . . . ?'

'This is not just a house-warming party,' said Cassie, 'this is also a *birthday* party. As far as I recall.'

After Cassie's presents had been opened, they toured the apartment, establishing, several times, that: there were six apartments in the building, that this one was on the *ground floor*, that they were almost finished renovating and that Marbie had only been joking when she said they were going to tear down the outside bathroom wall and bathe *al fresco*. Then Cassie suggested they play Pass the Parcel.

They played Pass the Parcel, Musical Chairs and Pin the Tail on Grandpa Zing. Cassie had painted a picture of Grandpa Zing for the purposes of this game and Grandpa Zing was a good sport about it.

Later, they sat down, still breathless from the games, and ate banana treats.

'I'll never get out of this beanbag,' said Grandma Zing now and then.

Nathaniel took Radcliffe and Grandpa Zing on to the roof of the apartment building to see where the air-conditioning vents came out. Grandma Zing remembered she had a house-warming present and returned from her car with a fig tree. Marbie watered the tree and Fancy made cocktails. She used vodka, vermouth, apple juice and apple gratings, then she put a curl of apple peel on the edge of each glass.

'Look,' she said, carrying the glasses carefully, as their contents lapped over the edges. 'I've invented an apple martini.'

Listen took Cassie and Lucinda into her bedroom so they could play Cassie's new game of Valerio Rock. You took turns composing melodies on the keyboard, sang into the micro-phone, and then waited while the game added beats and back-up singers so that you were, for a moment, a rock star. After that, the game became complicated and you had to spell, mime, draw pictures and do the hokey-cokey.

'Hang on a minute,' said Cassie, and she ran into the living room, where she announced to the room: 'Listen is *such* a great dancer', before running back into the bedroom. 'Keep dancing, Listen,' she ordered, 'until everyone comes and sees.'

In the main bedroom, Grandma Zing admired the curtains, and then took them down so she could redo the hems.

The game of Valerio Rock ended, and Listen said, 'Cassie, your nose is bleeding.'

'It'll stop in a minute,' said Cassie. 'It's because it's summer.'

'She just needs a cloth,' explained Lucinda, 'and I have to put a key on the back of her neck.'

Listen gave Cassie a cloth and the front-door key and left the girls to work on the bleeding nose.

In the living room, Marbie put on a Red Hot Chili Peppers album and asked Listen to teach Fancy how to dance. Listen jumped on the spot to the music, shaking her head wildly, and Fancy obediently copied.

Quietly, Grandpa Zing and Radcliffe retreated to the porch.

In the bathroom, Cassie leaned over the tub and allowed her nose to bleed. She tried to write her name but it just went: spot . . . spot . . . spot, each spot leaking in a different direction.

Lucinda sat on the edge of the tub, holding the key against the back of Cassie's neck and watching the blood with interest. Every now and then she reached to turn the taps on and wash the blood away.

Later, Grandma Zing asked Listen how she was finding Clareville College these days, and whether she had made any new friends.

'She likes her old friends, don't you, Listen?' Nathaniel said affectionately. 'They're doing her homework for her today so no wonder she likes them.'

Everyone congratulated Listen on having such generous friends.

'Tell us about your teachers, Listen,' Fancy said. 'Tell us some funny teacher stories.'

'Well,' said Listen, slowly. 'There's a Food Technology teacher who taught us how to make lamingtons. It's not a funny story, but I could make some now?' She was walking backwards towards the kitchen.

'But will you need eggs?' said Marbie. 'Because I used them all in the pavlova.'

'Yes,' said Listen, hesitating again. 'I'll need eggs.'

Fancy looked at her watch. 'Gosh,' she said. 'It's eight o'clock. Let's go to the corner store and buy some eggs for Listen. Marbie?'

'Tell us about Year 2 while they're gone,' Grandma Zing said to Cassie. 'How's your teacher, darling? What do you think of your teacher?'

'I prefer Mr Woodford to our teacher,' chatted Lucinda. 'He's the other Year 2 teacher? And he's REALLY funny. I wish I was in his class instead.'

'Do you?' Grandma Zing regarded Lucinda, and then turned back to Cassie.

'I like *my* teacher,' declared Cassie. 'She's nice.'

'That's my girl,' said Grandma Zing. 'Come here and give me a hug.'

Cassie gave her grandmother a hug.

'We might be a while, OK, everyone?' said Fancy, drawing a black chiffon scarf from her handbag. 'Because I think we should go into Baulkham Hills for the eggs, don't you, Marbie?'

'I agree,' said Marbie.

'Be careful, eh?' said Nathaniel, reaching for a handful of peanuts.

'Over there, behind that station wagon,' Fancy pointed, and Marbie pulled over.

'Have you got it?' said Marbie.

'It's in my scarf.'

'And the new code?'

'Apparently it's in the mint.' Fancy opened the back door

and reached into a wicker basket. 'Got it.' She fell into step alongside Marbie.

'Final check,' said Marbie, drawing out her pager and tapping in a number. They walked on side by side, until a cat gave a faint 'miaow' from Marbie's pocket. 'That's it,' said Marbie. 'You OK?'

'You bet,' said Fancy, and they separated smoothly, Fancy floating into the distance. Her earrings glinted in the moonlight.

Lucinda had fallen asleep on her beanbag when Fancy and Marbie returned.

'Here we are,' said Fancy, opening the front door.

'All right?' said Radcliffe.

'All right,' agreed Fancy.

Listen reached out for the eggs.

Part 6

The Story of the Watercolour Painter

15

Once upon a time there was a watercolour painter who thought he could invent a parachute.

This was in the early days of parachutes.

Out in the meadow with his easel and his brushes, he saw an early parachutist dripping from the sky.

'How was it?' he cried, jogging up to the gathering crowd.

'Oh,' cried the parachutist, tangled in the parachute, 'I feel *sick*.'

But this was in Paris, so they spoke in French.

Those days, parachutes had a design flaw: they did not float gently to the ground, they spun through the air at dizzying speed and parachutists turned an olive green.

So, the watercolour painter went home and put up his feet for a coffee and a think. *How can we stop these brave falling men feeling sick?* is what he thought.

After thirty-five years of thinking, he figured it out. He put down his coffee, picked up his sketchpad and called to his wife. 'Look,' he said, calm with pride as he tilted the sketch towards her.

His wife squinted, and her eyebrows bounced, for his parachute was *upside down*! Instead of being shaped like an 'n', it was shaped like a 'u'.

'Will it work?' she mused.

'Of course!' he exclaimed. He made a parachute out of her handkerchief to prove it. The handkerchief flopped to the floor but, as he pointed out, it didn't spin.

So convinced was he that *this* was the solution to the spinning parachute he decided to make one of his own. He ran it up on his wife's sewing machine. Next he persuaded a friend to let him try it by jumping from the basket of the friend's hot-air balloon.

He was so excited that he didn't test it first with a dummy (or a cat), which would have been the custom in those days; he just strapped himself in and jumped.

He plummeted straight to the ground – like a vase knocked from a shelf – and was killed.

When she first heard this story, Maude Sausalito (aged eleven at the time) felt a cold gust of sadness for the painter. Then she imagined (yearningly) the things he might have landed on which would have saved his life.

A haystack; a pond; a freshly turned garden bed.

A vat of mulberries!

A gigantic banana milkshake!

A stack of blueberry muffins!

(She was hungry.)

If only, she thought – and she still thinks this often, even now – if only the stupid, overexcited man could have caught an updraught in his useless parachute! If only the updraught could have carried him high into a zinging blue sky, over a hill of whipped butter, across a maple-syrup pond. And finally, gently, deposited him on a buttermilk pancake bed.

Years later, after the terrible thing had happened, Maude lay in bed for several weeks. Loss and pain were put into context at that time: broken hearts, blisters, paper cuts, scaldings; all grains of sand pouring calmly through an hourglass. She was used to them. But this new thing was a sharp rock lodged in the neck of the hourglass, choking the flow. No time, no breath, just monolithic pain holding everything still. If only she could pick up the glass, shake it loose, throw away the pain as she had thrown away that life.

Sometimes she dreamed herself out of the hourglass and into the basket of a hot-air balloon. But then she could only watch helplessly as an inverted parachute fell from the basket and crashed through the air to the ground.

Part 7

The Last Few Weeks of Term

16

It was well known at Redwood Primary that Warren had a wife up the coast. He just hadn't mentioned this, specifically, to Cath.

In fact, in the weeks after the Borrowed Cat, it seemed to Cath that 'Warren's wife, Breanna' was the subject of constant conversation at Redwood, *even among her friends*. For example, Suzanne would say to Lenny, 'What are you up to this weekend, Len?' To which Lenny would reply, 'Going up the coast to Terrigal, I think.' To which Suzanne would declare, 'Terrigal! Isn't that where Warren's wife, Breanna, lives?' To which Lenny would demur, 'No, Warren's wife, Breanna, lives at Avoca. It's the next beach around.'

Or, for example, Mr Bel Castro (teacher, Year 5A) would say, 'These muffins are delicious!' To which Ms Waratah (teacher, Year 4B) would reply, 'Oh, thank you! The recipe is Warren's wife, Breanna's!' To which Mr Bel Castro would say 'Gosh.'

That's how it seemed to Cath in the weeks after the Borrowed Cat. *Warren's wife, Breanna* was like one of those new phrases you learn and then find that it's been kicking around for years.

Of course, the night of the Borrowed Cat itself, she only knew that Warren had kept the wife a secret, and then sprung it on her, cheerfully, like a novelty mousetrap. Driving home that afternoon, she felt a flash of terror at how stupid she had been. Then the terror became a fierce blush of self-loathing at how VERY VERY STUPID SHE HAD BEEN.

The blush lasted almost all the way home and blazed up again when she found her favourite dress set out neatly on the ironing board. Also, her black opal necklace, whimsically looped around the fridge-door handle as a reminder to herself to wear it. She opened the fridge and slammed it so hard that the kitchen shook.

Then she opened the fridge again and poured herself a glass of apple juice in order to calm down. 'So what? He's married. Big deal.' She wandered carelessly into the dining room, where she stamped once and flung the juice at the window. It dribbled over her reflection.

At her law class, tears welled in her eyes. She realized, drawing sad little squiggles in her notebook, that there would be no shy, meaningful glances tonight, no bluesy conversation. No! There would be Warren-and-his-Wife-Breanna. They would sit opposite her with their hands intertwined.

Actually, now that she thought about it, it would be *more* than just Warren-and-his-Wife. It would be the whole gang!

'Come along', he had written in his quiz at the Monday assembly. 'Come along to see the Carotid Sticks, *where we will meet a jolly circle of my friends, my wife, incidentally, among them*!'

That's what he had meant. It was so obvious, she was blinded by her tears, and her breathing became tangled. Doctor Carmichael, the lecturer, leaned towards her from his podium and his turban almost fell off.

Warren's friends, she realized, would stand up noisily when she arrived, their ashtrays and drinks in a clutter. There would be a shortish woman in a large-collared blouse, who would swap a cigarette to her left hand, and squint a smile at Cath through the smoke. There would be two skinny men in corduroys, each saying 'Hi!' in a witty friendly way. Also, a little later, breathless from the Central Coast train, there would be Warren's wife, Breanna.

By the time Cath reached the Borrowed Cat, she was furious with Warren and his gang. *Don't you smoke in my face,* she commanded, angrily, as she pushed open the door. And: *What's with the corduroy, boys?* she sneered as the waitress welcomed her.

The Borrowed Cat was in a basement. An unexpected spotlight roamed the room, but otherwise it flickered darkly like a shaded candle. The waitress led Cath to a corner table where Warren was sitting alone.

She gave him a vicious, complicated smile, which he returned with a dazzling beam, stretching out his arms in welcome.

'You're not late at all!' he said.

'Yes I am. I am *fifteen minutes* late.'

'It's OK, they're not starting for another hour,' he reassured her.

'Where's your wife, Breanna?' she said archly. 'And everybody else?'

'There is nobody else,' he apologized. 'And Bree just called. She's not going to make it and she's disappointed. She wanted to meet you. She said to say "hi", OK?'

Cath was so shocked she sat down and snatched the menu from Warren's hands.

That night, their knees touched under the table several times, and each time she moved away abruptly. She drank a reckless pitcher of sangria, and she made a little monster out of Warren's bread roll so he couldn't eat it. Also, she told him the facts of some brutal murder cases, all the time glaring and glowering at him, while he leaned forward, delighted.

When the Carotid Sticks began playing, she turned her chair around so she could see the band, and fell asleep against his shoulder.

When she woke, she told Warren that the band was *crap*

and that was a word she never used. 'I only agreed to come,' she said, 'because I was thinking of the Clotted Creams.' He shouted with laughter and suggested they see the Clotted Creams together some other time. 'No,' she said, 'because you have a bony, uncomfortable shoulder and I hardly slept a wink.' He shouted again and then apologized sincerely.

While the band packed up, she asked a lot of ironic questions about the wife. *What does she do for a living? Oh, and why does she live up the coast? Uh-huh, and where did you two meet?*

The wife was a psychologist, and was having trouble finding work in Sydney, so she lived up the coast during the week. She did relationship counselling up there. They had met through friends or something dull like that. Breanna had a late appointment that day and would come down on the early train tomorrow. Usually, she arrived Fridays, on the seven fifty-three.

'Ah,' agreed Cath, 'the seven fifty-three.' She felt wonderfully cutting.

But the following week, back at school, Cath discovered the wife's renown and felt contrite. It was not Warren's fault. He must have assumed that she knew about the wife! He had just kept her out of the conversation!

The weather shifted one shade down: the sky cast a light that was cautious and reserved, and the air took on a disapproving chill. Cath walked around in cardigans and in a dull, private shame.

With Warren, she became gentle and polite, as if she had discovered he had a terminal disease rather than a wife.

Often, he looked at her in a puzzled and disappointed way as if to say: what has happened to my friend?

But, she cried in the middle of the night, *he is married! How can I continue as his 'friend'?* At the same time, she wondered what had happened to their friendship. Could it just end like that?

Coincidentally, the day after one such sleepless night, Cath attended a law class on:

Principles of Statutory Interpretation: Lesson 1

She always began her law notes with a flamboyant heading. Begin as you mean to go on. After a while, though, the lecturer's voice would drift, taking its own meandering path, and her notes in turn would grow drowsy. Today, Cath's notes paid attention, at least for the *first* principle of statutory interpretation.

> *Generalia specialibus non derogant*: if a special Act is followed by a general Act, the special Act remains as an exception to the general.

Doctor Carmichael explained: 'For example. Let us say Parliament enacts the Care for Pigs Act. This is an act requiring all pet pigs to be dyed a lurid shade of orange.'

He paused, but nobody ever laughed in law class.

'e.g,' Cath wrote in her notes, '<u>Care for Pigs Act</u>. Must dye pigs orange.'

'And one month later,' continued Doctor Carmichael, 'Parliament enacts the Care for Animals Act. This act requires all *pets* to be dyed blue. OK, guys, let's say you have a pet pig. What colour do you dye your pig?'

'1 mnth ltr,' Cath wrote. '<u>Care for Animals Act</u>. Must dye pets blue.' She waited with her pen poised for the lecturer to give the answer.

'Come on, come on,' said Doctor Carmichael, looking around the room. 'Take a guess! Do we dye our pig orange or blue?'

Ask the pig, thought Cath, *which it prefers*.

'Orange,' said Doctor Carmichael, calmly. 'You must dye your pig orange.'

'Dye pig orange,' wrote Cath and doodled a pig.

'You see?' Doctor Carmichael had bright blue eyes and wisps of orange hair escaping from the edges of his turban. 'The first Act was *specific*, so it stays on as an exception to the second. Your dogs and cats and turtles must be blue, but your *pig* has *got* to stay orange.'

At this point, Cath's notes faded into half-finished words – 'dog, cat, turts, bl'. Then she wrote: *Surely it is wrong to dye a pig any colour at all?*

She drew a circle around the question mark, and added petals to the circle. The petals made her think of Warren. *We have bought a DeLonghi Sandwich Maker together*, she remembered sadly. *If I can't have an unfurling romance, why can't I at least have the friendship?*

But she knew that the special little act, the purchase of a DeLonghi Sandwich Maker, had been eclipsed by his announcement: 'My wife.' She could never be friends with him again.

Generalia specialibus non derogant.

Aha! Cath realized, with a sudden thumping heart: *If a special Act is followed by a general Act, the special Act remains as an exception to the general!* So it's all right! Her face was burning. The sandwich maker is allowed to carry on! It remains as an *exception* to the Wife!

After that, with some relief, Cath returned to her jocular ways with Warren, and he also seemed relieved to have her back. They started having takeaway lattes again, and sometimes hot chocolates with marshmallows. And they spent a lot of time kneeling in front of the staffroom radiator trying to turn it up.

Since their sandwich-maker friendship had never included

discussion of the Wife, Cath did not raise her in their conversations now. Neither did Warren.

One Wednesday afternoon, they worked in the staffroom until the sky was heavy with darkness. Walking to the parking lot, through the empty, echoing school grounds, cold fog curled around their ankles. 'Like my cat,' suggested Cath. Warren gave a chuckle, and kicked a pebble towards Cath. She kicked it straight back.

'Don't our cars look lonely?' said Warren. 'We should park them next to each other when we work late like this.'

'So they can get to know each other,' agreed Cath.

They were now at the edge of the parking lot – Cath's white Mercedes Sports gleamed from the far right corner; Warren's rusting Corolla glinted from the left.

'Holy baloney, I love your car,' breathed Warren. 'Remind me how you scored that again? Some wealthy former lover?'

'I won it in a competition.'

'Lucky girl,' whistled Warren, and then swiftly: 'Remind me when you were planning to take me for a ride in it?'

'Right this moment,' said Cath, clapping her hands together once like Mary Poppins. 'You don't have any plans, do you?'

'*Plans*,' said Warren, sadly. 'I'm as lonely as our cars are tonight. I was going to see a movie actually. But what kind of a fool would choose a movie over a ride in *your* car, Cath? What kind of a fool, what kind of a tool, what kind of a *drool*-ing mule?'

'I could drive you to the movie if you like. I'll see it with you.'

Warren leaped into the air. He was tall enough already: Cath imagined his leap would take him right into the stars.

Then, suddenly, Katie Toby (teacher, Kinder A) was

standing beside them. Cath shrieked, and Warren said, 'Holy *jacaranda*, woman, where did *you* come from?'

They both stared down at Katie Toby, who was little, with a dimpled, round face and a reputation, among parents, teachers and children alike, as: *sweet as a toffee apple.*

'Hi, guys,' she giggled. 'Sorry to scare you. I've just come from my classroom. Going to a movie, are you?'

Cath nodded uneasily.

'What movie?'

'Ah, the Valerio retrospective at the Chauvel,' said Warren, after a beat. 'It's *Pie in the Sky* tonight.'

'Oh yeah, *great*. I'd love to see that again. What time? On your way right now?'

'Well,' said Warren, 'it starts at nine.'

Then there was a silence as Katie dimpled at them until Warren said, 'You want to come along?'

'Oh *no*!' cried Katie. 'I'm off! My bicycle's just over there! Stay joyous!' and she skittered away into the darkness.

Cath and Warren approached Cath's car in silence, but as soon as they had each pressed the car doors closed Warren said, 'Thank Christ she didn't accept,' and Cath felt such a gust of relief that she fell into a fit of giggles. She couldn't get the keys in the ignition, she was giggling so helplessly. Warren sat beside her, laughing happily and looking around at the upholstery.

Then, just as Cath had calmed enough to sniff and wipe her eyes, Warren's phone rang.

'WHERE *ARE* YOU?' cried a tinny voice.

It was Warren's wife, Breanna. Inside Cath's car. Cath gave a little shiver.

'I'm in a beautiful Mercedes Sports car next to the lovely Cath, and we're going to the movies,' Warren explained promptly. 'How about you?'

'I'm *here*! At *home*! I've come down for a surprise visit! I've got candles and *everything*!' Breanna's voice rushed along in a high-pitched gabble. It was unnecessarily loud and was filling Cath's car. She opened her window.

'You're joking,' said Warren, his voice deepening and softening at once. 'You're here? My beautiful Bree, within *minutes* of me? On a week night?'

'I was starting to worry about you! What kind of a job does he have, I thought. I thought he was a teacher! A laugh of a job! I was wrong! Come home! Come on! I've got Indian!'

'I'll be there in five.'

He returned his phone to his pocket. 'Sorry, Cath. Another time?'

As he walked towards his own car he blew a passionate kiss her way, which she almost took for herself. Then she realized it was for her car.

Driving home, Cath passed the ice-cream van that was always parked across the street from her apartment block and thought: *That van is NEVER open.* What if she wanted an ice cream right now? Even if it *was* after eight, and a cold, foggy, blustery night. She would, in fact, like an ice cream.

She walked into her apartment and the silence seemed to catch her like a hangnail.

I like the way he walks, thought Cath, one late afternoon, watching Warren cross the playground. *He looks good in that linen suit, too, with the open collar. I wonder when I'll get to kiss his collarbone?*

She watched as he approached their building.

It's not wrong to think about kissing his collarbone. That's probably healthy. You have to fantasize about someone's collarbone; it could be Brad Pitt, let's say, and you know you're never going to kiss his collarbone. So why not dream about Warren's?

Warren was now running up the steps to the Year 2

125

balcony, and Cath thought fiercely: *Turn right, turn right towards my classroom.*

He did. He leaned in to her open classroom door and said, '*There* you are! I've been looking for you everywhere!'

'How come?' She busied herself away from the window. 'I'm just taking down these pictures of polar bears.'

'Because I want to take you out to dinner tonight,' explained Warren. 'I've got a reservation at Tetsuya's, and Breanna was coming down especially, but she just cancelled, if you can believe it, so you're not allowed to say no, OK?'

Cath regarded him.

'And also,' said Warren, 'it's my birthday today.'

'OK,' said Cath. 'I'll come.'

After Tetsuya's, they took a taxi to the Shangri-La Hotel for cocktails. The taxi nudged through traffic and gathering rain, and Warren Wishful Woodford unfurled his long thin body, and unfurled his words ('How much?' to the driver), and his body and his words were like a banner, or a long royal carpet, thought Cath, gazing through the steamy taxi window. He was standing on the pavement waiting for her, and she was inside the taxi thinking that his words were like a pathway through the woods.

As she gathered up her handbag, he opened her door, taking the steamy taxi window with him, and letting in the traffic and the cold. She walked beside him silently, her legs moving smoothly like the wheels of a cart through the furling, ferny fronds of a forest. (At Tetsuya's there had been a nine-course *degustation* menu, with a wine to match each course.)

At the cocktail bar, it was so crowded they had to lean in close to hear one another. They talked for a while about how wicked it was of Breanna to cancel on Warren's *birthday*, even *if* a pair of clients had phoned her to say they had made a joint suicide pact and were having trouble with the catch on the gun. 'Birthdays come but once a year,' said Cath, sternly, 'but suicide pacts?' She gave a dismissive shrug.

'A dime a dozen,' agreed Warren.

'Hey,' said Cath, changing the subject and looking up at Warren from her frothy strawberry cocktail (she reflected that her eyes would be shining in this light). 'I need your teaching advice. You know Cassie Zing?'

'How could anybody not know Cassie Zing?'

'Well, today she said "tax audit" five hundred times.'

'Of course she did.'

'Well,' agreed Cath, doubtfully, 'she does this all the time, you know. She chooses a word or a phrase to say five hundred times, and sometimes I think the best thing is to ignore it and she'll get over it, but she doesn't.'

'What other words?'

'You know, negative things. Like eczema or garbage disposal or penalty notice. Kind of negative in a small, itching way. Things from around the home that you don't usually talk about – anyway, now I think about it, maybe she's casting a kind of spell over the classroom, I mean a *good* spell, where she's taking all the evil out of the world by chanting away the ugly little things so there's nothing left for us but *good*, so maybe I should just, you know, let her cast her spell.'

'Does she take requests? Because I've got an ingrown toe-nail.'

'Seriously, do you think it's a spell thing? Or do you think maybe I'm drunk?'

'Well, she's either casting a spell or she's obsessive compulsive, and you are gorgeous when you're drunk. And you're the experienced teacher – I'm just making it up as I go along. Do you want me to ask Bree about Cassie? She used to work with kids before she got into relationship counselling.'

Bree was in the conversation a bit too much tonight, Cath thought, disgruntled.

'Oh no,' she said, 'I'll ask Lenny. Good idea! Professional help! I always forget that Lenny's the school counsellor as well as the Year 6B teacher. I'll ask her advice.'

'She'll be distracted,' said Warren, signalling for the bill. 'Sleeping with Frank Billson must be very – distracting.'

'You can't pay for this too, Warren. This will be me paying. This will be your birthday present from me. Watch me pay, OK? And HEY, HOW DO YOU KNOW ABOUT LENNY AND BILLSON? IT'S A SECRET!'

Warren slid the bill from underneath her hand and said, 'You coming out with me tonight? *That* is my birthday present from you. And I know about Lenny and Billson because Lenny and Billson are blindingly obvious. Everybody knows about them, Cath Murphy.'

'Do they?' Cath said, wonderingly, enjoying the way he just said her full name and scraping at the sides of her cocktail glass with the straw.

'Maybe not Heather Waratah,' conceded Warren. 'Heather Waratah probably doesn't know about Lenny and Billson. She's too busy baking muffins. Don't forget your jacket there, eh? Here, let me take your arm.'

Later that night, Cath lay awake replaying Warren's sentence: 'You coming out with me tonight? *That* is my birthday present from you.'

The next day Warren passed on Bree's 'eternal gratitude' to Cath, for taking care of Warren on his birthday.

Zooming from school to her law lecture, and then from the lecture to Feminist Discussion, Cath felt she had a full life. Her windscreen wipers dashed back and forth, trying to keep up with her full life.

She ran through the rain to the cafe and sat in the comfortable plum-purple chair. 'Hi,' she whispered and 'Sorry to be late', and Leonie mouthed back a quick 'No worries!'

Leonie Marple-Hedgington was an old friend of Cath's from teachers' college. She had purple hair, polar-white skin and the settled, mistaken belief that Cath was the kind of person who would want to go to Feminist Discussion. Cath did not like to correct her and so attended every session.

Leonie leaned forward, bonily, cardigan pushed up to her elbows, to say, 'I thought today,' (a little shy to start), 'I thought today we might find a way to deconstruct the rational/irrational duality?'

Everybody nodded, including Cath, but as she nodded she thought of Warren Woodford and his own special nods. His own sideways thinking nod, his own hearty, rapid nod, his own slow, *perhaps* nod, his nodding nod-nod.

'As you know, there's a crit group who call themselves the *irrationalists* so as to reclaim the word "irrational" and invest it with something powerful and good,' continued Leonie.

Irrational, thought Cath, and she thought, immediately, of the word: *affair.*

How irrational an affair would be! Even, let's say, if Warren planned such a thing. I would NEVER let it happen! It would be wrong, but more to the point: IRRATIONAL. I've read the books, I've seen the movies, I've read the magazine problem pages! Don't even worry about it. He'll keep promising to leave his wife, but he NEVER EVER will.

'Doing no more than exploring the boundaries of the admittedly nebulous notion of sense, of course.'

And of course, I wouldn't WANT him to leave his wife! That makes no SENSE. Because, see, if he's the kind of guy who leaves his wife, he's not a nice guy, and why would I want a not-nice guy? Plus, I would never want to hurt another woman like that. I'm at Feminist Discussion! If I had an affair with Warren, I would betray my own KIND!

'What we still have to do, you know, is to pin down the power/knowledge paradigm, and colonize Foucault, make him our own. Keeping in mind the Balkanisation of the issue, of course,' finished Leonie.

'Hmm,' agreed Cath, nodding along with the others.

In the last week of the school term Cath sat on her living-room floor, wrapped in her quilt, and played with the hole in her tooth with her tongue. It was so cold that the windows had fogged over, and her small electric heater did not know what to do. It made hysterical hissing noises.

Cath had to make a dentist appointment. She leaned out of her quilt to write in her Filofax, choosing the second Tuesday of the holidays to – *Make dentist appointment*. Then, efficiently, she closed the Filofax. So, that was done.

'Now, I'm sure you will *all* have noticed that Sydney is experiencing *record-breaking* lows even for winter – and this is only autumn!' the weatherman interrupted her. She looked at the TV and nodded her agreement.

'And you might *also* have heard some buzz around that *snow* might come to Sydney. You know what? I'm going to put my eggs in that basket too.'

'Snow!' said Cath, scornfully. 'It doesn't snow in Sydney!'

But still, imagine if it did! The weatherman was waving an arm over his map, and talking about ground temperatures, a cold front and moisture on its way. 'Or,' he was saying, 'let me go out on a limb here – I would not be at all surprised if this turned out to be *freezing rain*!'

She changed the channel to MTV. There were Things-To-Do clumped all around her, and her cat, Violin, trod from Thing to Thing; disrespectful, indiscriminate, like the weather. She took Violin beneath her arm, the bell on his collar jangling, and surveyed her Things-To-Do.

130

1.   A pile of egg cartons for Art and Craft at school. (Cut out the egg cups so that the kids can glue them to popsicle-stick rafts. Think up a reason why.)
2.   Cases and Materials on Torts. (Read Chapter 7. Trespass and Assault.)
3.   Letters from my Staffroom Pigeonhole. (Open.)

She decided to begin with the Letters from the Staffroom. The first envelope was addressed in elegant gold:

Cath Murphy, Teacher, Class 2B,
Redwood Primary, Castle Hill Road,
Kellyville

Dear Ms Murphy,
You may be pleased to know that my daughter (Cassie's) loose tooth has come out. And the Tooth Fairy has come and gone.

I hope you will forgive me for writing again so soon, but I have a small favour to ask.

I have just learned that Cassie's 'cousin' will be 'attending' Redwood next term — she is one of the Year 7 students from Clareville College, where, as you may have heard, there has been a flood! Apparently, there was a faulty connection which caused a water pipe to burst. So, after the holidays, she and her classmates are being 'shipped out' to your school for a month or two.

I say 'cousin', by the way, rather than cousin, for this reason: I have a sister, Marbie, who lives with a man named Nathaniel, along with Nathaniel's daughter. Do you see? And it is this daughter — Alissa Taylor, better known as 'Listen' Taylor — who is the 'cousin' of whom I speak.

In any case, I am wondering if you might keep an eye on Listen for us? She is beautiful, but perhaps not in the way that young people understand. And she seems to us a very quiet little thing. If you could just look in on her, once or twice – make sure she is not lost in the system – I would be so grateful.

Again, thank you for being such a delightful teacher to our Cassie, and again, I am longing to meet you at Parent-Teacher Night!

Best wishes,
Fancy Zing

'Well,' said Cath, rereading the part about what a 'delightful' teacher she was. She had heard something about seventh-graders using the new portable classrooms at Redwood next term, but she had only thought, wisely: *Billson would never have allowed this if it wasn't that he's distracted because he's so in love with Lenny.*

Now she drafted a polite reply to Fancy Zing, agreeing to look out for 'Listen', and pointing out (for the sake of something to say) that she herself had a toothache today, and wished it was a matter for the Tooth Fairy! (*Who ARE you, Cath Murphy?* she scolded as she wrote.) Then she turned to the next letter in her pile.

Cath Murphy
c/o Redwood Primary

Dear Ms Murphy,

The Harvey K. Whatsmeyer and Dorothy
P. Ruckleman Scholarship in Part-Time Law

It is with great pleasure that we inform you that you have been awarded the Harvey K. Whatsmeyer and Dorothy P. Ruckleman Scholarship in Part-Time Law.

This scholarship covers the full cost of tuition for your part-time law degree and offers a textbook and photocopying allowance each term.

It is awarded to students at the Barhill University School of Law who are studying law part-time and seem to be particularly brilliant. Congratulations! We are very glad to have you join the 'prestigious' and 'exclusive' club of Harvey K. Whatsmeyer and Dorothy P. Ruckleman Scholarship in Part-Time Law holders!

Your tuition will be paid directly on your behalf, and we now enclose your first textbook cheque.

Kind regards,
The Trustees
Harvey K. Whatsmeyer and Dorothy P. Ruckleman Scholarship in Part-Time Law

Cath read the letter over again, noting that the paper was thick, the font elegant, and that a bank cheque was pinned to the back. Her cheeks began to ache from the smile of it all. She turned the TV up loud, danced with her cat and danced into the kitchen to make celebration chocolate-chip cookies. This is wonderful, she danced, wonderful!

Still, she thought, in a more reasonable voice, *it's not all that surprising.*

Chocolate chips spilled in a shower to the floor. What did she mean by that? Why should it not be surprising? Certainly, she had never applied for the Harvey K. Whatsmeyer and Dorothy P. Ruckleman Scholarship in Part-Time Law. She had never even heard of such a thing. But she had to admit that she had won a scholarship like this every year of high school and every year of teachers' college. So that, even the other day when she was talking to Warren and Suzanne about how worried she was about the cost of tuition – even then, she was more *impatient* than actually concerned.

Violin skidded among chocolate drops as Cath reflected that this sort of attitude – *impatient to win a scholarship!* – was both conceited and spoiled. Furthermore, such an attitude – *unsurprised when she actually won one!* – was likely to ruin the excitement of almost *any* happy event. So she collected her excitement about her again, danced the chocolate-chip cookies on to the top shelf of the oven and danced back to the TV.

There was one last letter waiting for her, an *internal* letter, a two-word CATH MURPHY envelope, in handwriting that she knew. She had known that it was there all along, and *partly*, the careful piles of Things-To-Do and the chocolate chip excitement at her scholarship letter – partly, all those things were nothing more than self-imposed suspense.

> Cath,
>
> This is just something ridiculous that I made for you. It's to say thank you because you helped to make my birthday so special the other day.
>
> How about we have dinner this Thursday night? In honour of the end of the term. I have a favourite Moroccan restaurant which would do the trick. The 442 takes us to the door if you don't want to take that Merc of yours.
>
> Warren

Cath looked at the letter as a rectangle of paper. She looked at the handwriting as angles and curls, and finally, she looked at the enclosure. It was a cross-stitched bookmark, stitched with a crescent moon and three stars, all in midnight blue.

No, well, of course I cannot go. A Moroccan restaurant! The idea! This Warren Woodford had such long, skinny legs that his head was stuck up in the sky. She grew angry at him for a moment, because what did he think he was playing at? What was he doing to her face and her cheeks, and her forearms and the space behind her knees? WHAT DID HE THINK HE WAS DOING when he sent her the *moon and the stars*?

She would, of course, say NO. Sternly and firmly: NO.

But Warren Wishful Woodford had long, skinny legs and wishful flecks of gold in his wistful eyes. Warren Wishful Woodford was as *good* as *gold* can be, and his long thin fingers had taken up a needle and some cloth. These long thin fingers had taken *her*, Cath Murphy, and threaded her, like cotton, through the needle. He had thrust her (Cath Murphy) straight into the cloth (her eyes closed tight against the shock) – then gently, his long thin fingers had tugged her through the other side. Then down again, and gently, up above the cloth, these fingers had transformed her into Moon and into Stars.

Cath Murphy had a beanbag and a slender cat. She had the Harvey P. Whatsmeyer and Dorothy P. Ruckleman Scholarship in Part-Time Law. She was *delightful*, she was *brilliant*, she was lucky as a cat, and everything was sewn in midnight blue.

She took up her pen to reply.

On Thursday night, at dinner with Warren, Cath leaned forward and told him it was her destiny to be a lawyer. He poured her another glass of wine, and she explained that each year in high school she had received a special award, and it had always turned out to be a book about justice or the law.

'Every single time?' said Warren.

'Every single time.'

'Well,' said Warren, 'who chose the books? It was probably the Legal Studies teacher or something.'

'I don't know,' said Cath, confused, 'I don't know who chose them, but listen to this!'

'Listen to what?' He poured himself some wine and held the bottle above the glass, allowing it to drip, drip, drip, until a waiter saw and said, 'Shall I bring you more?'

'Yes, please,' they both said together.

'Every single career guidance counsellor I ever had told me I had to study law!'

'Hmm,' said Warren.

'And once. Once! A palm-reader told me I was going to be a lawyer. And my star sign *often* tells me that. And Chinese fortune cookies – no . . . But once I had a swimming coach, Ella her name was, I think, she was some former Olympic champion or something, anyway, Ella told me I did backstroke like a lawyer. 'Forget the swimming,' she said, 'you go straight to law school, little one.' I was only ten or eleven at the time. And plus, I just remembered, I got offered a scholarship to study law in my last year of high school! Without applying for one! What do you think about *that*?!'

She ate a mouthful of couscous.

'But you still became a school teacher,' said Warren, admiringly. 'You know what you are? You're a *destiny fighter*.'

'Thank you,' she blushed.

'So what happened? How come you started law this year, Cath Murphy?'

'That doesn't count,' she explained. 'I had a broken heart. And then I got this leaflet in the mail about a new law school, and the classes were at convenient times, and it was easy to fill in the application form. But, you know, I had a broken heart so it doesn't really count.'

'You can't fight destiny if your heart's not in it,' agreed Warren. 'But what I want to know is, what brain-dead moron broke your heart? Look at you! Would you just look at you! And tell me, *who* could break that heart?'

136

'Do you believe in omens?'

'Yes,' he said. 'Don't you?'

Their eyes caught for a moment, and held, and continued to hold until Cath felt her whole body tremble.

'Why?' said Warren.

'I don't know. It's just that we got the 442 tonight, and the Friendly Bus Driver was driving.'

'The *friendly bus driver?*'

'Yes, didn't you notice him chatting to me when we got on the bus?'

'Cath, I'm sorry, but who is the Friendly Bus Driver?'

'You don't *know* the Friendly Bus Driver! He comes by Redwood every afternoon – he drives the Glenorie bus? And he always leans out and chats to me while the kids get on board, and he is *so* friendly, Warren.'

'And so,' said Warren, gazing at her. 'And so, it's an omen that he drove us here tonight. An omen of what?'

He leaned forward on his elbows and stared at her, waiting, while she stared back.

'Guess what,' she panicked suddenly. 'I'm always cutting competitions out of magazines!'

'Are you?' said Warren archly, leaning back into his chair again and straightening the napkin on his lap.

'Yes, and guess what else? I practically always win.'

'Like what? Like what competitions?'

'Like, I won a free flight to go see my parents in Perth last year, and that's from a coupon I cut out of a magazine. Always cut them out, Warren. OK? I don't mean from big newspapers like the *Herald* – I never win those competitions, but small ones, like *Travel Schmazzle.*'

'Small ones like *Travel Schmazzle?*'

'Right,' she said, nodding excitedly. 'Or *Cat Nap.*'

'Never in my life have I heard of a magazine called *Travel Schmazzle.*'

'Or *Cat Nap*?'

'No, not *Cat Nap* either, as a matter of fact.'

'The *Journal of Dreamy Window Boxes*?'

'Cath Murphy, you are priceless. Come home with me tonight.'

'Well, how about *Elf Epistles*? I won a blender from them. Just the other day.'

'Cath, you are beautiful. Come home with me. Please.'

The next day, the last day of term, Cath watched Warren through the window of the classroom and felt the chill of the ice storm in her chest. Because: *what if that had been her only chance?*

She had not gone home with him. She had ignored his invitation. At the end of the night, she had held her head haughtily and climbed into the taxi while he watched her through narrowed eyes. Then he slowly pressed her taxi door closed, took one step back, turned his shoulder to the wind and flagged down a taxi of his own.

At first, in her taxi, she had felt proud, but she quickly found herself appalled. Her lips ached from not having kissed. She held her arms around her body to comfort it. Because the next day it would be Friday! Breanna would be down from the coast! Then two whole weeks of school holidays, during which time Cath would be alone with the empty space where his body should be. Two whole weeks, during which time Warren would forget their flirtation and remember himself and his wife.

Cath, you are beautiful, come home with me, please. It had been her last chance. If she had just stepped back from the taxi for a moment and kissed him, just that, the kiss might have held him for the holidays.

She watched him now in the lunchtime playground through

the iced-over windows of her classroom. He seemed to have agreed to referee a game of rounders.

Marcus Ellison took the bat, Severino lined up with a tennis ball, and then, in a whirl out of nowhere, there was Cassie Zing. She had been sprinting on the iced-over asphalt, and now she could not stop and was caught in a wildfire skid. Cath, behind the window, gasped.

But Warren Woodford, calm as snow, took two long strides towards the wildfire. He lowered his body, caught her in her skid and dusted the ice from her hair. Then, crouching crookedly, he spoke to the children, who moved in closer to hear. Cath saw some of them grinning. She wanted to be there herself, hearing Warren speak.

Now she saw Cassie hopscotching back towards her friend Lucinda, who caught her just before she fell.

From the window, Cath watched as Warren Woodford stood and smiled like a gentle king, and clapped his hands once, meaning: 'Right! Play on!'

Later, sharing bus duty with their shoulders close against the cold, Cath pressed her fingers together through her gloves. What could she say that would hold him until next term?

'What are you and Breanna doing tonight?' she tried, hopelessly.

Warren cried: 'Don't *tell* me you haven't heard! How could you not have heard?'

'Heard what?'

'Lenny D'Souza is *leaving*, and wait, there's more, she's leaving *today*!'

While Cath stared, Warren explained that Lenny and Billson had had a HUGE fight about ABSOLUTELY NOTHING, in front of EVERYONE, in the STAFFROOM, at the end of RECESS that day.

'And she *resigned*?' whispered Cath.

'She resigned! But she left a message saying she's having a farewell party at her place tonight, and everyone's invited.'

'Including Billson?'

'No, Cath. Not including Billson.'

'Well!' said Cath, importantly. 'Lenny's my *friend*. I have to get over there, right away. She must be wondering where I am. And she must not realize that you can't have a farewell party and then change your mind about resigning. I have to stop her!'

'Don't stop her,' said Warren. 'I feel like going to a party tonight.'

'You're coming?' cried Cath, startled, and almost giddy. Then she said, lightly: 'So you'll bring Breanna along? I finally get to meet her!'

'Cath Murphy,' said Warren, 'where exactly have you been all day? Has it passed you by that the weather is *really weird*? That this is Sydney's first *ice storm* on record? Have a look at these school buses here, Cath, and tell me what's happened to their tyres. They have *chains* on their tyres, Cath. Do you think they'd let trains run? How exactly do you think Breanna's getting down from the coast tonight? And another thing, how exactly did you get your class to talk about anything *other than weather* today? You're a better teacher than I am, that's for sure.'

Cath giggled and said, 'I wonder how we'll get to Lenny's party?'

Then she explained, casually, that she lived down the road from Lenny's place. She and Warren might as well drink hot chocolate in the staffroom now and then share a taxi from school to the party. After the party, he could take a taxi home, and she could walk.

Warren was pleased with this idea.

*

Lenny wept into Cath's neck.

'Oh my God, Cath! I *loved* my job! I *loved* that man! I will *miss* you so *much*!'

Cath, on the couch beside Lenny, tried to balance a gin and tonic around her sobbing shoulders.

Warren was as plastered as a wall, he said. Cath said that she was too.

They caught one another in the kitchen, and made some rude sentences with the magnet words on the fridge. Katie Toby (teacher, Kinder A) and Jo Bel Castro (teacher, Year 5A) wandered into the room, and Katie Toby said: 'Ice? Where's the ice?'

Jo Bel Castro put a friendly arm around Katie's shoulder and declared, 'Where *would* a person find ice?'

Warren opened the dishwasher and took out the cutlery container. 'Not here,' he shrugged, and put it back.

Katie Toby stared and frowned. 'Thank you, everyone,' she said and left the room. Jo Bel Castro raised an eyebrow and walked in the other direction.

Cath giggled and fell against Warren, on purpose more or less by the fridge.

Warren held her up with his arm around her shoulder and pressed his face into her hair. He was saying something.

'What?' she said, not wanting to let go. 'What are you saying?'

'Thank you,' he murmured, in his muffled voice. 'I'm saying thank you for last night. For not coming home with me. Cath? I don't trust myself around you any more.'

Cath stayed still. His nose was pressed just above her ear and the warmth of his face was in her hair. 'Well,' she said, eventually. 'What does that mean?'

'It means,' said Warren, 'that I'm relying on you. You have to be the strong one, OK?'

'Right,' said Cath. 'Right.'

She pressed her whole body against his for a moment, as hard as she could, and then she stepped clean away.

'Right,' she said. 'I'm going to the bathroom.'

Lenny's bathroom had an apricot theme and an art nouveau pattern around the tiles. Cath looked at herself in the mirror and immediately knew that she was drunk: it was just as she'd suspected.

'Nine times seven is sixty-three,' she said to the mirror. So she was not all that drunk. She was still there, inside her head, doing her nine times tables. *But that woman there, that woman in the mirror? Who is that, Cath Murphy, who is that?*

Seven times nine is –

In reverse, it was not so good.

'You'll never get a cab in this.'

It was snowing outside.

'Freakish weather!' whispered Katie Toby, gazing through the window. Then, to the room: 'Snow in Sydney! I mean, maybe a few flakes once in a blue moon! But *heavy* snow! I mean, it's really kind of *heavy*? You know? Ha ha!'

'Promise me something,' said Warren, who was holding his phone to his ear. '*Never* lose that sense of humour.'

'OK,' said Katie, dimpling. 'I'll try. Thanks.'

Importantly, Cath explained to the room: 'Warren is going to get a cab.'

'He'll never get a cab in this,' said Lenny.

Warren had decided to go home and was holding his cellphone patiently to his ear. Lenny looked up at him and repeated: 'You'll never get a cab in *this*!'

They looked through the window at the glow of white, and Cath turned back to watch Warren. 'Nobody's answering,' he mouthed at her. And she nodded, solemnly, with her face and her heart singing over and over: *Do not answer, do not answer, do not answer.*

Cath's boot tap-danced the icy path home. One boot, *thud,* one boot, *tap.*

'I have a couch that turns into a bed,' she told Warren, proudly. 'It's in the living room. I have linen too. One hundred per cent cotton. It might even be Egyptian cotton, you never know. Plus I have a spare quilt.'

Snow feathered about them. Warren's head was hunched into his shoulders. 'I'm hungry,' he said. 'Let's get some food.'

'It's midnight,' said Cath, 'and you're always hungry.'

'This corner store,' suggested Warren.

'It won't be open.'

But it was. They bought chips and salsa for a midnight snack, and behind the counter the corner-store girl with the plaits to her hips said, 'Hello there, *you*!' as usual to Cath, and 'Hey!' in a friendly way to Warren.

'Hey,' said Warren, friendly back – and Cath thought: *I like a man who's friendly to strangers, and friendly to corner-store girls!*

'Right,' she said aloud and confused. Warren and the corner-store girl looked at her.

At that moment Warren's cellphone rang, and Cath panicked, thinking it might be the taxi company calling to try to take him home. She and the corner-store girl watched in suspense as he answered and said, 'Bree! Hey! Do *not* worry yourself. Couldn't get a taxi so I'm staying at Cath's place tonight, OK? We're just on our way there now. You OK? Keeping warm? It'll all be melted by tomorrow, trust me on that.'

'My wife,' explained Warren when the conversation finished, smiling at the corner-store girl.

'Crazy, huh?' Cath jutted her shoulder at the window while she paid.

The corner-store girl flung her plaits over her shoulders and said: 'You bet! But you know what? I'm *out of here*!' It turned out that tomorrow she would take a week's vacation to Byron Bay.

'Lucky!' Warren and Cath said at once, and the corner-store girl began to nod her plaits, as if to say more, but stopped, becoming distant and glassy-eyed. Warren and Cath quietly gathered their things to leave.

'Look!'

Cath wanted to show him everything, suddenly, frenetically. Photos of her mother, her father and the family Alsatian. Photographs of Violin, her cat. Violin, the cat in living form. ('Violin! Come here and meet Warren! Violin!') A new ceramic casserole dish she bought a month ago. The rewind button on the VCR, which was jammed. The new DVD player she had won in a contest just last week! Warren moved his legs carefully among her books and chairs. At each thing she showed him he said, '*Mmm*,' with fascination and a crunch on a corn chip.

'This window is all smeared,' Warren observed, standing by her side in the dining room.

'Yeah,' she agreed. 'I threw some apple juice on it. A few weeks ago.'

They both stood and stared at the smears.

'Hang on,' said Warren. He went into the kitchen and came out with a glass of water, splashed water at the window and then rubbed the window with a cloth. It squealed, but soon was crisp and clear, and their reflections leaped out at them sharply. Vaguely, beyond the reflections, was the eerie white of snow.

'No way,' said Cath, in awe. 'Shouldn't we be building a snowman?'

She gazed up at Warren. Then she ran back into the living room and sat down on the couch, leaving space for Warren to sit beside her. But he chose the armchair.

She lifted her foot on to her lap and looked to see what was making her boots go thud, tap, thud. 'Look!'

It turned out a pebble had embedded itself deep within the rubber of her heel. Cath showed Warren and then tried to dig the pebble out with her fingernail.

'Here,' said Warren. 'Let me try.'

He swooped a corn chip full of salsa, ate it in one go, and then took her foot on to his lap. He scratched industriously at the pebble.

'Wait,' said Cath. She unlaced the boot and took it off. 'This will make it easier. I should have taken them off right away anyway. I'm walking snow all over the apartment.'

She passed him the boot, which he took with one hand, gulping his beer with the other. He put the boot down and took her foot on to his lap.

'Yes,' he said, 'that's better,' and pressed the sole of her foot.

'No,' explained Cath. 'That's not what I meant.' But she left her foot in his lap, safe in its ankle sock, and had a sip of beer of her own.

'Look!' she cried suddenly, taking back her foot and leaping to her feet. 'You want to see my Criminal Law essay, Warren?'

'Not really,' Warren frowned. 'Give me back your foot.'

Cath flicked through papers on the dining-room table. 'Warren, look at my Criminal Law essay.'

'All right,' accepted Warren. He looked:

'Lovely,' said Warren. 'Where's the rest?'

'That's it. I've only done the cover page. I did it weeks ago.'

'That's it!' Warren cast aside the page. 'Give me back your foot.'

Cath sat down and gave him her foot. Warren began with her instep.

Then he moved on to her toes, one toe at a time.

'Massage the bit that matches my knee,' Cath suggested. 'You know the way you can cure yourself by massaging certain bits of your feet? Like the bit for the liver and the intestines and that? Get the bit for the knees.' She crunched on a corn chip and added: 'Please.'

'Because I've got a problem knee,' she explained when he ignored her, continuing with her toes. 'I had two operations in high school and my knee's got metal bits in it now, but they've never set off the X-ray machine at the airport. It's all about the small things, you know. Like my little toe, just press my little toe and my knee is cured.'

'OK, listen,' said Warren. 'I'll rub your foot a tiny bit at a time and you tell me when you feel your knee begin to heal.'

'All right. But let's talk about my essay some more.'

Warren ignored her and peeled off her sock. 'You probably have to kiss it anyway,' he suggested and kissed one toe.

'Warren! I've had boots on all day. Don't kiss my *toes*.'

'Maybe I have to kiss the knee directly?' said Warren. 'Maybe the foot won't do?'

'I don't know,' admitted Cath.

He stopped for a moment and stared at her. He moved to sit beside her on the couch and kissed her.

'That's my mouth,' said Cath, blinking at his face, 'not my knee.' But she kissed him back in a fury of relief.

17

> Irritating Things About My Husband # 12
> Let's say it's an ordinary week night, I'll be
> cleaning up the kitchen, and I've just about
> finished – the dishwasher stacked, detergent neat
> in its compartment, only the large baking tray left
> to rinse – when Radcliffe, right on cue, will step
> into the room and announce: 'Leave it –' grandly –
> 'I'll do the rest.'

The Monday after Cassie's birthday, Fancy closed her secret notebook and leaned back in her desk chair. She would now spend twenty minutes working on her prize-winning novel. It was 10.23 a.m.

Having read several prize-winning novels, Fancy was confident that she now knew the recipe:

1. Write a simple narrative.
2. Make a long list.
3. Scatter the contents of your list throughout your narrative.

So, for example, in the prize-winning novel that Fancy had just read, the author had done the following:

1. He wrote a simple narrative in which two people fell in love, then the man left the woman and the woman cried.

2. He made a long list of leaves.
3. He scattered the story with his leaves.

So 'Tears fell from her eyes' had become: 'Tears the shape of sugar maple leaves fell (like so many blackjack oak leaves falling on an autumn day) from her eyes.'

Voilà! A richly textured (prize-winning) novel all about love and leaves.

There was no harm in mixing the recipe around a little, Fancy believed. (She had flair in the kitchen.) She would begin with the *list* and then write the narrative around it. Although she was not yet at the stage of making her list, she was well under way with her list of things to list.

This was on the back of an old phone bill which she carried in her handbag wherever she went. It was stained with splats of cranberry juice.

List of Potential Lists

- sounds
- things that are very hot
- delicious things to drink
- foreign currencies
- fish

'Hmm,' she said, running her fingernail down the list. 'Fish?' She had a slight zing of excitement then, and picked up her pen, quickly scribbling: 'Tears the shape of trout fell (like a school of those darting, glassy fish that you see in tropical waters) from her eyes.'

Pleased, she turned to her computer and typed the word 'fish' into the word processor's thesaurus. 'Angle', it suggested promptly. And 'trawl'.

'No, no,' she chided gently. 'I meant it as a noun.'

She reached for the phone and dialled the Castle Hill Gym. A man with a husky voice answered.

Clear your throat, thought Fancy. But aloud she said, 'Hello. I'm just ringing to enquire about the hours of your swimming pool there. I'm hoping you might tell me when the pool is quietest.'

'The *quietest* time,' said the man with the voice, 'would be Friday mornings from nine thirty to eleven thirty, but then . . .'

As he talked, Fancy circled the first word on the list ('sounds'), and tapped it with her pen, frowning. That category was much too broad.

The man on the phone was laughing in a rasping, unpleasant way.

'All right,' she said briskly, 'thank you.'

Then she hung up, crossed out 'sounds' and replaced it with 'UNPLEASANT SOUNDS!!!' She looked at the clock on her computer, which said 10.42 a.m. After she had watched for a while, it said 10.43 a.m.

'So, that's that,' she declared, pleased.

In the back seat of the car, Cassie wore the middle belt so she could lean forward between the two front seats and talk to her dad or mum.

Her mum was driving and her dad was changing the radio stations. Dad tipped his head sideways to listen carefully to the news. Mum was behind her glasses and you couldn't tell if she was listening to the news or not.

Cassie looked through the groceries in the box beside her, which they had just picked up from Coles. They were extremely boring. Celery sticks and milk, cauliflower and toilet paper.

'Mum?' said Cassie.

'Shh,' said Dad, listening to the news with his head on his shoulder.

'Radcliffe,' said Mum, 'it's just the weather.'

'I want to find out if there'll be good sailing weather this weekend, *actually*,' said Dad, with his calm voice. 'There's a cold front coming in the next week or so, so this could be our last chance for a while.'

'We can't go sailing this weekend!' said Mum. 'There's the Bellamys and Samsons for dinner on Saturday and then your parents on Sunday!'

'We don't need to see the Bellamys and the Samsons,' said Dad. 'We can cancel.'

'I think you'll find that we do, actually,' declared Mum.

'You know I don't like *routine*, Fancy.'

'It's not a *question* of *routine*, Radcliffe. It's a question of *manners*. You can't *invite* people and then *uninvite* them because you feel like going *sailing*. And, besides, what do you *mean* when you say *routine*? It's been *ages* since we had the Bellamys and the Samsons!'

'That rhymed, Mum,' said Cassie from the back seat. '"What do you *mean* when you say *routine*?"'

'I also don't like being told what I can and cannot do,' her dad said coldly.

'Radcliffe, would you not be ridiculous? Please?'

'There is no point in our having this discussion,' said her dad, shrugging. 'I just *do* and *don't do* exactly as I please. Thank you very much.' He switched off the radio so he could be angry in peace.

'No point in having *what* discussion?' muttered her mum.

Cassie thought she should be quiet, but first she had to murmur, softly: 'What do you *mean* when you say *routine*? What do you *mean* when you say *routine*? *What* do you mean when you *say* routine?'

'The light's green, Mum,' Cassie interrupted herself.

'Thank you, Cassie,' said her mother and made the car jump forward.

*

151

Fancy flipped open a notebook, took the top from a thin black marker and instructed her husband: 'Radcliffe, tell me some sounds that are unpleasant.'

'Right then.' Radcliffe leaned back in his television chair to think. The TV commercials blazed.

'The sound of a fingernail on a blackboard,' he declared after two commercials had gone by.

Fancy replaced the top on her marker. 'I'm not writing that down.'

'Why not?'

'It's very common, Radcliffe. I think I need something original.'

'Too common? Well then.' He thought again. 'The sound of your voice!'

Fancy and Cassie both cried, 'HUH!' and Cassie said, 'Mum's got a *beautiful* voice!'

Radcliffe shrugged: 'Show's back on.'

'You have no imagination,' Fancy declared, closing her notebook.

'No need for one,' Radcliffe replied, amiable, tilting his wineglass towards his mouth. 'That'll be the telephone,' he announced next, as it had just begun to ring.

'Dressed in black?' said Marbie.

'Oh really? *Tonight?* What for? It's *cold*!'

'For the maintenance,' explained Marbie. 'Mum just paged me. It's blurred, remember? We can do it easy if we leave right now. Meet you at the ice-cream truck?'

Marbie was not at the ice-cream truck when Fancy arrived. She was in the tree above the truck.

Fancy pretended to consider the range of ice creams (single cone, double cone, single dipped in chocolate with a Flake on the side, etc.) and then squinted up into the darkness.

Marbie gave the sign for 'All set' (both hands flat on the head). She almost lost her balance and had to grab noisily at clumps of leaves.

Fancy gave the sign for 'Great and I've remembered all the tools' (a playful twirl of her handbag) then clipped across the road to the apartment block. Without pausing, she firmly pressed in the security code and entered the building.

She and Marbie had both learned to pick a lock when their fingers were fresh and nimble. She got into the apartment in less than three seconds, smiled at the cat and slid silently from room to room in a quick Emptiness check. (There had once been a plumber in the bathroom, but Fancy, ingeniously, recruited him on the spot.)

In the dining room, she opened her handbag, reached in for the nail file and accidentally took out her telephone bill. The cat miaowed.

'Hmm,' she murmured and sat down at the dining table, turning over the telephone bill. There was a clutter of papers there, which she shifted slightly so she could study her List of Potential Lists.

- ~~sounds~~ UNPLEASANT SOUNDS!!!
- things that are very hot
- delicious things to drink
- foreign currencies
- fish

Except that the word 'fish' was now caught in a tangle of lines, each linking 'fish' to various fish species. *Objects in a family home*, Fancy wrote at the end of the list. The cat miaowed again and Fancy said, 'Hello,' and added *cats* in a flash of inspiration. Beside it, she scribbled – *(Include lions, tigers, panthers, etc!!! also, basic domestic cats?)*.

Miaow, miaow, said the cat.

'Are you hungry? Is that it?' Fancy murmured soothingly, reaching out her left hand to stroke the cat but not being able to find it.

She looked up and the cat was standing way across the room in the doorway, its collar bell whispering faintly.

'How . . . ?' began Fancy.

Then she gasped, took out her pager (which miaowed at her even as she pressed the message button) and read: GET OUT *NOW*.

At which exact moment, a key turned in the lock.

On Friday night at Grandpa and Grandma Zing's, Fancy sat on the carpet next to Listen and said, 'Tell me some sounds that you don't like to hear.'

'The sounds of cars crashing,' offered Nathaniel from the dining-room table.

'Not you,' Fancy said, but she wrote it down in her notebook. 'I'm asking Listen now. I'll ask you later.'

Listen thought hard.

'You have to think outside the box,' advised Radcliffe drily. 'Otherwise, she cuts you to the quick.'

'Oh!' cried Grandma Zing. 'Radcliffe! Was she mean to you?'

'Not mean,' said Radcliffe, thoughtfully. 'More malicious.'

'The sound of a puddle,' Listen said now, 'going splat when you just accidentally stepped in it with your sneaker.'

'Good!' Fancy wrote fast.

'The sound that our school library computer makes,' Listen said calmly. 'Kind of a mean-sounding BLEEP? When you return your book and it turns out it's overdue. Does that count?'

'Perfect!' Fancy scribbled frantically.

'Come on, Fancy!' Grandma Zing called. 'We're all going out to the shed!'

'Fancy,' beckoned Radcliffe, at her mother's shoulder, 'come on, hon.'

From the slightly raised platform at the far end of the shed, Grandma Zing frowned at her clipboard.

Fancy turned to her sister. 'Tell me some sounds that you don't like to hear.'

'I think your mother wants to start the meeting.' Radcliffe sat straight in his chair. He had his reading glasses on.

'No, no,' said Grandma Zing. 'Carry on, I'll just be a moment.' She flipped through documents piled in a box.

Marbie thought. 'Some people,' she said, after a moment, 'make this kind of grunting sound. This sound kind of like *uh*, when they're reading or thinking and they don't even know that they're doing it.'

Fancy wrote the word: UH.

'I imagine the sound of a *key* in a *lock* might be a sound you don't like to hear,' said Grandma Zing, with a glint in her eye.

There was a clamour at this as everyone cried, 'How did you make it out the *window*?' and 'That was *such* a close one,' and Radcliffe said bossily, 'We should discuss this at the appropriate time in the meeting, shouldn't we?'

'Oh *God*,' said Fancy, closing her notebook again. 'How did I let it happen? I think I must have lost my touch!' (There was another clamour as everyone assured her she had not lost her touch.)

'Look at the way you opened the window, closed it behind you, jumped into a tree and climbed down without being seen,' Marbie said. 'I think you're amazing. And anyway, Fancy, it was my fault – I didn't notice the car coming down the street until the last moment.'

'Why didn't you notice it?' said Radcliffe pointedly.

'I was distracted.'

'Distracted by what?'

'But still,' interrupted Fancy, 'it was so lucky she switched on the TV right away and stayed in the front room – if she hadn't . . .'

'Gotta change that pager sound,' said Radcliffe.

'And we all thought that it was the cat's miaow,' offered Nathaniel.

Everyone groaned and Marbie hit his leg, but then she embraced him proudly, while Grandma Zing said, 'Shall we start the meeting? We have an *edict* today!'

'Worn-out brake-pads,' whispered Grandpa Zing, leaning over to Fancy, 'make an awful squealing sound.' He pointed at Fancy's notepad and she mouthed, 'Thanks, Dad,' and wrote it down.

Fancy was at her computer working on *Love Among the Wildebeests* while Cassie played on the floor by her feet. She tapped the space bar several times, sighed, turned away from the screen and took up her pen to write to Cassie's teacher.

> Dear Ms Murphy,
> You may be pleased to know that my daughter (Cassie's) loose tooth has come out. And the Tooth Fairy has come and gone.

She stopped. She had already written about Cassie's asthma, her allergy to bees, her aversion to gingham. What else was there?

Cassie sat on the floor behind her, threading plastic beads on to a string and saying now and then, 'Mum? Will Listen *really* come to my school next term?'

Fancy swivelled around and looked at Cassie. 'Any more loose teeth, darling?'

'No,' said Cassie, sadly. 'Wait.' She tested each tooth with her tongue. 'No. No loose tooths.'

'Teeth! You know that. Cassie, anything *interesting* happening at school?'

'No,' asserted Cassie confidently.

'Hmm.' Fancy turned back to her note and stared at it for a while, while Cassie continued to chant, 'Mu-um, will Listen *really* come to my school after the holidays?'

'Right then,' Fancy said suddenly. 'I'm trying to work, Cassie, and you should be in bed!' Then her eyes roved over the pink plastic beads scattered on the study floor like sugar drops. 'Sorry, Cassie! Yes. Marbie called today to tell me that Listen is going to your school next term. After the holidays, Listen will be at your school for just one term. Because her classrooms got flooded.'

'Thanks,' said Cassie solemnly and stood up at once, ready to go to bed.

Fancy had a happy flash of inspiration then, and continued her letter:

> I hope you will forgive me for writing again so soon, but I have a small favour to ask.

Cassie was climbing under the covers and her mum was picking clothes up off the floor.

'*Cassie*, these are your sports clothes! You should have put them in the wash!'

Cassie said, 'Whoops!', slid under the *Harry Potter* quilt and squashed her cheek against the pillow. Her mother shook out the clothes, frowning at them. She folded them over her arm, pulled the curtains tightly closed, patted Harry Potter smooth and switched off the light.

In bed, Cassie imagined her own school flooded. She thought of papers, teachers, desks and bottles of White-Out

bobbing along in a river. Ms D'Souza in a life raft, Mr Woodford in a row boat, Ms Murphy treading water. She thought
of blackboard dusters, whiteboards and pink chalk; overhead
projectors, flower vases, cardboard boxes. She thought of the
school turtle, swept out of his pond, paddling and honking in
alarm.

The whole thing seemed suspicious to Cassie, and also,
absolutely strange.

On the Monday of the final week of term, Fancy found an
unlidded purple marker in the pocket of Cassie's sports shorts.
A purple butterfly bloomed at the hip of the shorts, but Fancy
attacked it with Pre-wash Stain Remover and watched as the
wings began to dribble.

In inky purple marker, on a piece of tissue paper, she then
listed as follows:

Objects in a Family Home
• oatmeal soap
• a bucket containing a pink sponge
• a puddle at the base of the washing machine
• washing machine

On Tuesday, Fancy found a coffee filter filled with ageing
coffee grounds quietly wilting in her coffee-maker. 'Oh, *Radcliffe*,' she said aloud.

On Wednesday, she sat at the kitchen table, scraped at
candle wax and looked idly around the room. After a moment,
she reached for a notebook and a pen.

Objects in a Family Home – again/some more
• elastic bands
• calendar with photos of Canadian Rockies
• port decanter

- doll's underwear
- Hong Kong two-dollar coin
- glue stick
- nail file
- tube of sample MUSK perfume
- spots of candle wax

On Thursday, Fancy reached for her handbag to choose something new to be listed.

Her List of Potential Lists was not there.

'Ah,' she sighed, moving into her study to check her desk. It was not there either. *Hmm!* she said, with a jaunty frown.

She was not concerned because she remembered exactly what was on the list. It would be easy to rewrite on the back of another phone bill. Nevertheless, she began a thorough, cheerful search of the house: the kitchen, the laundry, the bedrooms, the garage, the car. She found herself running up and down the steps, searching in random places such as the cutlery drawer and the liquor cabinet.

It's probably in a pocket somewhere, she realized. *Now, when did I last have it?*

And then it came to her. The last time she had it was at the Intrusion. The *near-disastrous* Intrusion – when she had failed to notice Marbie beeping her, had come within a cat's whisker of getting caught and somehow had climbed out of the window. *So, it would be in the pocket of my black pants, of –*

But there was the strangest sensation in her cheeks: as of automatic doors closing slowly towards her nose. Because there were no pockets in her black pants.

She had left her List of Potential Lists on the dining-room table by the window inside the apartment. And her phone bill was on the back.

*

Her mother, when she telephoned with shaking hands and teary voice, was remarkably professional. 'There was a pile of papers on the dining-table there?'

'Yes,' Fancy quavered.

'Chances are it's still exactly where you left it,' said her mother contentedly. 'I'll put out a Request for an urgent Distraction. You let Marbie know what's going on. And we'll have an Intrusion under way before the end of the day, you mark my words.'

'I'll sit by the phone,' promised Fancy.

'Don't worry so much, darling. Just go about your day as planned but keep your pager with you. We may have just a slight margin.'

Of course, Fancy could not possibly leave the house. She was agitated and hysterical all day, gasping whenever the phone rang and whenever she heard leaves rustle (that was the new pager sound). She called Radcliffe and asked him to fetch Cassie from school as she was too overwrought to drive. Radcliffe tried to reassure her but the excitement of disaster bristled in his voice. She called Marbie several times to confirm that she would leave work early: Marbie laughed and was serene about the whole thing when Fancy first told her, but even she seemed to grow a bit tetchy after Fancy's fourth phone call.

When their mother's alert finally arrived, Fancy's heart was playing thrashing rock.

But it went surprisingly smoothly.

There was nobody around, Marbie climbed her tree safely, the code worked, the apartment was empty and dark, and the List of Potential Lists was sitting safely on the dining-room table, underneath some kind of legal assignment. Once she had folded the List into her handbag Fancy was so relieved that she decided to do the maintenance work she had not completed on the last Intrusion.

'Sleep well,' said Marbie kindly as she dropped Fancy back at home. 'And have a nice, relaxing day tomorrow. Get an aromatherapy massage.'

But the next day, Friday, the last day of the school term, Fancy woke in such a state of jitters that she had to spend some time deep-breathing. *It's all right, it's all right, it's all right*, she chanted.

Her hands fluttered from her mouth to her elbows to her ears, and sometimes to nothing.

'Are you all right, Mum?' said Cassie as Fancy drove her to school.

'Yes, darling, perfectly fine! Have a nice last day at school! Holidays tomorrow! Hooray!'

Cassie looked back at her suspiciously.

Driving home again, Fancy knew that she must *take action* against this hysteria. Otherwise, it would manifest itself in some physical way such as a heart attack or hives. *Swimming*, that was what she needed. The serenity of gliding through the water.

And how about that, it was Friday morning and that man on the phone had told her that *this* was the quietest time for swimming.

The Canadian was standing on his porch.

'I haven't seen you for a while!' she chatted as she reached her front door. 'I guess it's been too cold for your breakfasts on the porch. I never got a chance to thank you for that delicious cake! Cassie *loved* it, by the way. She took a piece to school as a treat.'

'Never too cold for me,' he said, 'to eat breakfast on my porch. I've been away, is the explanation. And that's the nicest thing I've heard in a while that Cassie took a piece of my maple cake to school as a treat.'

'Tell me,' said Fancy, suddenly. 'Now, a sugar maple leaf, that would be a Canadian sort of leaf, wouldn't it?'

'They have sugar maples elsewhere as well,' said the Canadian formally. 'But yes, the maple leaf is on our flag. So you could say it's Canadian.'

'Then tell me,' Fancy repeated, 'would a teardrop ever look like a maple leaf?'

The Canadian considered this. 'I would have to say,' he said slowly, 'I'd choose a different leaf if I wanted to describe a teardrop. I'd choose a leaf with your more traditional leaf shape. Such as that eucalyptus leaf, right there. Now, I suppose that a teardrop might fall *splat* on to a page – say you were reading a book and having a weep – a teardrop might fall *splat*, and the mark that it left on the *page* might, if you were lucky, resemble a sugar maple leaf. But otherwise, I would say no.'

Fancy felt a rush of love for the Canadian-next-door.

'Thank you,' she said, blushing, and walked into her house.

Driving to the swimming pool, Fancy felt calm. She allowed herself to imagine she'd invited the Canadian along. And he had said, *Swimming, I love to swim!* And run inside to get his bathing suit. Perhaps he'd have come back out wearing it! To prove that he was Canadian and could get about bare-chested in grey and icy weather. And then they'd have driven chattingly along, her bare hand on the gear stick, so close to his bare legs.

She entered the gym and asked for a token for the pool.

'Sorry.' It was the man with the rasping voice. 'Sorry,' he said, 'the swimming pool's closed for cleaning. Nine thirty to eleven thirty every Friday.'

'No,' said Fancy emphatically. 'No, I phoned a few weeks ago. This is the *quietest* time to swim.'

'That was you calling? What I said,' declared the man with

a grin, 'was that the swimming pool is *quietest* at this time! Of course it is! There's nobody there! They're cleaning it!'

Fancy stared at him. That a person could play such a trick! She felt entitled to continue staring, with amazed, accusing eyes for as long as she liked.

'I did explain,' he said defensively, 'I did go on to explain why this was the quietest time. You mustn't have heard me.'

'If the pool is being cleaned now,' said Fancy with a proud swing of her head, 'then I don't *imagine* it's all that quiet. I *imagine* the cleaning equipment makes quite a racket!'

She flounced out of the gym.

Behind the wheel again, Fancy felt so foolish that she had to cry a little. The rain was strange on her windshield: it seemed to land with an icy skid rather than a normal sugar-maple-leaf-shaped splat.

She felt especially foolish at the idea that the Canadian might have been with her. How she would have wasted his time. She was cold with fear at the thought. Of course, he might have found her mistake adorable and suggested a hot chocolate instead. The car skidded and slipped on the road, and some of her jitters returned.

Back home, the day seemed endless. She tried phoning her mother, and they had a brief chat about whether to cancel the Zing Family Secret Meeting that night because of the weather. They decided they should cancel, so then her mother had to hang up to let the others know. Fancy wandered from room to room, picking up objects from the floor and then letting them slide back in different places.

And all the time that sad little sentence played itself over in her head: *How is your ocean bream, my love? How is your ocean bream?*

Anything but this. Fancy jumped up from the living-room floor, tripping over photo albums, and strode down the hall to the front door, throwing it open.

She stepped on to the porch and something whacked her face like a leather glove: that's how cold it was. The mat, when she stepped on it, crunched with ice. A shudder spiralled through her and pinched her shoulder blades. The sky was low, pale and plaintive, like Cassie when she was coming down with something. The Canadian's porch was empty.

Back inside with the door firmly closed against the cold, Fancy stared down the hall. She should hoover.

Then she remembered that her vacuum-cleaner was in the repair shop.

I wonder if the Canadian has a vacuum cleaner I might borrow? she thought suddenly and earnestly. At that moment, the vacuum repair truck turned into her driveway. Fancy accepted the repaired vacuum with cold politeness, and, as soon as she had closed the door, she plugged it in.

She vacuumed: the hall, the lounge room, the TV room, Cassie's room. And now she was in the main bedroom. Her lower back ached, the room roared with vacuum cleaner groans, she used her knees to shove the bed to the side and she busied herself with the skirting boards. Crouching down to the floor, she fed the nozzle way under the bed, but then there was a gasping, choking sound and she switched the vacuum off. There was something caught in its mouth which she gently removed.

It was a dusty purple sock. Stitched at the back of the ankle with a simple purple daisy.

She held it up and frowned at it. This was not Fancy's sock. Nor was it Cassie's sock. Certainly, it was not Radcliffe's sock. So now, whose sock would be deep under their bed like that?

In the post-vacuum quiet, Fancy rocked back on her heels, looking from the sock to the window to the ceiling to the vacuum. The vacuum had no reply, but there was something wide-eyed about the room.

This sock belongs to another woman, Fancy whispered to herself. *Radcliffe is having an affair.*

Immediately, crouching on the floor by the bed, she laughed to herself. Radcliffe having an affair! It was so unlikely that the word – 'affair' – was immediately surrounded in her mind by a circle of witty prompt cards. Each card contained a rhetorical question, such as: *When would this affair take place, Fancy, given that you work at home each day?*

I know, I know! *When?* (She laughed along.) Although still (she noted, politely) I often *do* go out – on Zing Family Secret business, for instance, or for coffee with Marbie or Mum. He's only ten minutes away and often slips home to surprise me for lunch. He could easily slip a pretty woman home.

But, FANCY, what sort of a pretty woman would have sex with Radcliffe? I mean, seriously.

Me, for a start (she thought, tartly). He's not that bad. He has an unexpected charm. And there are plenty of women at his work. There's *Gemma*, for instance, in the pay office, who spills her drinks at Christmas parties and gets all the moles zapped from her arms.

Yes, but a purple sock? Why would she leave a purple sock behind?

Here, Fancy had to pause. She had never believed for a moment in bits of gossamer lingerie or single diamond ear-rings. No woman would have a dalliance with someone else's husband and then flit off in a taxi without her underwear and earring. No woman! The wind would blow cold against her buttocks! Not to mention her diamond-less ear.

But a purple sock. This she could believe.

Let's say Gemma (it might as well be Gemma) – let's say Gemma only works afternoons. (Gemma does only work afternoons – Radcliffe mentioned that.) All right, so let's say one morning Fancy calls Radcliffe to tell him, 'I'm going to have coffee with Marbie today so I won't be home!'

Radcliffe makes a furtive call to Gemma: 'Are you still at home, my darling? Haven't left for work? The wife's gone out. Meet me at my place in ten.'

Gemma, dressed in morning attire of shorts, sneakers and purple socks, arrives breathless. Her work clothes are in a gym bag over her arm. They hurry up the stairs for a few moments of passion, Gemma showers steamily, then she throws her work clothes on (stockings, skirt, lipstick) and off they rush to work. So easy to forget a purple sock!

Well, but really, why would you imagine that Radcliffe is having an affair? You've never thought a thing like that before.

The question (frostily) is why have I *not* considered it before. Recollect that Radcliffe cheated on me when we were fifteen years old and had only just begun going out. If he could not last a single month, why do I imagine he can last a lifetime?

And now she found the word 'affair' gleaming and proud, surrounded by fallen cards. It waited patiently for her to fill in the details.

It *was* with Gemma! Of *course* it was! Remember how Radcliffe spoke of her? So tenderly, so fondly. 'You must remember Gemma,' he had said. 'No,' she had replied. And then he had explained how Gemma had the moles zapped from her arms. Why should he know that? Why would Gemma from the pay office tell Radcliffe about her moles? Didn't people in the pay office stay behind closed doors, filling up envelopes with pay?

He must have brought her home on the day Fancy met Marbie and Listen for coffee in Castle Hill. On that day, Radcliffe had come home from work to 'surprise' her for lunch. *But*, she realized now, *she had phoned to let him know she was not there.* He came home BECAUSE *she was not there.* He came home with Gemma in purple socks!

And on that day, she recalled in a rush, he had broken a

glass. He had broken the vacuum cleaner trying to clean it up. Trying to clean away *the evidence of his affair*!

No! It was *Gemma* who had broken the glass. Gemma was clumsy. She spilled drinks at Christmas parties. He only mentioned his sojourn at home and the breakage of the vacuum cleaner *weeks* after the event. It was a slip! How strange and awkward he had been when he told her. And then how kind and loving as they carried the vacuum in to be repaired.

All this time, her vacuum cleaner had been trying to let her know about the affair. First, it choked on the broken glass, then it caused Radcliffe to slip up and reveal he had been home that day, and now, today, it had come home to her from the repair shop. *On purpose, to swallow the purple sock.*

Fancy lay flat on her back on the bed, and thought with clarity: *Radcliffe is having an affair.*

Oh *stop* that, she cried, sitting up with a final burst of scorn. *It's just a sock!* She looked at it on the palm of her hand, so flimsy and frail. How could this mean something so immense as an affair?

But then she thought of her recipes: an accidental touch of egg yolk in her meringue, an eighth of a teaspoon of cayenne pepper in her mango dressing – these tiny things had such an impact! Small things, she realized, *can* mean something immense.

Suddenly the sock felt moist in her hand, a scaly, alien thing, and she flung it back on to the floor. It lay there, seeming to wriggle, like a fish too small to eat.

18

The day after Cassie's birthday party, Listen sat at a window desk in Castle Hill Library. Her dad and Marbie thought she was meeting the others here to collect the work they'd done for the assignment.

There was no assignment. But she did have English homework.

She was supposed to be defining 'irony', but all she could do was stare at the traffic lights outside, thinking about how ironic it was that Donna had held her strategy meeting before Cassie's party.

The party had been her idea. She had wanted to show Donna and the others her new life. Now, finally, she had a mother, and what a beautiful, dreamy mother Marbie was. Now, also, she had a family, and what an amazing, crazy family the Zings were. She had a family secret too, even if she didn't know what it was. Somehow, she thought, Donna and the others would have realized there was a secret – something to do with the connection between family constellations – and then they would have found out what it was. (Donna could be very persuasive.)

Probably, Listen thought, drawing stars all over her English homework, the Zing family were undercover agents. When you walked into the garden shed, it probably looked like a regular office with white walls, green carpet and a receptionist wearing chunky earrings and typing at a desk. If you knew the password, the receptionist would pull a leaf from a pot plant on the desk. The floor would open up. You'd fall smoothly down a slide to a basement deep underground, with walls of computers, flashing lights, spy cameras, disguises and machine guns. The Zings would be sitting at an oval table dressed in black.

Imagine if she could have taken Donna and the others into the shed and down the slide! Let them dress up in disguises and play with the guns. They would have loved her forever!

But the party had come too late.

Donna had already had her strategy meeting, and now her friends would never meet Marbie, or the rest of the Zings, or learn the Zing Family Secret.

It was ironic.

Another ironic thing was that the Zings seemed to think that she, Listen, was special. They were as blind as her dad had always been. He and Marbie and the Zings looked at her with such admiration, and said things like, 'You're so popular!', and 'You're so pretty! I bet the other kids are jealous of you!' They asked her questions about school and life as if she was the expert on Year 7. When, in actual fact, she was a failure.

Donna had called the strategy meeting because she thought that Listen might jeopardize their chances of survival at Clareville. 'I'll go through her reasoning for you,' Joanne had offered, on the phone. 'OK, number one, you dance too much. The thing is, you never stay still. You're always swaying and clicking. Personally, I hadn't really noticed but some of the others have been pretty embarrassed about it. Also, you kind of wear the wrong clothes. Caro did point out that that's not completely your fault because you've only got your dad to buy clothes for you and you never had that much money, but then we were thinking that Gabrielle doesn't have much money either, but she's still got the right personal style.

'But the main thing is, you're too quiet. It's like your name says. You just listen. You don't talk. Which is obviously not your fault, I guess, but it still means you're kind of like a taker. Not a giver? And Donna was saying, well, you know how Donna's mum got divorced? Well, her mum says that love can die, and Donna was thinking that *like* can die too. Especially when the person you used to like doesn't talk.'

Joanne reassured Listen that the others argued with Donna for a while, trying to point out Listen's good features, but to be honest they were having trouble thinking of any besides the fact that Listen was a nice person. 'There's a lot of nice people in the world,' Joanne had explained wisely. 'It's just not all that special.' And Sia had remembered that they had tried to help Listen dress better by giving her clothes for her birthday, but even then Listen didn't wear them right. Like the jeans she and Gabrielle gave her were too long but Listen hadn't got them taken up.

So, she was a lost cause.

Listen could never let her dad or the Zings know what had happened. They would be so disappointed to hear she was a lost cause. She would have to protect them from the truth.

There was another ironic thing. That Joanne had thought she, Listen, had to know the truth about the strategy meeting. When it was actually kind of upsetting.

Still, she was right to let her know, in a way, because now Listen could improve. 'You could try asking a lot of questions,' Joanne had suggested, 'if you're too shy to think of things to say yourself? You've got to start talking, that's the point.'

Asking questions hadn't worked with Angela's group. Maybe she was asking the wrong questions? Starting tomorrow, she would have to hide somewhere at recess and lunch until she came up with a plan for making friends.

The idea of tomorrow made her put her head down on the desk.

*

When she sat up again there was her dad's car sliding up outside the library. She threw her books into her bag, ran to the sliding exit doors, slowed down and walked out with a big smile on her face. At the last moment, while her dad was watching and just before the doors closed, she turned back, waved and called, 'See you tomorrow, guys!'

The Monday after Cassie's party, the neighbour's black cat crossed Marbie's path and tripped her up in such a way that she stumbled underneath a ladder. The ladder was leaning quite deliberately against the neighbour's house. She stood under it for a moment, trembling. As far as she could recall, it was the first ladder she had ever walked beneath. There was now no point going to work.

'Are you up yet?' she called, knocking on Listen's bedroom window. Listen seemed to have slept in. She appeared in her frayed pyjamas, rubbing her eyes.

'You look tired,' said Marbie.

'I just woke up,' Listen explained.

'Still,' said Marbie, 'you need a break. Let me take you to the seaside and buy you a sarong. Soon, autumn will begin and the sun will start to fall from the trees and become little shadows at your feet. We should wear sarongs until that happens.'

'OK,' said Listen, 'good idea.'

'I'll write a note and say you've got rabies.'

While Listen found her beach towel, Marbie phoned work and explained about the cat and the ladder. Tabitha was very understanding. 'You stay right where you are,' she said. 'Don't take a step towards the office.'

Then Marbie phoned the aeronautical engineer and said she could not meet him after work that night.

'Can't meet me?' said the A.E., with a slurping sound. 'I'm

sick anyway. Hear this? I'm sucking a lozenge. So, better off not meeting me, but aren't you the one who arranged this?'

Marbie was silent on the phone, thinking about this, so after a moment the A.E. made a crunching sound and said, 'Ouch. Bit through the lozenge and now it's got sharp edges. What say you to Wednesday next week instead?'

Again Marbie was silent, considering this. If she met him again, she could formally explain: *No more tennis.* Or invite him over for a cocktail so she could alter the tone of the thing: 'Here, Mr Aeronautical Engineer, meet Nathaniel and Listen! The A.E. is a sort of colleague of mine.' Then the A.E. would drive away, and she would hold Nathaniel's hand on the doorstep, already talking about something else, such as dinner.

'I say OK to Wednesday next week,' she agreed and put down the phone. She had a habit of simply hanging up rather than making some conclusive remark such as 'Great! See you then. Keep smiling!'

Friday night was Listen's first Tae Kwon Do class. She was embarrassed to be wearing the 'dobok', and suddenly frightened that Donna or one of the others might walk by the window and see her. But that was unlikely. Also, the other three beginners were admiring the way they looked in the mirror and had started doing a slow-motion charade of a kung-fu fight with each other. It was pretty funny. She started laughing but remembered that she was being a taker, laughing without being funny herself, so she stopped and just looked serious.

Afterwards, two of the other beginners decided to practise with each other. And the third walked up to some kids from higher grades and joined in their conversation.

Listen wondered how you ever got to be that brave.

*

The following Wednesday, the A.E. arrived in a chatty mood.

He sat down, chuckled to himself, picked up his beer and made a *brmmm* sound as he flew the glass towards his mouth. Foam spilled over the edges. 'Here comes the aeroplane!' he said. Then he told Marbie that his father used to be a pilot.

'Huh,' said Marbie.

'So this is how he always fed me,' he explained, 'when I was a baby. And *that's* why I studied aeronautical engineering!'

'Hmm.' Marbie wondered if she should mention that babies all over the world are fed by aeroplane spoons.

Instead, for the sake of politeness, she told him she had been to several festivals of hot-air balloons. She picked up her beer and floated it towards her mouth like a hot-air balloon. He chuckled, then remarked that hot-air balloons were 'terrifically significant' in the development of the principles of aeronautics. She said she once heard that Leonardo Da Vinci figured them all out, all the principles of aeronautics, in sketchbooks five hundred years ago. He said that this was a common myth, such as the myth that William Shakespeare wrote his own plays.

So then Marbie said she thought that myth was actually true, that William Shakespeare did write his own plays. And even if somebody else *had* written the plays, did it matter? Who really knew William Shakespeare these days? He could be a compilation of people, couldn't he, and it would still be William Shakespeare?

'Whoa!' said the aeronautical engineer, making his eyes sparkle to show his fascination and confusion at her point.

Also, she continued, talking about William Shakespeare, she herself came from a family of writers. For example, her father once travelled to Ireland for a year to write a novel (although he then threw the manuscript, one page at a time, into the ocean) and her sister, Fancy, was a writer.

The aeronautical engineer looked almost shifty at the news

of her family of writers. He did not express environmental concerns when he heard that her father threw his novel into the sea. (That was the usual reaction.) And he did not ask what *kind* of writing Fancy did, which was also a common reaction. Instead, he shifted (shiftily), looked into his beer (sadly), then looked up at Marbie (sharply) and said: 'I don't know if I should tell you this or not.'

'Of course you should,' said Marbie emphatically.

'I don't know,' he said, 'I don't know,' shaking his head and trying to get something out of his eye for a moment.

'Just count to ten and then tell me,' suggested Marbie.

He looked embarrassed, and gazed at her with unexpectedly vulnerable, baby eyes.

'I'm a writer myself,' he breathed eventually. And looked back down.

'What?' she said, although she had heard him.

So that's when he told her. He said he had invented a new form of poetic self-expression which he called the 'vision'. He said he had written exactly 1,449 of these 'visions' and that he intended to publish them, as a collection, once he had reached 2,000. He had never told anybody this before. Also, he had a selection of his favourites in his pocket right that moment.

Politely, Marbie said, 'Can I take them home and read them?'

'OK, but promise you won't lose them?'

'I can't promise that,' explained Marbie, 'because it's in my nature to lose things.' She suggested he make photocopies before he loaned them to her.

'These *are* copies,' he admitted. 'It's just I'm scared they'll get lost and someone'll steal the ideas, and, you know, *publish* them.'

Marbie said, don't worry, ideas can't be stolen, that's illegal.

174

So he let her borrow them to take them home.

'By the way,' she said as she pressed the visions into her bag, 'there was something important I wanted to say –'

At that, her handbag miaowed and her hand jumped out in surprise.

'UP FOR SOME MAINTENANCE?' said the message from her mother. 'CONFIRMED 3 HR MARGIN AS OF NOW.'

'Got to go, sorry.' She looked up at the aeronautical engineer. 'Got to phone my sister and then leave!' She slid out of her seat and floated away from the table.

Left behind, the aeronautical engineer watched as she took out her cellphone and idly turned back to his beer.

Marbie read the first of the A.E.'s visions later that night while sitting in the tree above the ice-cream van. She had watched Fancy safely enter the building and had surveyed the empty street for a few minutes. There were never any problems on Intrusions these days, and being Lookout was boring. Also, they were well within the '3 hr margin' and her mother never sent them in without confirmation.

So Marbie opened her handbag for a mini Mars Bar, and her hand found the A.E.'s scroll of visions. The first, curling at top and bottom, was vision # 263.

THE VISIONS OF AN AERONAUTICAL ENGINEER
VISION # 263

DEEP ON THE INSIDE OF MY FRIED-EGG BRAINS I SEE:
THIS! I SEE THIS, I SEE THIS.
I SEE A FENCE ALONG A ROADSIDE (AN IRON RAILING FENCE),
SHARP ARROW TOPS ARE SNIPPED ALONG THE FENCE,
AND DEEP ON THE INSIDE OF MY FRIED-DEAD BRAINS I SEE:

> THIS! I SEE THIS, I SEE THIS,
> I SEE THIS FENCE WITH ITS SHARP ARROW TOPS AND
> I TRIP ON A SCUFFLE OF MY BOOT-LACE HEEL,
> AND I FALL EYE-FIRST ATOP AN ARROW TOP!
> FIRM ATOP AN ARROW TOP ATOP AN IRON FENCE!
> BUT:
> DEEP ON THE INSIDE OF MY FRIED-VANILLA BRAINS I SEE:
> THIS! I SEE THIS, I SEE THIS.
> I SEE MYSELF JOGGING CALM
> ALONGSIDE THE FENCE,
> AND I'M BREAKING OFF THE ARROW TOPS, ONE BY ONE,
> AND THE ARROWS SNAP AWAY JUST RIGHT,
> LIKE FRESH ASPARAGUS.

Marbie felt curious. She shook her head, trying to shake herself back into herself. She read the vision again and felt even more curious. For she had *never told the aeronautical engineer* about her lifelong fear that long sharp items (such as umbrellas or fence posts) would somehow end up in her eye. *She had never even told him about the event with the flying beach umbrella.*

And yet here, curling in her hand, was a *vision* containing not only her fear, but also the *solution* to her fear. He was going to break the arrow tops *off the fence*! Like the ends of fresh asparagus.

Her hand, which was holding the travel torch, trembled violently and the torch slipped and rustled through the branches to the ground. She looked down. And there was the car in the street beneath her, turning into the apartment garage.

'GET OUT *NOW*' Marbie typed into her pager, fingers shaking. She sent the message thirteen times before Fancy finally acknowledged it. A few moments later, she saw

Fancy leaping smartly from the window to a tree and elegantly stepping down its branches.

Marbie phoned the A.E. from work the next day and expressed wonder at his vision. He did not seem surprised at her wonder. In fact, he seemed despondent because, it turned out, he *hated* writing his visions. He said that, as a writer, one felt a *compulsion* to write, much like the compulsion that some people have to tear out their own hair. He would give anything, he said, *not* to be a writer, for writers have *expression* in their soul, which is tearing and scratching to get out! Worse, he said, far worse, to tear something out of your soul than simply to tear it from your head.

It was his secret anguish, his writing of visions, and it surprised him too, this anguish, given that he was generally practical, objective, logical; just as an *engineer*, a *scientist!* should be. But the artist, sadly, was in him.

At school, Listen was a sentry.

In most of her subjects, she had found places to sit away from Donna and the others, although in Science she was not allowed to change benches. So she still had to sit with Donna and Caro, and when they did experiments together they were very polite.

At lunchtimes she hovered around the tuck-shop door, like a sentry. She stood on the tips of her toes, scanning the crowd at the counter. *Where are my friends?* her facial expressions said. *Why so slow?* She had to open up her sandwich and eat it, all the time watching and guarding the door. Then, finally, when she had finished her sandwich she gave up and went to the library until the end-of-lunch bell rang.

Recess was the most difficult time because there were fifteen minutes to fill and you were not allowed into the library. You were never allowed into a classroom: everybody had to sit outside on the lawn even though it was so cold these days that girls huddled together, or rubbed each other's hands between their own to make them warm, or sometimes groups of girls got up and did the can-can in a row.

The point was, there was nowhere to hide and fifteen minutes to fill.

Sometimes Listen thought about just going out on to the lawn and joining a group of huddled girls. If she stayed completely silent, they might not notice.

Sometimes, also, she thought about going out there on to the lawn, among the garlands of girls, and simply sitting on the grass. She could sit alone, eat an apple, read a book and *who cares what anybody thinks?*

There was never a single person eating lunch on the lawn alone. *I am the only one in the entire school with no friends*, she realized. Or if not, where do they go? Where are the other lonely people? Why can't we join up and be friends?

It was exhausting enough filling up the time at school. She also had to hide in the Vodaphone shop in Castle Towers on weekends so that Marbie and her dad would think she was out with her friends.

Marbie read the A.E.'s other visions, but none of them spoke to her in the same direct way as the one about the sharp fence posts. That particular vision she pinned to the corkboard above her desk and read each morning like a mantra.

It is curing me, she thought to herself, in wonder. Whenever she feared a long, sharp item these days, she would close her eyes and imagine the aeronautical engineer prancing plumply alongside a fence, snapping off the sharp bits one by one. In her imagination, he turned to her with an armful of fence ends clutched to his chest and he blushed and lowered his head.

One Tuesday afternoon, Marbie looked at the phone on her desk and thought: *Well!* Because why had he not called?

She had not had a chance to say: *No more tennis*, so why had *he* decided no more tennis? All of his own accord. (Did he have a *vision* that she had meant to say it?) Of course, the weather had turned grey and chill and there was talk that it was going to get freakishly cold, so maybe tennis was no longer appropriate. Bare legs would goose-bump as they ran towards the net. Still, he could have called for a chat.

She phoned Listen to see how she was. The night before, she had said to Nathaniel, 'There's something going on behind Listen's eyes.' And Nathaniel had agreed that Listen seemed different.

'I'll try harder to get her to talk,' Marbie promised. 'I'm kind of sad because I thought she and I would hang out together, but she's always out with her friends.'

Now, on the phone, she said, 'What are you doing tonight?'

'Going ice-skating with Donna and the others,' Listen said at once. 'It was so great when we went on the weekend? Sia was, like, super fast, but Caro wouldn't let go of the gate. Me and Donna held hands and just spun around and around till we got dizzy. So, we're going again tonight; maybe every Tuesday night from now on.'

'Sad,' said Marbie. 'I was going to see if you wanted to come to the movies with me.'

'Huh.' Listen was quiet. Then she said, 'Maybe another night?'

Marbie hung up and called Nathaniel. 'I just have to come to terms with it,' she said. 'Listen prefers to be with her friends, so probably that's why she seems depressed when she's with us. She's so sweet and polite, though; when I asked her out tonight she suggested we do something another night. I guess I should leave her alone.'

'Me too,' Nathaniel agreed. 'If she's in that phase she definitely doesn't want to hang with her dad.'

Marbie wandered out of her office and suggested to the others that they go for a drink.

Remember me?

I'm writing from the 73 bus. There's a huge sweaty guy beside me, and his big butt takes up more room on the seat than it deserves. It's Wednesday, 2 p.m, and I should be at work but I'm not.

Here's what happened.

Last night, I went to the Night Owl with the girls from work. The girls left – Rhamie and Abigail to their husbands, Tabitha and Toni to Step. I had my drink to finish, so there I sat, and behind me? Leaning over my shoulder, breathing beer into my cheek, two hairy hands on my shoulders?

The aeronautical engineer.

I hadn't seen him for a fortnight at least. Not since he gave me his visions. I'd almost forgotten him.

But there he was in the Night Owl Pub.

'Hello,' he said, leaning over me, a murmur of a smile around his beery lips.

'I have a suggestion,' he said.

'Not tennis,' I said.

He pretended to look shocked. He mimed a tennis ball hitting him in the stomach, but recovered quickly, and the smile was less a murmur, more a shout.

'All right,' he agreed, 'not tennis. I had this idea, is all.'

Then he leaned closer and spoke into my ear: 'Slip out of work and come to my house tomorrow afternoon. Take the 73 bus, it stops outside my door.'

It was Wednesday, they had made cheese soufflé in Food Technology, and Listen was hopeful. The bell had rung for recess and they had not even washed up! The other girls groaned, while Listen quietly filled her sink with soapy warm water.

'Never mind, girls!' cried the teacher generously. 'Out you all go! I'll clean this up later!'

Listen pretended not to hear and concentrated on the cheese chunks in the grater.

'Come on, Listen, I'm sure that's clean,' called the teacher, ushering the last girls from the room. 'Go along and get some fresh air!'

Outside the classroom, Listen checked her watch. It was ten forty-six. There were still fourteen minutes to fill. She leaned over, untied her shoelaces and retied them, went to the end of the corridor and retied them again. Then she took the long route to the bathrooms, around the back of the building, always hurrying, sighing and checking her watch, so that if anybody saw her she was just rushing off to meet her friends.

At the bathrooms, she washed each hand with soap and dried them at the heaters with great care. Now it was ten fifty-one. There were still nine minutes. She hesitated outside the bathrooms, looking both ways along the empty balcony. One direction would take her into the admin office, where she could pretend she had lost something and fill in a lost property form. The other took her to the Year 7 classrooms, where they were not supposed to be. Her eyes wandered the locked doors of 7A, 7B, 7C and 7D and then stopped at the next door along. She had never noticed that door before.

It was a darker grey than the other doors and did not have a number or letter. As she watched, it was slowly opening. A school handyman was emerging, his arms stretched wide around a large cardboard box. Once out of the room, he looked both ways, kicked the door closed behind him and grunted. Then he disappeared down the fire escape. She did not even make a decision. She just strode along the balcony, opened the grey door and walked inside.

It was cramped, dark and smelled like mushrooms. She could see the shadowy shapes of boxes stacked precariously, shovels, rakes, and shelves lined with aerosol cans. Also, against the far wall, a tiny bulb illuminated a panel of switches. *Fuse box*, she thought, and felt pleased with herself. Growing up in a camper van, she had learned how to change fuses, tyres and halogen lights. She had helped her dad install a dishwasher once.

She had a moment of pleasure at that thought, and then the pleasure faded like a pilot light burning out. *What if the handyman came back?* What reason could she give for being here? She could be practising her Tae Kwon Do. She could say that she had a grading right after recess and this was the only place to practise.

For authenticity, she tried a spinning hook kick. As she did, something happened in her mind: *I can't even make friends with the other kids at Tae Kwon Do.* They were funny, some of the other kids, and she planned to contribute something herself one day. But when she thought of funny things she worried, 'Is it funny enough?' By the time she had decided it was, the conversation had moved on. So she never said a word.

I am a lost cause. She swivelled and tripped on a tangle of cords. She fell against the fuse box and slid to the ground with a sound like someone flicking through playing cards. She stood back up in a panic and flashed her eyes over the fuses. Some said OFF and some said ON – which ones had she knocked?

They should probably all be ON. She flicked them all, breathing hard, and backed out of the utility room, closing the door behind her.

There was nobody on the balcony. There were distant sounds of girls laughing and chatting on the lawn. Somewhere, teachers were also chatting, in deeper, more sardonic voices. She used up the last five minutes of recess standing at the bag rack outside 7B and leafing through the contents of her school bag.

Walking home from school that day, hunched against the pale cold sky and the thin waves of rain, Listen thought: *Don't worry, there are only two more days until the end of the week.* Also she thought: *Don't worry, soon I'll find a new group to join.*

As she stepped around the edges of muddy puddles, Listen tried once again to go through the different groups of girls in her year, but instead found herself remembering a particular day from a weekend a few years back. On that day, she and her dad had taken a ferry ride on the harbour. Alongside a ferry wharf she had seen a large yellow sign, which announced, in black letters:

CAUTION
Submarine cables

Reading the sign, she had shivered with delight. *There was a submarine right beneath her!* She imagined it must be slender and silver, and inside, a group of harried sailors hunched over long low tables, sipping black coffee and studying maps. The submarine would be tethered to the sea floor with a cable which might trip you up.

Later, her dad explained that 'submarine' just meant 'below water'. The sign was saying: 'Caution: underwater cables'.

As she stepped up on to the apartment porch, Listen thought: *There is nothing magic in the world. There are no flying motorbikes, just aeroplanes. There are no shooting stars, just satellites. There are no submarines, just underwater cables. There are no eternal pacts.*

Then, as she found her key in her pocket, she thought: *I don't think I can make it to the end of the week.*

Inside the apartment door, she had to stop as the weight of her school bag had become too much for her shoulder. There was a noise down the hall. 'Hello!' called Marbie's voice. 'Is that Listen or a burglar?'

Marbie was sitting at the kitchen table, and the radiator buzzed at her feet. The room was so warm it was like a velvet hug. 'It's my beautiful Listen!' cried Marbie, leaping to her feet and throwing her arms into the air. 'Look, I've got you a welcome afternoon tea!' She swept her arms back and forth across the table, which was set with a lace cloth, a chocolate bar arranged in pieces on a saucer, wedges of orange in a bowl and a steaming cherry pie.

'Wow,' said Listen, dropping her school bag. 'How come you're not at work?'

'Do you think you could take the rest of the week off school?' said Marbie, ignoring the question and pushing the saucer of chocolate closer to Listen. 'I'm about to call Nathaniel and see if he can close the Banana Bar. Because guess what? I heard on the news that it's snowing in the Blue

Mountains! So I've arranged the De Luxe Package for the three of us at the Hydro Majestic. There'll be flowers and chocolates on arrival! And there are fireplaces in the rooms! And we can toboggan down gentle slopes, and then we'll come inside for spa baths and hot chocolate and marshmallows, and we'll all play Pictionary or whatever game you like. What do you think? Would you like to take the rest of the week off school? I'll write a note and say you've got mad cow disease!'

Listen laughed so hard she started crying.

On the train home from the mountains, while Listen was asleep, Marbie and Nathaniel talked again about how remote she was. They decided it was her age. This was the sullen phase, and next it would be drugs and vandalism.

'I thought she might skip adolescence,' Nathaniel reflected.

A lot of things were changing in her life, they realized: new school, new home, new family, new way of spending Friday nights. It was not surprising that she was retreating into such a busy social life with her friends.

Marbie said she thought the best approach was to be as loving as possible. They should praise her constantly. Nathaniel agreed.

The following week, Listen arrived at school with a snow burn and found that the Year 7 classrooms had been flooded. Every-one was as excited as if it was a holiday, and they had to take their lessons in the Science labs or even outside on the lawn. The teachers laid plastic sheets on the grass to stop them getting chills in their kidneys.

She sat in the school library at lunchtime and watched as a fat teacher wearing a kaftan and spectacles rolled out a poster for the wall. A lot of the teachers at this school wore spectacles, she realized. Was it just Clareville College or was it high school? Did it cause some kind of eyesight problem for adults?

A group of Year 7 girls stopped outside the library door. Listen slipped down in her seat so they would not see her. One of them was tipping out another one's pencil case; one was making a song out of her timetable; one was writing on another one's school bag; one was complaining that she had forgotten a textbook. None of them seemed to be listening to any of the others. All of them were shouting. A librarian sighed and closed the door.

It was a mystery to Listen: why could she not just walk out the door and shout along with the other girls? Why could she not relax, the way she did when she was with the Zings? Just last Friday, at the Zing dining table, she had been answering Fancy's questions about school. Fancy had turned back to the table to declare that they all had to help Listen choose a topic for her Science assignment. 'Choose two creatures of the sea,' Fancy recited, while Listen had nodded her encouragement. 'They may be mythical creatures and they need not be fish.'

'They *need not be fish*,' murmured Grandma Zing, impressed.

'Ocean bream and rainbow trout,' suggested Grandpa Zing at once.

'Mullet and mermaids,' tried Grandma Zing.

'Blowfish and stingrays,' said Listen's dad.

'Fish and chips!' Cassie giggled.

'Blue-eyed cod and . . .' Radcliffe clicked his fingers a couple of times.

'I was thinking that I'd try to do something kind of oppo-site,' Listen had explained. 'Like one thing very big and one thing very small.'

'Whales then,' said her dad.

'Definitely whales,' Listen agreed.

'Do a little bit of seaweed,' said Cassie, 'or a tiny, teeny, little sea grape.'

'Good idea, Cassie, but I was thinking of seahorses.'

'You already know what you're doing,' Grandpa Zing observed. 'Whales and seahorses. See that, everyone? Whales and seahorses. So why is she asking us?'

'I *didn't* know until this moment,' argued Listen. 'You all just helped me decide. Thank you.' She looked around and everybody nodded, except Fancy, who was thinking.

'Does it have to be creatures of the sea?' said Fancy, looking dreamy. 'Can't it be, I don't know, *dragons* and *dodo birds*?'

'I don't think so,' Listen had apologized. 'It's for our Ocean unit.'

It was just as if she lived in parallel universes. In one, with the Zings, she said whatever she liked, and her words became part of a stream of words, and they praised her and found her fascinating. In the other, she was at school or at Tae Kwon Do, and she never said a word.

The first universe must never find out about the second. The Zings would look at her in a completely different way. Their universe would disappear.

Nathaniel reached under the driver's seat to adjust it back. 'You must be shorter than you look,' he commented to Marbie, who was in the passenger seat beside him.

They were driving home after a Zing Family Secret Meeting.

'How was the meeting?' said Listen, from the back seat.

'OK,' said Nathaniel. 'How was your movie with Cassie?'

'Fine,' agreed Listen. Passing headlights striped all three in turn.

There was silence in the car, except for the tching of the indicator as they waited in a right-turning lane.

'How's school anyway, Listen?' Marbie said.

'Fine.'

Nathaniel and Marbie each sighed slightly.

'Looking forward to the holidays?' Marbie tried next.

'Yep,' said Listen. 'Oh, did I tell you I'm going to a party at Sia's place tomorrow night? Is that OK?'

'Of course!'

'You've got such a busy social life, Listen,' Marbie said. 'You're a lot cooler than I was at school.'

'Her friends have always loved her,' Nathaniel confirmed. 'How is Sia anyway, Listen?'

'Fine.'

Marbie and Nathaniel winced. There was silence from the back seat.

Then she surprised them, as Nathaniel took the corner, by asking, 'Marbie, can you tell your swimming-pool story again?'

'Well,' said Marbie, at once. 'I was five years old and this was a hot summer day. I was playing on the swing that Dad had hooked up for us, as a goodbye present when he left to go to Ireland, you know, the swing that hangs from the big gum tree down the back of the yard? So, I was swinging back and forth, trying to pick up a breeze to cool me down, so higher and higher I swung and the higher I went the more I could see: Mummy's flowerbeds, our old trampoline, the tops of small trees, the tops of taller trees and the roof of the garden shed. Higher and higher I swung until I could even see the roof of our own house, and then, of course, I started to see the neighbourhood – the empty school yard of Bellbird High next door, their basketball court and its goalposts, their tennis courts, their old stone buildings, the sloping lawn at the back of the school, how it falls into scrub and forest, and then, with one final *swing* of my knees, I went higher than I ever had before.

And that's when I saw the spark of something blue in the bush there.

'That night, I waited until everyone was asleep, and I climbed out of my bedroom window and ran down the back of our house. I found a gap in the fence between our place and the school, and I ran down into the bush, and there were rocks and dried grass that hurt my feet but I didn't notice because I wanted to find out what it was. And what it was, of course, was the school's new swimming pool. I was hot and dirty from running through the bush so I jumped in and swam around a bit. Then I went home and went to bed.'

'And then for the rest of that summer –' prompted Listen sleepily.

'And then for the rest of that summer, every night, after midnight, I would slip through the gap in the fence and go for a swim in the pool. I thought it was my own secret pool. Of course, after a couple of years I stopped being able to fit through the gap in the fence, which is why –'

She turned around to the back seat, but Listen was fast asleep.

It was exhausting having a secret.

Saturday night, Listen sat shivering by the Bellbird High swimming pool. The pool was covered and the signs were face down on the frosty ground.

It was a mistake coming here to hide out. She had thought it would cheer her up, sneaking into Bellbird like she used to with Marbie and her dad over the summer. Now it was just cold and dark.

She looked up and there was something impossible in the sky. A magical, pulsing blue light; something enchanted or maybe a spaceship. Her heart leaped up on to its toes and she trembled with excitement.

Then she realized what it was. It was a screen advertising cars on the side of the Goodyear blimp.

On Wednesday, an intriguing pink envelope was tossed on to Marbie's desk by the mailboy. Her name appeared on the front in swirling purple.

Inside: a large piece of paper bearing two yellow sticky notes. The first sticky note said in scratchy pen: JUST WROTE THIS AND YOU CAME TO MIND. SO HERE IT IS FOR YOU.

On the large piece of paper, vision #1451 was neatly typed.

THE VISIONS OF AN AERONAUTICAL ENGINEER
VISION # 1451

DEEP WITHIN THE ICICLES OF MUDDY, CRUDDY SPACE
I SEE THIS, I SEE THIS, I SEE:
GOSH!
I SEE YOUR FACE! YOUR OWN PRECIOUS FACE!
I SEE BLACK CATS, UMBRELLAS AND STREAKS OF SPILLING MILK.
I SEE A FOOTPATH CRACK, A BURNING EAR, A LADDER AND A WOODEN DOOR –
A NECKLACE CLASP IS GLINTING FROM BENEATH A DIMPLED CHIN!

The second sticky note said: TOMORROW NIGHT. MY PLACE. HERE'S YOUR SECOND CHANCE.

The next day, Thursday, Marbie sat at her desk and unwound paper clips. A little pile of ragged wires formed on her desk. Every now and then she took one from this pile and tried to bend it back into paper-clip shape. It was never possible.

The yellow sticky note was on her corkboard: TOMORROW NIGHT. MY PLACE. HERE'S YOUR SECOND CHANCE. Each time she read it, she felt a chill breeze waft through her mind: *You must not go! You must not go! You must not go!*

Of course not! She gave a contemptuous laugh, but continued to unwind paper clips. The telephone rang. It was Fancy.

'Marbie!' Fancy's voice was urgent and breathless – and Marbie felt at once that Fancy knew. *You must not go!* Fancy would instruct her. 'Of course not,' Marbie would reply.

'Marbie, something terrible has happened! I left a *phone bill* of mine on the dining-room table at the last Intrusion! I just realized! I have to go back in and get it! But what if it's too late? I can hardly breathe! I've called Mum and she's put out an Urgent Request for a Distraction. So, if we get one, is tonight OK?'

'Of course,' agreed Marbie. 'I'll leave work early and wait for your call. I'm sure it's not too late or we'd have heard something. Just calm down and breathe and have a foot massage.'

Well, she said to herself, hanging up after several minutes of calming Fancy down. *So that's that then. But a phone bill! Why did she take a phone bill along to an Intrusion?*

She sent a text message to the A.E. ('CAN'T MAKE IT'), took down the yellow Post-it and scraped the misshapen paper clips into the bin.

Then she got on with her day's work.

Listen was allowed to do the next spell on the last Friday of school before the holidays. She would do it as soon as she got home: like a beginning-of-the-holidays reward. On that day, they had Science first, and the teacher made an announcement: 'Guess what, girls, I've just got word that all Year Sevens are allowed to go home at the end of this lesson!'

Everyone said, 'Wha-a-a-at?!' and 'No way!' and the Science teacher explained: 'It's obviously much too cold to take

191

lessons outside –' he was interrupted by noisy agreement – 'and the weather, as you will no doubt have noticed, has become, shall we say, quite strange. The bus companies have hinted that they may be shutting down in the next few hours – so – hush, hush, no need for hysterics – so, we're arranging a staggered collection throughout the day, and you poor little homeless Year Sevens, yes, yes, I know – you poor little homeless Year Sevens have been selected as the first lot to go!'

After that, of course, the lesson was upbeat and hilarious, with nobody paying much attention to the teacher. At Listen's bench, Donna and Caro passed each other's homework diaries back and forth between them, writing the names of unlikely movie stars in large red hearts. Then they would show the other what had been written in her diary, and the other would shriek and try to scribble out the name. *Well really,* thought Listen, *why do you keep letting each other write in there if you know you're both going to write something stupid?*

'Hang on, hang on,' said Caro, 'I *promise*, this time, I *promise* I'm going to write something normal.' Donna passed her diary back, and Caro wrote in large letters: 'BE ALERT. THE WORLD NEEDS MORE LERTS.'

Listen, reading over Caro's shoulder, giggled. At this, Caro grimaced as if she had been asked to dissect a frog. She closed the diary and slid it back along the bench towards Donna, who gave her a sympathetic pat.

'Excuse me for living,' murmured Listen and shifted her stool a little further from them.

As the period drew to an end the teacher's voice rose again. 'OK, guys, the bell's about to go, so, while I have your attention, *two* things! Obviously, I don't need to remind you that you must all report to *Redwood Primary* at the start of next term! I know! I *know* that it's a primary school, but I expect you will survive. And I *also* expect to see your assignments that *very* day! I assume you're already *well* under way!'

192

Everybody laughed.

'Well, who can remind me what the topic is? Nobody? Choose two creatures of the sea. They may be *mythical* creatures and they need not be fish!'

Donna raised her hand and said, 'How can they be creatures of the sea and not be fish?'

With an elaborate sigh, the teacher declared: 'Donna Turnbull. Is it possible that you have not heard a single word of what I have said today?'

Donna shrugged and said, 'It's possible,' and beside her Caro made a snorting noise. Donna kept a straight face, but it crinkled around the edges.

'Donna,' said the teacher, 'have we been talking, this lesson, about *whales*?'

'Have we?'

'And, Donna, is a whale a type of *fish*?'

Donna stared, while Caro grabbed at her arm. The bell rang shrilly for the end of the lesson.

'OK! Nobody steps out of that door until someone has told Donna what kind of animal a *whale* is!'

Then half the class shouted, 'It's a *mammal*,' while Donna opened her mouth wide, and Caro slithered down in shrieks of giggles. Next thing they were all tipping their chairs backwards, talking and reaching for school bags, and leaning for pens which had dropped on to the floor.

Listen Taylor, however, sat at her desk for a moment, as if she had forgotten where she was, watching the girls packing up to go, and also watching Donna and Caro helping each other through the classroom door, both by now crippled with laughter.

Marbie stood in the corridor with Tabitha, Toni, Abi and Rhamie, and watched Tabitha talk about her pregnant sister. The other girls were shaking their heads, so Marbie joined in when they did. But what she was really thinking was: *I am the luckiest girl in the world. I am so lucky that Fancy called yesterday and we had to do another Intrusion last night so that Fancy could get her phone bill back. Because that meant I couldn't go to the A.E.'s house. I can't believe I was even considering it. Just because he sent me a vision about my superstitions. A lot of people are superstitious, you know. I am SO lucky.*

'That's your cell, isn't it, Marbie?' said Tabitha.

'Sorry!' said Marbie and slid into her office.

She had missed the phone call and there was no message. But as she stared at the '1 MISSED CALL', a text message arrived: '2DAY THEN, MY PLCE, 1 P.M. LV WK NW.'

She stared at this for a while. 'LV WK NW.' *LV WK NW.* What did that mean? Love wake new? But what did *that* mean?

Leave work now, she realized.

At which moment, Tabitha leaned into her office and said, 'Leave work now, Marbie! It's all over the news! They're expecting *freezing rain* or *snow* and if we don't leave now, we will *never get home*! They're about to cancel *all public transport*!'

HELLO AGAIN! said the Spell Book. 'Hello,' said Listen, automatically, and then stopped.

Hasn't it been ages? Well, and how do you feel today? I hope you feel fine. I myself feel JUST fine. Here is the next Spell.
This is a Spell To Make Two Happy People Have a HUGE Fight Over Absolutely NOTHING!

Here are the instructions:
1. Do twenty star jumps.
2. Take some pieces of paper, write the heading

> 'Things that Make Me Sad', then fill the pages with
> the *things that make you sad.*
> 3. Fold the papers and bury them at the bottom of a
> full box of tissues.
>
> *Close the book, put it under your pillow and we'll see
> you again for the next Spell TOMORROW!*

Listen lay on her bed, on her side, and read the spell over twice. And what she was thinking was that this spell was easy and quite good exercise. She was thinking that she wouldn't mind writing out the things that made her sad and burying them in the bottom of a tissue box. She was thinking that *tomorrow* was an unusually short time to wait for the next spell.

But what she was *really* thinking was: *Why would anybody do a spell to make two happy people have a fight?*

Before she got time to think of an answer she was already on star-jump number five.

Things That Make Me Sad. Listen poured herself a glass of juice, sat at her bedroom desk and stared at the heading she had written on a blank piece of foolscap paper. Then she moved her pen to the line beneath the heading and began.

'Donna has a table-tennis table in the basement of her house,' she wrote, 'and once Sia's mother made us all eat spaghetti squash. The first thing that makes me sad is that I'll never get to play table tennis at Donna's place again. Caro and I used to be the best team when we played doubles. The second thing that makes me sad is that they had a strategy meeting at Donna's place without me.'

She continued writing. 'The thirty-third thing that makes me sad,' she concluded, 'is that there isn't any point in my existence.'

Then, as the Spell Book requested, she buried her sadness in a Kleenex box.

The aeronautical engineer met Marbie at his doorway with one red rose and a kiss. He was on his front veranda, waving at the bus. Marbie was skidding on the icy path to his doorway. The red rose was waving in his hand, clutching at rain and dipping at wind. The kiss was quick and met Marbie's lips.

Too soon! thought Marbie.

He took her by the hand into his hallway, where she sat on the cold tiled floor to unlace her boots.

He murmured in her ear, in a tickly way, 'You are cold, my princess. Let us to the fire!'

'Oh, well,' Marbie explained, 'I haven't taken my other boot off yet, you see?'

'Come along!' he said, shrugging expansively at her one boot, and took her tripping to the fireside, where he made her sit on the floor.

Too soon! thought Marbie. *Too soon!*

He seemed to sense her owlish tune, and paused now, kneeling at her feet. Marbie sat, demure by the fireside, her arms around her knees. He unlaced her boot, criss-crossing down among the eyelets. He went too far. He slid the entire lace out until it leaped from the boot. Surprised, Marbie said, 'Do you not understand how shoelaces work?'

But he had taken a glass of champagne from the mantelpiece and in one smooth move had the cold glass in her hand.

'Champagne?' said Marbie. 'What's it doing on your mantelpiece?' She took a sip while he hit the 'PLAY' button on the CD player.

'Jazz,' said Marbie. 'A lot of people like jazz. Not so much myself. I'm not what you'd call a jazz kind of person. Fancy is. My sister Fancy? You wouldn't think it because –'

'All right,' interrupted the aeronautical engineer, leaning back to the CD player, 'no jazz then.'

The CD tray slid open slowly, presenting the CD like a waiter with a plate.

'Marbie,' said the aeronautical engineer, sitting cross-legged next to her. 'How long do you have?'

'Just the lunch hour, really,' she lied. 'I'll have to go back to work.'

He moved towards her, in a sort of slide across the carpet on his bottom.

She felt alarmed.

'Well –' she began.

But he leaned down and stopped her with a kiss.

'Look at it on the trees.'

He stood at his door with a towel around his plump waist, and a cold and hairy chest, and pointed. 'That's freezing rain, is what that is.'

'You'd better get inside,' Marbie told him. 'You'll freeze.'

He said, 'Look at the ice on the trees. Have you ever seen Sydney look like this? No, you wouldn't have. Nobody has. That's your bus now, at the lights on the corner. I think they should cancel the buses. I bet they do any moment now.'

'You'd better get inside,' Marbie said again. 'What happens if the freezing rain hits your chest? The hair will turn into curly icicles and you'll have to snap them off.'

'I'll watch you on to the bus,' he said. 'You be careful on that ice, won't you? It'll be a skating rink out there. Deadly.'

'Don't wait for me,' said Marbie. 'You'd better get inside.'

'Kiss me,' he said.

This was only fair.

Freezing rain crackled on the edges of the twigs and shark-toothed its way along the turrets and the grooves. The ice was like lace, or like Spanish moss, or like hand-blown glass on the trees.

Marbie sat at the kitchen table and waited for Nathaniel to get home. He was driving Listen to Tae Kwon Do. When he returned, she would tell him. She was surprised at how simple this was. She had thought it would be anguished indecision: should I tell him, should I not, should I tell him, should I not? But, at once, as she reached for the change for the bus, as she stepped from the bus to an iced-over puddle that soaked through her boots to her toes, at once! she had known.

She sat at the kitchen table with a Twix chocolate bar and a glass of lemonade. These were for Nathaniel.

After a moment, she opened the wrapper and ate the Twix bar. She had never eaten a whole one like that before, in big greedy bites, like a starving Charlie before the Chocolate Factory. Then she drank the glass of lemonade in one thirsty, greedy gulp. She had never done that before either. The fizziness, for a start, would have stopped her in the past. Now her mouth was chocolate sugar and her eyes were startled red. She was so frightened it made her want to giggle.

She reached into the kitchen drawer and took out the corkscrew, and then she began to play with it, rotating the top so that its arms rose up and then down, up and then down, like a person crying out for help. Giving up, crying out, giving up, crying out, the long thin body in an anguish of perpetual twisting.

There was the sound of a key in the door. She dropped the corkscrew with a clatter. But then there was a tumble of voices in the hallway: *Listen was home.*

'What happened?' Marbie called down the hallway. 'What happened to Tae Kwon Do?'

'Cancelled!' cried Listen. She danced, excited, and Nathaniel seemed excited too.

'Teacher left a note on the door,' he explained, opening the fridge. 'We should have thought of it. Traffic was hell. We were skidding all over the road. There's *ice* out there, Marbs, you should go have a look. Still, we weren't the only ones, were we, Listen? There were other kids hanging around there waiting. They hadn't seen the note. They were all trying to hit on Listen. Hey, Twix. I love Twix.' He was staring at the wrapper on the table.

'I know you do.' Marbie felt terrible guilt. 'I'm sorry. I ate it all. I'll get you another one tomorrow.'

'Ah well.' Nathaniel turned back to the fridge.

'I'm *hungry*,' Listen danced. 'They were not *hitting on me*, Dad.'

'Well that kid with the giraffe tattoo on his wrist was,' said Nathaniel, pulling up a kitchen chair. 'He's got it for you bad, kid.' To Marbie, Nathaniel indicated how the giraffe's neck ran from the boy's wrist to his elbow.

'That's Carl Vandenberg. He's going for his black belt. No way he likes me.'

'What say we go out for dinner?' Nathaniel said. 'We can walk down to that new Indian restaurant, to celebrate.'

'Celebrate what?'

'The ice storm. And the Zing Family Secret Meeting being cancelled. Not that I don't enjoy the meetings. It's just a reason, see. And Tae Kwon Do being cancelled,' suggested Nathaniel.

Listen pirouetted. 'But I like Tae Kwon Do.'

Alone in the kitchen again, Marbie thought sadly about buying another Twix for Nathaniel, only it was too icy outside. She had pretended she was too cold to join them at the restaurant, but now she was too frightened to do anything. She couldn't even make herself a curried egg sandwich for dinner.

*

'Come on to bed.'

Nathaniel sat up against his pillow, and Marbie stood at the foot of the bed, staring at him.

'You know how Arnold Schwarzenegger can kill a person by applying pressure to exactly the right part of their neck?' she said eventually.

'He's just an actor, Marbie,' Nathaniel said gently.

'And a governor,' agreed Marbie. 'But, well, he used to play characters like that sometimes, and the thing is, Nathaniel, you know how I sometimes give you a neck massage?'

'Not very often.'

'But *sometimes* I do, and the thing is, what if I accidentally pressed the bit that kills you and accidentally killed you?' Her voice broke.

'Marbie, I would tell you if you started killing me and then you could stop. OK? There's nothing to cry about. Look out the window, why don't you? I think it's snowing. I think I can see something white, and if I'm right, we should wake Listen and go outside.'

'It doesn't snow in Sydney,' said Marbie tragically, tears now streaming down her cheeks. 'But I could accidentally kill you with one little touch of my finger. Or what if you developed a spontaneous allergy to seafood, and I gave you a stamp to put on an envelope, and you got a reaction from licking the stamp because they use tiny fragments of fish bones in the glue? They do, Nathaniel; I read that. Or anyway they used to. And that could happen – you could die from a postage stamp.'

'I'm sure that's snow.' Nathaniel was leaning forward. 'Open the curtain.'

'It doesn't snow in Sydney,' Marbie said again listlessly.

Finally, Nathaniel paid attention. 'What's up, Marbie? Tell me what's wrong.'

'OK, I'll tell you,' said Marbie through her tears, and she did.

Part 8

19

Extracts from the Zing Garden Shed

(From 'Minutes of ZFS Meeting', November 1986)
- Mrs Z asks: 'How do we get rid of her?'
- Radcliffe makes a joke: 'A broken ankle or wrist might do the trick' (e/body laughs).
- General talk.
- *Resolved* that sub-committee be formed, consisting of:

Part 9

Snowstorm

20

The first day of the winter holidays, Cath woke up in a ruffled, empty bed and thought: *Of course, he has already left.* She wondered if there would be a single red rose on his pillow as a poignant goodbye but there was not. Instead, looking around her bedroom, she noticed a strange, almost exquisite light.

Then, as she watched, Warren Woodford appeared in the doorway. There was snow woven into his eyebrows.

'I've been for a walk,' he said, hesitating. 'If you can believe it, there's still snow on the ground outside.'

He was carrying a cardboard tray of takeaway coffees. His face was grey and frightened.

'It doesn't mean a thing,' Cath reassured him, sitting up against the bedhead. 'We were drunk and it didn't mean a thing.'

Warren raised an eyebrow.

Then he moved into the bedroom, closing the door with his boot. He put the coffee cups on to her bedside table and sat down on the side of the bed. He placed one cold hand on her forehead, as if he was checking her for fever, and his gaze was so troubled and so searching, she realized that it did mean a thing.

The first day of the winter holidays, Fancy woke when Cassie jumped on to her bed.

'There's *snow* outside! THERE'S SNOW OUTSIDE! MUMMY! THE WORLD'S GONE *WHITE*!'

Radcliffe muffled his voice straight into his pillow: 'Cassie, just lie down, honey, and have a little sleep.'

Cassie bounced on her father's ankle and he yelped.

Fancy blinked in the strange, almost secretive light of the room. Could there really be snow outside? Her daughter's shouts faded into a curious middle distance, and Fancy stretched her arms like a ballerina. Why did she feel so poignant and so graceful? Then she remembered: *My husband is having an affair.*

She had not yet confronted her husband about his affair. He had arrived home early the night before and found her sitting on their bedroom floor, the sock hidden safely in her pocket. He stage-whispered, 'If you're working on a book idea, I'll leave you to it,' and tiptoed out of the room.

One day, soon, she would tell him that she knew. In the meantime she would consider this poignant, graceful mood. Actually, she recognized the mood. It was the same strange, detached feeling that she had experienced at all secret yet significant times of her life: *I am not a virgin any longer; I am on the Atkins diet!; I think I may be having a child.*

'COME OUTSIDE AND PLAY IN THE SNOW, MUMMY!' Cassie's shouts began to penetrate. 'MUMMY, CAN I GO OVER TO LUCINDA'S PLACE AND THROW SNOW AT HER AND SHE COULD THROW SNOW AT ME?!'

'Well,' began Fancy, slowly and gracefully, but then the telephone rang.

The first day of the winter holidays, Marbie woke to a strange, almost haunting light which clouded her vision. For a moment she lay flat on her back, trying to see.

A buzzing sound gave her a flurry of hope: *It was all a dream! I never slept with the aeronautical engineer! I never told Nathaniel about it! Nathaniel and Listen are out in the kitchen making banana milkshakes!* But then she realized it was the sound of a leaf-blower somewhere outside.

Slowly, she wandered the apartment, gazing at the empty spaces: the doorknob where Listen's coat belonged, the shower rack where Nathaniel's shampoo should be standing. How thoroughly they had packed in the middle of the night!

She opened the front door and gasped at the strange little patch of white on the porch. It must be a message from Nathaniel. But what did it mean? She crouched down and touched it: it was icy cold. Had he hacked at the ice in the freezer, scraped it into a bucket, then tipped it out on the front porch? Meaning what? That her heart was as cold as an ice patch? That he would return *when the ice had melted*?

Then she looked up and saw that the white patches were everywhere. The white had dabbed at fence posts, letter boxes, tree branches. It sat on car roofs and bonnets, spread itself across front lawns and tipped over the edges of the gutters. Across the street, two little girls were aiming at the white with a leaf-blower.

Panicked, Marbie backed through the door into her hallway and reached for the phone. Her fingers shook as she dialled her sister's number.

'Can you meet me at Mum's place,' she whispered, 'right away?'

In Grandma Zing's kitchen, Marbie hyperventilated, her mother baked a carrot cake and Fancy sipped wisdom from her coffee cup.

'He will return,' was Fancy's wisdom. 'He won't be long.'

'I suppose he will.' Grandma Zing measured a teaspoon of dried ginger. 'But Marbie, darling, what were you thinking?'

'That's the thing.' Marbie sat back up, wide-eyed. 'I don't think I was thinking.'

'Someone as special as *Nathaniel* –'

'Stop it, Mum,' interrupted Fancy. 'Nathaniel will come back eventually, Marbie.'

'No, he won't,' murmured Marbie, turning to her sister. 'You didn't see his eyes. He was so *calm*. He listened to what I said, and then he got out of bed and took out his suitcase and packed. He folded his clothes like they were going on display in the window of a shop. And then he slept on the couch, and in the morning when I got up, he and Listen were gone. *And the snow was here.*'

'Never mind,' Grandma Zing comforted, 'the carrot cake won't be much longer now. I'm about to put it in the oven.' She glanced over to confirm that the oven was preheating. 'We'll leave your dad in the TV room for the moment. He loves that game show of his, doesn't he? And he's spent all morning in the shed.'

'Look,' said Fancy, firmly. 'It was just once, wasn't it, Marbie?'

'Yes,' agreed Marbie. 'Just the once.'

'And you don't plan to see him again, do you? This aeronautical engineer of yours?'

'No,' insisted Marbie. 'Never again.'

'Well now!' It was settled. 'Nathaniel will come back.'

'No, he won't.' Marbie shook her head, with tears blurring her eyes. 'No, he won't.' Then she dried her eyes, looked thoughtful for a moment and added: 'I admire his resolve.'

'Gosh,' said Fancy, 'it's still *here*.'

They were standing at the front door staring at the snow which was, she thought, like icing on a wedding cake, or cappuccino froth. It stared back at them, a little defiant, as if it knew it shouldn't be there at all.

'Honestly,' said Grandma Zing, 'I think you should both stay put now that you're here. I think it was dangerous of you to drive over unless there was an emergency.'

Then she looked at her two daughters and added politely, 'Of course, I understand that this *is* an emergency, Marbie.'

'If you drive slowly it's OK, I found,' said Fancy. 'Although I was skidding all over the road. Really, everywhere.'

'It's safe,' declared Marbie, 'because no one else is driving.'

'Yes, well, they're saying on the news that you should stay in your own homes and only come out to get necessary supplies such as torches and blankets and so on,' Grandma Zing confirmed.

They stood quietly on the porch for a moment, considering this, while up and down the street children and adults shrieked and played in the snow. Snowmen grew, snow fights flourished, and one or two people wandered around their gardens in their skis.

'I might stay here for a while,' conceded Marbie eventually.

'I have to meet Radcliffe for lunch,' Fancy declared.

'I'm going to go and lie down,' said Marbie.

'What are we going to do with that girl?' said Grandma Zing, at the window of Fancy's car in the driveway.

'Look at that!' said Fancy, surprised. 'The windscreen's completely frozen! The wipers aren't making a difference. I suppose people in cold countries have some kind of a scraping device for situations like this.'

'Let me see if I can get it with my fingernails,' offered Grandma Zing. 'Ouch! Turn off the wipers will you, darling? Fance, who on earth is this aeronautical engineer? And Nathaniel will forgive her, won't he?'

'I don't know,' admitted Fancy. 'He's so nice and sensible, so – then again, men can be funny about affairs.'

Her mother gave a sharp breath of laughter and said, 'Still. At least we don't need to worry about Nathaniel and the Secret.'

Fancy was playing with the vents in the dashboard, but at

this she said, 'I completely forgot about the Secret! It must be because you're right. He's not that type.'

'It was going along so nicely,' sighed Grandma Zing, 'what with Project 78 getting under way. Oh, and Fancy, I suppose I shouldn't bring this up now, but you know, it happened again. Just last night.'

'Again!' exclaimed Fancy. 'It's blurry?'

'No, it's just slipped. I don't suppose you and Marbie would be interested in another Intrusion for some Maintenance just now?'

'Not in the middle of a snowstorm,' said Fancy firmly. 'We'll wait until it melts.'

Fancy drove away from her parents' place, skidding on the snow and listening to the radio. It was a State of Emergency, the radio said, the roads and public transport were in chaos. Also, some areas had lost power, and there were concerns about homeless people freezing to death. Still, things were in hand because Sydneysiders were battlers. 'If there's one word to describe a Sydneysider,' the premier was saying in a recorded message, 'it's the word *battler*. I didn't say bull-headed there. We're not too proud to turn to our countrymen for advice – Aussie battlers in colder climes than ours. Tasmanians. Canberrians. We're not too proud to turn to *other* countries for advice either. Norway. Finland. Trust me. We have this in hand.'

'There you have it, people,' said the announcer, coming back on air. 'And let me say this one more time: have as much fun as you can in your own back gardens, but stay *off* the roads!'

'Oh blah,' said Fancy, stabbing at the radio buttons. Four centimetres of snow! What must *immigrants* be thinking about this hullabaloo! She blushed to think of the Canadian next door – how he must hoot as he sliced his kiwi fruit.

Fancy kept her own secret, Radcliffe's affair, buttoned up tight in her cardigan. She hadn't told anybody yet, but it was affecting the way that she moved. Her elbows, for example, as her hands gripped and skidded with the steering wheel, stuck out at a curious angle.

'What's happened? What's happened?'

Radcliffe was excited as the waiter led them to the table. The restaurant's lunchtime crowd was spilling out the door. It was the only place open in the neighbourhood, and people wanted to bustle into public spaces and chat with strangers about snow. 'Magic, isn't it?' a man said to Radcliffe, shaking his head at the picture windows. But Radcliffe only half nodded: he wanted to know Fancy's news.

'Something has happened,' Fancy had said mysteriously, when she phoned from her parents' place to suggest that they meet for lunch.

'Well!' said Fancy, then paused as the waiter took her coat for her, and paused as he drew out the chair for her, and paused as he swooped out the napkin for her.

'Well!' she repeated. Then the waiter jutted the menu at her nose, and she had to pause again.

'Can I start you off with a drink?'

Radcliffe ordered champagne.

The waiter allowed her a moment to continue by setting off to fetch their drinks.

'It's not a *celebration*!' she remonstrated, on account of the champagne. 'Something *awful* has happened!'

'Well, I wasn't to know,' Radcliffe grumbled. 'You didn't tell me what it was. You *sounded* like it was something exciting on the phone. Besides, we could celebrate the snow. Look at it out there! With the sun sparkling! It's like diamond-flavoured ice cream, isn't it? Don't you think?'

'Hmm.' Fancy pressed her hair behind her ears and announced: '*Nathaniel* has *left* Marbie!'

'He has not!'

He was so perfectly sure of this that Fancy began to doubt.

'He has!' she exclaimed, remembering. 'Marbie's been crying all morning. It turns out she's been having an affair.'

'Ah,' said Radcliffe, 'that I would believe.'

'Radcliffe!'

But Fancy had to stop because the waiter was back and wanted them to decide what to eat. Radcliffe chose Braised Lamb in Oyster Sauce. Fancy wanted the Atlantic Salmon.

'It wasn't an affair, really, anyway,' Fancy said, as soon as permitted to continue. 'It was just once, yesterday. With an aeronautical engineer, if you can believe it. And she told Nathaniel about it right away, that very night. Last night.'

'Good for her,' said Radcliffe.

'Yes,' agreed Fancy, staring at him carefully. 'It's the right thing to do. To tell. You should always tell.'

Radcliffe smiled slightly and looked down, which at first set off a panic in Fancy's chest (*he's about to tell me!*) until she realized he was thinking back in time. He had always been proud of himself for telling Fancy, when they were teenagers, that he had kissed another girl.

'But he *left* her!' Radcliffe exclaimed. 'Whatever for?'

Fancy regarded him shrewdly. 'You know,' she said, 'confession isn't everything.'

Radcliffe nodded.

'He moved out right away.' Enthusiastically, Fancy tore her bread in half. 'And she thinks they've moved back to the camper van where they used to live. You know, the one behind the Banana Bar?'

'Good God!' Radcliffe was impressed. 'Back to the *camper van*?'

'Yes,' agreed Fancy. 'Just when the renovations were

practically done.' Something occurred to her. 'Poor little Listen,' she began. 'Imagine how it must be for her – living in that awful camper van again, just when she's starting high school –'

But the waiter interrupted with their food.

Once he had gone, Fancy said idly: 'Who do you think you'll work with on Monday?'

Radcliffe had his mouth full of crunching snow peas, but he tilted his head sideways to show confusion.

'The usual, I guess,' he said, eventually.

'Gemma?' Fancy stared at him. 'Will you work with Gemma?'

'Gemma?'

Fancy squinted scornfully. 'The one who had her moles zapped,' she reminded him and peered at his mouth, his cheeks and his eyes.

'Oh, *Gemma*, yes. She works in the pay office. I wouldn't usually work with someone from the pay office, Fance. The moles! I remember. She also got her eyes zapped. You know, that laser operation where they burn open your eyeballs and scrape away whatever makes you short-sighted and then you don't need glasses any more? She had that done.'

This conversation was not actually part of Fancy's plan, and was suddenly exasperating, so she stopped and looked around for the waiter.

'I think I might drop by the Banana Bar,' she changed the subject as she looked, 'and see how Nathaniel and Listen are. Or is it too soon?'

'Aha,' nodded Radcliffe. 'Remind Nathaniel of his respon-sibilities *vis-à-vis* the Secret, eh? Remind him of all those confidentiality documents he signed?'

'Well, no, Radcliffe, we don't think Nathaniel's the vindic-tive type. We're not worried about him and the Secret. I just want to see if he's OK.' She raised her eyebrows at the waiter as she spoke and wrote her signature in the air, including the flourish she always added to the 'g' in 'Zing'.

'Ha ha,' chuckled Radcliffe, 'not worried, eh? Because he seems like such a nice guy, such a gentle, laidback, easygoing guy? You mark my words, Fance, it's the *quiet* ones you've got to worry about. Underneath all that *gentle wit* is a seething mass of resentment.'

'Well, I don't know about *that*.' Fancy frowned at him sternly, but also with a flicker of unease.

'Aren't you going to have dessert?' said Radcliffe. 'I was thinking of a coffee and now it's too late. You've gone and asked for the bill.'

'It's never too late,' said Fancy mysteriously. 'Nothing is *ever* too late, Radcliffe.'

'OK,' he agreed, and when the waiter put down a slender leather wallet containing two chocolate mints and the bill, Radcliffe said, 'Might I add an espresso to that, do you think?'

'Easy,' said the waiter and smoothly whisked it back.

'Hello!' said Fancy, brushing snowflakes from her jacket as she jangled the Banana Bar door. 'Busy today?' She sounded odd and bright.

'Nope,' said Nathaniel. 'Not one single customer. The weather, I guess.'

'Well!' (She could not stop the brightness.) 'I'll be your first! I'll have a banana milkshake, thanks.'

'On the house.'

'No! No!'

And then Fancy looked at him meaningfully to indicate that she knew, and Nathaniel shrugged to himself.

'So,' continued Fancy, building on her meaningful glance, 'I just wanted to see how you *were* – see if there's anything I can – and about the camper van – isn't it a bit too cold?'

'We won't sleep in the camper van. We've got a generator

for the shop, so we'll sleep out the back there. And also, if your mother's worried. I understand about the Secret. The Zing Family Secret. I would never –'

'Nathaniel! No! Of course we're not worried about *that*. I'm just hoping it will work out again. I mean, Marbie . . .' She was going to say that Marbie was a brat, a fool, a wicked witch, but one with the right sort of heart – only there was something about Nathaniel's eyes when she said the name. So she changed the subject. 'Where's Listen? How is she?'

'She's not so happy.'

'Did you tell her about – about Marbie – about . . .'

'I just said that Marbie and I had a fight. I said I didn't think we'd ever get over it. The fight. I said that was most probably it between Marbie and me.' He took Fancy's milkshake back from her, although it was not quite finished, and dumped it in the sink.

'Ah,' said Fancy.

Their eyes met for a moment and they both looked up at the giant plastic bananas hanging from the ceiling.

'She's out the back now in the camper van, I think. Practising her Tae Kwon Do.'

'OK,' said Fancy, standing and gathering her purse. 'Well, lovely to see you, Nathaniel. Make sure you call if you need anything. Or if you want to talk . . . And give Listen my love, won't you? Tell her to –'

But she didn't know what to tell Listen and simply waved.

It took years before you could do a proper flying side kick. Carl Vandenberg could do one, but he was going for his black belt, and even he looked messy in the air. The other day Listen had been one of the four people who crouched on the floor in a row so that Carl could jump over them and kick the piece of board held by the master.

Listen had decided she would secretly teach herself the

flying side kick. Out in the cold, she ran, leaped and fell on to her face. Her feet were bare. She wore summer pyjamas. She ran, leaped with her leg tucked under and fell face forward in the snow. She leaped and fell; leaped and fell.

When she got up, she could not feel her face, except her nose, which ached. Her hands were purple, her fingers were stinging, her knees and elbows were bruised or grazed and all the time she thought: *I deserve this*.

Because she had ruined everything. She was a stupid, selfish person and she stamped her bare feet in the snow to prove this and found herself stamping up the stairs into the camper van to burn the book.

A SPELL TO MAKE TWO HAPPY PEOPLE HAVE A HUGE FIGHT OVER ABSOLUTELY NOTHING.

She could not believe she had done a spell like that. She could not believe it meant her dad and Marbie. She never thought these spells even worked.

She took the Spell Book from her backpack, where she had packed it in the middle of the night last night, and slapped her hand scornfully against the lime green cover. She would *never* open it again. Excuse me, but why had she even bothered? The spells were useless. A spell about making somebody catch a taxi. A spell about breaking a *vacuum cleaner*. And then, the first spell that actually worked was an evil spell to make two happy people have a fight.

She was supposed to do the next spell today but she was actually going to throw the book away, burn it, tear it up or maybe just throw it in the recycling bin.

She would drown the book. She slammed it down into the tiny camper van sink, although it only made a slow popping sound, not the THWACK she wanted, and she reached for the tap, but of course nothing happened. The waterpipes had frozen.

It was then, looking down into the sink, that she noticed

tiny silver italics at the bottom of the back cover. She picked up the book and squinted at the words.

This Book will make you Fly, will make you
Strong, will make you Glad.
What's more, this Book will Mend your
Broken Heart.

She read this over, her face throbbed cold and goosebumps pricked her pyjama sleeves. She opened the Spell Book and read the next spell.

A Spell To Make Someone Give Someone a Rose

Put your finger on your nose and say: 'Golly!'

This Spell will work on a Thursday afternoon in about eight weeks or so. You can do the next Spell next Saturday!

'Cassie, honey, you know you don't need cushions and things for the snow. It's OK to fall on it. It's soft.' Fancy explained this as she drove Cassie home from Lucinda's place, keeping the car in low gear and skidding to the wrong side of the road occasionally.

'Not soft enough. See, there's not enough snow so you have to get the pillows and take the cushions off the couch and put them around on top of the snow so you can fall on them.'

'Hmm. Well. I'm sure that's wrong.'

'And we used Lucinda's mum's cake tins and frying pans to slide on, but you had to push yourself along with your legs because they don't really have any kind of hills in Lucinda's backyard.' Cassie drew a picture of herself on a cake tin in the window steam. 'See, Mum? This is how we pushed ourselves along.'

Fancy glanced over and said, 'Oh!', then, a few moments later: 'I suppose that's OK, about the cake tins. I suppose you can't really hurt them.'

'But I think we broke their VCR.'

'Oh, Cassie, I thought you were outside playing the whole time.'

'We were. We broke the VCR when we were sliding on it.'

'Cassie! Did Lucinda's mother know about this?'

'No,' explained Cassie. 'Lucinda hid the VCR under her bed. They should get a DVD player anyway.'

'Well,' said Fancy, 'I suppose so.'

Then they listened to the radio together for a moment: all over the city, people were tripping over, tobogganing down Martin Place, catching skis on parking meters, and leaving ski poles outside shops.

'Brrrrrrrrr,' said Cassie as they walked through the front door.

'Here's trouble,' exclaimed her father. 'Cass, you're walking snow into the house, kiddo. I think you ought to take your shoes off. Call me old-fashioned.'

'Come and sit on the steps beside me,' her mother offered. 'I bet this is what they do in cold countries. They take off their shoes on the steps. Radcliffe, shouldn't we put snow chains on the tyres?'

'I'll ring up the *Living With Snow* helpline,' agreed Radcliffe.

'There's a helpline?! So they think the snow's going to last?'

'I think we should have chicken noodle soup for dinner,' suggested Cassie, 'and then roast beef and roast potatoes, and then cherry pie, and then we should get a fireplace with a fire and marshmallows and games. That's what they do in cold countries when it snows.'

*

Over the next few days the snow slowly melted, but the weather stayed exceptionally cold and everyone expected more to fall. Just in case, the city of Sydney commissioned a series of television ads under the slogan *Living With Snow.* The ads advised on such things as shovelling the driveway and not wearing slippery shoes. Also, they pointed out that snow was designed to be 'fun' so nobody should panic if it did happen again.

Meanwhile, the Bureau of Meteorology cautioned that more snow was *highly unlikely* since snow in Sydney was a *freakish event.* It could not resist adding now and then: *but still, you never know!*

Each morning, the Canadian sat on his front porch, dressed in his overcoat and a black woollen hat, drinking coffee and breathing mist as he answered Fancy's queries about cold.

Each morning, Marbie woke at her parents' place, tangled in her childhood bed. She could not bring herself to go home, or to go to work. She took long hot baths and showers, left long phone messages for Nathaniel at the Banana Bar, and asked her parents whether he had called back while she was in the bath. He never had.

One morning she woke from a dream of Listen dancing, and she yearned to replay the night of the snowstorm: herself at the table with the empty Twix wrapper, Nathaniel and Listen home from cancelled Tae Kwon Do, Listen dancing through the kitchen. Then, later, telling Nathaniel about the A.E. *What had she been thinking?* She had been acting at the level of stupidity she'd learned about back when her sister told her parents she'd revealed the Secret to Radcliffe! How had she forgotten that lesson? If you do something wrong you keep it to yourself! You don't tell people!

If only she'd not told Nathaniel! If only she'd not eaten the Twix bar meant for him!

If only she'd not slept with the aeronautical engineer.

She stopped for a moment, staring at her high-school swimming trophies and wondering if she might have got the meaning of stupidity wrong.

But something was catching at the edges of her wonder, something significant and wrong.

She realized what it was.

She fell out of bed, ran to the phone and called Nathaniel.

Listen's dad wanted to build a snowman. Neither of them had ever built one before, and they were surprised by how difficult it was. The snow wouldn't roll into a ball; it kept crumbling in their hands.

That was another thing: they didn't have gloves.

While they were taking a break to blow on their hands and consider the problem, Listen's dad said casually, 'So, this is a real bummer, eh? Being back in the camper van after finally getting a place of our own?'

Listen laughed as if he'd made a joke and fell on to her knees to try a snowball again. As she scraped snow together, she thought of her brand new bedroom in the apartment. For the first time in her life, she'd had a chest of drawers, a lamp, a desk and a bed with two ends. Marbie had helped her choose the furniture.

Now she was back in a corner with a curtain for privacy, and a bathroom in the back of the Banana Bar. Also, no ironing board. Her Clareville College uniform would always be crumpled from now on.

'It must make you pretty angry though,' her dad persisted. 'Being back here. Would it help if I promise I'm going to get us out as soon as I can? We'll find a place to rent for a while. Who needs a mortgage anyway?'

He was collecting pebbles and bark now, choosing eyes and a mouth, maybe thinking that if he got attractive features ready the snowman would be grateful and appear. Watching her father frown in concentration, Listen felt so sad for him. His mouth trembled a little whenever he said Marbie's name these days, but each time he quickly smoothed out his face into a smile.

And he was so clueless about Listen herself. He had actually thought that the guys at Tae Kwon Do were 'hitting on her'. In fact, they were just talking to each other while she stood nearby. It was true that Carl Vandenberg had spoken to her. He had asked her for the time. She'd held out her wrist to show him her watch. Then her dad had arrived and that was that.

'Doesn't make me angry,' Listen said. 'But you could try to make up with Marbie, couldn't you? I mean, if the fight was over nothing? You could phone her up?'

'I guess there's one good thing,' her dad said as if he hadn't heard her. 'No more meetings at the Zings' on Friday nights. You get to go out with your friends instead of sitting with Cassie. Hang on, I think that's the phone.'

He opened the back door of the Banana Bar, stamped his feet on the mat, and went inside to answer the phone.

'Nathaniel, she doesn't dance any more.'

'Marbie?'

'Yeah. It's me. I have to –'

'Marbie, you can't keep phoning me, OK? I'm sorry but you can't.'

'OK, but I have to tell you something. Listen doesn't dance any more. I woke up and remembered she was dancing on Friday afternoon, the day I – the day before you moved out. Remember she was dancing in the kitchen when she got home from Tae Kwon Do?'

'So she does dance. What's your point?'

'But that's the first time I've seen her dancing in weeks.

She'd stopped dancing completely, Nathaniel, then the first day of the school holidays she starts again. I think it's a problem at school. I think there's something wrong at school.'

'She's fine, Marbie. School is fine. She'd tell me if it wasn't. And if she's stopped dancing, maybe that's a good thing. Maybe it was a nervous habit? I really need you not to call. I'm hanging up now, OK?'

While her dad was on the phone, Listen gave up on the snowman and went back to the camper van to get warm. She almost slid on the aluminium step up to the doorway and remembered the WELCOME mat with the picture of a curled-up cat at Grandma and Grandpa Zing's.

Suddenly she knew what the Secret was.

It was nothing to do with espionage and undercover agent work.

It was the Secret to family life.

The Zings spent Friday nights exchanging recipes and making shopping lists. No. The garden shed was a replica of an average suburban house, and Friday nights were spent redecorating: reupholstering furniture and pasting friezes around the walls. *No.* On Friday nights, they leaned their heads together and discussed the ingredients of love and happiness: how to stay together and keep children entertained. (That's why Cassie was always making jewellery from pink beads.)

Actually, it was more than that.

The Zings were the Keepers of the Family. Friday nights, they painted the stars that the children of real families see through bedroom curtains. They curled the smoke from chimneys; they slipped into homes and put doll's houses in corners, cushions on window seats, placemats on tables, pot plants and lemon-thyme soap in guest bathrooms.

Now that she was back in the camper van, the Zing Family were no longer her Keepers.

On the first Friday of the holidays, Fancy visited her parents for morning tea.

'Marbie's still asleep,' explained Fancy's mother, sitting down and taking the teabag out of her cup. 'And your dad's in the shed. He's taking it hard, this break-up of Marbie's – you know how fond he was of Nathaniel and Listen – and really, I wonder what Marbie thinks she –'

At that moment, Marbie walked into the kitchen, wearing slippers and her mother's pink dressing gown.

'Hello,' said Marbie, seeing her sister. 'Did you bring Cassie?'

Fancy raised her chin towards the kitchen window, and Marbie turned around. In the back garden, Cassie and her friend Lucinda were stamping around in the mud.

'Oh,' said Marbie vaguely. 'I felt like talking to her.'

'Never mind, darling. Have some ginger cake with us. It's still warm!'

'Why aren't you at work, anyway?' Fancy wanted to know.

'Well, I phoned Tabitha on Monday, she's my supervisor, and I told her what happened and she said I should take as much time as I need, and –'

'You can't stop working,' interrupted Fancy, pointing her teacup at Marbie, 'just because you've got a broken heart. It's no excuse. It's like when you have a hangover. You have to go to work even then.'

'I would think it'd be pretty quiet at Marbie's office these days,' their mother soothed, 'what with this funny weather.'

'Actually, imagine how many claims are coming in with all the skidding cars,' Marbie admitted thoughtfully.

'Cassie and Lucinda have been outside playing every day,'

said Fancy. 'They've adapted to the cold, and my point is, Marbie, there are some things you just *have* to do.'

'I'm going to have a bath,' Marbie said to her mother. 'See if you can find out what's wrong with Fancy. She's gone all right wing and Protestant.'

'Well,' said Fancy, 'if the *children* can get on with their lives . . .'

'Nathaniel? Is that you? It's me. I'm calling from the bath.'

'Marbie, you'd better stop phoning me, OK?'

Marbie was quiet.

'Marbie? Did you hear me?'

'You prefer me not to call?'

'That's right. Please stop leaving messages. OK? This is not going to work.'

'I can't even leave messages to say I'm sorry?'

'Not even that.'

'But it makes me feel better.'

'That's not really a concern of mine.'

'How's Listen? Is she dancing?'

'There's not much room in the camper van to dance, Marbie.'

'Oh, God, can I speak to her?'

'No, you can't. She's at the library working on her assignment.'

'Choose two creatures of the sea?'

'That's the one.'

'Is she still doing seahorses and whales?'

'I'm hanging up now, OK?'

'Really?'

'Marbie, I'm hanging up the phone.'

Seahorses

A lot of people don't know this about seahorses, but they are 'monogamous'. That means they stay together with their one true love for their entire lives. Each day, the seahorses link tails and go for walks along the ocean floor. Then the male seahorse gets pregnant.

Whales

It is commonly known that a whale is a mammal, not a fish. Some scientists even think that whales used to live on land, and had legs and fur, like enormous wolves. They waded into water, their legs turned into tails and their arms turned into pectoral fins. If that is true, it was not the best decision the whales ever made – they can't breathe underwater, and they have to spend most of their lives thinking about that.

It's Saturday! So you're allowed to do the next Spell.
Well done for waiting!
I hope you have been well.
This is a Spell To Make Someone Find Something
Unexpected In a Washing Machine!

Go for a walk and shout HOORAY whenever you see
something that looks strange, or lovely, or orange.

*The Spell will work on a Thursday afternoon in about
seven weeks or so. You can do the next Spell next
Saturday.*

In the second week of the school holidays the weathermen and women gave up hope of more snow. But it remained record-breakingly cold.

Fancy and Cassie fell into the habit of sleeping in, then deciding on an outing for the day while eating porridge with brown sugar in the kitchen. They had already seen all the holiday movies in the first week, and Cassie was beginning to complain about Lucinda, so they had to use their imaginations.

Of course, by the time they left the house each day, the Canadian had finished his breakfast and was nowhere to be seen.

Friday night at the Zing Family Secret Meeting, Fancy told Marbie she had run into Nathaniel at Coles the previous afternoon. He was buying tangerines. He looked sad. He had bleached his hair white-blond with sprouting black roots and a jagged short cut. Also, he was wearing a long black overcoat which floated, moodily, to the laces of his ankle-high boots.

'How terrible,' Marbie said, about Nathaniel's bleached hair.

'No,' said Fancy thoughtfully. 'No. It works. It's entirely sexy.'

'Nathaniel? It's me.'

'Oh, hello.'

'Don't hang up, OK? I just wanted to let you know that I'll get the mortgage payments on our apartment, OK? While you're – until you get back, I'll cover them, OK? In case you were worried. You know how it's due next week?'

'Yep.'

'Everyone misses you, you know. The meeting last night was stupid without you, it was so – And Fancy says she saw you at Coles and you've changed your hair, and she says it looks good.'

'OK. Two things. First, I told your sister not to worry about the Secret, so I'll tell you that too. It's safe with me, OK? Second, in relation to the apartment: when you can afford to refund my half of the deposit, send me a cheque, and I'll transfer my share to you. Everything else, you can keep.'

He had carved off most of his voice, and the leftover bit was as cold as a dental instrument. Marbie had to close her eyes.

'Uh-huh,' she breathed, with her eyes still closed. 'If that's what you think.'

'That's what I think.'

A dwarf pygmy seahorse is only about 3 centimetres long. That's the size of my little finger. A blue whale can grow to a length of 28 metres. That's three times as tall as our school library.

'Hey, Nathaniel, it's me.'

There was silence.

'Nathaniel? Can you hear me? It's me. It's Marbie.'

'I know who it is.'

'I just forgot to say something when I called earlier.'

'What did you forget to say?'

'I forgot to say, um, happy Saturday. It's Saturday today.'

'Yes, Marbie, it's Saturday.'

'Can I speak to Listen?'

'She's busy.'

'I want to tell her good luck at Cassie's school on Monday.'

'She's in the camper van. She didn't want to be disturbed.'

'Nathaniel? Can I see you? So I can tell you how sorry I am?'

'Nope.'

Marbie was still staring at the phone, wondering at its power, when it rang again. It was the aeronautical engineer.

'Come for lunch?' he said. 'Today? I've got a picnic!'
'I haven't heard from you for two weeks,' she said.
'I know!'

---

*A Spell To Make Somebody Eat a Piece of Chocolate
Cake*

1. Take up rock climbing!
2. Stop rock climbing!
3. Take it up again!

*This Spell will work on a Thursday afternoon in
about six weeks or so. You can do the next Spell on
Friday, seven weeks from now.*

The aeronautical engineer greeted Marbie at the door of his
house. 'At last! I get to see you again! It's been two weeks!'
He did not try to kiss her, but kept a respectful distance.

'I have to tell you something,' Marbie said at once.

'What do you have to tell me?' He ushered her into the
living room, where he had the following items set out neatly
on a picnic blanket on the floor:

- pickles
- sundried tomatoes
- two large radishes
- crackers and cheese
- bottled water
- corned beef sandwiches
- boiled eggs
- a salad made of spinach, crumbled bacon and anchovies.

'A lot of food,' she said, surveying this.

'What do you have to tell me?' He took her coat.

'I have to tell you about my family,' she said in a breathless rush, and then frowned at the voice in the back of her

head, which was saying companionably, *Marbie, where is your mind?* She would have to speak louder, to drown it.

'I HAVE TO TELL YOU OUR FAMILY SECRET!' she yelled, and he took a step backwards. 'OK, LISTEN FAST, IT'S THIS. We spy on a second-grade school teacher named Cath Murphy! WE HAVE A CAMERA INSTALLED IN HER DINING-ROOM WINDOW and she *does not know that it is there.*' She quietened down in surprise at herself.

'Wo ho!' He was grinning, holding both hands to his ears like a comedian, and then gesturing that she should sit cross-legged on the floor like him.

'Yes, yes,' she did as he instructed. 'So, we have a camera in her dining-room window and one other camera around the apartment, but it's . . . anyway, earlier this year, she knocked out the camera when she washed the windows, so we had to go in and replace it. Then she made it go blurry by throwing apple juice at it. So we had to go in again. It slipped *again* two weeks ago, at the start of the school holidays, *so we don't have a clue what she's been doing for the last two weeks.*'

'Marbie! Marbie! Why did I wait so long to call you?'

'And I don't feel like doing a Maintenance Intrusion to fix it.'

'You're a riot and I don't understand a word! Eat, my princess! Dig in!'

'No,' said Marbie, watching as a radish slowly rolled across the blanket. 'I have to tell you more about the Secret.'

Part 10

The Story of Professor Charles

21

Once upon a time there was a physicist who thought he could invent a balloon. This was in 1783, and the physicist's name was Professor Jacques Charles. To his wife, the Professor made a promise: 'I shall build a balloon made of taffeta, twelve feet in diameter, covered in India rubber and inflated with hydrogen gas!'

'Oh!' said his wife, not understanding, until, early one rainy March morning, the Professor and his friends paraded the balloon through the streets of Paris on a wagon. They inflated it with hydrogen gas and let it loose. It rose to enormous heights, astounding a crowd in the rain on the Champ de Mars.

It is said that Benjamin Franklin (an old man at the time) was among that crowd on the Champ de Mars. Benjamin Franklin, as is widely known, invented such things as: bifocal glasses, a urinary catheter and a 'long arm' for reaching books from the tops of bookshelves. Invention was an interest of his.

'What's the use in that?' exclaimed a passer-by scornfully – meaning the balloon.

Ever wise, Benjamin replied, 'What use is a newborn baby?'

He meant, Maude understood, that newborn babies grow up to be men, just as balloons would, eventually, grow up into jet-engine planes.

Maude Sausalito was sixteen years old and the moon was just a slither tonight, a sliver of leftover soap. She was jogging gracefully, her high heels in her hands, stockinged feet on the damp dewy grass of people's lawns. *The Mickey Mouse Show* chanted to itself from the window of every house she passed. A sharp piece of gravel glanced against her toe, and she slowed slightly.

She was not all that late. But her new boyfriend was coming to dinner at her family's place that night, and she wanted to make potato casserole. Her favourite thing, at the moment, was to peel and slice potatoes and layer them with salt, pepper and cheese. Then bake for forty-five minutes.

The little white moon, Maude noticed now, was actually tucked into the corner of a big dark circle of moon. She was not pleased about this: it undid the idea of fresh and changing moons: plainly, now, there was just one moon, presenting itself like a dull set of slides in differing angles of light.

At present, Maude was saving to buy herself a piano. Also, she was growing her hair (which now curled up around her ears) because she wanted it to swish down to her shoulders. She expected this would keep her warmer on cold nights, like a cheap and never-lost scarf.

The new boyfriend's name was David. He worked in the novelty corkscrew shop next door to the bakery where she worked. He himself was vibrant, energetic, bouncy, and leaped about his life like the tail of a kite. But his *family* was remarkable. Stretching back to great-great-greatness and beyond, *every single one was an inventor*. Every surface in David's house bristled with patent certificates.

Although the family had not made any money, Maude and David were both looking forward to David's first invention. They wondered what it would be.

Maude herself was reading a lot about balloons these days and secretly hoped that David might invent something balloon-related.

Also these days, Maude was planning the journey in a hot-air balloon which she would take on her honeymoon with David.

David, once he had grown up and invented a thing or two, would probably become a diplomat. Then he would propose to her. Floating along in their honeymoon balloon, they would play chess for long, languid hours. As the sun set each night, David would mix cocktails, gazing at her over slow, careful stirring with the swizzle stick. He would bite his lower lip seductively, and then wink, surprisingly, once.

As for the Professor's balloon, it landed in a field, where peasants found it and poked it with pitchforks. Upon smelling the horrible hydrogen smell, they panicked and beat it to death.

Consequently, the French government issued a 'Warning To The People On Kidnapping Air-Balloons'. *If you see a black moon in the sky,* said the Warning, *do not panic! It is not a monster, it is just a bag of silk.*

Part 11

The First Six Weeks of the New Term

22

On the first day of term after the holiday Cath arrived to a brisk, blue-sky day. She stepped over ridges of mud in the car park and turned when she heard her name.

'Cath! Cath! How *are* you? How was your *holiday*? What about the weather! Were you cold?'

It was Suzanne, rolling down her window as she pulled into a spot. Cath waited as Suzanne spilled out of her car and gave her a welcoming hug.

'Wasn't it *cold*!' Suzanne exclaimed, falling into step alongside Cath. 'My big old house was just *freezing*! How about your apartment?'

Cath explained that her landlord had installed gas central heating, with a vent in every room, just before the start of the holidays.

'Lucky duck!'

'Hello there.' A deep voice moved against the back of Cath's neck like slowly warming sunlight. They both turned and there he was: Warren Woodford, smiling down.

'Warren!' cried Suzanne. 'How was your holiday?'

Warren explained that he had attended a K-2 Cognitive Learning conference in Bowral for the whole two weeks, so it was not, in fact, a holiday. He then interrupted Suzanne's exclamations to ask after *her* vacation.

'Me? Oh, I spent a lot of time with Lenny, poor old Lenny – what was up with that anyway? They seemed so happy. I'm just *wrecked* about that fight. Hey, I left my briefcase in the car!' Suzanne rolled her eyes affectionately at her own forgetfulness and skidded back towards the car park. She held a hand flat in the air behind her, meaning they should wait. Obediently, Warren and Cath stood side by side watching her.

'Well,' murmured Warren, without turning his head. 'I myself am not *wrecked* about that fight. I myself am fairly *stoked* about that fight.'

'You can't be glad,' said Cath promptly, eyes still on Suzanne, 'about two happy people having a fight.'

'But I am. I'm glad they had a fight, because then Lenny had a party, and then I went to your place, and then – and look who's back again!'

Suzanne hurried up to them, grinning and waving her briefcase.

In her classroom, waiting for the class to settle down, Cath watched the playground through the window. A long line of girls in blue tunics were marching out of the assembly hall in pairs. What was that all about?

Of course! It was the seventh-graders from Clareville College, rescued from their flooded classrooms. She had forgotten all about them. And yet there was something *important* about them – something she herself had to do – what was that? She could not remember.

They began with News, so that everyone could tell about their holidays. It turned out that most of the children believed the snow had happened to them alone. While each child told an *amazing* story about waking up on the first day of the holiday and finding *snow* outside!, the rest of the class daydreamed quietly to themselves.

Cath recalled the first day of her own holiday, how she woke in a ruffled empty bed and looked for a single red rose.

'Well,' Warren had said, sitting on the side of her bed with one hand flat on her forehead and a takeaway coffee in the other, 'I promise I'll leave you a single red rose when I plan to say goodbye. But wild horses could not make me say goodbye. If, let's say, wild horses wanted to.'

Then they had run away together. They went to a K-2 Cognitive Learning conference in Bowral. Warren was already going to the conference, because Breanna, it turned out, was on a psychology seminar herself. The strange weather meant there were plenty of cancellations, so it was easy for Cath to get a place.

They attended all the same lectures, sitting side by side and writing notes to one another in the margins of their handouts. They ate lunch and had coffees together. They walked the streets of Bowral, looking for the gardens and sweet shops that inspired *Mary Poppins*.

They never touched in public, except for one afternoon when they were caught in a downpour and had to cling together to share the umbrella as they ran for the shelter of a cafe. At the cafe, a woman said sadly, 'It's only rain.'

In the evenings, they said 'See you tomorrow' in the courtyard, in the presence of other conference attendees. Then they went their separate ways to their own rooms. Warren's room was in the north wing; Cath's room was in the east wing. There was a laundry in the basement, which was accessible from all the wings.

Each night, Cath went down to the laundry room in her pyjamas, and, when there was nobody looking, took the staircase to the north wing. Each night she passed the same sign:

BOWRAL FUNCTION CENTRE
LAUNDRY FACILITIES

- Please remember that these machines are for the use of *all* conference participants.
- The machines take $2 coins only – *no* change is available at the front desk.
- Please clean lint from dryers after *every use*.

It was the sweetest, most emphatic sign she had ever read.

Cath smiled around her classroom and decided she should listen for a while. Cassie Zing was standing out front, talking to the class about fairy penguins and ice creams. Also, she was explaining that her mum had let her keep some snow in the freezer at home. She opened the lid of her lunchbox to show off a little pool of water.

Cassie's mum was *always* writing notes. Cath wondered if there would be one today – perhaps about the incident in which Cassie scooped snow into the lunchbox. Perhaps it would say, 'Sorry! I couldn't resist! Hope it doesn't spill all over the floor!'

Of course! That's why she had to remember the seventh graders. She had been asked to keep an eye on one. Some kind of relative of Cassie's? One with an unusual name. What was that name . . . ? She would have to check.

She and Warren had not discussed what would happen now that they were back in the real world. Breanna would be down for the weekends, and they would both have school work to do in the afternoons. Perhaps it would all be over? Perhaps it was just a two-week interlude? But that was impossible.

Later that day, Cath was walking home from a dentist appointment at Round Corner when a rusty station wagon slid along the street beside her. She glanced over. The passenger door was opened from the inside.

'Get in,' said Warren, looking straight ahead like an under-cover agent. Then he drove them to her place for the night.

Over the next few weeks they fell into a pattern. During the day they practically ignored one another, except for occasional acquaintance-friendly chats. But late each evening, Monday to Thursday, Warren found his way over to Cath's place. He returned to his own home early the next morning. When Warren had a soccer match, he arrived muddy in his soccer clothes and took a shower while Cath made dinner. When Cath had a law class, Warren let himself into her apartment and got dinner ready for her return. He liked to wrap things in filo pastry – chicken, eggplant, goat's cheese – and then bake it alongside a tomato. They watched movies, listened to music and did school work sitting side by side at the dining-room table. But mostly, they spent their time in bed.

Warren chipped a tooth slightly at Cath's place once.

They were cooking together on a Monday night, in Cath's kitchen, which was crowded with ingredients. She made him dance with her to her favourite Suzanne Vega song, while the ingredients waited. They were sleepy, wearing bathrobes, drinking red wine and eating occasional olives.

Cath was telling a story which included an impersonation of Billson, the School Principal. The impersonation made Warren laugh so suddenly that he bit down on an olive stone and chipped a tooth.

Later that night, Cath made Warren look through her family photo albums. He was very obliging and remarked on such things as the healthy fur of their family dog and the resemblance between Cath's and her mother's hair colouring.

At that, Cath unlocked her secret box and explained that she had been adopted. She only had this one photograph of her biological parents: they had been killed in a fire which burned down their house in the outback. The photo was hazy, as if the smoke had seeped into its edges. Warren stared at it for a long time, and eventually said he could see that Cath's parents were in love.

The only other photo Cath had was one showing the firefighter who had rescued her, a sleeping baby, from the fire.

*

'Do you think we should stop?' Cath said occasionally in the early dawn light as Warren buttoned his shirt.

Warren always considered the question grimly and always said the same thing: 'You're right. We should stop. We should stop soon. But I can't.'

And in the silence that followed, they would think the same thing:

This affair has parameters. It's only the weekdays. It's only at Cath's place. It's a secret from everyone else. We have plenty of chats about *guilt,* about *marriage,* about *lost opportunities* and *fate* ('If only we'd met sooner!', 'We're so *right* for each other!', 'I never thought I'd do this kind of thing'). This affair has an end date! Soon it will finish! The moment Breanna gets a job in the city we will call the whole thing quits. But for now, why should we stop? The betrayal has already occurred: on the night of Lenny's party, the marriage was broken. If it's already broken, why stop? With parameters in place, why stop?

Two or three times, Breanna phoned Warren on his cell late at night and he pretended to be at home. 'Something's wrong with the home phone,' he explained. 'For some reason I don't hear it when it rings. Don't worry though, you can always reach me on my cell.'

Then he and Breanna would talk as Cath waited in bed, staring at his naked back in the darkness of her hall. She could hear the chatter of Breanna's voice, saying things like, 'Can't wait until the weekend! Oh God, I miss you!'

Afterwards, they were both silent for a while. Warren sat on the side of the bed with his head in his hands. Cath kept her body careful and separate.

Eventually, Warren would say 'I'd better go home', and

Cath would say 'Yep', and he would dress in heavy silence and go home.

Thursdays, they made mulled wine to say goodbye for the weekend. Warren had a crisis and Cath agreed at once to end the fiasco. Warren always looked crestfallen and torn.

Then he decided: 'No. Let's keep going until she gets a job in Sydney. Why stop now when we have come this far? When she gets a job in Sydney we will stop. But until then, I just can't.'

Cath always said: 'Are you sure?'

And Warren said: 'Yes.'

Then, Cath had her own crisis. What exactly did he think he was doing? He was cheating on his wife! And every weekend, he was cheating on *her*! But the worst thing of all was Breanna's voice. When she heard the voice on the cellphone in the hallway, it was as sharp to her as a paper cut. But imagine if Breanna knew he was allowing his *lover* to hear those conversations! That was the worst betrayal, worse than the physical part. Breanna believed her voice to be safe within her husband's home, safe within their private, married world – when instead it was here, on display, in the hallway.

He listened fiercely to every word and agreed, nodding his head. She put special emphasis on the word 'lover' in her attacks, embracing the word, loving it.

He listened, and then he explained, over and over, how sorry he was, how shocked he was at his own behaviour, that he could not hurt his wife, that telling her would kill her. And Cath pounced. *I don't WANT you to tell your wife, I don't WANT you to leave your wife, I've never ASKED you to leave your wife.* And he said, *Yes, but it's coming apart at the seams.*

It didn't have long, their marriage, he said, it was coming apart at the seams. Then she would relent, and they would look at one another and say, 'This is all so stupid, because you and I are *right* together.' And: 'I'm sure that it's going to work out.'

Cath spent the weekends pacing her apartment, trying not to think of Warren and Breanna, the closeness of their bodies and hands. In the dark of night, she would wake in a panic of disbelief. In the cold light of day, she would shake her head in wonder at her own behaviour. She had always been opposed to mistresses. She was a vixen, a villain, she was betraying her own kind. She was a home wrecker!

But she didn't really mean these lectures to herself and quickly rallied to her own defence:

If she doesn't know, how can it hurt her?
I haven't told a single person!
If nobody knows then it's not really happening!
Besides, I only get him on the weekdays – she gets the fun days, the weekend days.
Why should she get him, anyway, just because she met him first?
Anyway, I love him, so I can't. I cannot stop.

And all the time, she was really just waiting until Monday, and her heart was beating quickly and excitedly, because she knew that it would all work out. Somehow, it would all work out and nobody would end up getting hurt.

Sometimes, of course, she worried vaguely about the job in Sydney. 'I'll give you a rose as a poignant goodbye,' Warren joked, 'the moment she gets herself a job.' What if she did get herself a job? But, really, Breanna had been looking for work in Sydney for months. She was probably not trying very hard. She probably didn't even want to spend the weekdays with

Warren! Besides which, it *was* a joke. The idea of saying good-bye! It was funny.

Meanwhile, the weather grew steadily warmer and the only remnant of the strange Sydney snow was the fact that ski poles occasionally washed up on Bondi Beach.

Strangely, Cath did not think of the pact about the rose when she found a short-stemmed rose in her pigeonhole on Thursday afternoon. She simply blushed and thought: *That's a risk!* Because people would wonder where she got it from. Then she sat at the table ready for the staff meeting. She would slip the rose into her handbag when nobody was watching, as soon as the meeting finished.

Billson started with a joke about the seventh-graders and how nobody expected them to hang around *this* long! The one Clareville teacher attending smiled warily.

Cath kept her eyes away from Warren. She was talented at pretending there was nothing going on (he was always telling her this).

Billson suggested a new format for the school newsletter, and a couple of teachers had far too many thoughts on this theme.

Cath wanted Billson to get a move on. It was Thursday and they had to go to her place for their crisis and mulled wine.

'A temp is a temp, as fine a temp as Mrs Rory has been.'

Billson was nodding at the temporary Year 6B teacher: the emergency replacement for Lenny. Cath watched his face carefully for signs of a broken heart when he said Lenny's name. He seemed perfectly all right. Perhaps he was an *actor*, like Cath?

'And as you all know,' Billson continued, 'we have put our heads to the wheel on this particular one.'

'Heads to the wheel – ouch,' murmured Warren from

across the staffroom table, which gave Cath an excuse to look at him and smile.

'Excuse me,' said Ms Waratah, raising her hand slightly. 'I think the phrase is *shoulders* to the wheel.'

Billson ignored her and continued: 'And Mrs Rory has agreed to become permanent! As you all know, she's had plenty of experience, she's rock solid and she's loads of fun!' Mrs Rory smiled modestly, and everyone said congratulations.

'So!' Billson got a move on, gathering his papers. 'So, that's Year 6B taken care of! And –' He held both hands high, to still the stirring room. 'And, here's some news!' He had trouble keeping his smile in check. 'You remember how Lenny used to be Year 6B teacher *and* school counsellor? Well! Never let it be said that we don't fly with the times here at Redwood!'

The teachers paused with their bags and their jackets at the ready.

'Guess what?' Now Billson was beaming. 'We have reached a decision to employ a *separate* school counsellor. A *full-time* school counsellor! And guess who we have chosen?'

Nobody could guess.

'A woman by the name of Breanna!' Billson practically whooped as he beamed his delight about the room. 'The psychologist wife of our very own Warren Woodford here!'

'Huh!' cried the room, and, 'Congratulations, Warren!'

Warren leaned back in his chair and took a bow.

23

Returning home after dropping Cassie at school the first day back after the holidays, Fancy paused to look at the vacuum cleaner. She had placed it in the hallway alongside the umbrella stand, as a cryptic message to Radcliffe that she knew about his affair.

The vacuum cleaner gazed back at her, its hose neatly coiled at its side. *I was once broken*, it said. *I choked on the shattered pieces of a marriage. A glass had been broken by the husband's lover; the husband used ME to clean it up. But no, I choked on his deceit. Now the repair man has fixed me: can the same thing be said of the marriage?* So far, Radcliffe had not appeared to hear.

Fancy pushed it a little further out into the hallway: if Radcliffe tripped over it, he would surely get the message. But, of course, her plan was more concrete than that, and now that Cassie was back at school she could set it in motion.

First, she ran upstairs and crawled around her bed, peering into the darkness for further clues of the affair. As usual, there was nothing. She returned to the downstairs hallway and picked up the phone, her heart beating gently.

'Radcliffe!' she said, when he answered. 'Just thought I'd let you know that I'm going to the city for the day. I'm on my way out the door right now. Doing some work for Mum. So, don't bother coming home for lunch, will you? I won't be here *all day*.'

Radcliffe thanked her and she hung up, walked out the front door and sat down on the porch.

The way she walked out the door and sat down, with her

head oddly tilted and her posture straight, it was as if she was a ballerina. *My husband is having an affair.* She smiled softly and hugged her knees. She could have been wearing a gossamer gown.

The Canadian was not on his porch. She longed for it to snow again. Imagine this, she thought, imagine that this is now a *city of snow*. Imagine that *everything* has changed: there are caribou, polar bears and squirrels. In fact, helpfully, Cassie had left footprints in the muddy front lawn, which could almost resemble claw marks. Bear prints!

Imagine this, thought Fancy: a black bear moving gracefully, as if the bear had glandular fever, or as if the bear's husband was having an affair, is making its way up the street. It passes open curtains, parked cars and For Sale signs; pokes its snout into letter boxes; sharpens its claws on telegraph poles. Its movement is silent in the snow. It pauses now and then at distant sounds: a truck on the highway, somebody's screen door.

The fantasy was complicated slightly, Fancy realized, by the presence of a man in a pale grey T-shirt and jeans, standing inexplicably still by the side of the house next door. When the bear approached, that man would have to be warned.

It was the Canadian, looking at the wall of his house.

'Hello!' she shouted.

He turned slowly and waved. 'Just checking for structural damage,' he called. 'I had a *minor* explosion in my basement just now. Did you hear it?'

'No!'

'Great!'

He turned back to the wall and stared some more. After a while, he waved and smiled at Fancy again and then disappeared into his house.

Fancy waited on her front porch until 3 p.m. that day, but

the Canadian did not reappear. Nor, for that matter, did Radcliffe and his lover.

Over the next few weeks Fancy's days fell into a pattern. She would drive Cassie to school, return home, phone Radcliffe and tell him she was out for the day and then she would sit on her porch. After a few days, she remembered that Gemma-from-the-pay-office worked afternoons, so she decided she could stop around lunchtime. Any liaison must surely take place in the morning.

This was fortunate because she needed the afternoons to work on her prize-winning novel, or on the Zing Family Secret, or to go to the gym. Meanwhile, her sister Marbie kept arriving unexpectedly at dinner time and asking frantic legal questions.

Very occasionally, on her morning vigils, the Canadian would emerge on to *his* front porch and sit at his breakfast table. These days he was eating blueberry muffins and breadfruit with his coffee. He never seemed to wonder at Fancy's presence on *her* front porch, simply chatting to her about this and that, and Fancy felt that her neck was slender and that her hands, when she spoke, were like butterflies.

One day the Canadian had a small portable stereo alongside his blueberry muffin. 'Hey, Fancy,' he called, 'you want to help me out with this?'

'OK!' she called back happily.

It turned out that he was required, for some reason, to compare two different versions of the song called 'Love Cats'. One version was the original, by a band called The Cure. The other was a more recent cover, by a man called Tricky. Such a jumble of intriguing words and names! Fancy felt nervous and excited.

'Which one do you think is slicker?' the Canadian called. 'Which one is more powerful? Which is more beautiful?

Which one makes you want to dance? Which one do you think is sexier?'

He played the two songs over and over, facing the stereo towards her porch, and the space between their houses filled with drumbeats. Fancy answered his questions solemnly, and he jotted down her words, nodding with interest.

'I like them both a *lot*,' said Fancy.

'Tell you what,' offered the Canadian, 'I'll make you a copy.'

'Thank you!' said Fancy, tears in her eyes.

Not once did Radcliffe's car appear in the driveway and nor did Gemma arrive to reclaim her purple sock. Meanwhile, Fancy's prize-winning novel had stalled. She had reread the book about love and leaves and had made a discovery. The author had done more than simply list leaves, he had also provided information about them – there were entire sections of the book devoted to pigmentation and photosynthesis.

It was not just lists that were required, Fancy realized, it was *language*. By the time that a reader reached the end of a prize-winning novel, she or he had to know a new language: photography, geography, topology. The language of fly-fishing, Malta, or bread-making.

Fancy was not sure she knew any languages worth teaching and sensed that she ought to learn one. Meanwhile, each new prize-winning novel released took another language away – the better books, the *Booker*-winning books, often used four or five.

One day, Cassie's mum collected her from school and took her to the dentist.

'This is not the way to the dentist,' said Cassie.

'You have an excellent memory, darling,' her mother declared. 'You're right. It's not the way. But we're going to try a new dentist at Round Corner. On the way, tell me how school is going.'

'OK,' agreed Cassie. Then she thought about other things for a while.

'How's Ms Murphy?' tried Mum. 'Do you still like her?'

'Uh-huh. She's pretty nice, actually.'

'Mmm. Do you think she's good friends with any of the other teachers at your school?'

'Well,' said Cassie, thinking and staring out the window. 'She's got two friends. Mrs Barker and Mr Woodford.'

'Mr Woodford, eh? He's the other Year 2 teacher, isn't he? What's he like?'

'He is *so* funny.' Cassie swung back from the window. 'Everyone's always laughing at his jokes.'

Actually, she thought, Ms Murphy laughs the most. But she didn't mention that to her mum.

At the dentist, Mum held out her toothbrush. 'Here,' she said. 'Run to the bathroom down the hall and clean your teeth.'

Cassie took the toothbrush, and the woman at the desk said, 'Cassie? Would you like a treat?'

By treat, the woman meant the tiny plastic zebra she was holding up. Cassie did not want a plastic zebra, but she said, 'OK.' The zebra could be a trick. The woman might have a fun-size Mars Bar hidden in her other hand.

Fancy sat in the dentist's waiting room, took out her cellphone and selected her mother's number.

'I'm here,' she murmured. 'Nobody else in the waiting room. Perfect layout. Now is good.' She hung up.

Almost immediately, the phone behind the reception desk rang.

'Round Corner Dental Centre,' the receptionist said. 'How

can I help you? Uh-huh? Oh, gosh! Hang on then. No, I'll – wait right there and I'll be out!'

She stood up and hurried into the corridor. The lift doors opened and closed.

Fancy moved behind the reception desk, opened the top drawer of a filing cabinet, and flicked through manila folders. Her fingers landed on: MURPHY, Cath. She slid the folder out and glanced around the room. She opened the folder, held her wristwatch over the first document, and clicked the side of the watch. A flash flickered. She turned to the second page, and clicked again. She closed the folder, returned it to the drawer and sat back down in the waiting room.

She was reading a magazine when the receptionist returned. 'Funny,' said the receptionist to Fancy as she resumed her seat, 'a courier just phoned and said she'd backed her van into our service entry and couldn't get it out! But when I got down there, she was gone. Must have got out on her own.'

'Oh,' agreed Fancy. 'She must have.'

Cassie in the dentist chair felt small because the dentist was a giant. 'Well!' he giant-voiced, wheezing and buzzing a button which made the chair bend backward. Going to the dentist would be fine if the dentist wasn't there, and you could just be alone and play on the chair.

'Well!' the dentist boomed again, buzzing another button, which made the chair rise slowly upwards. It practically hit the spotlight on the ceiling. The ceiling itself was good, she noticed. It was painted green, like a jungle, with a lot of elephants, monkeys, lions and giraffes. So you had something to look at.

Cassie thought about offering her puffer for the dentist's wheezing. But then he would put it in his mouth.

'How old are you, Cassie? What is it: seven, eight, nine?'

'Seven,' replied Cassie from her sticky leather chair.

'Seven!' The dentist seemed to find this funny. 'Let's have a look here, shall we?' He chuckled away and leaned over her with a wheedly, 'Open wide.'

The dentist began to play with her teeth instead of the chair. 'Rinse out,' he said.

She did not want to rinse out because the dentist's water was pink and warm, but you had to.

'Mrs Zing?' The dentist was wiping his hands on a towel at the doorway.

'How is everything? Everything all right?' Her mother appeared, looking cheerful.

'A teeny little hole, just the one,' boomed the dentist with a chuckle, probably still thinking about her age. 'I can do it now if you like. Won't take a minute. Shall we have happy gas? And then the fluoride treatment and we're done.'

'*Fluoride*,' said Cassie from the chair. 'Mum, you know that makes me cry.'

Her mum just laughed, agreed to happy gas and happily returned to the waiting room to wait.

Cassie breathed slowly into the happy gas mask, sank into the chair and stared up at the jungle pictures. She took herself from the chair into the jungle for a moment. A pair of cheetahs, she saw, were running side by side towards the edge of the ceiling as if they planned to escape. That reminded her of something. She did not know what. Only, there was something about those cheetahs that Cassie found deeply troubling.

During those weeks of the new school term, when Fancy spent her mornings on the porch, difficulties arose in relation to the Family Secret. Specifically, Marbie refused to attend Meetings or do Maintenance. This meant that the camera in the dining-room window of Cath Murphy's apartment remained broken. The other camera which they kept in the apartment had never been any use.

Meanwhile, Marbie still kept appearing at Fancy's front door in time for dinner and asking frantic legal questions.

Another night, over spinach soufflé, Marbie said, 'As soon as she's a lawyer, she'll sue, won't she?'

'What's the charge?' said Radcliffe.

'Who's going to sue?' Cassie had her hands around her strawberry-and-orange juice, just about to drink.

'Nobody, darling.' Fancy gave Marbie a meaningful look. 'What do you think of the juice, Cassie? It's new!'

'Wait,' said Cassie, 'I'll try it.'

'Ever heard of the Convention for the Protection of Individuals with Regard to Automatic Processing of Personal Data?' pounced Marbie.

'Gosh!' said Fancy. 'Is there really such a thing?'

'*That!*' Radcliffe was scornful, scraping at the burned bits of cheese on the edge of the serving bowl. 'That's to do with computer processing. Government databanks, that kind of thing. For big corporations. Nothing to do with us.'

'Seriously?' said Marbie. 'But I guess it's illegal to break into –'

'Who says we're breaking in?' Radcliffe interrupted. 'We're the landlords and it's all in the lease. In the fine print, I admit, but: "Access shall be granted blahdy blahdy maintenance blahdy blahdy nice and vague".'

'It's not bad,' said Cassie, replacing her juice on the table and wiping her strawberry mouth. 'You try it.'

Fancy, Radcliffe and Marbie reached for their glasses.

Later, while Radcliffe was playing computer games in the study, Fancy said, 'What's going on with you, Marbie? We've always known the Secret is illegal.'

Marbie was stacking Fancy's dishwasher. 'I kind of forgot,' she said.

'So you also forgot that we let Radcliffe believe we're safe?

He believes in all these loopholes, otherwise he'd be a wreck. But really, we'd go down in a million different ways if we got caught! There's trespass, stalking, all kinds of surveillance offences and breaking and entering, of course. The fine print in the lease would be worthless to us! Tenants have rights, apparently. We'd all end up in prison, and the civil suits would ruin us if we got caught!'

'This is making me feel much better,' Marbie said.

'The thing is,' Fancy said, 'we're not getting caught.' She leaned over and retrieved a teaspoon that Marbie had placed in the dishwasher's cutlery rack. 'It's too little,' she explained, holding up the teaspoon. 'It falls straight through and gets lost in the works.'

Nobody knew what was going on with Marbie but they supposed it was connected with Nathaniel. The fact was, he *still* had not returned. They were all taken aback by that, so Marbie must have been reeling. She was probably worried that he might use the Secret against them somehow. He would never do that, they all agreed, uneasily.

Radcliffe offered to replace Marbie on the Maintenance Intrusion, but Fancy said she would not feel comfortable. She and Marbie worked so well together. Besides, she added kindly, Radcliffe had spent *hours* on the desktop publishing lately. Everyone agreed that the latest issue of *Elf Epistles* looked fantastic. Such glossy pages!

'Still,' said Radcliffe, 'I'm surprised at Nathaniel. I would have sworn he'd have forgiven her by now.'

'Would you just?' said Fancy coldly.

'Well,' said Radcliffe, shelling pistachio nuts and piling the shells on to his thigh, 'wouldn't *you*?'

'I miss chatting with Listen,' sighed Fancy unexpectedly.

*

Coincidentally, Fancy saw Listen at the gym the next day. She had been climbing on the elliptical machine for half an hour.

'Two minutes to go,' said the machine.

I should hope so, thought Fancy, climbing the stairs.

The machine provided her with a workout summary and released her, and she ran into Listen at the water fountain.

'Well, *hello*!'

'Hi, Fancy!' Listen seemed shiny-eyed and sweaty, cute in tracksuit pants and a singlet top.

'You don't *work out* at the gym, do you?'

'No,' Listen explained, 'I'm doing rock-climbing classes. In there – see that fake rock wall they have in there? I just climbed it.'

'Ha! How about *you*! Mission Impossible! James Bond!' They smiled at each other for a moment.

'Anyway,' said Listen, 'I'd better go now – Dad's picking me up. Say hi to Cassie for me, would you? I see her around at Redwood sometimes but she always looks kind of busy.'

'OK, sure. We all miss you so much, Listen, especially Cassie. I hope we get to see you soon.'

And Listen, running up the stairs to the gym's front doors, her ponytail bouncing behind her, turned back and gave a strange grin. Afterwards, Fancy wondered if it was more a grimace.

Finally, after several weeks of sitting on the front porch, Fancy decided that she needed a new tactic. It was obvious that Radcliffe had moved his affair to a different location – perhaps the incident with the vacuum cleaner had been enough to scare him away? Dangerous, after all, to bring a clumsy woman like Gemma into his home. They were probably spending all their time at Gemma's place – breaking *her* crockery.

This realization came to her one Thursday afternoon while she was sitting on the front porch and waving at the postman.

He was wheeling his bicycle along and had just pressed a handful of letters into their mailbox. Fancy stood, still waving, thinking to herself: *I need a new tactic*, then began to walk across her lawn to fetch the mail. It was then that she realized that her gestures were no longer graceful: they were awkward, uneasy, jerky, like a puppet on uneven strings. She blinked and even her blinking had an arrhythmic twitch.

Here was the problem, she thought, calming herself as she drew out the mail. She was about to lose hold of the affair. Over the last week, there had been days when she wondered where she got the idea in the first place, there had been days when she doubted that a purple daisy sock could *really* mean so much, there had even been days when she *completely forgot* that her husband was having an affair.

She needed to focus, to give the affair the right sort of attention, pin it down, line it with sandbags. Otherwise, she felt, it would slip from her grasp, rise out of reach and drift away forlornly like a helium balloon.

Looking down at the handful of mail, she saw her answer. It was on a flyer at the top of the envelopes.

Relationship Counselling
- Affordable
- Discreet
- Confidential
- Guaranteed

Winston Hills Family Counselling Centre (see reverse for contact details)

Of course! The plan came to her in a tumble: she would set up some sessions with a counsellor. She would surprise Radcliffe with these sessions. Tell him it was a kind of gift certificate for their marriage. In fact, the idea would be to ensure an anchor, a controlled environment. Within that environment she could tell Radcliffe that she knew of his affair. The counsellor would ensure that the affair did not skitter away. It was 'Guaranteed'! She went straight inside to make an appointment.

Relieved, having restored the graceful swish to her movements, she decided to hang some laundry out. It was breezy and sunny, the chill almost gone. She leaned and pegged, leaned and pegged, then crossed to the other side of the line where yesterday's clothes were ready to be removed.

Grevilleas were blooming, she noticed, as she unpegged a pair of her own cotton underpants, apricot in colour. Spring was certainly here. The return of the graceful, floating feeling meant that her hands did not quite grasp at things so that the wind, when it breezed by, found it easy to take the underpants from her fingers and fling them through the air. Whoosh! Up into the sky! Whoosh! Over the fence and into the neighbour's yard.

She ran to the fence in time to see her underpants blow into the face of the Canadian next door. They flattened against his face and then dwindled towards the ground. He was surprised but caught them before they hit the grass. He had a peg out ready himself, she saw, and was hanging his own laundry.

Specifically, he appeared to be hanging out three pairs of women's underpants: tiny, multicoloured G-strings, like colourful lizards.

He turned to face her, smiling, holding up her underwear.

'And you,' she called, apologetically, 'with all that pretty underwear!' Then she wondered at herself.

But he laughed and clumped over his lawn, companionably, to the fence. 'Your panties?' he offered graciously.

She took them from him, thinking that the word 'panties' was the most intimate thing she had ever heard. She, a writer

262

of wilderness romance. 'Sorry to blow them in your face,' she said.

He gave a chin lift of laughter and leaned against the fence, and they both turned back towards his clothes hoist to stare at the line of frilly panties. Which was when Fancy saw it. A single purple sock, hanging from his line, flickering slightly in the wind.

'Excuse me,' she said, 'but may I see that sock?'

'Well, sure,' he agreed, and clumped back over to his clothesline. Good-naturedly, he unpegged the sock and brought it back.

Yes, it was the one. It was the pair. A purple sock stitched with a daisy.

'Where did you get this from?' she said, realizing that her voice quivered melodramatically.

'That's a funny question.' He remained good-natured. 'I found it in the bottom of my washing machine just now. Unexpected. It belonged to my ex-girlfriend. Ex-*ex* girlfriend as a matter of fact. I guess she left some of her laundry behind, and this sock was maybe stuck in the bottom of my washing machine for a while. You know socks.'

'Well, the thing is,' said Fancy, 'the thing is that I found the pair to this sock in my bedroom a few weeks back.'

'Did you *really*?'

They both stood still for a moment, while the wind dabbed at their clothes and at their hair. They found themselves gazing at the cotton underpants in Fancy's left hand and the purple sock in her right.

'I guess,' said the Canadian reflectively, 'that Tammy's sock might've got blown over the fence one time, just like your panties did today. I guess I might have hung the one sock up to dry while the other one was stuck in the machine, and the line one got blown over the fence and mixed up with your laundry.'

Fancy was doubtful. She was caught up in much more vibrant explanations: a threesome between Radcliffe, his affair and this *Tammy*, for example. Or: kinky Canadian climbs into her bedroom in the middle of the night and hides his girl-friend's sock under her bed.

'I guess that could have happened,' she conceded eventually. 'I *do* sort my laundry in the bedroom sometimes, so I guess I might have sorted it there and the purple sock fell and got kicked under the bed.'

They were still again. The sun sat on their shoulders.

'Funny,' said the Canadian, 'me finding the sock in my washing machine like that on the day your panties blow over the fence.'

'Shall I get the matching sock for you?' suggested Fancy. 'So you can send them back to – Tammy?'

'Ah, forget it,' he shrugged, endearingly. 'Tammy can live without her purple daisy socks, I guess. She didn't turn out all that nice. Now, *Gina* . . .' he continued, looking back at the underwear frill along his line. 'But she had to go back to Naples in a hurry. I'm sending on her valuables,' he added vaguely.

'Say "out and about",' said Fancy, out of nowhere.

'Out and about,' he obliged, at once. But then, as he strolled back to his clothesline he turned and called, 'Oot and aboot!' and rolled his eyes in a friendly way.

There is no purple sock, thought Fancy as she smiled her thanks at the Canadian. There is no purple daisy sock belonging to a woman from the pay office at Radcliffe's work. Radcliffe's affair – she thought next, with a strange little thud, like a book falling off a bedside table – Radcliffe's affair is over.

My husband is not having an affair.

24

The day after the picnic on the living-room floor, the first day of the new school term, Marbie hit snooze on her alarm clock just as the telephone rang. It was the aeronautical engineer.

'Don't call me *at home*!' she hissed, pretending that Nathaniel and Listen were still there.

'If your boyfriend had answered I'd have just hung up. OK? Just chill, OK? Can you talk?'

'No.'

'Well, can you listen for a moment? Marbie, you are a riot. What *was* that yesterday? Showing up at my place, telling me a story about spying on a second-grade teacher and waltzing right out the front door? You didn't even touch my picnic! I thought to myself, who *was* that?'

'Well,' said Marbie, 'it was me.'

'OK, whatever, I just want to say one thing. I want to say that you are gorgeous, and I want to say how happy I am about the decision that I made way back when I first met you at the Night Owl Pub.'

'That's more than one thing. And you didn't meet me at the Night Owl Pub. You met me at work.'

'Huh. Yeah, I remember that too. Your paper aeroplanes! Wo ho! Dodgy! But what I'm talking about here is my *decision*. At the Night Owl Pub? When I saw you sitting there? All your pals were gone and my car had just got towed. So I asked you what the time was and "Five o'clock" you said, in that voice of yours – and right away I made a decision. The best decision I ever made.'

'What decision?'

'The decision to get a taxi. I thought – like *shazam!* – I thought: *I'll get a taxi*. I was running late for a meeting, see, and I knew I'd miss the bus if I stayed. So I was about to say "See ya", but then I thought: *Shazam*, I thought: a *taxi*, that'll do the trick! And it was the best decision I ever made.'

'OK. Well, that's great. I think I should hang up now.'

'Sure. That's all I wanted to say anyway. Just that.'

'OK.'

'Oh, and Marbie, you've got to come by my place tonight and explain what you were going on about yesterday. You can't tell a spy story like that and just leave me hanging. You hear me?'

'I can't?'

'No.'

'Because I was thinking that I could. I was thinking you could forget I said a word, and get on with your life. OK?'

'No, because I heard every word, and now I need an explanation or who knows *what* might happen? See you tonight. Another thing, if there's anybody there with you now, just say that this was a wrong number.'

'That's stupid.'

'Righto, gorgeous. Bye.'

Marbie hung up and clutched her pillow tightly to her chest. Quite simply, she did not know why she had slept with the A.E. in the first place, let alone told him the Secret. She looked around the room in confusion. The night before, she remembered, it had suddenly seemed clear that she must tell him, and that this would be the answer. But how could it have been? Here she was, Marbie Zing, embracing an irrational existence. She looked down at the pillow in her arms and thought: *My existence is a pillow*. She did not even know what she meant.

She threw the pillow away and dialled Nathaniel's number, but there was no answer. She left a message saying that she just wanted to wish Listen good luck again for her first day at Redwood Primary, and also, if Listen needed anything, well, she, Marbie, was right here in the apartment, except when she was at work.

The seventh-graders were marching down the path at Redwood Primary. They had been welcomed at the assembly hall and now they had to go to the portable classrooms.

'In pairs!' shouted the teachers. 'March in pairs!'

But actually the teachers did not care if they walked in pairs or not, and Chloe, who was next to Listen, faded back from her and joined the two behind. Listen had just said, 'How was your holiday?' but at the same time someone had shouted 'GIVE ME MY HAT!' so Chloe had not heard.

There were Redwood Primary kids at the windows of classrooms, opening their mouths to stare. Listen tried to huddle with the pair in front, so the kids would not think she was alone, but she couldn't because they patterned out and took the whole path.

Two's company. Three's a crowd. She thought this sadly, and then there was a glint of sunlight on the buckle of her school bag and she thought it again: *Two's company, three's a crowd*! Of course! Let's say somewhere in her year there was a group of three friends? Well, two's company, three's a crowd. So, they would need a fourth. She could be the fourth.

The teachers tried to teach like a normal day, but the girls messed around like this was a vacation. It should be a vacation; it was the first day back and this was a primary school.

'That doesn't mean you have to *act* like primary-school students,' the teachers said over and over. When the bell rang for recess, it was not a high school electric bell, it was a strange, clanking primary bell.

On the muddy grass outside the classroom, Listen pulled her jumper sleeves over her hands and said, 'Hi, Kelly.'

Kelly Favoloro, who was walking past, looked surprised and said: 'Hi.'

Listen said fast, in a metal-flat voice, 'Can I hang out with you guys, maybe, just today?'

Kelly looked around for her two friends, Amber Tang and Sasha James, and all three raised their eyebrows.

Then Kelly said, 'Sure, yeah, OK.'

Quickly and politely, the other girls said it too: 'Sure, Listen, yeah!'

Listen said, in a serious voice, 'Just say no if you want.'

'Don't be stupid.' Kelly twirled Listen's ponytail around her hand. 'Why would we say no?'

In her bed in the camper van, Listen had a bumping heart of frightened happiness. This plan could work. She had sat with Kelly and the others at recess and lunchtime that day, and Kelly had admired her hair. It's so soft, Kelly said. She suggested Listen wear it in a French braid. Also, Amber told a long story about how her father lost his job during the holidays but then talked his boss into giving him a *promotion* instead. Sasha told ballet stories: she loved ballet so much that she carried her slippers around with her all the time, like a long, drooping bracelet.

The second day of term, Listen felt both frightened and safe. At recess and lunchtime she sat outside in the winter sun and watched while Kelly Favoloro took turns arm-wrestling with Amber and Sasha. She passed around her bag of Valerio honey-mustard crisps, and everybody took one. She asked Amber two questions about her father's promotion, and Sasha three questions about ballet.

The next morning, while the History teacher read to them

from the textbook, Judith Sierra, who had braces and a ruler-straight fringe, turned around and whispered, 'Listen?'

'Yeah?' Listen whispered back.

'Who d'you hang around with?' Carefully, Judith regarded her.

'Kelly Favoloro and Sasha and Amber.'

Judith looked concerned. 'Um,' she whispered, 'cos they were talking to me before school, and they're really worried. They thought you only wanted to sit with them for one day – they didn't think you meant, like, forever.'

'It was just until today,' Listen explained. 'They don't need to worry, it was just until today, and that's it.'

Judith looked relieved. 'I'll let them know. They were really worried. See, Kelly likes you but Amber and Sasha aren't so sure because you kind of like just ask questions? Like you're a school teacher or something? And they could tell you kind of wanted to *buy* them as friends, the way you kept offering food.'

'Just the crisps,' Listen said. 'I only offered them honey-mustard crisps.'

Judith blinked. 'So, anyway,' she said, 'Kelly felt guilty about saying you could join.'

'OK,' said Listen. 'Thanks.' She smiled for reassurance and Judith smiled back.

Marbie would have to go to the A.E.'s place to begin repairing her mistakes. Maybe she could shout 'April fool!' and pretend it had all been a trick? But it was not April, and when she arrived, she saw that it was too late to pretend.

His eyes, when he opened the door, had a glittery, greedy look.

So, sitting straight-backed in his lounge chair, Marbie explained the Secret again, more succinctly this time, and with emphasis on confidentiality. She spoke in a soft, serious voice, to show that reverence was the appropriate reaction, rather than feverish excitement. He assumed a grave expression. She concluded by explaining that the Secret was an honour which was rarely bestowed. He smiled and assured her he was worthy of this honour.

Then he served the lasagne and things began to go wrong.

She noticed that the A.E. was frowning. He was staring at his fork, and there were at least thirteen different cracks and creases in his forehead. It was unnecessary, that many cracks and creases.

'So, basically, you spy on this woman without any kind of authorization, or I don't know, police protection? Right?'

'Right. It's just us. But "spying" is the wrong –'

'And this woman is not only a teacher, she's also a lawyer, you say?'

'Not a lawyer. She just studies law part-time.'

His frown was like a freshly broken mirror. 'I've got to say, Marbie, you're playing with fire there. What happens when she finds out?'

'Who says she's going to find out?'

'Well,' said the A.E. with a maddening shrug. Then, as he reached for more lasagne, he said, 'Come to bed with me?'

'No,' replied Marbie, 'thanks all the same.'

Over the next few weeks Marbie's days fell into a pattern. She would arrive home from work, phone Nathaniel, get his answering machine and go over to the A.E.'s place. The A.E. would ask difficult questions about the Secret and try to persuade her to go to bed with him. The next day she would go over to Fancy's place to find answers to the A.E.'s questions, so that, on the following day, she could go to the A.E.'s place again.

It was exhausting but she could not see how to stop. The A.E. had the Secret, and he kept setting little brush fires with it. She had to go over and put them out.

*

Mopping the shop floor in the Banana Bar one late afternoon, Listen discovered that her mind was humming: *Two's company, three's a crowd! Two's company, three's a crowd!* – in a cheerful, mocking tune. *All right,* she thought, *so the plan didn't work. You don't have to sing about it.*

She looked at her dad, who was counting money at the register, and thought, with a thud: *Two's company, three's a crowd.* That's why Dad and Marbie broke up! Because *I* made them into a crowd!

She mopped savagely for a few moments, tears in her eyes. Then she calmed down, because she knew what her dad would say if she mentioned that to him. She knew she was being stupid. She wouldn't even waste his time by raising it.

But she would ask something one more time. 'Dad,' she said, and he looked up, mouthing *twenty-three* as he did so. 'What did you and Marbie fight about?'

'Ab-so-lute-ly nothing,' he said, with a smile, and returned to his counting.

She squeezed the mop into the bucket. It was too much of a coincidence: a Spell To Make Two Happy People Have a Huge Fight Over *Absolutely Nothing.* Even when she reminded herself that there was no such thing as magic, and also that, as far as she knew, the first two spells had not worked (a Spell To Make Someone Decide To Take a Taxi, a Spell To Make a Vacuum Cleaner Break) – it was *still* too much of a coincidence.

The only hope was the promise on the back of the book: *This Book will make you Fly, will make you Strong, will make you Glad. / What's more, this Book will Mend your Broken Heart.* As long as she finished *all* the spells, the book would somehow fix its own mistake.

She wondered if the next three spells would work – as far as she could figure out, they were all supposed to happen in a few weeks at the same time. A Spell To Make Someone Give

Someone a Rose (maybe Dad would give Marbie a rose?), a Spell To Make Someone Find Something Unexpected In a Washing Machine (hmm), and a Spell To Make Someone Eat a Piece of Chocolate Cake (maybe Marbie would drop by the Banana Bar for cake?).

At least, if those spells worked, they wouldn't hurt a fly.

While she waited for the Spell Book to work, she just needed a new strategy for school. For a start, she would stop asking questions and offering honey-mustard crisps. But it was more complicated than that. The fact was, she had never actually belonged to Kelly Favoloro's group. She asked them questions, but they never asked her one. They arm-wrestled, but never with her. Why hadn't they joined her in with the arm-wrestling? Why had she not held out her hand and said, 'Now try me'?

Waiting to start Tae Kwon Do the other day, Carl Vandenberg and some of the others had been having thumb wars. Listen had stood apart from them, watching. She could never hold her thumb out and say, 'Now try me.'

But then Carl had sidestepped towards her, fixed her with a fierce gaze and grabbed her thumb with his own. Next thing she'd been having thumb wars with them all.

Whatever she had done at Tae Kwon Do that day must have been right: she must have been standing in a cool way while she was watching the others. Or she had the correct expression on her face. So, the strategy was: while at school, pretend you're at Tae Kwon Do and stand or sit in exactly the same way.

Actually, the master at Tae Kwon Do had told her that she was stronger than she looked. She would have beat Kelly and Amber in arm-wrestles. Maybe not Sasha. Sasha had muscular wrists.

*

'Playing with fire,' A.E. said, wanting to talk about the Secret again. 'Crash down on you like a house of cards.'

'What do you mean exactly?' Marbie was slicing up an onion. 'The house of cards will catch on fire? Or the house of cards will fall on our heads? Because guess what, a house of cards *would not hurt a fly.*'

A.E. sat on his kitchen counter, drumming his heels against the cupboards and watching as Marbie chopped the onion. The frown was in the centre of his forehead again.

'Ton of bricks then,' he adjusted. 'Crash down on you like a ton of bricks. You don't think a lawyer's going to pull any punches, do you?'

'What's the charge?' pounced Marbie. She spoiled the effect by sneezing seven times.

'Hay fever?' said the aeronautical engineer.

'So?' said Marbie spitefully.

'You've probably got a cold. Not hay fever at all. As for the basis for her legal action,' he continued, 'ever heard of the Convention for the Protection of Individuals with Regard to Automatic Processing of Personal Data? Hmm?'

'What in the world makes you think I'd have heard of such a thing!' cried Marbie with a flurry of onion skins.

There were disadvantages to being at Redwood Primary. For example, there were no laboratories or kitchen facilities, which meant that in Science and Food Tech they did nothing but theory for the term. A lot of the girls complained about this and the effect it might have on their futures. Also, although Redwood was only five minutes' drive from Clareville College, some teachers could not make it there in time for a class. So they often had substitute teachers, and once, they even had a Redwood teacher step in at the last moment to take Commerce.

His name was Mr Bel Castro. His own class, he said, were doing Gym.

'Excuse me, sir,' said Donna Turnbull, pretending to be polite. 'Can I just check with you about something?'

'Of course,' said Mr Bel Castro, also polite.

'What *year* do you teach normally?'

'Year 5,' he said.

'So,' Donna continued, slowly, 'don't take this the wrong way or anything, but could I just ask, have you ever had any, kind of like, *experience* with teaching high school – I mean, students like us?'

Anxiously, she looked around the room as if concerned about the fate of her class. Beside her, Caro giggled.

'Teaching students like *you?*' said Mr Bel Castro, pausing as he picked up a marker. 'Well, I don't know about students like *you*. I did spend five years teaching Economics to Year 12 at Riverview before I came to Redwood. So, I don't know, which would you say are more like *you* – my senior students from Riverview or my Year 5 students here?'

Everyone laughed and someone said, 'Haaa, Donna, he got you good.'

Then Mr Bel Castro wrote his name on the whiteboard and moved straight on to teaching. Afterwards everyone said he was better than their regular teacher. In fact, he seemed to have a whole lesson stored in his head which he taught by asking questions.

'You've been doing advertising?' he began. 'Consumer awareness and so on? Well, who here thinks that the Valerio empire is messing with our minds?'

He smiled when everyone said, '*Huh?*', and soon had them shouting out Valerio products from their homes and their days, including Valerio toys, pies, cars, computers, TV shows and cleaning products. Then he waited while they began reciting Valerio jingles and lines from the recent Nikolai Valerio biography, which had outsold the Harry Potter series in the first two weeks of its release.

'OK, you've got Valerio jingles jumping around in your minds and Valerio's book on your shelves. You've got Valerio films on your TV screens and Valerio junk mail in your letter boxes. Who thinks the Valerio empire might be invading their privacy?'

This led to a discussion about whether you could invade somebody's privacy by getting products and words inside their mind. Also, whether it made a difference if people chose to buy the products and watch the movies. Kelly Favoloro pointed out that you sometimes *couldn't* choose because Valerio shows were the only things worth watching on TV. 'Good point,' said Mr Bel Castro.

Then Angela Saville said, 'But isn't it really the other way around, and *we* invade the Valerio family privacy?'

'Aha!' said Mr Bel Castro. '*Interesting!* Well, let's see how much we know about the Valerio family. Who's in the family for a start?'

Of course, everyone knew the Valerio family: Nikolai, his wife Rebekka, and their three handsome, grown-up sons. Nikolai and Rebekka had now retired of course, and liked to play tennis and gin rummy in their South Carolina mansion. They had their own bowling alley! Nikolai had been a beautiful young motor mechanic working in New York, with a smear of motor oil on his nose, when he was discovered by a movie producer. His seven films were generally considered the best ever made. He became an icon and a sex symbol immediately after his first film. He designed a line of Valerio underwear which was an instant smash. When he married Rebekka, a Romanian model, after his first film, women all over the world threw themselves off buildings. There was a famous photograph of Nikolai and Rebekka dancing in a

275

buttercup meadow *in bare feet*. Bees buzzed close to their naked toes.

Nikolai and Rebekka's three sons, although still young, ran the family empire. Each of the sons had been troubled by drugs and shoplifting in the past, but had recovered after treatment in a Swiss resort. The eldest was only twenty-one, but was always Bachelor of the Year.

'So,' said Mr Bel Castro. 'Do you think Rebekka can paint her toenails without somebody noticing? Can Nikolai buy a hamburger? Could any of the three Valerio sons take up guitar without *you* finding out?'

'Yeah, that's a true point,' said Donna, 'but I'd put up with being watched all the time if I had about one quarter of the money they've got.'

'It's because they're like the royal family of the world,' said Angela, 'because Nikolai made his seven movies in seven different countries so it's like he spread himself all over the world, like peanut butter, and now *everybody* loves him.'

'But not everybody loves peanut butter,' somebody pointed out wisely.

Listen was quiet, thinking about how much work it was to hide from the eyes of the girls in her year, and the teachers, and her dad. She had to hide because if they saw her alone, they saw this: a girl with no friends. Once they had seen her in that way, they could never see her any other way. She couldn't change it. She couldn't make it stop.

'I don't think it's worth it,' she said, without even putting up her hand. 'You'd forget how to be yourself.'

'Yeah,' said Angela. 'But Nikolai *chose* to be a movie star.'

'That's just one choice,' said Listen. 'After that, the world decided he and Rebekka were *perfect* people, and they wouldn't let them change. They were like a king and queen because that's what everybody wanted. Then they had three sons so that's a fairy tale. So now they're a fairy-story family, and there's nothing they can do to make it stop.'

Everyone was quiet and surprised. Listen Taylor rarely spoke in class.

'Huh,' said Mr Bel Castro, 'sorry, I don't know anybody's name – you are . . . ?'

'Her name's Listen Taylor,' said Angela.

'Her name's not actually Listen,' said Donna.

'It's *Alissa*,' Caro added. 'She just *calls* herself Listen.'

Mr Bel Castro looked from Angela to Donna to Caro, and then back to Listen. 'She just calls herself Listen?' he said. 'I like that.' He smiled at Listen, and nodded his approval.

One night, watching *Law and Order: Criminal Intent*, the aeronautical engineer laughed at something Marbie had just said and murmured, 'Maribelle, you are a riot!'

'Who's Maribelle?' said Marbie from the floor, where she liked to watch TV.

He continued to watch the screen, leaning back on the couch. After a moment he said, 'Isn't Maribelle your name?'

'No, Maribelle is not my name.'

'Well, what else could Marbie be short for?'

'What else?! And you call yourself a visionary. It's short for Marbleweed.'

'Marbleweed!' He laughed so much that he had to mute the TV. 'Why would your name be Marbleweed?'

Marbie explained about her mother – how she had wanted to give them gifts with their names. She gave Fancy the gift of *imagination* and Marbie the gift of good luck.

'Good luck!' cried the aeronautical engineer. 'With a name like *Marbleweed*?'

Marbie explained that 'marble' was, in fact, *excellent* luck, according to a book on witchcraft which her mother once owned. If marble grew like weeds, her mother thought, you'd end up with a surfeit of good luck.

'*And*,' Marbie added, 'it worked. I've had *excellent* luck all my life.' Then she frowned for a moment, considering this, and cleared her throat.

'Marbleweed,' he whispered, shaking his head at her. Then he giggled and began singing the name, over and over, humorously.

A few days later, the aeronautical engineer fell asleep, lying flat along the couch, while Marbie watched *Survivor: Cook Islands* from the floor. When it finished, she tried to wake him to tell him that the Convention for the Protection of Individuals with Regard to Automatic Processing of Personal Data did not apply to the Zing family. It was irrelevant.

And even if it technically applied, she thought, exasperated as she tried to formulate this thought, even then, what did the law or legal documents have to do with her family and its meetings in the shed? The Zing Family Secret was a family matter, far too complex, emotional, private, fragile and delicate for the application of *rules*.

'Hey,' she said. 'Hey. Wake up.'

He gasped in his sleep, said 'Huh? What? Huh?' and turned on his side. A cushion fell off the couch.

She found this display extremely affected.

'Oh, *forget* it,' she said, and went home.

One night, after dinner at Fancy's place, Marbie asked her sister when Nathaniel would return. 'You said he'd come back,' she accused.

'Well,' said Fancy, cheerfully. 'Has he had an affair with someone else yet?'

Marbie gasped.

'Because,' Fancy explained, 'he won't come back until he's had an affair of his own.'

'But I only slept with the A.E. once!' cried Marbie.

'And you're not seeing him any more, are you?'

'No!' she lied.

'Still, that's just a technicality. As soon as you slept with your aeronautical engineer, you gave Nathaniel the right to sleep with someone else. It's a rule.'

Although Marbie begged Fancy to change her mind, she refused.

'He *has* to,' she said, gently. 'Otherwise it's not balanced. Didn't you realize?'

'I would die if Nathaniel even touched someone else.'

'You should have thought of that before.'

'Stop it, Fancy, it's not funny. I don't *want* him to have an affair. Come on, please?'

'It's not up to me. Revenge is his right.'

Oh God! thought Marbie, breathless with panic. Nathaniel's hands on another woman's hands, Nathaniel's thighs against another woman's thighs! Nathaniel playing the astronaut game and moonwalking across another woman's bed! Why had she not thought of this before?

If he had to get revenge – and Marbie supposed that he did, because Fancy was generally wise – if he had to get revenge, then couldn't the revenge be something else?

The next day, Marbie slept with the A.E. again.

For weeks he had seemed perfectly content to ask her, now and then, if she would like to 'give it a whirl again'. Each time he asked, she would pretend to consider, politely, and then say, 'No. Thanks, though.' But on this day she arrived to find him wearing nothing but boxer shorts and a bow tie. He was carrying a bottle of champagne.

'Marbie,' he said, as she walked in the door and raised her eyebrows at him, 'Marbie, this can *not* go on.'

'Can't it?' she said.

'No, my beautiful, it cannot. You *cannot* sleep with me once and then not again. You *cannot* use those pouting lips to tell me your delicious family scandal and then keep your lips away from mine. You *cannot* come over, night after night, with those sexy legs and that husky voice, and *not* sleep with me again.'

She gazed at him for a few moments. 'All right,' she said. 'But not on the living-room floor.'

For the next few days, Marbie stayed at home. She explained to the A.E. that she had to do 147 Business Activity Statements for the various Zing Family Secret corporations. (This happened to be true: she had an excellent mind for corporate structures and formalities.) She phoned Nathaniel and offered to do the Banana Bar BAS, as usual, but he said he had found an accountant.

The next time she saw the aeronautical engineer, it was in the Night Owl Pub, after her work friends had gone. He did not even sit down. He whispered in her ear, 'Have a drink on me,' and placed a schooner of beer in front of her. Then he took out a curl of paper, tied with a pink ribbon, and added 'One of my new visions' before he slipped away. Marbie opened the vision and read it. It left her somewhat cold.

THE VISIONS OF AN AERONAUTICAL ENGINEER
VISION # 1562

TRAPPED WITHIN THE COBWEBS OF MY COUNTER-INTUITIVE CHIN,
I SEE THIS, I SEE THIS, I SEE THIS.
I SEE, WITH STARTLED CLARITY, FOR JUST A WHISPERED MOMENT:
BI-DIRECTIONAL EVOLUTIONARY STRUCTURAL OPTIMIZATION.

The following Thursday was a difficult day for Marbie. Things such as this kept happening: she made a call to get somebody's number, scribbled the number on a Post-it note, and then lost the Post-it note. Also, her nose and her eyes were itchy, and she was always on the verge of a sneeze.

She was almost relieved when the A.E. phoned in the afternoon and asked her to slip out of work to meet him at a cafe.

She ordered a piece of chocolate cake.

'Whoa,' said the aeronautical engineer when the cake arrived. The waitress smiled, as if it was a compliment. 'You gonna eat all that by yourself?' He himself had only ordered an espresso.

'You can share it if you like,' said Marbie, politely.

'Heeeee-uge.' He whistled between his teeth, and shook his head: 'No thanks.'

Marbie adjusted her chair slightly and took up her spoon.

'You'd better get stuck in,' he advised. 'I mean, we don't have all *day* here; sure, if you wanted to share it with a starving nation, you might just –'

She touched his thigh to make him stop.

'Ho ho!' he said, looking at her hand on his thigh with a grin. 'Ho *ho*!'

When she returned to work, the day continued exactly as before. Worse even: one of her toenails had developed a sharp edge and was cutting into the next toe.

Later that night she drove to the A.E.'s place to watch TV.

'I'm hungry,' she said, during an ad break.

'After that piece of chocolate cake!'

'That was hours ago,' Marbie pointed out.

He raised his eyebrows. '*I'm* not hungry,' he declared.

'I assume you realize,' Marbie said spitefully, 'that your not being hungry doesn't make you a better person than me?'

He chuckled and leaned back on the couch, stretching out

an arm as if to parallel park. Marbie stood up. She stared at him.

'What's up? Feeling fragile today?'

Formally, she announced: 'I'm leaving. Sorry, but we have to end it now.'

'Come on,' he smiled wryly. 'You're ending it because of a piece of chocolate cake?'

'Because of a piece of chocolate cake,' she agreed, and she gathered up her handbag and her shoes.

Part 12

The Story of Madame Blanchard

25

Once upon a time there was a man named *Monsieur Blanchard*, who fell in love with hot-air balloons. By lucky chance, he also fell in love with a woman (*Madame Blanchard*), who herself was enamoured of balloons. Together, they cast their ballooning spells, performing sky shows all over France.

Madame Blanchard was a sensitive soul who could not stand the clamour of noise. Often, of an evening, she took her balloon into the sky, and remained there, with the moon, until dawn.

Sadly, Madame Blanchard died in a balloon crash. It was during a fireworks display over the Tivoli Gardens in Paris. From the basket of her balloon, Madame Blanchard sent gold! and silver! in cascading stars to the delight of the crowd below, and then she sent a great burst of fire. The crowd cheered happily, not understanding that this burst of fire was an error and signified disaster: in fact, the balloon was on fire.

She crashed on to the roof of a house in the Rue Provence, and broke her neck.

Maude Sausalito, now older, and married (and in fact not Maude *Sausalito* any more), wore her hair long and flat like a shawl. She was telling her husband about the Blanchards, the legends of ballooning, while he polished his shoes. She herself was icing cupcakes on the one clear corner of the kitchen table; he had spread newspaper across the remainder and was nodding as he dipped a brush in polish. He had just been promoted to assistant-manager-in-training at the menswear store where he worked, which is why shiny shoes were important.

When Maude told how Madame Blanchard took to the sky of a night, her husband, David, chuckled to himself and said, 'Not a bad idea!'

They both glanced down at their first child, Fancy, who was sleeping in the pram that Maude had found abandoned on the street (David had refurbished it completely). Lately, Fancy had been teething, so that their nights had become precarious affairs: they did not sleep so much as teeter in suspense. The baby's cries were so sharp they both felt the cut of the tooth.

Maude and David had married two years before and honeymooned in a tent in the Hunter Valley. Maude had secretly arranged a dawn balloon ride for the second day of the honeymoon, but, during the wedding reception, David's brother made several jokes about his vertigo.

'What's vertigo?' Maude whispered.

'A fear of heights,' David whispered back.

He had never told her! Secretly, she cancelled the balloon ride.

They never mentioned his vertigo, but both acknowledged it silently – for example, when Maude's kite got caught on the chimney she herself climbed up to retrieve it, while David watched, trembling and pale.

Generally, David was happy to hear her balloon stories, but when Maude finished the story of the Blanchards, he said sternly, 'She died in a balloon crash? That's not a nice story, Maude. Why tell me that story?'

'OK, here's a nicer story,' said Maude at once. 'About *Monsieur* Blanchard. The husband. About how he crossed the English Channel in a balloon! Just rock the pram with your foot, would you? We'll trick her into going back to sleep.'

As she told the story of Monsieur Blanchard, Maude daydreamed about the journey they would take in a hot-air balloon, once David was cured of his vertigo. (If she told enough balloon stories, then surely . . . ?)

The pilot would have long curling hair, almost to his shoulders. In the creaking basket of the balloon, one night, he would point out a powerful owl. 'Is that actually a bird?' David would say. 'Isn't it just a bit of dust?' But the pilot, his muscular arm reaching up to tug a rope, checking the wind with a private little nod, would steer them closer to the dust, which would turn into a powerful owl. He would glance at her reaction, shy for a moment, but then he would grin, mischievously, and turn to the care of his balloon.

Blushing, she would look down at the slice of lime, perched on the side of her martini.

Part 13

The Story of the Trip to Ireland

26

When Fancy Zing was eleven years old, her father went to Ireland for a year. The day that he was due to return she sat at the kitchen table to write a poem:

'Today! Today! My Daddy's Coming Home!
At last! At last! Fetch the Cheese and Honeycomb!'

The thick black lead of the HB pencil slipped when the table wobbled, and the 'Cheese' spilled its 's' across 'Coming'.

Fancy examined the table. It was cracked, and scribbled with words such as 'MARBIE ZING' and 'COW!' She lay her hands flat and rocked the table to pinpoint the wobble, tore a corner from her poem paper and crouched next to the table leg. As she crouched, she stopped and swirled her skirt, making it touch the floor in a parachute circle. It was a brand new second hand skirt, to Welcome Daddy Home.

Her mother had said, 'New jeans?'

And Fancy had said, 'I think I'd like a skirt.'

'A skirt!' cried Mummy. 'Aren't we growing up!'

Then she took most of the money from the St Vincent de Paul box on top of the fridge, took Fancy's little sister, Marbie, by the hand, and all three walked to the bus stop. Only, Mummy realized she didn't have exact change for the bus fare, so they walked into Castle Hill.

At Pre-Loved Fashion, Fancy's mother bought herself a pale green scarf, which floated in the air when she tossed it about, making up her mind whether to buy it (and she leaned towards Fancy and explained, 'A little pink lipstick and a pale green scarf, and you'll find you win any man's heart!' 'Will you?' said Fancy, surprised). They also bought a purple T-shirt for Marbie, and for Fancy, a skirt in the colours of a rainbow lorikeet.

Now Fancy stood up from the floor, graceful, a flamingo, and felt the skirt rest against her legs.

The wobble was gone when she sat back down, and she took up her pencil again. But here was the problem. She could not write the poem too fast because she had to be there, writing it, when her father arrived. She had to be sitting at the table, her pencil chatting poetry, frowning as she worked on the last few words.

He would walk through the door and say, 'Fancy! Hi! Doing homework?'

And she would say, 'Writing a poem to welcome you home.'

She would stand, her skirt would fall against her legs in a great spray of colour, and he would say, 'You're all grown up!'

And she would say, gracefully, 'Welcome home, Daddy.' And present him with the poem.

So she sat at the table and drew tiny flowers in the space between the lines of her poem. Then she wrote the heading: 'WELCOME, DADDY' in bubble letters, and made a 3D effect by shading around the edges.

The telephone rang and Mummy shouted from the laundry, 'Get that, would you, Fancy?' But Marbie came skidding through the back door and grabbed it from just beneath her fingers. 'Hello?'

Fancy whispered sternly: 'Good afternoon, Marbie Zing speaking.'

Marbie shivered her muddy face and turned towards the wall. 'Yes,' she said to the receiver. Then, 'Ye-e-e-e-s! Of course!' Then, 'Uh-huh, Uh-huh. OK. Bye.'

Fancy said, 'You're all muddy, Marbie. Who was that?'

'Nobody.' Marbie squirmed past and ran down the hall-way.

'It can't have been nobody,' Fancy murmured to herself. She followed Marbie at a more stately pace.

'Who was it?' Mummy asked.

'Guess.'

Mummy stood up slowly from the laundry basket, carrying a pair of Marbie's shorts. She put her hands in both shorts pockets, one at a time, and took out crumpled tissues and dirty handkerchiefs. 'Look at you, Marbie,' she said, shaking her head. 'Look at your lovely new T-shirt.'

Marbie looked down and said 'Oops!' to see the purple T-shirt splattered with mud specks.

'Oops is right, young lady.' Mummy took an apple core from Marbie's shorts pockets.

'Who was it?' Fancy demanded. 'On the phone?'

'But it already had that mark on it when we bought it, remember, Mum?' Marbie licked her fingers and began scraping at the mud.

'Stop that,' said Mummy. 'You'll only make it worse. Here, take it off right away and I'll put it in with this lot. Marbie, who was on the phone, darling?'

Marbie lifted her T-shirt up over her face and from behind the purple she said, 'Daddy.'

'Daddy?' Fancy cried.

'Hang on,' said Mummy. She had noticed something deep in the washing machine. Being quite fat, she had to reach over her stomach before she could get into the machine. Marbie and Fancy waited. 'Hm,' she said, coming back out and holding up a sock. She tossed it into the basket and turned around to reach for Marbie's T-shirt.

'Yeah,' said Marbie. 'Daddy. And he says he's still at the airport now because the plane was late, and he'll come home soon, OK?'

'Right,' said Mummy, bending to the basket once again. 'We may as well get dinner started. No sense in us starving, is there?'

'I'll start dinner, Mummy,' offered Fancy.

The chicken and chips were sitting on the counter, wrapped in a great white bundle. Fancy took the aluminium tray with its burned biscuit stains, and let the food tumble from its paper on to the tray. She switched on the oven and placed the tray on the centre shelf.

Ceremoniously, she moved to the table, took her HB pencil and crinkled her forehead at the poem.

27

When Marbie Zing was five years old, her father went to Ireland for a year. Every night that he was gone, Marbie crept into the school yard next door and took midnight swims in the pool. During the days she sailed paper boats in the kitchen sink.

The day that her father came home, Fancy wrote a poem, Mummy washed the curtains and Marbie turned the hose on to the trampoline.

It was Marbie who answered the phone when he called from the airport.

'That's Marbie, isn't it?'

'Yes.'

'Do you remember your old dad?'

'Ye-e-e-s! Of course!'

They ate chicken and chips for dinner, and their mother said, 'Let's get this place looking perfect for your dad!'

Fancy threw away the chicken bones, and Marbie, accidentally, threw away Fancy's poem. Mummy hung freshly washed curtains in the kitchen windows and stood back. 'Girls, what do you think!'

Fancy said, 'Beeeautiful.'

Marbie said that the curtains looked crinkled and raggedy.

'Did anybody see my poem?' said Fancy, shifting magazines around.

Mummy took another step back and bumped into Fancy. 'Maybe you're right. I should iron them.'

'They look beautiful, Mummy,' Fancy said. 'Leave them. But I can't find my poem. Did anyone see my poem?'

'Only I don't know if I have time.' Mummy looked at the kitchen clock, the curtains and the closed front door. 'Oh dear.'

'Maybe you should just throw the curtains away,' suggested Marbie.

'That's not the answer, precious one,' said Mummy, then: 'Fancy! What are you *doing*?'

Fancy had the kitchen trash can tipped upside down. She was sitting among chicken bones, tin cans, paper towels, tuna fish, carrot peels and corn.

'My poem!' Fancy cried. 'I can't find my poem!'

'The floor!' Mummy cried.

Headlights flashed through the kitchen curtains and an engine grumbled in the drive.

'He's *here*!' Fancy shrieked, and Mummy and Marbie jumped. 'And I'm all ruined, and I can't find my poem and –' Then she found her poem.

'My *poem*!' Now she was crying properly. 'It's *ruined*, it's got *chicken grease* all over it and LOOK AT MY SKIRT.'

Which is why, when Daddy got back from Ireland, the first thing he looked at was Fancy's new skirt.

'That's tuna on your skirt there, isn't it?'

Those were his first words. He was carrying a large brown suitcase, and his face, Marbie thought, was like a fat pink balloon. Fancy stood up in a tumble of garbage and ran from the room in a sob.

'I hope you're not hungry,' Mummy announced. 'We've eaten all the chicken and chips.'

'Have you got presents?' said Marbie.

'Of course I've got presents!' said Daddy. 'I'll put my suitcase away, and then we'll all go sit in the lounge.'

In the lounge, Daddy gave them presents: bags of M&Ms and packets of crisps. They waited hopefully, but that was it, so they started eating the M&Ms. Daddy looked around the room and began picking up objects and putting them back down.

'Just leave that one,' said Mummy suddenly, but Daddy had put down a photo frame and picked up a magazine. When he did, a dried flower fell on to the floor.

'Oh,' said Daddy, 'sorry,' and he tried to pick up the pieces of the flower. 'Just leave it,' Mummy said again.

Meanwhile, Fancy sat on the carpet in her dirty skirt and sniffed. 'I wrote you a poem,' she said eventually, 'but it got thrown away and now it's ruined.'

'Here, come sit on my lap,' Daddy suggested. 'You can write me another poem if you like!'

'But I can't . . .' Fancy burst into tears and nobody heard what she said next.

'We can't hear you,' Marbie explained. 'You have to stop crying.'

Fancy kept crying anyway, and Mummy said, 'Hush now,' and leaned forward to stroke her hair.

'I can't sit on your lap, Daddy.' This time they heard Fancy. 'The couch is broken and we'll fall right through because I'll be too heavy and my skirt's too dirty.'

'Rubbish!' cried Daddy.

'Yes,' Marbie explained, 'it's rubbish. All over her skirt.'

'Come along.' Daddy patted his knees. 'I think on this special day you can sit on my lap, no?' So Fancy did. Daddy shifted so he wasn't sitting on the broken spring.

'Where did you go for a whole year, Daddy?' said Fancy, wiping away her tears.

'I went to some islands, Fancy, off the west coast of Ireland.'

'How many islands, Daddy?'

'Three.'

'What are they called?'

'Inishmore, Inishmaan and Inisheer.'

'What are they like? Are they nice?'

'The soil is almost paved with stones,' said Daddy, clearing his throat, and continuing, 'so that in some places nothing is to be seen but large stones with openings between them, where cattle break their legs. The only stone is limestone and marble for tombstones. Among these stones is very good pasture, so that beef, veal and mutton are better and earlier in season here than elsewhere.'

'Interesting,' said Mummy.

'Yes,' agreed Daddy.

'What did you do on the islands, Daddy?'

'I wrote my novel, Fancy.'

'Can I see your novel, Daddy?'

'No. Once I had finished my novel, Fancy, I took the pages, one by one, made each into a paper boat and sent them all to sea. Because, Fancy, my novel took me away from my family. So I washed it away in the waves.'

'Daddy!' whispered Fancy, then: 'Welcome home.' She cried again and threw her arms around him.

'Little Fancy,' whispered Daddy, 'little Fancy.'

Marbie blinked her eyes to make herself cry. 'What's the matter, Marbie?' said her mother. 'Don't tell me you're allergic to the carpet?'

Part 14

Thursday Night

28

Late Thursday night, Cath closed the door on Warren, and sat on her couch to imagine.

She had driven straight home from the staff meeting that day, without touching the rose in her pigeonhole, and had waited, breathless, for Warren to arrive. When he did, she threw open the door and said, '*What's going on?*' Then she laughed at her own melodrama: he was sure to have an explanation.

It turned out he did not. The truth was set out in his solemn face: Breanna had a job at Redwood Primary, beginning Monday. In fact, he could not even stay tonight – he had to go home and get the house in order. Her furniture would arrive the next day. The affair was officially over.

'Why didn't you tell me before?' she said.

'I didn't know until today that it was definite.'

'But why did I have to hear it from *Billson*?'

'I tried to warn you. I left you a rose.'

'But why didn't you *tell* me?'

'I'm sorry,' said Warren. 'You're completely right. But it was up in the air until this morning, and I just didn't want it to be true. Really. I left you a rose.'

'But at our *school*! Why didn't you stop it from happening?'

'I couldn't stop it – how would that have looked? When it came up a couple of weeks ago, I didn't think it was serious. I really didn't think it could happen.'

They spent the evening sitting on the couch, while Cath tried to cry. She found that she could not. There was nothing to cry about. Here he was beside her. The idea of his not being there was absurd.

'It's just that I think I love you,' she murmured eventually into his shoulder. Then she panicked: it was the first time this had been said between them. It was the first time she herself had ever said it first.

'I think I love you too,' he replied and stroked the hair behind her ears.

'It feels impossible,' she said.

Warren agreed. His voice was sad, but practical. 'I can tell we'll be together one day,' he said. 'Some day, soon, it will all work out.'

'You're married,' she reminded him, but in a teary, smiling voice.

'Yes,' he replied, 'but it's coming apart at the seams.'

Then he left, pausing at the door. They stared at each other fiercely and then laughed, and he placed his hand on her forehead as if checking for fever.

Cath returned to the couch to imagine the affair being over. She pictured a train screeching to a halt with a jolt and a *tick-tick-tick* into silence. (The sound of a window squeaking open and a passenger blustering: what *now?*) But, in her vision, the train slid back into motion almost at once. She could not imagine it simply standing still.

It would be *intellectually* interesting, she decided, but otherwise would probably not hurt. It was not as if he was leaving *her*, he just had to return temporarily to his wife.

They had always agreed that contact would cease when Breanna moved to Sydney. Otherwise they would have to sneak around like people having an affair. And, although she would miss his body, this would be altogether different to broken hearts of her past. After all, she and Warren were in love. They had just admitted it. Shortly, the marriage would unravel.

Warren would still be around. She would be able to see him, talk to him, tell him her secrets. 'It will be fine, won't it?' she confirmed with her cat, Violin.

Late Thursday night, Fancy stood at the long, narrow window by her front door and gazed out across the shadowed lawn.

Radcliffe had driven to the corner store for milk, and Cassie was asleep. For the first time that day, Fancy had a moment to consider how she felt about the end of her husband's affair.

Instead, she thought about hotel foyers.

Ah, she thought, *hotel foyers!* The smooth integration of elevator doors, marble floors and granite reception desks! The concierge behind his helpful little glasses, which glint in the chandelier light. The glass shopfronts with their indoor plants and neat subtle lettering: *Armani, Gucci, Dolce & Gabbana*. The wine bar in curving stainless steel with dashes of electric blue (martini glasses!); and the bathrooms, especially the bathrooms! Their frosted glass and their clever taps, towels folded in neat white piles, dried flowers, and the sensors! Everywhere the sensors! Hand driers, toilet flushers, doorways!

As generally happened when she thought of hotel foyers, Fancy's breathing slowed. She calmed enough to return to her own front hallway. *Your husband is NOT having an affair*, she reminded herself. But watching the front lawn and hearing the occasional gear change of passing cars, she felt herself jolted back to the imaginary foyer.

Immediately, she ran into a man in a pale grey T-shirt.

She thought she might kiss him deeply. No! She would lean in to kiss him and he would turn away! She saw him, the man (not quite his face, more his T-shirt), and she longed for his touch: please, put your hand on my wrist! But he refused.

Jolted again, she was back in her home. She shrugged deeply, feeling the spasm of the stranger's non-touch by touching her own arms with her fingertips.

Was that him now? Had he followed her out of her dream? That was a car!

She peered beyond her reflection into the night. A car *was* pulling into the driveway. There was a succinct click as the headlights turned off. The engine was quieting. It *was* him! The man from the hotel foyer! They were *his* strong hands unbuckling the seatbelt, his thumb on the button of his keys: *Bip-Bip!*

His shoes were moving on the gravel – a quiet crunching, a few running steps up the stairway – and now he would knock! 'That was you in the hotel foyer,' he would accuse, enigmatically.

'Won't you come in for a drink?' she would reply, breathless, and –

Fancy jumped as keys rapped on the window.

'Fancy that!' cried a voice. 'My Fancy is at home!'

Radcliffe leaned around the door with a grin, holding up a carton of milk.

Late Thursday night, Marbie drove home from the A.E.'s house, relieved she had finally ended the affair.

She walked down the hallway of the empty apartment, switching on lights and checking behind doors for intruders. Then she sat down on a beanbag in the living room to think.

The A.E. was not attractive, kind, intelligent, poetic or interesting, she thought. In fact, he was mostly annoying. Despite that, she had slept with him twice, told him the Secret and spent several nights in his home. All the time, she had been conscious of a mild voice asking, *Excuse me, but where is your mind?* She had treated the voice in the same way you might treat a person asking, *What's that burning smell?* You might look vaguely towards the kitchen and then turn back to the TV.

Now she would suffer the consequences. She would wake each morning, conscious of the fact that she had failed to pay attention while her house burned to the ground.

Part 15

Friday Night

29

In the camper van, Listen watched her father emerge from the back door of the Banana Bar. He turned, locked the door, lifted his head to the night sky and sighed. She could see the sigh because it took his shoulders with it and then slumped them down. He leaned against the door now and lit a cigarette.

He gave up smoking years ago.

Now he would get cancer and die, and this would be her fault. Everything was her fault, she realized, with amazement. She was pretty sure she had caused the flooding of the Year 7 classrooms at Clareville: something to do with those fuses she had knocked in that storage room.

She had broken up her dad and Marbie with a spell.

When you thought about it, she had *caused* Donna and the others to break their eternal pact. They had to break it. She jeopardized their survival.

Right this moment, she and her dad should have been at the Zings for the Friday Meeting.

Her dad flicked his cigarette between his fingers, and Listen realized something: she'd been wrong when she decided that the Secret was about family life.

In fact, the Secret was a murder.

The Zing family had murdered somebody and now they had to cover it up. They had to shovel graves and bribe police and blackmail witnesses. They spent Friday nights organizing robberies to cover the costs of the cover-up. The garden shed was a bare concrete floor with a wooden table in the centre. The family sat around the table and smoked, squinting at maps and plans of bank vaults. They were jumpy, looking up uneasily when a bird landed on the shed roof.

Eventually, they would have recruited her to a life of crime. That would have been appropriate too. There was something wicked and wrong about her. She was connected to the Zings by her shame.

If you put a baby seahorse in an aquarium, she thought, it will swallow an air bubble and die. If a whale ever falls asleep, she thought, it will forget to breathe, and it will die.

She watched her dad stamp out his cigarette and brush his hands together.

Part 16

The Following Week

30

The following week, Cath found out how it felt, the end of her affair.

It felt: suspenseful, frightening, surprising, confusing, obvious, outrageous and eventually like despair. These emotions arrived individually or in clusters, and sometimes one would brush the surface for a moment before eliding into another. On the first day, Monday, the primary emotions were SUSPENSE and FEAR.

Three significant events took place that day:

1. Seeing Breanna for the first time
2. Being introduced to Breanna
3. Having coffee with Breanna

At Monday assembly, she sat in her usual place, mistaking the suspense and fear for an exciting arriving-at-the-theatre sort of feeling. Warren ran in late, as usual, and sat beside her, with a friendly yet restrained 'Hey, hey'. His face was grim and grey, and her excitement increased. She ignored Billson's introductory remarks, but then tuned back in when she realized he was no longer talking, but was breathing, unpleasantly, into the microphone.

'I'm *waiting*.' He held up his thumb and then his pointer. He was going to count ten fingers, while the children whispered and giggled. 'All right,' he said, growing bored with the game. 'Let's show our newcomer how well behaved we are at Redwood! A round of applause to welcome our new school counsellor, Breanna Woodford!'

And there at last was Warren's wife. She was moving forward to the front of the stage, and she was, on first impression, cheerful and breezy – but then, Cath realized, she also looked extremely nervous about being on a stage. This gave Cath the strangest stab, and she had to look away.

After the assembly, on her way across the playground to her classroom, Cath felt terrified as Billson approached, beckoning Breanna to follow him. Breanna would surely see the truth in her eyes! Or hear it in her voice? Or sense it in the way she held her shoulders?

'Oh, *you're* Cath Murphy,' said Breanna, friendly. 'I've heard so much about you!' She swung her right arm forward, as if to shake hands, but instead clapped her own hands together as if she was very excited.

Recklessly, Cath said, 'I've heard a lot about you too!'

'I was really looking forward to meeting you at the Carotid Sticks?' said Breanna. 'Remember? It was such a shame I couldn't make it down in time.'

'I know!' exclaimed Cath, but Billson was bored by their chatter and wanted to whisk Breanna away to meet somebody else.

'Do you want to have coffee after school today?' Breanna called over her shoulder, to which Cath replied: 'That's a great idea!'

Watching Breanna hurry away, Cath felt another strange stab. 'I know!' she had said about the night when they almost met. And 'That's a great idea!' about coffee. It was all so cheap and deceptive.

At coffee, Breanna chose a couch instead of a hard-backed chair and slumped in it as if determined to relax. They were in the shopping mall across the road from the school, with a view over the highway.

'I'm so relieved to get this job,' Breanna said, stirring her coffee. 'I didn't know how much longer I could stand being away from Warren for the weekdays. Do you know what I mean? I don't know if it's good for a marriage, for a start.'

Cath breathed in for a moment, her mind looping backwards on itself as she tried to figure out a response. *What would I say, in this situation, if this situation were what it's meant to be?*

'Mmm,' she said, and then tried to change the subject. 'So, you've worked with kids before, have you?'

'A few years ago,' said Breanna. 'And actually mostly with teenagers, but my thesis was on nine- to twelve-year-olds.'

Cath prolonged this for as long as she could, asking after Breanna's thesis topic, where she went to college, who her favourite teachers were, whether she took good notes. She enjoyed the conversation. She almost forgot who Breanna was, but the FEAR and SUSPENSE always buzzed just below the surface.

'Anyway,' said Breanna, 'Warren tells me –'

'Oh, hang on!' panicked Cath. 'Have you heard there are some Year 7 girls at our school? Because their classrooms got flooded? Do you think you'll be their counsellor too?'

Breanna knew about the seventh-graders but she didn't know if they were part of her job description. They probably had counsellors of their own.

'The thing is,' said Cath, 'I've been watching one of these girls, because she's somehow related to a girl in my class. And every time I see her she's alone, and she looks sad to me. I think she might not have any friends.'

'Well,' said Breanna, 'I don't see why I shouldn't try to help. Do you know her name?'

Oh God, thought Cath, *there is nothing to dislike. She is kind and obliging, she has pretty eyes and nervous hands, and there is nothing, nothing, nothing to dislike.*

But then Breanna took the subject back to Warren.

'Warren's as excited as I am about me moving down to Sydney,' she said. 'He's like a little boy. You know what? He even secretly went and bought a new bed to welcome me! And he surprised me with it! A four-poster. He put a sign on it saying "WELCOME HOME". Isn't he gorgeous?'

After these three distinct events, the week fell into a haze, and Cath walked around a step or two behind herself.

On two separate occasions, she saw Warren take Breanna's hand, and together they ran across the road. Once, she saw Warren beckon Breanna across the playground, and then tip up a small bag of chocolate sultanas, filling Breanna's palm. She also saw Warren demonstrate the staffroom coffee machine. Breanna stood beside him, concentrating so hard that he laughed and told her this was not life or death. She giggled, embarrassed, and shook her shoulders to loosen herself up.

Meanwhile, the other teachers stopped talking about 'Warren' and started talking about 'Warren-and-Breanna'. *Look at me*, Cath wanted to shout. *Everybody see what I have been to Warren! Everybody say 'Warren-and-Cath'*. But they kept telling Cath what a nice person Breanna seemed to be, and how fun it was to meet Warren's 'other half'.

Cath began to feel that the ground was shifting slightly and that the sky was not quite fixed to the earth. *Now then,* she thought, trying to stay calm, *who am I? Where do I belong? Where are my family? Who are my friends?*

She phoned her mother and chatted about her dad's middle ear and her mum's Tai Chi and a girl in her own class with a piercing in her nose. When her mother eventually asked, as usual, 'Any young men on the horizon?' Cath wanted to dissolve. Or to pour herself into the holes in the telephone receiver and sprinkle herself, like pepper, into her mother's arms. She wanted to tell her mother everything, but what could she say? 'I had an affair with a married man and now his wife has come to take him back.' Imagine her mother's silence across the continent. Imagine the slide in her mother's view of Cath.

Cath's parents thought of her as a well-behaved, innocent girl. A quiet girl, courteous, respectful of other people's things.

'Of *course* his wife has come to take him back!' her mother would say, after the silence. 'What did you think?' There would be such disappointment in her tone.

She thought of her three best friends from high school, who, oddly enough, had all ended up in remote, exotic locations: Lucy in Nepal, Kristin in Mongolia and Sarah in the Sahara. She wrote them a long email with the subject: 'HELP!' But Lucy, Kristin and Sarah rarely got access to the Internet, so she did not expect an answer for a month.

She tried to study her law notes, but could not concentrate. For example, when she read the chapter on larceny, she decided to steal Warren from his wife:

'A asked B to lend him a shilling' (she read). 'B agreed and handed A a coin. Both thought it to be a shilling, but later it emerged to be a sovereign. A kept the sovereign.'

Aha! (She looked up from her book.) She would ask Breanna for a loan of a *sovereign*, and by mistake, Breanna would hand over a *Warren*. Cath would carry him away on a white horse, wicked laughter echoing; too late, Breanna would discover her mistake!

There was one day during that week – possibly Wednesday – which she thought of as the Day of Letters. The first letter was handed to her in the playground before school had begun. Cassie Zing, sprinting past, suddenly skidded to a stop and said, 'I forgot to give you Mum's note!' She took an envelope out of her pocket and handed it over.

> Dear Ms Murphy,
> Just a note to let you know how very much I am looking forward to meeting you at the Parent-Teacher Night this Friday.
>
> Very best wishes and kind regards,
> Fancy Zing

Cath looked up in surprise. This note was so warm and unnecessary! Such a kind, pointless thought from a stranger! She felt suffused with comfort – *all would be well*. But then she saw Breanna smiling at her and she had to crunch the letter in the palm of her hand. *You do not deserve such kindness*, she thought.

This was confirmed when she checked her email and received a reply from Kristin in Mongolia: 'CATH!! YOU POOR BABY. DON'T FEEL GUILTY. THIS IS NOT YOUR FAULT. IT WAS HIS CHOICE. IT'S ALL HIS FAULT. YOU DID NOTHING WRONG! YOU DON'T DESERVE THIS! WILL SEND LONGER EMAIL SOON. AM RUNNING OUT OF MONEY!!!!!!'

But it *is* my fault, she said to the computer screen. And of course it was wrong. She was a grown-up and had always known that affairs are wrong. While it was happening she had told herself: *There is no right or wrong. This is passion! It transcends morality! The rules do not apply!* But why had she thought she could slip outside the rules just because she felt a powerful desire to do so? She'd been trying to steal Warren from the start. No wonder she could not tell her mother about the affair. You can't tell your parents you're a criminal.

Then, in her staffroom pigeonhole, she found a large pink

envelope addressed in swirling purple. At first she felt excited, but then she opened it and read:

> DEAR MS MURPHY,
> I KNOW SOMETHING ABOUT YOU.
> SOMETHING SECRET AND UNFORGIVABLE.
> MEET ME FRIDAY, 1 P.M., AT THE VALERIO COUCH POTATO
> CAFE ACROSS THE ROAD FROM YOUR SCHOOL.
>
> A STRANGER

So it was true. She was evil and she could not be forgiven. Self-loathing crept down her spine.

Then she read the note again and panicked: what was this letter about? *Was it suggesting blackmail?* She and Warren had been so convinced that nobody knew! They had even been proud of their subterfuge! How had they been caught out?

It must be someone from the school. Who else could possibly know? She hunched over her pigeonhole, examining the letter, and then glanced furtively around the room: Heather Waratah was eating a blueberry muffin. Jo Bel Castro was reading the paper. They both looked innocent.

She thought she should search for Warren and show him the letter, but decided against it. The only thing that she and Warren had left now was their secret. Telling Warren about the blackmailer was like telling him there was no secret. Anyway, it would be unbearable to see him panic about Breanna finding out. She, Cath, would deal with it on her own.

That night, Cath arrived home and found a fourth letter in her mailbox. This one was from her landlord, and said that the landlord had purchased the two apartments adjoining Cath's. He intended to knock down the walls between all three, creating one grand apartment. Naturally, Cath would be welcome to continue living in the grand apartment, which would, incidentally, include a sewing room and a sauna. The letter continued:

> Of course, renovation can be noisy and inconvenient! We therefore offer you free accommodation in a penthouse suite at the Winston Hills Tudor Arms for the duration.
>
> Rest assured that, despite the additional comfort which we endeavour to provide with these alterations, your rent will remain as it is for the remainder of your lease.

A sewing room! A sauna! What would she do with such things?

But it was exciting, and she reached for the phone to call Warren. Of course, she remembered, she could not.

It occurred to her that this was a common feature of break-ups – the not being allowed. When boyfriends had broken her heart in the past, the worst of it, when she saw them again, was not being allowed to touch. Not being allowed to smooth their eyebrows, or take their hand at the traffic lights, or touch the end of their nose. Not being allowed to phone up and say, 'Well! You're not going to *believe* what's happened!' Instead, you had to explain yourself. You had to say, 'Hello, this is Cath, how are you?' And that was assuming you were allowed to phone at all.

Of course, all along she had been denied the right to hold Warren's hand in public – but now she was not allowed to see him on week nights and she was forbidden to phone.

She reread the letter, to comfort herself – *at least her landlord seemed fond of her* – and noticed, as she did, a pale little footer in the bottom-right corner of the page. 'Project 78' said the footer.

Project 78. Now what did *that* remind her of?

She ran into the kitchen, opened a few drawers, leafed through recipe books and found it: a letter she had received a few months before, offering a free course in 'Healthy & Delicious Cooking for the Young And Young At Heart'. (She had not taken the offer but had abandoned it in her recipe drawer.)

And there it was – a pale little footer in the bottom-right corner of the page. 'Project 75' it said.

She had a strange, scary feeling for a moment – *how was her landlord connected with a local cooking school?* – but then she smiled: what a coincidence!

The coincidence comforted her. It suggested a world in which everything was connected by faint dotted lines. There was a grand scheme to things, a gentle, controlling destiny. Life was a series of projects – Project 75, cooking; Project 78, renovations.

She returned to the dining-room table, picked up the letter about proposed renovations and traced her finger slowly around Project 78. Things that were meant to be would happen. Some day, somehow, it would all work out.

She almost reached for the phone again, to call Warren and let him know.

After the Day of Letters, Cath found that her week was clenching into RAGE.

'What's going on?' she said to Warren in his empty classroom at the beginning of recess. He was tacking paintings on the wall, ready for Parent–Teacher Night the next day.

'I think,' said Warren, 'I think it won't be too much longer. Things are just falling apart. Bree and I are both sensing something's wrong.'

'Mmm,' said Cath. Then, as he continued tacking paintings to the wall, she said: 'If it's falling apart, why did you buy a new bed? And put a sign on it saying: "Welcome Home, Breanna".'

'She told you that?'

'Uh-huh.'

Warren was silent now, gazing at the thumbtack which was lying on its side in his palm.

At lunchtime that day, Breanna found Cath in the staffroom, sat down beside her and said briskly, 'I just wanted to let you know that I spoke to that Year 7 girl, the one named Listen Taylor? The one you were worried about? I spoke to her yesterday.'

'Wow,' said Cath. 'That was quick.'

Breanna looked pleased so Cath continued to praise her: 'Seriously, thanks so much for doing that. That was really nice of you. You're so efficient!'

'Anyway,' said Breanna, opening up a packed lunch, 'I think you were right. She seems unhappy to me – she didn't want to talk about her friends, but she's going through a tough time with her home life at the moment. Her dad brought her up, you know – apparently, her mother ran off to explore the world and have adventures when she was just a little baby. Poor kid. You wonder what effect that has, losing a parent when you're a baby. I mean, do you rememb –'

Breanna stopped, gasped slightly and said in a low voice, 'Oh, sorry, Cath. You lost *both* parents when you were a baby, didn't you? They died in a house fire?'

'Right,' said Cath, frowning slightly and trying to turn the frown into a smile. 'But it sounds weird to me, hearing you say that. My adoptive parents are my parents, really, and I haven't lost them. I don't remember my biological parents at all.'

'Yeah,' agreed Breanna. 'The only thing you've got left of them is a faded photograph? Is that right?'

'Mmm.' Then Cath remembered that she should be back in

her classroom preparing for tomorrow's Parent–Teacher Night.

When Warren saw Cath at the doorway to his classroom, he said, 'You OK?'

'Sure,' said Cath, with a *snap* like a ring binder. 'You told her I was adopted. You told her about the photo of my parents.'

'I'm sorry, Cath. I didn't know it was a secret.'

'You didn't know it was a secret? I got out the photo from a locked jewellery box. We *both cried*. And that didn't seem like, I don't know, a *confidence*?'

'Cath, all I can do is say I'm sorry.'

'Stop saying my name,' snapped Cath. 'You both keep saying my name. You and your *wife*, she does it too.'

Warren looked surprised, and Cath said, 'You can't *do* this –' her voice became trembly – 'you can't have an affair with me, and then go back to your wife, you can't say that it's coming apart at the seams and then buy a four-poster bed. It's not *allowed*.'

She reached towards him, and he took one step back.

'I'm sorry, OK? I can't do anything about it now – it would kill Breanna. I know this sounds arrogant but the fact is she's really in love with me.'

'Oh, cut it out,' said Cath. 'She's not in love with you. She doesn't even *know* you.'

'Well,' he said gently, 'we've been married for three years.'

'She doesn't know you,' Cath repeated. 'You're a man who cheated on his wife. She doesn't know that, so she doesn't know you.'

He bowed his head while Cath's shaky breathing filled the room.

'I can't leave her,' he whispered, after a moment.

'I'm *not asking you to leave her*,' she almost shouted. 'I *like* her, she's *nice*. *I don't want you to leave her*. You said it was *falling apart.*'

'It is,' he said. 'I swear, we just have to wait.'

'Well, while we're *waiting*, do you have to keep *touching* her? Do you have to keep holding her hand? I saw you *massaging* her *feet*. Have you *thought* about how *that* makes me feel?'

'Please don't cry,' he said

'This doesn't make me cry!' Haughtily, she stalked out of the room.

That afternoon, she tried to study criminal law but decided, instead, to murder Warren Woodford. She would smother him with cross-stitched bookmarks, or watch, with a smirk, as he drowned in the syrup of his words. She chose her defence in advance: 'Provocation' (Chapter 5). The accused, transported by passion, was simply not mistress of herself.

Later that night, sleeping on the couch, she dreamed that Warren told her he was in love with Breanna again. 'It's over between you and me!' he confided, warmly, happily. 'I'm in love with my wife again!'

She shouted at him and punched his chest: 'You are *not* in love with your wife! You're in love with me! Warren, don't you understand? It's not real! You *think* you're in love with your wife, because she's so *happy* and so *bright* and so *nervous* and so *sweet*. Whereas me? Look at me! I'm so *cold* and *angry* and *bitter* and *sad*, but I'm *not,* Warren, if you'd just come back to me, *I* would be the happy person that you want, if you'd just, if you'd just, I'm *not* this brittle, this – Warren, this *does not count.*'

On and on she argued in the dream: passionate, ferocious, eloquent, ingenious. Her arguments sliced the air, but still he smiled his contented smile and shook his head.

*

By Friday, she had settled into DESPAIR.

Watching through her classroom window in the morning, she saw Warren and Breanna walking from the car park. *I hate you*, she thought. He was facing away from her. *Look at me*, she thought, *turn around*.

But he reached his hand back like a beckon, and Breanna hurried forward like a reply.

I love you, Cath thought plaintively. He was swinging Breanna's hand.

At lunchtime that day, Cath sat calmly in the Valerio Couch Potato Cafe and waited for her blackmailer. She took one sip of coffee and slammed it down on the table, thinking: *I hate these chain store coffee shops! Why couldn't the blackmailer have met me in a REAL cafe?* But really she was thinking: How dare Warren tell his wife my secrets!

She remembered the night she told him she was adopted. He had played soccer that afternoon and had come straight to her place from the game, his skinny legs streaked with mud and socks pulled lumpy over shin guards. He carried two cold beers, opened one while he talked and handed it to Cath, opened the other for himself and sat down on the couch. Then he stood to explain how a tackle went wrong and his knee twisted around during the game.

'You see?' he said, pressing his muddy knee against her knee, to demonstrate. 'You see what went wrong?'

They had made pasta together, and he had chipped his tooth on an olive. She had shown him the photo of her biological parents later that night. He had run his finger gently over the outline of her parents and that of the brave, burly firefighter, and tears had formed in his eyes.

Cath's eyes blurred as she looked at her watch. It was two o'clock and the blackmailer was nowhere to be seen.

*

Later, while her class was doing Music, she tried to read her lecture notes from 'Principles of Statutory Interpretation'.

'*Ejusdem generis*' (she read), 'of the same type', and then she had written, cryptically: 'Is a crowbar the same as a mask, disguise or letter?'

Her notes did not explain themselves. Instead, they descended into pictures. She had drawn an elegant mask, a swooping cape, a letter sealed with wax and a crowbar. Her crowbar was set aside slightly from the other more romantic objects.

It's a crowbar, Cath thought, sadly: it will never belong to the same club as a mask, a disguise, or a letter sealed with wax. All this time she had believed that her affair was something wonderful and clandestine: a detective novel, a cloak-and-dagger mystery. But an affair, she realized now, is as blunt and as common as a crowbar.

That afternoon, she sat in the staffroom correcting school work, waiting for Parent–Teacher Night to begin. Just along the table, Warren and Breanna leafed through Ikea brochures and giggled at furniture pictures.

'No,' murmured Breanna. 'No, you can't have chrome in the living room – we've got a pine coffee table, remember?'

'You're right,' agreed Warren. 'I just really like the look of those shelves.'

'Tell you what,' suggested Breanna. 'What about the study?'

'Or too big?'

'No! Look. Here's the measurements. See the scale?'

'EXCELLENT WORK,' Cath wrote in an exercise book, 'WELL DONE!' And she made a monster tick across the page.

'Hey, Cath,' said Warren, turning in his seat beside Breanna. 'We should be getting over there now, shouldn't we?'

Cath agreed – it was almost five and the parents would soon begin arriving.

Breanna said, 'Oh, Cath, before you go – I wanted to tell you something. I was showing a new Year 7 girl around the school this afternoon, and, anyway, I introduced her to your Listen Taylor. You never know. Maybe they'll be friends?'

'Huh,' said Cath, 'that's great, Breanna. Thanks.'

'See you at home, OK, Warren?' Breanna was picking up her bag. 'I'll stop by the hardware store and surprise you with curtain rings!'

The Year 2 interviews were held in Cath's classroom: Room 2B. Warren set up a table at the back of the room, and Cath used her own desk.

The first parent to arrive was a man who introduced himself as Radcliffe. 'I'm Cassie Zing's dad!' he said before he even entered the classroom. He was wiping his feet on the doormat. 'Call me Radcliffe. And you must be Ms Murphy.'

'That's right,' agreed Cath and looked around Radcliffe. 'Your wife?' she said. 'She's not coming? She writes a lot of notes . . .'

'*Does* she?' cried Radcliffe, pausing, and placing his hands on his hips. Then he grinned and walked into the room. He stood still before Cath and continued to grin, shaking his head slowly. Then he remembered himself: 'Ah yes, Fancy, my wife. Well, something's come up, I'm afraid, and poor old Fancy couldn't come. Cassie got – well, we had a little incident with Cassie, but she'll be fine. Fancy took her to the doctor.'

His words seemed blustery, overexcited, and they hurried in a stop-start shuffle. He picked up the chair, spun it around and sat down with his arms around the chair back.

'Well,' said Cath, straightening her voice. 'Thank you so much for coming in then, Mr – ah, Radcliffe. We all adore Cassie – she has a great deal of character. In reading, she –' But she stopped, as the man was gazing at her face and rocking slightly on the chair.

'So you're Cassie's teacher then?' he said, as if she had not spoken. '*Cath Murphy*, eh? Wonderful to meet you.' He reached out to shake hands, but she was too surprised to offer her own. 'Not giving you any trouble, I hope?' he tried, settling back into his happy rocking motion.

'Trouble,' repeated Cath, with an effort. 'Well, no, not really.'

'Not really!' He beamed.

'I just worry a little,' Cath explained. 'She seems, sometimes, to be – angry at the world? And she uses – strange words. She *chants* strange words and phrases.'

'Oh, that *game* of hers,' agreed Radcliffe. 'I know! Where she chooses a word and then repeats it? My wife and I don't have a clue what to do about that.'

'I've tried several different strategies to deal with it,' said Cath – someone had to be the professional here – 'but nothing has worked so far. Also, I've done a bit of reading – and I found that children sometimes develop a sort of obsession with things that seem *negative* or *forbidden*, if they sense something dark and negative around the home. Or if they are excluded from – if there is – sorry, I don't mean that any of this applies to *your* family – but, this sometimes happens if there is some forbidden, shadowy region of family knowledge?'

Radcliffe continued to gaze at her.

'Anyway,' she added, embarrassed, 'they're the words that were used in the article I was reading and I like them – the words – the forbidden, shadowy –'

'Is that right?' Radcliffe interrupted, his voice fascinated. 'You're saying that kids pick up on family secrets and get – what was your word? Obsessed with things that are forbidden? Is that the case?'

'Of course,' blustered Cath, 'I don't mean that *your* family has a secret, I just wondered if . . .' She tried to change the subject. 'Her writing skills are really coming along . . .'

But the man was simply staring at her. She looked down, searching for other topics, but when she looked back up, he was standing, as if it was all decided. Or as if he was too excited to keep still. *Good heavens*, thought Cath, and also stood up.

'Look,' said Radcliffe, reaching into his pocket. 'Here's my business card. Any time you need to talk about our little Cass, give me a call at work. My advice is to leave my wife well out of it. She's under a lot of stress at the moment – so best, by far the best, if you call me. All right?' He pressed the card into her hand. 'Just *wonderful* to meet you!'

And then he was outside the classroom door, but facing inward and wiping his feet on the mat, confused. 'Ha ha,' he said, pointing down. Then he spun around, waving, calling, 'Looks like rain!' as he headed out into the night.

'Good grief,' murmured Cath and glanced to the back of the classroom.

Warren did not have a parent with him yet, and had been bowing his head, listening to the interview. He grinned now, widening his eyes, and she widened her eyes in return. Then he pulled one of those faces of his, one side of the mouth down, the other side up.

Oh God, thought Cath, laughing. *I am still in love. He is still in love with me.*

Then a gathering of parents arrived.

Afterwards, while the last parents were opening their umbrellas at the doorway, ready to run into the rain, Warren joined her at the front of the room. Outside it was dark and heavy with rain. Inside it was warm with a strange, orange light. Cath felt his breath and his body next to her and believed he was going to kiss her. As soon as the parents' voices faded, he would close the space between them.

But when the voices faded, Warren remained apart, watching the rain. In a slow, heavy voice he said, 'I don't know what to do.'

'No,' agreed Cath.

But she did: close the space, Warren, that's all.

Warren stood still at the edge of the space, and Cath stood beside him, her arms by her side, and waited.

31

There was something important in the jungle on the dentist's ceiling, but Cassie did not know what it was. Something about the two cheetahs, running away from the jungle.

'Can I go back to the dentist, Mum?'

'Whatever for?'

They had just pulled up outside the school gate on Monday morning, and the engine was running.

'Nothing,' said Cassie. 'But can I?'

'Does your tooth hurt, darling? You must tell me if it does.'

'Which tooth?' said Cassie.

'Any tooth, Cassie. Any tooth at all. Have you got an umbrella? Have you got your note for Ms Murphy?'

'Yes,' said Cassie listlessly.

'Yes, umbrella? Yes, note? Don't forget the note now, will you? Give it to Ms Murphy the moment you see her, OK? Darling, your uniform's all funny!'

Cassie, standing on the footpath outside the car, untwisted her uniform until her mother was content. After her mother drove away, she twisted it back around again. It was warmer that way.

In Fancy's opinion, a choice had to be made when your husband said something unkind. Specifically: be cruel, be strong or sulk.

'Be cruel' by saying an unkind thing back.

'Be strong' by choosing not to mind. But to do this, you have to use up a piece of your love. You have to shave off enough of the love to forgive. After a while, the piece might grow back, but sometimes not. And if you shave off all the soft curves, you'll be left with a sharp-edged love.

'Sulk' by sulking. Sulking is simply delaying the choice to be cruel or strong.

On Tuesday morning, Fancy woke and remembered she had made a counselling appointment. She lay in bed sadly for a moment, realizing that she ought to have cancelled it – there was now no point in going. Radcliffe was not having an affair. Still, she thought, it was odd she had *believed* it for so long.

And then, almost immediately, she found herself imagining a discussion with a counsellor. 'I set up this meeting because I started to think that my husband was having an affair. Stupid, isn't it? I had absolutely *no reason* to think it, but I just couldn't stop!'

In response, the counsellor flinched slightly and said, 'Oh, *Fancy*, I'm so sorry to tell you this, but women *do* know when their husbands are cheating. Even if there seems to be no evidence, you just *sense* it.'

'Really?' Fancy said tearfully.

'Really,' the counsellor confirmed.

With a flutter of hope, Fancy called to Radcliffe in the bathroom: 'Radcliffe! I need to ask you something. Are you busy today? I need to talk to you.'

Radcliffe was surprisingly cheerful about the marriage counselling, even at such short notice. 'Huh,' he said, naked, both hands on the shower taps. 'A *refresher* course for the marriage, eh? Why not?'

But in the apple-green office of the Winston Hills Family Counselling Centre, it did not go according to plan. For a start, the counsellor was a pale, thin, bald man who crossed his legs, and then twisted his ankles as well. As if he wanted to braid his legs.

Bravely, Fancy began her speech: 'Well, I set up this meeting because I started to think that my husband was having an affair. Stupid, isn't it? I had absolutely *no reason* to think –'

Beside her, Radcliffe was gaping. '*Fance*,' he began, 'what on *earth* –'

The counsellor interrupted by slowly unplaiting his legs. 'Well,' he said, smiling kindly at Fancy, 'that's *one* thing for us to work through. First, let me assure you, Fancy, that irrational fears like this are common at this stage in a marriage. You're approaching middle age, and I'd guess you're fearing that your husband is losing interest in you. You fear that he may be growing bored, looking elsewhere – am I right?'

Radcliffe and the counsellor both gazed at Fancy, waiting for her response. 'Approaching middle age,' she murmured. 'I'm only thirty-four, you know.'

The two men took this to be a joke and laughed appreciatively.

The counsellor spent some time asking Fancy about her days, and about her coping mechanisms.

'My coping mechanisms?'

'The place you go to when you start to panic about things like approaching middle age?'

Fancy admitted that she liked to imagine herself calming a pair of angry seagulls. Also, she liked to imagine herself in a hotel lobby. Finally, she sometimes liked to remember Radcliffe's marriage proposal.

The men were very quiet as she listed her 'coping mechanisms', and when she reached the marriage proposal she felt a hand squeezing her shoulder. It was Radcliffe: she turned and saw that his eyes had become misty.

'This is just the opener session,' the counsellor reminded them. 'Please don't expect *everything* to be solved today. Fancy, we will work through your stresses, be assured, and we'll work on your coping mechanisms. For now, we're just laying the table.' Then he gave them each a notebook and pen and asked them to write letters, which they would then exchange, explaining the things they disliked about each other.

'*Dis*like?' cried Fancy.

'Dislike. Trust me, OK?'

Fancy and Radcliffe sat side by side in the counsellor's office, resting their notepads on their knees. Radcliffe chewed on the end of the pen, chuckled quietly and began to write. Fancy hesitated. This could not possibly be right. Her own method – writing Irritating Things in a secret notebook which Radcliffe never saw – was surely superior. Afterwards, she might take the counsellor aside and suggest it as a new technique. Did he not realize the impact that exchanging these letters would have? Radcliffe would have to choose to be cruel, be strong or sulk. As would she. If either chose to be cruel, the cycle could go on forever.

Maybe you were supposed to answer cleverly, pretending to say what you disliked, but actually revealing the depth of your love. Like a job interview, when asked about your weaknesses.

On the other hand, the counsellor wanted the 'table laid'. Perhaps he meant them to 'express' their irritations for their own good? Very well, she would express herself, but she would do so in such a way that Radcliffe could never understand.

> Dear Radcliffe,
> Leave it! Leave it! I'll do that.
> Tap, tap, tap.
> Tap, tap, tap.
> Fancy! Ha! My dog –
> Fancy! Grrr, just clear my throat!
> Leave it! Leave it! I'll do that!

Tap, tap, tap.
Tap, tap, tap.

Lots of love,
Fancy

DEAR FANCY,
I WOULD MUCH PREFER TO SAY THE THINGS THAT I LIKE
ABOUT YOU, FANCE. BUT UNFORTUNATELY THE ASSIGNMENT IS
THE THINGS THAT ARE ANNOYING. SO, HERE GOES.

- TO BE FRANK, I AM NOT FOND OF YOUR MOLES.
- OCCASIONALLY, YOU DON'T ASK ME HOW MY DAY WAS.
- YOU SHOULDN'T SIGH SO MUCH WHILE WASHING UP. EITHER
  DO IT OR DON'T, BUT DON'T SIGH.
- I DON'T LIKE YOUR SULTANA CAKE.
- IT'S WASTEFUL THE WAY YOU DON'T DRINK ALL THE WINE
  THAT I POUR INTO YOUR GLASS. IS IT HYGIENIC TO TIP IT
  BACK INTO THE BOTTLE? NO.
- YOU ARE SOMETIMES A BIT BORING AND REPETITIVE.

ALL MY LOVE,
RADCLIFFE

On Wednesday, Fancy dropped her car off at Valerio Auto for
a wheel balance and alignment and caught the bus home.

While she was waiting on the bus stairs to pay her fare she
noticed the driver's ID photo hanging from his rear-view
mirror. The photo showed a man in his fifties with a handsome, well-structured face and a winning smile. But when it
was her turn to pay the driver, Fancy saw a *different* man. That
is, she saw the same man with the handsome, well-structured
face – only the face had a glowering scowl.

For the entire bus trip, Fancy watched the driver and his
expression remained the same. She imagined to herself the
time when the photograph was taken: how the man was

perhaps delighted to get the job, how maybe all his life he had wanted to be a bus driver and here was his dream come true! They were giving him his uniform and taking his ID photo: he was joking with the photographer and grinning in joy!

And then, what happened? Was it a personal tragedy? Or was it just the daily grinding of the gears, the folding and unfolding of the doors, beeping of buttons telling him to stop, tickets, inspectors, teenagers pretending to be younger than they were, people leaning forward to ask where to get off, feet on seats and spilling Coke cans? Was it just the day-to-day that did this?

Fancy cried the whole way home. She tried to comfort herself by recalling that this Friday she would meet Cath Murphy. *For the first time ever, I am going to talk to Cath face to face.* But this made her cry all the more.

Thursday afternoon, Fancy was working on her prize-winning novel. *Look for characters from everyday life.* She remembered reading that somewhere.

She thought of the scowling bus driver and wondered if he could be a character. It could be a sort of public transport novel. *Transport* could be the language that she taught her readers! Excitedly, she began to research 'transport' on the Internet. She scribbled down the addresses of various useful-sounding websites: why not just list the URLs at the start of every chapter? Why not – and here she became even more excited – *why not just refer her readers to GOOGLE?* 'If you are interested in any of the topics raised in this novel, please enter the following search terms in GOOGLE: bus, train . . .'

'Hmm.' Fancy paused in her frantic scribbling and looked up, frowning to herself.

A faint sound caught her attention. Cassie, she realized, had been standing at her office door, knocking gently, for some time.

'Hello, Cassie!' she said.

'Hello, Mum,' replied Cassie, nodding. 'Can I paint my bedroom ceiling, please?'

'What colour would you like to paint it?' said Fancy, spinning around in her office chair.

'A lot of colours,' Cassie explained. 'It has to be like a jungle. There have to be two cheetahs. But also monkeys, elephants, zebras . . .' Cassie listed the animals on her fingers, but her voice drifted away.

'Well!' said Fancy. 'Why not?'

She and Cassie drove to the hardware store and bought paint, brushes and a small stepladder. Fancy persuaded Cassie that they should put the jungle on one of the walls rather than the ceiling so they would not have to strain their necks.

She was painting stars in the jungle sky while Cassie added ladybirds to the jungle grass when Radcliffe arrived home.

They heard his car in the driveway.

Then they heard his voice at the front door: 'Fancy that! My Fancy is at home!'

Cassie held her paintbrush still for a moment and looked up. 'Mum?' she said. 'How come he never says "Fancy that, my Cassie is at home"?'

Fancy looked down at her daughter.

'Or else,' said Cassie, painting again, '"*Cassie* that, my Cassie is at home". How come he doesn't say that?'

'That's a good question, Cassie,' Fancy replied.

Friday afternoon, Fancy was choosing earrings to wear to the Parent–Teacher interview when Cassie appeared at her bedroom door, sneezing to herself.

'Hello, Cassie!' said Fancy, glancing at her in the mirror. 'I thought you were playing outside.'

'Hello, Mum,' said Cassie and coughed.

Fancy continued to hold various earrings against her ear.

'Mum?' said Cassie, after a moment.

'Yes, darling?'

'Can I show you my foot?'

'I've already seen your foot!' Fancy joked, and then, when there was nothing but quiet wheezing from Cassie, she turned around and looked at her daughter properly. 'All right then, let's see your – my *God*, Cassie, *what have you done?*'

Cassie's right foot was the size of a loaf of bread. Her face was swollen like home-baked banana muffins. She was scratching her arms and her stomach.

'I got stung by a bee,' she explained. 'And I'm allergic to bees, aren't I?' Then she slid down the door frame to the bedroom floor, whispering, 'I can't really breathe very well.'

Radcliffe arrived home from work just as Fancy was carrying her daughter out the front door.

'Bee sting,' she called, jogging across to her car in the driveway. 'I'm taking her to the hospital.'

Radcliffe slammed his car door. 'Did you give her the injection?' he said.

'And she's had an antihistamine,' Fancy nodded. 'She's already feeling better, aren't you, darling? We'll just get the doctors to make sure.'

Radcliffe approached and opened the car door for Fancy. 'But her eyes! Cassie, are your eyes all right?'

'They're just a bit itchy,' said Fancy breezily, closing the door on her daughter.

'They're getting better,' Cassie called through the window.

'Just relax there, Cass,' suggested Fancy, getting into the driver's seat.

Radcliffe hovered anxiously and said, 'I'll just stay here, shall I? Or shall I come along?'

Fancy put the car into reverse and pressed the accelerator to the floor.

*

When they returned it was ten o'clock and Cassie was fast asleep. Fancy carried her into her bedroom, changed her into pyjamas and then sat on the edge of the bed and watched her daughter sleeping.

Radcliffe hovered, whispering, 'She's all right?'

Fancy nodded.

They went into the kitchen for a cup of tea, and Fancy told him about the doctor's suggestion that they get Cassie into a desensitization program.

'I think her allergy's getting worse,' said Fancy, 'so maybe it's time we looked into that?'

Radcliffe nodded, but he seemed distracted. 'By the way,' he said, filling up the kettle for more tea. 'I suppose you're upset about missing the Parent–Teacher Night?'

'Oh,' said Fancy, remembering.

'Well,' said Radcliffe, 'good news! I called the school and managed to speak to Cath. I explained that you couldn't make it and asked if you could have another appointment. She promised to call you to arrange it.'

'You spoke to her?!'

'Only for a moment and only on the phone,' said Radcliffe firmly. 'Don't worry yourself, Fance. Just as we all agreed, *you'll* be the first to meet Cath in person. All right? And you'll get to do that *on your own*.'

'Well!' Fancy was moved. 'Thank you so much, Radcliffe.'

Radcliffe nodded and looked earnest for a moment. 'Like your mother says,' he declared, 'the restraint you've shown this year has been commendable. It would have been so easy for you to make an excuse to meet with her. But no. You exercised caution and waited till the proper time. All you have to do now is wait a little longer, and she'll give you a call.'

Fancy blinked the tears out of her eyes.

32

Monday lunchtime, Listen wandered, pretending she was going somewhere, but in her mind she was climbing the outside wall of the Redwood central building. She could see hand- and footholds all over that wall – window ledges, jutting bricks, waterpipes – and she was getting very fast at her rock-climbing classes.

Imagine this: there is a Year 1 kid trapped on a window ledge up there; Listen climbs the side of the wall and rescues the kid in an instant; most of Year 7 watches in awe from the school yard below.

Then, after lunch, at her Science class, imagine this: an intruder surprises them, planning to take the class hostage: silently, Listen slips out of her seat – 'Stay down!' she whispers, and girls hunch over their desks with startled eyes as Listen runs and leaps – a flying side kick across the *entire* classroom! It ends with a dramatic thump of her foot against the whiteboard, which sends the board spinning. This distracts the intruder so much that next she overcomes him with a series of spinning hook kicks, chair splits, side kicks (straight up), flying back kicks and double knifehand guarding blocks.

Breathless, one foot on the chest of the astonished intruder (now lying flat on the floor), Listen glances back at the class. They are weeping with fear and relief, but also applauding.

Another thing: that Redwood teacher – Mr Bel Castro – he happens to be taking the class, by chance, and he gazes at her in amazement and says, *I like that.*

Having walked out into the night, to post her letter to
Nathaniel, Marbie sat in her beanbag and reflected, against a
backdrop of growing alarm, on just how much she missed
him.

She remembered a time when she had arranged to meet
Nathaniel and Listen in Castle Hill but, half an hour before
the meeting time, she had seen them in the distance by chance.
Nathaniel had also seen her, and had stopped still, dropping
his shopping bags to the floor, opening out his face and his
arms in an enormous, wondrous smile, shaking his head, as if
to say: 'Look who's here!' while Listen giggled beside him.

Also, she remembered how patient he was with her nightmares and sleepwalking. How she would wake in a panic from
a nightmare and, from the darkness beside her, Nathaniel
would speak calmly in his daytime voice and say, 'Marbie? Are
you OK?'

She remembered that when she touched him on a knee or
a forearm, he would continue with conversation, but casually,
as he talked, he would cover her touch with a touch of his
own, the tiniest pressure from his thumb.

She remembered also the bursts of love she had experienced when she saw him hunched over papers, working on ideas for the Banana Bar. Or when she saw how kind he was with his daughter – how seriously he took her education and how he knew all the names and hobbies of her friends.

Now Marbie knew it was time to confront herself. Why had she started an affair with an aeronautical engineer? She sank deeper into the beanbag and closed her eyes.

Certainly, there had been a strange low buzz between them which she supposed was chemistry. He had seemed like an adventure parachuting into her otherwise dull work life. It was just as if a waiter had unexpectedly brought a hot bread roll. 'Wow, a special treat!' she might have thought, before she realized that they had heated the roll for a reason. The A.E.'s purples and paisleys, his visions and surprising invitations: they were all just hiding the fact that he was stale.

She made herself consider the theory of Toni from work. 'It's because you had just moved in with Nathaniel and his kid,' Toni had informed her. 'You were running for your life!' Could it have been about Nathaniel? Had she been reacting, subconsciously, to all the indications that here was the rest of her life? After all, she had bought an apartment with him *and* she had told him the Zing Family Secret. The level of commitment was impressive, and perhaps overwhelming.

That's just nonsense. I was ecstatic about life with Nathaniel. I considered him perfect. I was terrified of losing him! I thought I had to concentrate on keeping the luck – I was obsessed with ladders and black cats! I was afraid of making the simplest decisions – what to wear to work, whether to leave paper clips under my desk – just in case one tiny thing would end it. I saw catastrophe at every corner, and the suspense was killing me.

And there it was.

Marbie's eyelids fluttered as she shifted slightly in her beanbag. It was clear to her just for a moment. If she was going to lose Nathaniel at some unknown moment in her future, she had better make it happen at once. If a catastrophe was flying at high speed towards her, she would move to be directly in its path.

She found she was drifting towards sleep. Already, her revelation was splintering into confusion. She fumbled for its words, but found there was nothing in her mind any more except small, sharp images, the pinpoints of tiny paper clips skimming through the air.

Wednesday, Listen was summoned out of morning roll-call by a woman in a cardigan and wooden earrings. 'Might I borrow Listen Taylor?' said the woman from the door, and the roll-call teacher said, 'Why not?'

The woman introduced herself to Listen as they walked across the school. Her name was Ms Woodford and she was the Redwood counsellor. Her office was very small – the size of a broom closet – but every surface was covered with paper lanterns, paper swans, paper bears and paperweights. There was also a picture of a fox on the wall.

Although Ms Woodford seemed like a nice person, Listen was confused about what she herself was doing sitting in her office.

After chatting about how warm it was getting, and how difficult it was to remember the snow, Ms Woodford asked what Listen's parents did for a living. Listen explained that her mother was in Paris, or maybe Peru, and had been on vacation since Listen was a baby. Also, she added, since the counsellor seemed keen to hear more, also, she and her dad used to live in a camper van outside her dad's Banana Bar, then they lived with her dad's girlfriend, Marbie, but now they lived in the camper van again.

'*Oh!*' Ms Woodford was upset about everything. 'You

know, it's not your fault that your mum ran away when you were a baby, don't you?'

Listen nodded, intrigued. Of course it wasn't her fault.

'And you live in a camper van!' She seemed so upset by this that Listen had to reassure her: 'It's OK. I don't really mind. I mean, I miss Marbie and that. But it's fine.'

Ms Woodford played with a square of construction paper and turned it into a rose.

'Cool,' said Listen. 'How did you do that?'

'So,' said Ms Woodford, not answering. 'How's school for you?'

Listen looked at the rose and said, 'Fine.'

'Uh-huh. Plenty of friends to muck around with then?'

Muck around with, thought Listen. *What did that mean?* 'Yep,' she said, staring at the paper rose, which she now thought was maybe just a cabbage. 'I go to Tae Kwon Do and also rock climbing after school. I've got some friends there.'

'And friends at this school?'

'Well, this is not really our school, so it's all kind of different,' she tried.

'No, but I mean in your year? Your own year?'

'Yep,' said Listen, 'plenty.'

After that, Ms Woodford chatted about how happy she was to be a school counsellor at Redwood Primary, and how Listen could come and see her *any time she liked*, and then she was allowed back to class.

It was true that she had friends outside of school. Anyway, she was kind of friends with Carl at Tae Kwon Do. He sometimes spoke to her after class, and there had been that thumb-war incident. Also, the other day she had noticed a Bellbird High emblem on his bag, and she had actually walked up to him and said, 'I know the people who live in the house next door to your school.' Carl seemed surprisingly happy to hear it. 'Really?' he said, grinning like she'd told him she knew where he could get a year's supply of Gatorade for free (he was always tipping back an empty bottle of Gatorade when she saw him after class, trying to get the last drops). He seemed to want more information, so she added, 'I used to go to their place every Friday night.'

He said she should look out for him because he stayed back late on Fridays for violin. She didn't get a chance to explain that she had actually stopped going to the Zings' on Friday nights, because the others at Tae Kwon Do were laughing at Carl for being a black belt who played violin.

Furthermore, at rock climbing, there was a girl named Samalia Janz with a ponytail, who always said 'Hi' and 'See you' as if Listen were a regular person. Listen was pretty sure that they would soon have a real conversation. It had occurred to her that Samalia might be even more shy than she was. She herself was going to have to start the conversation.

After school that day Listen collected the mail from their post office box, but there were just two letters for her dad.

She walked the letters back to the Banana Bar and did not press the button at the traffic lights. Instead, she ran to the middle of the road, waited as a truck skimmed past her and then ran again.

Her dad was eating a chocolate-coated banana in the empty shop. He was sitting on the counter and swinging his legs. 'Whatcha got?' he said, trying to see the envelopes.

'Nothing.' Listen sat up beside him on the counter.

He leaned back and got her a chocolate banana of her own.

'Hey,' he said, when he had opened the first envelope. 'This is from your school. Did you know they were going to do this?'

'Do what?'

'A camp,' said her dad. 'They've fixed your classrooms so you'll be able to go back in a couple of weeks. And they're taking you all to the mountains the weekend after next, because you've been good sports. Good sports. It says it right here. See that?'

'How about that,' said Listen.

'I always knew you were a good sport, Listen. And now here it is in print. Wait a second. Now it says they're going to do some extra lessons at the camp to make up for the classes you've missed. So, the camp's also compulsory.'

'Compulsory?' said Listen. 'It can't be.'

'Which is it? Is it a special treat because you're such good sports, or is it compulsory because you're behind in school work?' Her dad was holding up the letter and shaking it: 'Make up your mind!'

'Who's the other letter from?'

He picked up the second envelope – it was brown, with strange pieces of bark and string embedded in the paper.

'Nobody,' he said, and put it in his pocket.

On the doormat there was a large pink envelope, addressed with the single word 'Marbie' in swirling purple ink. 'More poetry.' She frowned, recognizing the A.E.'s style.

Inside the envelope, just as she suspected, there was another of the A.E.'s visions.

THE VISIONS OF AN AERONAUTICAL ENGINEER
VISION # 1563

DEEP INSIDE THE TURNPIKES OF MY CRISPY FRAGRANT DUCK,
I SEE THIS, I SEE THIS, I SEE
ANGUISH, A BROKEN HEART!
ABANDONMENT!
ALSO, I SEE A MAN WITH A HAT UPON HIS HEAD.
AND A CAT UPON THE HAT,
AND A MAT UPON THE –
NO. WAIT. THAT'S NOT MINE.
LOOK. FORGET I SAID A WORD.

'Well,' said Marbie aloud, 'so much for *his* broken heart.'

Then she found a typed note glued to the back of the vision.

Marbleweed! I miss you! Come back to me!
In the alternative, please see the following:

RE: YOUR FAMILY SECRET

I HAVE ARRANGED A MEETING WITH CATH
MURPHY AT 1 O'CLOCK TOMORROW. AT THAT
MEETING, I INTEND TO TELL HER
EVERYTHING I KNOW!
DELIVER $50,000 IN CASH TO MY HOUSE BY
NOON AND I WILL STAND HER UP.
FAIL TO DELIVER AND THE GAME WILL BE
UP!!!!!!!!!!!
THE CHOICE IS YOURS.

Marbie sneezed hay-feverishly. She had suspected it was too much to hope that she could simply walk away from the A.E. and his little brush fires.

She stood in her doorway now, rereading the letter. Certainly, she would not allow him to blackmail her like this. That much was clear. She supposed she would have to resume her evening visits to his house. She would have to watch TV with him, and eat his crunchy lasagne, and argue with him about the Secret. 'But I don't want to sleep with him again,' she pointed out firmly.

Then she realized with a slow shock that she would *have* to sleep with him again. If she resumed her visits, eventually he would greet her in his boxers and bow tie again, and say, 'Marbie, this can *not* go on.'

'No,' said Marbie, raising her eyebrows, 'it cannot.' He *had* been blackmailing her. She just had not seen it.

She walked back into the house, clapping her hands

together softly, which was her way of thinking. Then she sat at her computer and began to type.

Sir,

I write with respect to a patient of mine (Marbleweed Zing). Ms Zing informed me recently that she had commenced a 'relationship' with you. I was delighted to hear it - her condition generally frightens the fellows away.

As she will have informed you, Ms Zing suffers from severe paranoid delusions, generally revolving around her parent's garden shed. When suffering from these delusions, she believes such things as: the shed appears only when it rains; the shed is used as a base for spying on a second-grade school teacher; aliens have eaten the shed (catalogued delusions: #32, #49 and #102) - and so on.

I hope that Ms Zing has not succumbed to any of these delusions in your presence; however, she can be absent-minded and occasionally forgets to take her medication.

It has occurred to me that you might like to assist her in this manner. Occasional, gentle reminders can do a world of good - as you no doubt know, she is somewhat embarrassed by her (anti-psychotic) pills (they are inconspicuous, small and red) and conceals them with her hay-fever medication. Take them out of the plastic! Dangle them good-naturedly before her nose! Tap her on the head with the box! Little things like this can only help.

Finally, Ms Zing mentioned that you write 'visions' because you have a sort of artistic 'beast' tearing away at your insides. My professional view

Marbie had sufficient software, precedent letterheads, thick stationery and authoritative stamps to make the letter look genuine. The Zings had stockpiles of such equipment.

Also, fortunately, she was accustomed to breaking into other people's homes. In fact, Intrusion and Maintenance used to be *her* field of expertise, until Cath got the cat, which made Marbie sneeze and affected her work.

Although the A.E. was a nuisance, she was happy to be doing another break-in, for old time's sake. She drove to his neighbourhood at 2 a.m., parked a block away, put the letter in his box, broke in through the bathroom window and planted, in his top bathroom cabinet drawer, a box of her hay-fever tablets. Inside the box she had hidden two small red pills.

Down the hallway, she could hear the A.E. mutter and grumble in his sleep. 'Tch,' she said to herself and climbed back out into the street.

She was home again by 2.15 a.m.

Afterwards, when the adrenalin had faded, Marbie lay in bed alone, wondering at herself. It had been foolish enough to get involved with the A.E. in the first place, but why had she entangled herself further by telling him the Secret? She had never told anyone before Nathaniel and requesting permission to tell *him* had seemed such a turning point. Her mother and

Fancy had formed a sub-committee who decided that she was sufficiently committed to Nathaniel, that he was sufficiently in love with her, that he was an all-round wonderful guy and that therefore she could tell him.

It was as if she had announced her engagement. Everyone congratulated her, and Radcliffe said mysteriously, 'You'll keep him forever now, you know – the Secret's got a lot of pull with your average bloke.'

Her memory of telling the A.E. was less clear. She recalled a sensation of urgency: a compulsion to tell. Yet she must have known the risk. He could have used it to ruin her family. Had she *wanted* to ruin her family?

Her drowsy mind began to toss images about: her mother pulling the shed door closed; her father squinting at surveillance equipment; Fancy leaping smartly from a window to a tree. She was confused. *There was something, she thought, so exquisitely fragile about these images. Her family, it seemed to her now, were always on the verge of catastrophe.*

Of course they were. Their entire life was built on the foundation of a secret. All it would take was one small slip and the foundation would collapse. *The suspense*, said Marbie's mind, *was killing you.*

This was a familiar idea. Had a lifetime of suspense about the Secret found its way into every corner of her life? Was she constantly pre-empting disaster by welcoming it in?

Or was it that she knew how foolish she had been to sleep with the A.E. in the first place? By telling him the Secret she made their connection serious. She changed the nature of their story: it was love! It must have been, otherwise why had she told him the Secret?!

Marbie's ideas began to fragment again: she saw sea urchins sink to the ocean floor; she saw Fancy, a teenager, standing in the beach house, declaring she had done something incredible. A chalkboard stood outside a beachside takeaway: rain fell against it languidly, washing away the specials.

Dearest Nathaniel,
J'll tell you one of the many things that J love about you.
    The way you can take two cans of Coke from the fridge in a shop, and carry them to the counter in one hand. You can hold two cans of Coke, one for me and one for you, in a single, outstretched hand.

Love,
Marbie

Early on Friday morning, Listen remembered she was allowed to do the next spell. Her dad was in the Banana Bar, so she had the camper van to herself. There were only a few pages left in the book, she realized, and the spell began by declaring itself to be the third from last.

> *Yep, only two more Spells after this one!*
> *And then? All will be well! Why, you may ask? Ask no questions and I'll tell you no lies. Curiosity and the cat, eh? No use crying over spilled milk? No use at all! Go ahead and mop it up! By the way, after this Spell, you can do the next Spell the Thursday after next!!*

The Spell Book was getting manic.

> *Anyway, here is a Spell To Make a Person Get Stung By a Bee.*

Listen paused. She had been determined not to do any more spells that could hurt people, and bee stings stung.

Still, only two more spells, and *all would be well*. And people were always getting stung by bees – it was no big deal.

```
┌─────────────────────────────────────────────┐
│                   Ingredients                 │
│                      You                      │
│              A Complete Stranger              │
│                                               │
│                    Method                     │
│    Introduce yourself to the Complete Stranger by   │
│  shaking the Stranger's hand, saying 'Hi!' and giving │
│    your name. Now, say the following things to the   │
│        Complete Stranger (in the following order):   │
│        • Are you, by any chance, the sorcerer?       │
│       • Do you, possibly, have the flying carpet?    │
│    • Do you happen to have the ingredients for carrot pie │
│                      handy?                    │
│     • Consider this, Stranger: I have hardly even caught │
│   your name, and yet I feel I know your every thought. │
│                 What can it mean?             │
└─────────────────────────────────────────────┘
```

'Oh, come *on*,' said Listen, and she threw the book on to the camper-van floor.

Later that day, the final bell was ringing when the counsellor put her head in the door of Listen's classroom and called, 'May I borrow Listen Taylor again?'

Listen followed her across the school playground but this time they did not go to her office. Instead, they stopped outside the library door. The Redwood school library was one small room with plate-glass windows, through which you could see a cartoon hippopotamus glued to the wall. A stuffed-toy zebra ate leaves from a crêpe-paper tree, and picture books were opened on display.

A girl stood just outside the library door. Her hair fell into her eyes and she was wearing torn jeans and a small gold stud in her chin.

'Here you are again,' said Ms Woodford, smiling at the girl as though she did not have a gold stud in her chin.

'Listen Taylor, I'd like you to meet a new student – this is Annie Webb. She's just moved to the area and will be joining your school next week! I've given Annie a quick tour, but I thought I might let *you* tell her all about life here at Redwood, not to mention life at Clareville College. OK?'

'OK,' agreed Listen, politely.

Ms Woodford hurried away towards the staffroom.

Annie Webb stepped away from the library door, so now they were standing in the middle of the path, staring at one another.

'So,' said the new girl, and scratched the skin around her chin-stud. They both turned and watched Ms Woodford crossing the playground.

'Mmm,' agreed Listen.

'Whatever,' said the new girl.

They both laughed.

'What was your last school like?' Listen tried.

'A rat-hole,' said Annie.

'Yeah,' said Listen. 'Well, this one is too. It's only temporary, because of the flood. Not that Clareville is any better.'

The new girl nodded slowly and swivelled on the heel of her shoe. 'I might not be coming to your school anyway,' she said. 'I didn't tell that teacher, but my mum and me are checking out a couple in the area today. So we can make a proper decision. Anyway, what did she say your name was again?'

Well, thought Listen, *I have nothing to lose.*

'Hi,' she said, holding out her hand to shake the new girl's hand. 'I'm Listen Taylor. Are you, by any chance, the sorcerer? Do you, possibly, have the flying carpet? Do you happen to have the ingredients for carrot pie handy? Consider this, Stranger: I have hardly even caught your name, and yet I feel I know your every thought. What can it mean?'

Annie Webb was staring. Eventually she whispered, 'Did you just ask for the ingredients of carrot pie?'

Listen bit her lower lip.

'Wow,' said Annie, shaking her head slowly. 'You really think you know my every thought?'

Listen was not sure how to answer or explain without breaking the spell. She tried to put a mysterious expression on her face.

'I have to go now.' Annie walked backwards away from her. She didn't seem to need to see where she was going; she continued to watch Listen carefully as she walked. 'My mum's waiting, so I have to go. Maybe I'll see you next week if I choose this school? Though I've got to say, I probably won't choose it. The uniform sucks.'

Listen nodded.

Anaphylactic shock, said Marbie to herself. It was late Friday night, and Fancy had phoned her from the hospital to let her know that Cassie had been stung by a bee.

'But she knows she's allergic,' Marbie said. 'What was she doing outside in bare feet?'

Fancy explained that she had actually been wearing sandals, but, according to Cassie, the bee had *wanted* to sting her.

'What I don't understand,' said Marbie, 'is why a bee would want to sting someone. Don't they die as soon as they use their sting?'

Fancy suggested that the bee did not know.

Now Marbie sat in the beanbag and thought about bees, wasps, peanut dust and funnel web spiders hidden in sneakers. She thought about how you could run over the cord of an electric lawnmower, or slip on an ice cube and knock yourself out, or accidentally leave the gas on and fall into a coma. A beach umbrella could stab you between the eyes. You could suffocate in this very beanbag.

Part 17

The Thursday After Next

33

Two weeks later, almost midnight on a Thursday night, Cath Murphy lay beneath her feather-down quilt and waited.

'We just need to wait,' Warren had promised, again, that morning. 'It's seriously coming to a head – Breanna and I don't love each other any more. It's gone. The love is gone.'

Cath sat up now on the side of her bed and stamped in sudden fury on the floor. Then she calmed herself and climbed back underneath the covers. She lay still, patiently.

A steamroller started at her toes and clanked against the bolts in her knees. Her thighs and her stomach were flattened now and her neck and her face quite crushed.

Almost midnight, the same Thursday night, Fancy Zing sat on the living-room floor and studiously turned the pages of a prize-winning novel.

Radcliffe wandered into the room, in boxer shorts and sports socks, nodded at her on the floor and picked up the crocheted blanket from the couch.

'That's the ticket!' He lay down on the couch, carefully positioning the blanket over his body and closed his eyes.

'Haven't heard from Cath yet, have you?' he said, after a while.

'No,' she said, and turned another page. 'I'm still waiting.'

'Well, she promised she'd call. I'm sure she will. Goodnight then.' He snuggled into the couch.

Fancy read on for a moment. Then she looked up at Radcliffe: at his socks with their ribbed ankles and the hole where his big toe poked out. His elbows seemed to stretch at the blanket. His eyes seemed self-consciously closed.

'I love you, Fancy,' said Radcliffe unexpectedly, in a sleepy drawl, without opening his eyes.

'Thank you,' she said politely, and she took a breath and added, 'Me too.'

Radcliffe chuckled and turned to face the wall. The blanket slipped slightly to the floor.

Meanwhile, Cassie lay in bed and reflected on the crankiness. There was so much around that she could hear it.

First, it had happened at school: Ms Murphy had talked in a loud smile like an ad for Kmart. 'Well now!' she had said. 'Let's say we talk about dinosaurs!'

'Let's say we bring in some dinosaurs for show and tell!' said Mark Baxter.

Ms Murphy screamed as if Mark had shown her a tarantula. But the scream turned out to be a laugh.

At home, her father had talked all night about pedestrian crossings. Her mother lined up the mugs on one side of the dishwasher, threw the dishcloth on to the floor and moved the mugs to the other side.

Now Cassie could hear the scritchy, angry noise of crankiness. It was a sound that scrabbled at the edges of other sounds. When she turned over in bed, for example, the rustle of her sheets and the elastic bounce of the mattress were exaggerated. Even the sounds she made herself – she made a 'hmm' sound to test it – even these sounds were louder than usual, collecting the crankiness around them. It was like those days when she had asthma and didn't notice at first – she'd be walking around happily and then would realize that an extra sound, the sound of her own wheezing, was scrabbling around the edges of her breath.

Almost midnight, the same Thursday night, Marbie twitched and clicked in her sleep. She was dreaming of a letter she was writing at work: the penultimate paragraph, in this dream, had dislodged itself from the rest of the letter and its words were clattering like marbles to the floor.

Marbie woke with a gasp at the sound of the marbles and peered into the deep spring darkness of the room. She waited for the shadows to take shape.

In the camper van behind the Banana Bar, Listen lay awake and thought of: recess, lunchtime, after school, before school, choose-a-partner, form-a-team and, worst of all, she thought: *school camp*.

The school camp would begin tomorrow morning. It would span the weekend and half of Monday. She had tried to persuade her father to send an excuse letter, but he took her education too seriously.

'I could stay and help in the cafe,' she had offered, 'and catch up on my homework. In the long run, it would be better for both of us.'

'I'm not letting you miss out on a camp to help in the cafe,' he had replied calmly. 'What kind of a father would I be? Don't worry, you'll have a great time. Donna and the others will be there, won't they?'

Now Listen's head was so heavy she was surprised that the pillow could hold it. She thought she might go outside, climb a telegraph pole and get electrocuted. Or else climb under the camper-van bunk bed where a snake might poison her. Anything was better than a weekend full of bus seats, cabins, free time, night-time.

- Bus seats – she would walk down the aisle of the school-camp bus past girls with their bags and their legs curled beside them, meaning: *This seat is saved for a friend.*
- Cabins – girls would crowd around bulletin boards filling in *ten* names, *ten* friends for a cabin.

- Free time – 'OK,' the teachers would say, 'everybody off now, out of our hair, *for the entire day*!' and girls would rush to the bush, to the bathroom, to the lake.
- Night-time – 'OK,' the teachers would say, 'lights off, everybody quiet!' and girls would cluster together for séances or smoking or climbing out through windows.

The clock-radio, which they kept on the camper-van sink, said 11.56 p.m. She had gone to bed at ten and was still not asleep. Only four more minutes until Friday, she thought sadly.

Then she realized that meant four minutes left of Thursday, and *she had not yet done the next spell*. The second last spell in the book. She had been so distracted by the school camp she had forgotten it. Now it would be too late. She could never do a whole spell in four minutes.

Unless it was one of those short spells.

She took the book from under her pillow and picked up her reading torch from the camper-van floor.

In her sleep, Cath waited, hopefully.

Fancy looked up from her novel and remembered one of her favourite conversations with the Canadian next door. It had happened just after the snowstorm.

'Did I tell you my mother swept up the snow on her front porch with a dustpan and broom?' she had said to him one morning. 'She tipped it into the kitchen tidy bin.'

The Canadian laughed. 'Wait till I write home about that,' he said.

'Where is home anyway?' she asked.

'Canada.'

'No, but where in Canada?'

'Where is Canada?' He looked concerned.

'No, no! Where *in* Canada?'

'Oh!' He was relieved. 'I grew up all over, but most recently Montreal.'

'Montreal? Does it snow in Montreal?'

The Canadian laughed again. 'Does it snow in Montreal?' he repeated to himself affectionately.

'OK, then,' said Fancy. 'What's it like, in Montreal, when it snows?'

Obediently, he reflected. 'Sometimes,' he said, 'you get as much as a two-metre snowfall. That's not just decoration when that happens. That changes everything. It changes the terrain.'

'The terrain,' agreed Fancy, pleased: 'It changes the terrain.' Then, since this reminded her: 'I made a chocolate *terrine* last night. Would you like some with your coffee?'

He was surprised, but agreed, and they each ate a piece of chocolate terrine, sitting on their own front porches, watching the melting snow.

Of course, that was back when Radcliffe was having an affair with a woman in purple daisy socks. All that was over now.

She stood up and walked out of the room, not looking at Radcliffe on the couch. She could hear him breathing very deeply tonight, using up everybody's oxygen.

A Spell To Make Someone Catch a Cold!
Simply place this Book under your Pillow, and Think, inside your Head, of Three Small Sharp Objects.

You can do the Next Spell – the Final Spell – tomorrow morning!

Listen did as the Spell Book said just before the clock flicked to midnight. Then she fell asleep, thinking: *bird beaks, thumbtacks, cuttlefish bones, bus seats, cabins, free time, night-time, bird beaks, thumbtacks, cuttlefish bones.*

Marbie fell asleep again, thinking, unexpectedly, of sharp little bird beaks, thumbtacks and pieces of cuttlefish bone.

She sneezed and clicked her throat.

Part 18

The Story of the First Trip

to the Seaside

34

Shortly after her father returned from Ireland, Fancy's family went to the seaside and stayed in a house on the hill.

Each morning, the family gathered their towels, buckets, spades, sun cream, T-shirts and beach umbrella, and tumbled down the hill to the beach.

Each evening, Fancy stood with her back to the mirror and turned her head to see her shoulders. She wore a purple sarong, which she tied in various ways: between her legs, over her shoulder, or around her waist so it flapped low against her ankle chain. Her shoulders, as she watched, turned golden brown.

But one day, Fancy's parents told her to take her sister to the beach on their own. 'We'll just be doing some cleaning here in the house,' said Mummy, 'don't worry about us.'

'Only swim between the flags,' said Daddy.

'Or in the rockpool?' said Marbie.

'Right,' agreed Mummy. 'And I've made you some buttered sandwiches, so you can buy hot chips for your lunch. Give them some money, David.'

'Stay at the beach until they take the flags down,' Daddy reminded them.

Two lifesavers in yellow-red caps marched past the girls, flag-poles on their shoulders, and Marbie said, 'Are the flags down now?'

Fancy, who was making Marbie's towel into a shepherd's veil, agreed, 'Yes. Let's go.' She frowned at her golden shoulders, which were peeling.

'Can I peel some of your skin?' said Marbie, swinging her shepherd's veil.

Fancy allowed her to take three pieces of skin.

They washed the sand from their feet and ankles and walked on the gravel road home. Fancy was carrying the suntan cream, the flippers and the beach umbrella, and Marbie was carrying her flip-flops.

'Put your flip-flops on,' said Fancy, 'or you'll stub your toe.'

'No,' said Marbie, 'because my feet are wet and that makes the flip-flops slippery. Whose car is that?'

From the bottom of the hill they could see their house, but it looked strange and unfamiliar. A long silver car stood in the driveway. They approached slowly and saw that the car was shiny, its windows dark. A sticker on the back window said: 'SEA LION'. Another sticker on the bumper bar said, 'If you can read this sign, back off'.

They ran up the stairs to the veranda and paused at the living-room window. Inside, they could see their mother, sitting on the couch with a straight back and a small, interested tilt to her head. Next to her was their father. And seated in a row of kitchen chairs, their backs to the girls, were three men dressed in black. One of the men, Fancy saw, was tapping a polished shoe on the floor.

Fancy and Marbie stood at the window and watched as Daddy coughed into his fist, Mummy laughed, and the three men in black each picked up a briefcase from the floor. There was a scraping of chairs, a shaking of hands, and the front door opened so that voices and light spilled out on to the veranda.

'Oh!' said Mummy from the front door, seeing the girls.

'We waited till the flags came down,' said Marbie.

The three men stepped out and lowered their heads. One of the men said, 'Girls,' but the others did not appear to see them. One man unlocked the car and opened three doors, politely. The men got into their car.

Then the Zing family stood in a mosquito-slapping row on the veranda and watched as the car slid away.

'Who were they?' said Fancy.

'Nobody,' her father replied.

35

Shortly after her father returned from Ireland, Marbie's family went to the seaside.

Each day, Fancy made Marbie's beach towel into a turban, a crown, or a shepherd's veil. She had to hold her head straight or the towel fell into her eyes, making the world a soft, speckled white. If she shivered slightly, it brushed against her shoulders like long hair.

One day, Fancy and Marbie were allowed to go to the beach on their own until the flags came down. Another day, they woke up and their mother was gone.

Their father was sitting at the head of the table waiting for them. He had placed the box of Coco Pops in the centre of the table, alongside the milk. On the table: three bowls with spoons in straight lines beside them.

Formally, he explained: 'Mummy had to go away for a few days. She will miss you very much.'

'Has she gone to Ireland?' said Marbie, and her father smiled.

The three of them went to the beach, as usual, and had fish and chips for lunch. Daddy wanted to participate in their beach games: he helped with a sandcastle, but wanted to build it higher than was necessary and also wanted to decorate the castle with sea grapes and Popsicle wrappers. The girls grew bored and went for a swim.

As they walked home together in the cooling light, Marbie said, 'Will Mummy be home when we get there?'

'No. Just a couple of days and she'll be back.'

In the kitchen, Fancy set the table for dinner while Marbie

spun in circles. She bumped into a chair, spun away from the chair and landed with her feet apart for balance. Then the room spun itself, the windows tipped, the couch capsized and the clothes rack draped in swimming costumes jumped.

She fell against the chair, which crashed to the floor.

'*Marbie!*' cried Fancy.

Daddy stood at the kitchen door and said, 'Stop it, Marbie. You'll make yourself sick.'

But it never made her sick.

They had sausages for dinner, which Daddy fried with smoke, a tea towel and a frown. They pulled out their chairs and sat down quietly. Daddy took a fork and put sausages on each plate, then cut a tomato into three chunks. Fancy and Marbie looked at each other about the tomato.

That night Marbie lay in her bed and thought that the sound of the waves on the beach was the sound of the silver car bringing Mummy home. Daddy was out in the kitchen, clanking the plates, sweeping the floor and switching off the lights to go to bed.

The next couple of days were similar. At the beach, they were allowed Splices, Chocolate Hearts and Chiko Rolls. Daddy built his sandcastles higher and higher. The girls swam between the flags but returned occasionally to admire Daddy's castle.

Mummy came home in a taxi at breakfast time one day.

Fancy and Marbie ran outside in their nighties, and Daddy emerged slowly behind them. The taxi driver was more excited than they were. He was chattering, laughing and opening doors.

Mummy's voice came from inside the taxi.

'Girls,' said Daddy, 'wait a moment.'

He leaned down to Mummy. When he stood back up he

was holding something like a pink shopping bag. Marbie thought it might be presents.

'Here we go!' cried the taxi driver. 'Look what we've got! Look, girls, see what your mummy's brought home for you!'

Fancy took one step and said, '*It's a baby.*'

'Not just any baby!' cried the taxi driver, but he had to stop as Daddy wanted to pay him the fare.

'Whose baby is it, Mummy?' Marbie said. 'Where did you get a baby from?'

'Just a moment, precious one,' said Mummy.

The taxi driver talked his way around to the driver's door. '. . . Congratulations! . . . . . . All the best! . . . You take care of Mummy now!' He seemed to continue talking as he drove away.

Daddy said, 'Do you think you can manage that box between you, girls?'

Fancy and Marbie carried the box, Daddy carried the baby and Mummy carried nothing.

Inside, Fancy and Marbie sat on the couch and took turns holding the baby. Marbie grew bored: the baby simply lay in its blanket and you couldn't scratch your knee. But Fancy crinkled her eyes and sang, '*Hello*, little baby, *hello*, little cutie baby, *hello*, little baby.' Mummy sat beside her, leaning over, watching.

Daddy and Marbie opened the box and it turned out to be a new basket for the baby. Daddy found baby sheets and diapers in a cupboard which Marbie had never noticed.

'I didn't know you were pregnant, Mum,' said Fancy, grown-up and casual.

'That's because I'm quite plump already,' explained Mummy. 'It doesn't show so much, see? Nobody knew, darling. Don't worry.'

'Is it *our* baby?' Marbie said.

'Well,' said Mummy, 'it is and it is not. This is where you have to listen carefully, now.'

Fancy was on the couch with the baby in her arms. Marbie was sitting by the empty box on the floor, and Daddy was standing at the kitchen door with his arms folded.

'This baby,' said Mummy, looking closely at the girls, 'is a secret baby. Do you understand?'

Fancy and Marbie said they understood.

'No,' said Mummy. 'It's more important than that. It's more important than anything ever before. It's a special Zing family secret. OK?'

Fancy and Marbie nodded.

'This baby,' continued Mummy, 'can only stay with us for one week.'

'*No!*' cried Fancy. 'Only a *week*!' She kissed the baby's forehead.

'I hope you will help to take care of her this week,' said Mummy.

'Of *course*,' said Fancy.

'OK,' said Marbie, thinking: *What about the beach*?

'What's her name?' said Fancy. 'What's the new baby's name?'

Mummy looked at the baby and straightened the folds of the blanket. After a minute, she said, 'I have decided to give this baby the gift of a normal life. So her name is Catherine.'

'Is it?' breathed Fancy.

'Yes,' her mother replied.

Part 19

The Story of Nikolai Valerio

36

Maude was making pastry when her husband, David, announced that he was leaving.

It was not surprising that she was making pastry: she was always making pastry in those days. She was determined to become a successful pie chef. Already, the local cake shop had said it would take a few pies now and then, and this had given her hope so she practised whenever she could. She could no longer look at a circular object without thinking of its use as a pastry cutter: teacups, breakfast bowls, steering wheels, balloon baskets.

'Hmm,' she said vaguely when David made his announcement. She was rubbing butter into flour, her favourite part of pastry making, fluttering her fingertips as fine crumbs emerged, neither flour nor butter.

'I'm so sorry,' said David softly. (It was after midnight and the girls were asleep.)

Now Maude paid attention. 'You can't *leave*,' she cried.

He explained that he had no choice, and as he talked – about how he needed time alone to figure things out; how he hoped it would not take long, the figuring out; how he also hoped, when it was done, that she would take him back – as he said all this, Maude slowly sank into a kitchen chair and thought: *Of course.*

Her pie-making must have distracted her. Her husband was fading into nothing. Where was the vibrant, vivacious boy with excited expectations of invention? She recalled how he used to spring down the aisles of department stores, looking for inspiration; then how he took to wandering, more slowly and thoughtfully. The wandering grew listless, and now he never wandered, except down the hallway of their home. Now and then he picked up one of Fancy or Marbie's toys, turned it over distractedly and put it back down on the carpet.

He had never lost his gift for electronics and gadgets, but he only used it to repair the girls' clock-radios or install dead-locks on the doors.

David's talent had been consumed by family life, Maude saw now. And here he was, a grown-up Zing who had never invented a thing. His parents and relatives commented on this now and then, but were friendly and forgiving. The invent-iveness had to stop *somewhere!* they said. Why not with David? He had, after all, created two lovely girls. That was enough for them!

But David spent hours watching TV, or playing Fancy's Donkey Kong game. His vertigo grew worse instead of better – these days, he could not even go to the movies. The seats were at such a steep gradient, he said, he feared he would fall into the film.

Now, as he talked and apologized, Maude considered all this and played with her flour-dusted wedding band. Eventu-ally, she pulled it off her finger and dropped it on the table between them. David breathed in sharply and buried his head in his arms. Maude regarded the wedding ring, imagining its use as a pastry cutter. Thousands of tiny pastry circles for thousands of tiny pies.

'Well,' she said, surprising him with the kindness in her voice. 'Well, I understand you have to go. But we'll say that you're going to Ireland. We'll say that you plan to paint pic-tures or write poems, or maybe a novel.'

Why Ireland? David wanted to know.

Maude thought it was the romantic sort of place where people ran away to do creative things. 'That way,' she explained carefully, 'if you happen *not* to invent anything, you can come back to us, without –'

'But people will ask me about Ireland when I get back,' David pointed out.

'You can look it up in a library book,' suggested Maude. She stood up again and returned to the counter where her pastry was waiting.

As a goodbye present for the girls, David hung a swing from the highest branches of the scribbly gum out the back. This tree had no low-lying branches. He stood a ladder against it to reach the closest branch and climbed the rest of the way up. This was the bravest thing he had ever done.

Fancy, who was a formal eleven-year-old, waved him off in the taxi, wishing him the best of luck on his trip to Ireland. She hoped he would write a good novel. She hoped he would come back soon. She would miss him *very* much. But Marbie was only five and didn't wish him anything.

David quit his job in sales and found a small flat in West Ryde. He promised Maude he'd invent something quickly and make a fortune for the family. Maude told everyone he'd flown away to Ireland to write a novel and immersed herself in pie-making. The local cake shop had been replaced by a laundromat so she had lost her only client, but she pinned notices to community bulletin boards, visited restaurants and even set up a table on the front lawn, offering pies to passers-by.

Unexpectedly, nobody wanted Maude's pies. Not even the students or teachers from the school next door. By now, David had used up half their savings on his rent and equipment for inventions that never materialized; Maude had used the other half as a down payment on an industrial oven. They were living on credit but neither would admit they were in trouble.

It was only by chance, while looking for a second-hand

vacuum cleaner in the *Trading Post* one day – thinking she could try house cleaning for cash and finding her own vacuum was broken – that Maude came across the ad. 'WANTED,' it said: 'Twelve Pie Chefs for Short-Term/ Full-Time Baking'. The pay was minimal, but it might just keep her afloat until her business took off.

It is well known that Nikolai Valerio's second movie, *Pie in the Sky*, was filmed in the western suburbs of Sydney. Despite careful secrecy, news of the shoot leaked to the press as filming neared completion, and mobs of hysterical fans began to form. They had to whisk the cast away to Lord Howe Island to wrap up.

The movie is a classic – gentle, yet ambitious; dangerous, yet ineffably sweet. As with all of Nikolai's movies, it swept the pool at Cannes and at the Oscars that year, and many Valerio critics rate it as his best. He had been polished by his first movie – yet he still exuded the naivety of the oil-smeared motor mechanic. Later, he lost some of that innocence.

Of course, Maude knew who Nikolai Valerio was, and, like most women, had seen his first movie several times. Like most women also, she had engaged in secret fantasies in which she imagined Nikolai greeting her at the auto shop. But when she auditioned for the pie-chef position, she had no idea it was for a Valerio film – that was still a secret. She thought she was going to help with a series of TV ads for Mama's Frozen Desserts.

Eighty pie chefs auditioned for the job, and twelve were selected. Maude was asked to pass a national security check and told to sign five separate confidentiality agreements. She began to suspect that this might be more than a series of ads for Mama's Frozen Desserts.

*

Maude, tonight, was wearing a silver Alice band in her hair. Her daughters were asleep and she was sitting in the living room, watching through the window. Her husband, David, had been away (*in Ireland, writing a novel*) for almost a year, and she, Maude, was having an affair. Specifically, she was having an affair with Nikolai Valerio.

Technically, Nikolai Valerio was also having an affair with her: he had recently married Rebekka. But, really, Maude thought, when you are as famous as all that, the same rules do not apply.

The affair consisted of odd fragments: messages in code; a fireplace in a sandstone pub; wet shaking hair; a frangipani flower which she pressed between the pages of a magazine; kisses in a claw-foot tub; silk sheets; Egyptian cotton bathrobes.

In her living room now, Maude was recalling her first days on the film set. All twelve pie chefs had been jittery with excitement until it emerged that their days would be spent in one dark trailer, seated together around a long table, ingredients and cooking utensils set out at each place, sweltering in the heat of baking ovens.

At break times, they stood around on the dry, dusty grass, trying to get a glimpse of Nikolai. Only it turned out that movie stars were rarely there when movies were made. Most of the day, the dull film crew walked around, measured things, talked to each other, set up equipment, looked at papers, frowned at the sky, shouted commands – as if building an imaginary skyscraper.

Nikolai and the other stars were whisked on to the field in dark-windowed cars only when the sets were ready for them. Even then, you could only see fragments – the top of a head, an arm reaching out – through the clusters of cameras and assistants.

It was not until the third week of shooting that Maude saw

Nikolai's face. She had been asked to help place some pies in the shot – *Pie in the Sky* called for a general backdrop of pies. As any film student will tell you, apple pies, pumpkin pies, cherry pies and pecan pies, each with golden crust, were artfully scattered in the distant background of every camera shot in the film.

Maude was carrying a steaming cherry pie in each hand when the limousine paused beside her. A window was rolled down. Nikolai Valerio was smiling at her.

A woman seated beside Nikolai leaned around him. 'He wants a piece of your pie,' she called. 'Can you give him a piece?'

Everyone in the car laughed, while Nikolai continued to smile at Maude.

'I'm sorry,' he said in his movie-star accent. 'I'm sorry, I keep seeing these pies everywhere I look. You make all these pies?'

Maude explained that she was only one of twelve pie chefs. He tilted his head, interested, and asked, 'Do you think I may have a piece of one? It doesn't have walnuts, does it? I am allergic and my lips will swell to the size of a balloon!'

She shook her head about the walnuts, but then she didn't know what to do: she had no knife for cutting, and no saucer or spoon on which to place a slice of pie.

'Here,' he said, reaching his hand out of the car window. 'I'll just tear off a corner if you – ow, this is a very hot – and I'll just – oh, this is cherry pie, I cannot explain how happy that – my god*father*, this is a beautiful *pie*! – and now, I will just straighten the edge, and *so*! It is still fine now . . . like nobody has touched it.'

The people in the car quietly watched all this and then they laughed and said, 'All right, Nikolai?'

'All right,' said Nikolai, smiling at Maude again. 'And the

best cherry pie I ever ate, did you make this cherry pie or was it one of the other eleven?'

'Me,' said Maude.

'And you are?'

'Maude,' she said. 'Maude Zing.'

Then the car moved away from her again.

She did not see any more than fragments of him for the next few days, until one night when most of the cast and crew had left. Nikolai and the leading lady remained for the midnight boating scene. Maude also remained – she had left her girls with a neighbour for the night – along with one other pie chef, and the two were extremely busy. The river had to be lined with pies. Furthermore, each pie had to look freshly baked, a twirl of steam rising from the neatly scored lines in its lid.

It was exquisitely intimate, this filming with only the two main actors and a skeleton crew: for the first time, Maude was able to watch and hear the slow unfurling of a scene. Furthermore, she was *part* of that unfurling. She heard an assistant comment, 'That coffee smells *great*', and he meant the coffee she herself had just brewed!

Then the two actors and the collection of crew wandered over to where Maude was laying out the pies.

'Hello, Maude Zing,' said Nikolai, remembering her name and holding the name, for one breathless moment, in his accent.

The leading lady was less friendly and seemed to be complaining to the director. 'Come over here,' said the director in a low voice.

Nikolai and a make-up lady tried to persuade Maude to let them eat one of her pies, and she jauntily refused. She found she was no longer nervous of Nikolai. He was an ordinary person with an accent. She was chatting with him! She was making him laugh!

Then there was an angry shout from the leading lady and she strode into the distance.

'Oh, come off it!' called the director. 'This is nothing. We're fighting about *nothing*. Come on, you've got to be kidding me!'

But the leading lady refused to return and disappeared in a long black car.

The director was distressed. The moonlight sprinkles were perfect on the river, and the scene was almost done.

Maude was trying to gather up her pies to keep them hot in the oven when she realized the director was staring at her. 'Turn your head slightly,' he instructed. 'Now back, now left, now right.'

It turned out that Maude's hair, the back of Maude's neck, the smooth curve of her cheek all precisely matched that of the leading lady. She would be the double, they informed her.

Which is how it came to be that Maude spent most of the night in a long slender boat being punted up and down the river by Nikolai Valerio. Nikolai chatted as he punted, applying his disarming accent to every word he said. He asked questions about Maude's daughters and about her life, and he told short, witty anecdotes about Hollywood actors who were close personal friends.

The night grew colder so the director let them drink glasses of port to keep warm; the port made them clumsy, so that when Nikolai tried to cross the boat towards Maude to fix a strand of her hair, he capsized the punt. This resulted in shaking wet hair, huddling together under blankets, shivery giggles, and patient amusement from director and camera crew all packing up to go home.

Nikolai suggested that Maude accompany him in the limousine to his hotel room, to bathe and to sit in a robe by his fireplace and dry her hair with his towel. Which was how the affair got its start.

*

380

In her armchair now, some months later, Maude felt that she was floating just above the chair. Nikolai would visit any moment: it would be the first time he had come to her home. For months, they had spent elaborately secret nights in his hotel suite. She had used her wages to pay babysitters for Fancy and Marbie, had stopped working on her pie-making business altogether and had spent luxurious evenings bathing in his claw-foot bath while he watched, turning the hot-water tap with her toe. Nikolai had listened to her stories, and had sworn he would fly her away in a gold-trimmed balloon one day. He wanted to know everything about her, he said, as his hands traced the curves of her body. He seemed, genuinely, to love her body. Even though it was quite plump.

Tonight, he had promised to come in a plumber's van, labelled 'EMERGENCY – 24-HR PLUMBING SERVICES', so the neighbours would not be suspicious. He was going to drive himself. He was going to wear a moustache and blond wig. She was going to make him pancakes while her daughters slept.

They were in love, she and Nikolai, but had always known that their affair could not go on. Often, they spoke in wonder of the strangeness of the affair: it was both essential and impossible. It must cease to exist for it floated between two realities: his star-spangled career, his beautiful wife, his collection of vintage cars; her daughters, her remote and troubled husband, her unpaid electricity bills, repossession warnings and the foreclosure notice from her bank.

Yet, although they had often blinked tears from their eyes, knowing the affair had to end, Maude had never believed that it would. The realm of the affair was too exquisite. In fact, for the past five months she'd kept a secret from him – easy enough with her plump body. She'd been waiting to share it, knowing that this secret, revealed at the right moment, would bind them forever. It would transform their gossamer love into something real.

The night before, she had told him the secret and his face had crumpled with joy. 'No more visits to my hotel, darling,' he had whispered. 'This changes everything. Tomorrow, I come to your house.'

Any moment now he would arrive. He would probably help her make the pancakes: he would watch in his reverent way as she cracked eggs, and measured out flour. That was the nature of their realm: a collection of precious moments. She loved him so much she felt that *they*, together, would become the pancake batter. Intertwined, they would spill into the pan and together they would breathe with slow new bubbles.

The moon tonight, Maude thought idly, was as round as a tablet. It would do very well for cutting pastry. As a matter of fact, so would Fancy's hula hoop, which she could see through the window, luminescent on the lawn. Or her own watch face, here on her wrist, showing Nikolai to be an hour late.

Part 20

Friday Morning

37

Early Friday morning, the sun just touching the sky, Listen read the final spell by torchlight.

> **Here it is!**
> **The Final Spell!**
> *Once you have completed this Spell, all will be well!*
> *It's a Spell To Make Two People Fall In Love Again*
>
> **Gather up the following things:**
> - **An overnight bag**
> - **Four candles**
> - **Flowers**
> - **A bottle of wine**
> - **Bread, cheese, olives and chocolate brownies**
>
> *That's it! Just by gathering these things together you will make the Spell take effect. (And by the way, you will* know *when the time is right to* use *these things!)*
>
> *Goodbye then. It's been a lot of fun.*
> *(In the next few hours, you should be sure to hide this Book some place you are never likely to see it again.)*

Listen crept out of bed and gathered everything on the list, packing them together in her overnight bag while her dad slept. By lucky chance, she found bread, cheese and olives in the Banana Bar fridge, chocolate brownies in the camper-van cupboard, and a bottle of wine in a crate underneath the table. Someone had given her candy pink candles as a Kris Kringle present last year. She added the Spell Book to the overnight bag so she could hide it somewhere later that morning, and she got back into bed. *A Spell To Make Two People Fall In Love Again.* It was perfect. She fell asleep through tears of happiness.

When she woke again, her dad was already up and gone. She was so excited she could hardly dress or clean her teeth. Maybe he was *already* with Marbie! Maybe he had driven straight to her place when he woke up!

Walking from the camper van to the back door of the Banana Bar, she tried to stay calm, but felt the sun on the back of her neck, saw the pale blue curve of the sky and thought: *It's the beginning of everything!*

As she walked into the shop, the phone was ringing and she reached for it, but her dad, who was behind the counter, called, 'Just leave it.'

The answering machine switched on, and there, as Listen knew it would be, was Marbie's voice. She reached for the phone again, but her father said sharply, 'Listen.'

So they both stood quietly while Marbie chatted: 'Nathaniel! Sorry, it's me. Sorry to bother you. Sorry, I'm sniffing, I've got a cold, and that's why I'm calling you, not really, that's not really why. But I decided I shouldn't go to work today, and then Mum called and said she and Dad are going away for the weekend to this Festival of Balloons somewhere in the Hunter Valley, and I thought, seeing as I'm not going to work I might as well go away for the weekend with them, and I thought, well! maybe Nathaniel and Listen want to come along! I thought it could be fun for you guys to see the balloons, and you know, and anyway, give me a call if you're interested. We're leaving in the next hour or so, so it's spontaneous. OK? Great. Hear from you soon, I hope.'

The machine clicked and whirred backwards. Listen looked

over at her father with shining eyes. Here, now, it was going to happen.

'All packed?'

She raised her overnight bag and swung it around slightly.

'You need to leave now or do you have time for breakfast?' he asked next.

'I guess I need to go now,' she said. 'But I've got a minute if you want to call Marbie back.'

'That's OK,' he said, and switched the sign on the Banana Bar door to 'BACK IN TEN MINUTES. 'Hang on,' he said. 'Left my keys in the camper van.'

Listen stood on the path in front of the Banana Bar, the hot wind brushing at her face. She leaned against the glass door to wait.

When her dad pushed the door open again, jangling his keys in her face, she said, 'So, are you going to call Marbie?'

'Nope.'

She watched his back as he opened the car door.

'What do you mean "*nope*"?'

'Listen, I'm sorry, I'm not going to call her.' He was standing with the door open, waiting for her to come across to the car.

'You should go to the balloon festival,' she said, beginning to panic. 'You *have* to go to the balloon festival. Don't you get it? Dad, it's perfect. I'm going away for the weekend; what are you going to do if you don't go to the balloon festival?'

'Run the Banana Bar, for one thing,' he said. 'Listen, I'm sorry, baby, I thought you understood. I'm not getting back with Marbie. Not ever. It's over. Finito.'

Then he slammed his car door closed.

They drove towards Redwood Primary, where coaches would collect the girls to take them to the mountains for their camp. Listen watched her father's profile, but it was set and calm. There was nothing she could do to change it.

She looked into her overnight bag, at her pyjamas, shorts, T-shirts, swimming costume, and beneath them, the glint of a bottle of wine, the lid of the jar of olives, the candy pink of the candlesticks.

She was not going to the school camp.

She knew where she was going instead.

It was just like the Spell Book had said. *You will know when the time is right to use these things.*

The time was now. She was supposed to hear Marbie's message, not because it meant Dad and Marbie would fall in love again, but because it told her that the Zings were going away. She would hide in their place for the weekend. She would hide in their garden shed. She would live on olives, bread, cheese and chocolate brownies for the next few days.

But what were the candles, flowers and wine for? They suggested some kind of ritual. Did she have to perform a ritual? She pictured the Zings' back garden: the large wooden shed, the sagging trampoline, the scribbly gum with its old rope swing. She thought of the old rope swing, how it swayed sometimes, white against the night-time, when she watched through the Zings' kitchen window. She thought of rituals with candles and flowers.

She thought: *A Spell To Make Two Happy People Have a Huge Fight Over Absolutely Nothing.*

It was her fault that Marbie and her dad had split up.

She thought of the school counsellor saying, 'It's not your fault that your mother left.'

But it must have been her fault. Why else would the counsellor have raised it? Who knew what she did as a baby to scare her mother away – maybe cried too much or didn't sleep enough. That was what she did: she caused mothers to leave. Her father would always be lonely as long as she was around.

She thought: *Two's company, three's a crowd.*

She thought: *You will know when the time is right.*

She thought: *This book will make you strong.*
And the whole thing fell into place.

Fancy found it too hot in the kitchen and took her breakfast outside for the breeze.

She sat on the edge of the porch, which burned her thighs, and carefully set her breakfast bowl, orange juice and coffee around her. Radcliffe had offered to drive Cassie to school on his way to work, which was unusual. But she expected him back any moment. He had forgotten his lunch: she had just seen it in the fridge.

She was thinking vaguely of her prize-winning novel. The book she had finished reading the previous night had employed a lyrical tone. The one she had finished last week was written with startling coarseness. You had to choose your tone, she realized. That was one of the rules. You chose slapstick, pastoral, melancholy, magical, lyrical, poetic or flatulent. But, she wondered, wouldn't you *increase* your chances of a prize if you combined some of these?

She began to formulate a sentence: – 'Pressing its delicate hoof into the mist-curling grass of the copse, the deer breathed the stench of gingivitis –' But then Radcliffe's car turned into the driveway, and he called through his open window: 'Hey, Fance! Can you grab my tuna sandwich?'

When she opened the front screen door again, carrying his sandwich in a brown paper bag, she had an 'Aren't you silly?' expression ready on her face. But he was standing on the porch.

'Oh,' she said. 'I was going to bring it to your car.'

The shape of him was dark against the sunlight.

'Right,' he said. 'But, Fancy, I've got to tell you something. I can't stand this deception.'

She felt the familiar leap of excitement – *He's having an*

affair! – but was so weary of that leap that she dispelled it with a breath of mocking air. 'Ye-e-s?' she said, almost tauntingly.

'Can we sit down?'

Obediently, she sat beside him on the edge of the porch.

He swivelled towards her, and began haltingly: 'The reason I offered to drive Cassie to school this morning was that – now, you might think it was nice of me to make that offer, but the *reason* was that . . .'

'Ye-e-es?'

Then he told her his secret in a breathless rush. 'The reason was that I didn't want you to see Cath Murphy! Because you're waiting for a call from her and maybe you would say something to her about it, but you're never going to get a call, Fancy, I made the whole thing up. *I* went to the Parent–Teacher Night in your place! When Cassie got stung by a bee and you took her off to the hospital, well, that's what I did. I just went. And I'm sorry, but I couldn't help it. I just couldn't stop thinking that the bee sting had happened for a *reason*. The reason being that *I* was meant to get to meet Cath. *Me*. A non-Zing family member. The first of us to meet her. *I* wanted to talk to her, to see her, to have *her* see me. *I* wanted *her* to meet me! Fancy, I am *so, so* sorry.'

Fancy stared at her husband. She shifted away from him slightly. 'So, I didn't get to meet Cath first,' she said. 'And Cath is not going to call me. Right?'

'Right,' he agreed. 'I am so sorry.'

'Fine,' she said, 'it's fine, Radcliffe. But can I just check something with you. When Cassie got stung by a bee – our Cassie who is allergic to bees, who could die from a bee sting – when that happened, Radcliffe, all you could think about was going to the Parent–Teacher Night?'

'Mmm,' he nodded mournfully.

*

Marbie left her message for Nathaniel, hung up the phone and breathed in sharply. The sound of the phone clicking back on to its hook had struck her with the truth. Nathaniel would never call her back.

She could send as many letters as she liked, she could leave apology messages, and messages inviting him to hot-air-balloon festivals, she could invite him on a trip to the moon, but Nathaniel was never coming back.

Then she had to stop this unfurling chain because she was sneezing. Her sneezes were immense and shivery.

She thought she might just get back into bed for a while before she packed for her weekend with her parents.

She saw herself in the bedroom mirror – bleary eyes, pink nose – and gathered her bedclothes around her. She had used up a whole box of tissues in the night, but felt around the cardboard bottom, hoping for a single loose tissue. She found something odd and crackling.

What was this crumpled piece of paper doing in the bottom of a tissue box?

Cath arrived early on Friday morning and sat on a bench in the sun.

The weather reminded her of her early meetings with Warren: the day he stood at the opposite end of the Year 2 balcony and pulled his funny face; the day he brought her a coffee, saying, 'White, no sugar, yes?'

Such a soft, warm breeze, such a tender, blue sky. It was spring and the weather had relented, promising gentle surprises. The warmth made her long for the touch of Warren's hands and, for the first time in a while, she was confident of that touch. Today could easily be some day!

A voice behind her said, 'White, no sugar, yes?', and a coffee appeared in the air.

Warren Woodford straddled the bench like someone riding a horse, and now he was facing her shoulder.

'Thank you,' she said, taking the coffee and smiling at him.

He smiled back. There was something so generous in his smile that she almost wept with relief. 'Cath,' he said, 'I need to tell you something.'

She continued to trust in his smile.

'This morning something happened,' he explained. 'Something amazing. Bree and I woke up really early and we looked at each other, and I'm sorry, Cath, but we fell in love again.'

'Ahah!' she said, kindly, as if a child had shown her a magic trick.

'I'm so sorry about all this, Cath, but I've got to say, for me, it's a relief, I couldn't go on this way much longer. It just happened, out of nowhere, we fell in love again.'

'You're not in love,' Cath began her speech, carefully but firmly. 'You're not in love because she doesn't know what you've been –'

'That's the thing,' said Warren. 'I told her last night. Well, she kind of already knew, she says. She says she sensed something – that there was a secret just out of her reach – and that's why she's been feeling so nervous and on edge. It's so much better to know than not know, she says. Still, she's pretty upset, but we talked and talked and we both cried and it was great. It was like we'd never talked before. And that's why, this morning, early, we woke up and fell in love again.'

'That's why, is it?' Cath was suddenly outraged. 'Lessons on how to save a marriage by Warren Woodford. Lesson one, cheat on your wife. Lesson two, tell her about it. She'll fall head over heels! You just *talked* and you *cried,* and now you're both in love, and I really, really think you should *trust* that feeling, Warren, that must be *so real.*'

She saw his panicked expression and adjusted her face. 'Warren,' she said, 'come on, seriously. I see how it must feel like a relief, but she *can't* love you now she knows. She must hate us both.'

'I'm sorry,' he said again, now in the voice of a teacher who needs to repeat a simple lesson. 'I'm sorry, but it happened. It's real. I seriously thought it was gone, but early this morning it came back. I am so sorry.'

She tried brisk: 'It's fine, Warren. I knew what I was doing. I never meant you to leave her unless it was really over. And I think it *is* over, Warren, this is just some kind of false hope. I'll still be here. I'll still be waiting, but please God tell me that Breanna isn't at school today. Because if she's not blaming you, then I swear to God, she must be ready to scratch out my eyes.'

'I'm sorry,' he repeated. 'She's in the staffroom. Probably watching us right now. I told her I was coming out to let you know. She's angry, but I don't think she would hurt you.' He was standing up and backing away.

'What happened to the seams?' she called.

'What?'

'Forget it,' she said. 'I'm trying to work.' And she looked down at her coffee.

38

On the edge of her wooden bench, Cath sensed the gleams of light on the staffroom windows, each window gazing fixedly at her. She had yearned to be seen and now felt the shock of exposure. *If Breanna knows*, she thought, *everybody knows, and the whole school is watching me.* Children's shadows crossed her body. *Here is the teacher who loved another teacher*, the shadows seemed to say, placidly enough, *she planned to run away with him but his wife arrived to take him back.*

Meanwhile, the wife was moving from window to window, stalking, judging, despising her, and all with perfect right. The sun was not gentle and tender at all, it was a spotlight.

On the Year 2 balcony, Cassie stood outside her classroom, watching the playground. Ms Murphy was sitting on a bench, curling her shoulders. The bell was ringing for school to start, and Ms Murphy hadn't even moved.

'You go inside,' Cassie told Lucinda. 'I just have to stay here for a minute.'

Fancy, alone on the porch again, now with a new cup of coffee, listened to the fading engine of Radcliffe's car. He had left for work with a final beseeching request that she forgive him. *Was that possible?* she mused now.

All her life she had longed to meet her baby sister – her mother had promised that she would be the first – and Radcliffe had stolen that away.

Still, she thought, did it matter? She could meet Cath

another time. She almost felt embarrassed for Radcliffe, as if he had revealed that he ate the last of Cassie's chocolate Easter eggs, and secretly, guiltily, elaborately covered it up. It was childish and greedy, but what was the big deal?

She thought she could forgive him. Which made her think: what else could she forgive? If Radcliffe *had* been having an affair, for example, would she have forgiven him? *Should* she have forgiven him? Wasn't she supposed to get revenge?

Be cruel, be strong, or sulk.

Of course! She had forgotten. Revenge was just one of the options. The rules were more complex than that.

All this time, waiting for confirmation of Radcliffe's affair so she could pounce with a counter-affair, she had forgotten she might have to be strong. As a matter of fact, strength was a more appropriate response when you were a grown-up with a house, car, garden hose and child. She sipped her coffee and felt the mug tremble in her hand.

Then again, she thought, as the coffee fanned out in her head, if you chose the 'strong' option you had to shave off a piece of love as fuel for the strength. And if great strength were needed, she might have used up all her love. But would she be *allowed* to –

Oh, stop it, she thought angrily, slamming the coffee mug on to the porch and burning her hand with the splash.

The paper crushed into the bottom of the tissue box was covered in Listen's curly handwriting. It was entitled, 'Things That Make Me Sad', and the text began: 'Donna has a table tennis table in the basement of her house, and once Sia's mother made us all eat spaghetti squash.' Even before she had finished the page, Marbie was reaching for the phone.

'Nathaniel,' she said into his answering machine. 'Sorry to call again. I know you won't come to the balloon festival, it's OK, it's not that, it's about Listen. I don't know how long ago she wrote this but there's stuff in here that's scaring me, maybe you know all this now, but if you don't, you should, and I can't believe what her friends have done –'

'Marbie?'

Marbie jumped at the sound of Nathaniel's voice.

'I'm here,' he said.

'Oh,' said Marbie, 'OK, hi, Nathaniel, well I just found this paper that Listen wrote, like a kind of diary, and did you know that Donna and those others threw her out of their group?'

'What are you talking about?'

'I'm just reading this and it's full of all the things those stupid girls said were wrong with her, and how she wants to cross highways in front of cars, and she walks through long grass hoping to get bitten by a snake, and switches on the power with wet hands, and how did we not notice, Nathaniel? What were we thinking? And I think she's going to hurt herself, so where is she? I really need to speak to her.'

'OK,' said Nathaniel. 'You have to calm down. I just dropped her at school for a camp. Hang on, I've got a customer.'

When she finally raised her head to confront the staring eyes, there was nobody looking at Cath. Children were running towards their classrooms, teachers were chatting in the doorway to the staffroom, even the staffroom windows had a blank, unseeing look.

The vulnerable, exposed feeling receded slightly, and she decided to be sensible. It was unlikely, for a start, that anybody else knew. Breanna had not become friends with anybody yet.

Anybody, that is, except Cath.

She could not possibly see Breanna. Her briefcase and cellphone were in the staffroom, but her car keys were in her pocket. She would just have to drive away.

Warren was emerging from the staffroom again, calling out something to somebody inside and heading across to their building.

'Warren,' she called, 'can you take care of my class for the morning?'

'Of course,' he said, grim, solemn and gentle all at once.

'I just have something to do,' she scolded and walked briskly towards the school gate. Warren hurried after her, and she quickened her pace. 'Are you all right?' he murmured as he reached her side. This was ridiculous. Now Breanna was watching them together again. She began to jog, but Warren actually jogged alongside her. 'I hope you can understand,' he begged.

From her hiding spot under the bag rack on the Year 2 balcony, Cassie watched a crowd of girls forming at the entranceway to the school. Dressed in jeans, they were kicking pillows at each other.

She turned back to Ms Murphy. Ms Murphy was gone from her seat. She was running towards the front gate, and Mr Woodford was running beside her.

It was the two cheetahs running away from the jungle! Finally, she understood the picture on the dentist's ceiling!

She clambered out from beneath the bag rack and rushed down the Year 2 stairs.

Cath and Warren had to pause as two coaches were pulling into the driveway. In fact, the entranceway was now a mess of girls and sleeping bags.

'It's the seventh-graders,' Warren said, 'from Clareville College. They've got a camp in the mountains this weekend.'

'Aren't you full of knowledge?' Cath snapped. 'Warren, I'm fine, please go back.'

He looked hurt, shrugged and hurried away, and Cath felt utterly bereft.

He had given up so easily.

She pressed her lips together, breathed a sigh through her nose and began to skirt around the seventh-graders. That was when she spotted that girl – Listen Taylor – the relative of Cassie Zing's. Listen was taking something out of her bag, crouching down and pressing it under a rock in the garden which edged the driveway. Strange. Was it a book? Now she was pointing out her name to a teacher with a clipboard and was stepping back into the crowd.

Watching Listen, Cath felt a rush of guilt. She had asked Breanna for help with this girl – now that Breanna knew about the affair, asking her for help seemed unforgivable.

She looked again for Listen in the crowd but could not see her. She was turning, then, about to head to the teachers' car park and her car, but something caught her eye.

Listen Taylor was slinking towards the school's front lawn – and had just ducked underneath the fence.

Stop it! Fancy thought. *Stop with these childish games and rules! You can't wait for permission to have an affair! You can't wait for permission to leave!* You have to be grown-up and make things happen on your own. You have to face the truth: *there is no love left.*

Now, trembling on the front porch, Fancy struggled to argue back, setting up the cue cards of her love for Radcliffe. But all she could see were squabbling seagulls, the inside of a hotel lobby and the neat italic type of that recurring sentence: *How is your ocean bream, my love? How is your ocean bream?*

*

Marbie, pressing the phone to her ear, waited through a malted milkshake transaction. She heard a brief exchange about cricket and the jangling of cash register and change.

'Marbie?' Nathaniel's voice was there again, and she could hardly breathe. 'Marbie,' he said. 'So, this sounds bad, but you know, she's at the school camp so she's OK, and maybe it's all better now. I bet she's got new friends. Kids go through bad phases, so maybe that was just one, so . . . Could you post me that paper she wrote?'

'OK,' whispered Marbie. His voice had turned cold and final again.

'Anyway,' he said, even colder. 'Why so interested in Listen? You weren't exactly thinking of her when you –'

He stopped. She tried to hold on to her tears.

'Marbie?' he said, now sounding almost rough.

'I hate myself for what I did to you, but I wanted –' She made herself speak, and as she did, her voice began to build. 'I wanted to be like a *mother* to Listen, and look what I've done.'

Now Nathaniel was silent, breathing quietly. 'You know, Marbie,' he said eventually, 'I'd have forgiven you almost right away if it hadn't been for Listen.'

There was the distant sound of a jangling door and Nathaniel shouted, 'WE'RE NOT OPEN!' His voice returned to the phone, softer and quieter. 'See,' he said, 'I'd have given you years to make up your mind about me and to have your adventures and affairs, if it wasn't for Listen. But she's already lost one mother to that world. I can't let it happen to her again.'

'But I've *made* up my mind,' said Marbie breathlessly. 'I know it didn't seem like it, but I didn't *want* to have affairs or adventures, I just wanted you. I can't believe how much I miss you. You and Listen *are* my adventure.'

Nathaniel was silent. 'Are you sure you should be going

away this weekend?' he said eventually. 'You sound like you've got a cold.'

'I know,' said Marbie. 'Maybe I won't go.'

Again, Nathaniel was quiet for a moment. 'So you met this guy at the Night Owl Pub?' he said, in a just audible voice.

'He asked me to play a game of tennis.'

'Tennis. How was he?'

'Well, a lot better than me. He said he played C-grade competition. But you played A-grade, didn't you? Nathaniel, if I could see you, I could try to explain. I swear I'd never do it again. Would you let me try to explain?'

There was a strange clanging noise, which could have been Nathaniel stacking and unstacking silver cups.

After a while he said, 'Maybe you should come by. So we can talk about Listen.'

Cath thought of calling out to Listen Taylor, but somehow, it seemed more professional to take the entry gate of the school and follow at a lurking crouch.

The girl darted across the street, and Cath darted not far behind her.

Now she walked fast along the footpath, turned down a side street and stopped at a bus stop.

Cath stepped back behind a hedge.

When she thought of squabbling seagulls, Fancy thought of Radcliffe being childish.

When she thought of hotel lobbies, she thought of herself running from Radcliffe, checking into glamorous hotels.

When she thought '*How is your ocean bream, my love?*' she pictured, suddenly, an ageing couple in a restaurant. The man was asking his wife, in a loving, interested voice: *How is your bream?*

And Fancy understood. She herself would never be part of

such a couple, because Radcliffe would never care about her bream.

Panicked, she reminded herself of Radcliffe's wedding proposal: the shoe-polish mud, the winding trees, and Radcliffe clicking a photo of her: '*I would like to marry you and everything about you.*' She waited for the usual rush of contentment – her husband loved her and everything about her! – but instead was amazed. Why had she never thought of this before?

I would like to marry you and everything about you.

He meant the Zing Family Secret.

He meant the Friday night meetings, the hidden cameras, the network of suburban spies. He meant the edicts from Nikolai Valerio, the labyrinthine corporate structure and the romantic ideal of Cath: a more beautiful, sculpted version of Fancy herself. He loved the Secret more than he loved her. He loved it more than his own daughter. He was so overcome with the thrill of meeting Cath he hardly gave a thought to Cassie's bee sting.

It was settled. Fancy was going to have to leave him.

The 382 pulled up and Listen climbed aboard. Cath leaped from behind the hedge and knocked on the closing bus door, which reluctantly opened to let her aboard. She slipped into the front seat and bowed her head.

Cassie skidded through the gates of the school in time to see Ms Murphy hop on to a bus. The bus pulled away at high speed.

Nice try, thought Cassie, with a grim little nod, and began to run. She would have to run as fast as a bus.

It was no trouble. Once, she remembered, she had been sprinting across the icy playground and had skidded into a game of rounders. Mr Woodford had caught her, and told all the kids: 'This is Cassie Zing. Future Olympic champ. I suggest you get her autograph now.'

She pounded the footpath ferociously, sometimes running across three lanes of traffic as a short cut.

When Listen got off the bus, Cath got off behind her. Listen skittered around a corner. Cath stopped at a real estate agent to smile at the pictures in the windows, but after an agonizing moment, she gave chase again.

Listen, she saw, had arrived at a blond-brick house alongside a local high school. But the girl did not go to the front door. She lowered herself to a crouch and darted around the back. Cath also lowered herself and darted around the house.

She stopped and looked around. It was a large backyard lined with a wire fence through which you could see the empty grounds of the school next door. In one corner of the yard there was a tall gum tree with a swing. A few metres away there was a timber shed, painted olive-green. The yard was empty. The girl must have gone into the shed.

Again, she paused. Then she walked slowly across the lawn. She stopped, changed her mind, returned to the house and considered knocking on the front door.

But the girl, she was sure, was in the shed.

She returned and knocked on the shed door instead.

There was no reply, so she opened the door. She wiped her feet on the 'WELCOME' mat and walked into the Zing Garden Shed.

39

She was vaguely surprised at what she saw. She had expected spiderwebs, rusty nails, mud-encrusted shovels. Also, possibly, red-bellied black snakes curled inside of gumboots.

Instead, the shed was a spacious, post-and-beam construction, with high ceilings and polished floorboards. A cluster of high-backed wooden chairs were set up in the centre of the room and there was a slightly raised platform at the far end. On the platform was a microphone and a white screen on a stand. The wall stretching away from the entrance was lined with filing cabinets in unexpected colours such as spearmint and lilac. A bank of television monitors was set up along the opposite wall. Also, there were pot plants in corners and vases of yellow tulips scattered about.

On either side of the doorway where Cath now stood, there were slender, ornate bookshelves, holding rows of photo albums and piles of manila folders. On the top shelf of each of these bookcases, candy pink candles stood in saucers, flickering dimly. The candles seemed curiously pointless because the room was lit like a film set with bright track lighting. There were no windows, although a beam of sun from a single skylight hit the far wall.

Just below this skylight, and behind the platform, the girl, Listen Taylor, was sitting on the floor and staring at her.

'Hello!' called Cath, squinting down the room.

'Hello,' said Listen, shifting slightly so that she was in the shadows.

She decided she had better approach Listen, but as she made her way across the garden shed she felt oddly foolish, like someone heading to the spotlight with nothing to perform.

Cassie ran along calmly. Her shoelace had come undone and as she ran she watched it flip from one side of the shoe to the other. She looked up to see Ms Murphy getting off the bus. Now she was turning into the road where Cassie's grandparents lived.

Cath saw an overnight bag on the floor by Listen's feet and standing neatly alongside the bag: a bottle of wine, a loaf of bread, cheese, olives and chocolate brownies.

'Hello!' she said again, standing opposite Listen, awkwardly.

The girl looked up at her.

'Having a party?'

She shook her head.

'I'm from your school!' said Cath, suddenly realizing that Listen might not know her. 'I mean, from Redwood. I'm Cassie's teacher, you know, Cassie Zing? I'm her teacher, Ms Murphy. And I saw you – I noticed you running away.'

Listen, she realized, was not looking at her. She was staring into space. They were both silent.

After a while, Cath said, 'Did you light the candles on the shelves there?'

Listen nodded. 'I'm not going to drink the wine, you know.'

'OK. Are you meeting somebody here?'

Listen shook her head. She was leaning against the wall of the shed, her legs stretched out before her, and now at last she looked Cath in the eye.

'Well . . . are you planning to spend the weekend?'

'No.' The girl was barely whispering. 'No, I'm not staying, I'm just – *can you please leave me alone?*'

*

'But I just got to work,' said Radcliffe reasonably.

Fancy, however, was insistent. She needed to meet him right away, at the Muffin Break in Castle Hill. He eventually agreed.

'I asked you to meet me,' said Fancy, taking a deep breath, 'because I want to talk about *us*.' She stirred her cappuccino into chocolate swirls. At a table nearby, two young women were looking through a pile of photographs.

'They've been to Fiji,' Radcliffe said, nodding at the women's table. 'Lots of tropical island shots.'

'How do you know it's Fiji? It could be Tahiti.'

Radcliffe turned back to Fancy, and assumed a concerned expression. 'This is about the Parent–Teacher Night, isn't it?' he said. 'I thought you were a bit too quick to get over that this morning. But seriously, Fance, I'll do whatever I can to make it up to you.'

'This is not about the Parent–Teacher Night. This is not about Cath.'

'See that?' said Radcliffe. 'They've taken some panorama shots. Doesn't Fiji look great?'

'I'd like a trial separation,' Fancy said.

The girls with the photographs raised eyebrows at each other and bowed their heads sideways to listen.

'Nonsense,' said Radcliffe, jocular. 'I said I was sorry. I'm going to fix it, Fancy. I'll set up a meeting with your sister somehow.'

'You don't understand. This is not your fault.'

'Well, whose fault is it then?'

'I think we should go home.' Fancy pushed her chair back.

'I need to go to work.' Radcliffe looked distracted.

'I'm trying to leave you, Radcliffe.'

'No you're not.'

*

'I'm sorry, but I'm not going anywhere,' said Cath.

'It's OK,' said Listen. 'I'm allowed to be here. This shed belongs to a family I know called the Zings. They're Cassie's grandparents?' She tried to shrug, casual, but stopped at the sound of a knock at the door.

A tiny figure stood in the doorway, dark in the sunlight.

'*There* you are!' she cried, pointing at Cath, and now they recognized her.

'Cassie! What are you doing here?'

'I didn't know you were here, Listen. We're not allowed to be in here, remember?' Cassie wandered into the shed. '*Finally*, I get to see it.' She gazed up at the high ceiling and along the walls. 'Who's the girl in that photo? Is that me?'

'Cassie, did you run away from school?' said Cath. 'Did anyone see you leave the school? How did you *get* here?'

Cassie had wandered over to a small framed photograph sitting on top of a filing cabinet.

'I don't think it's you, Cassie,' said Listen, joining her at the cabinet. 'It looks a bit like Fancy or Marbie though.'

'Look,' said Cath, getting up as well and marching over. 'Why don't we all get a tax – Who did you say that girl was?'

In the living room, home again, Fancy tried to convince Radcliffe that she wanted him to move out for a while.

'Like a holiday?' he said, dimpling, not taking this seriously. 'You want me to take a holiday? Fance, girl, aren't you the one who needs a break?'

'I need to stay and take care of Cassie!'

'Well . . .' He put his thumb to his mouth and played with his lower lip thoughtfully. 'I suppose I could go and stay in Nathaniel's camper van out the back of the Banana Bar. No! That's no good. Nathaniel's living there, isn't he? Marbie and Nathaniel have split up. Marbie had an affair.'

Fancy realized he was trying to give her a complicated message. 'I *know* you didn't have an affair,' she said. 'I know there's no reason. It's just something I have to do.'

Cath was staring fiercely at the photo in the frame when Cassie began opening filing cabinet drawers.

'I had a denim skirt just like that,' Cath said. 'And I'm *sure* I had earrings like – and that background, can you see what that sign says, Listen?' Politely, Listen examined the photo.

'Pets,' announced Cassie from the filing cabinet. 'Knee. Broken here – broken hee-arr. Broken *hearts*.'

Cath and Listen looked up from the photo.

'Cassie, are you allowed to be looking at those things?' Cath said, but as she spoke she was wandering over to Cassie and the filing cabinet. 'I mean,' she said, while her eyes moved over the files in the drawer, 'do you know what your grandparents use this place for? I guess it's probably private!' She glimpsed two labels as she closed the drawer: 'Nightmares' and 'Potential Recruits'.

Cassie, undeterred by Cath, opened the next drawer down and pulled out a handful of papers. 'Can you read this for me?' she said, handing a small piece of cardboard to Cath.

'Maybe you shouldn't,' murmured Listen.

'It's some kind of ad.' Cath took it in a teacherly manner and read aloud: 'Wouldn't it be better to know what's going on in your home or office at all times? Now you can! Our top-of-the-range pocket radio receivers provide superb sound sensitivity, so you can listen even to whispers! Range is up to 500 metres.'

'I wonder if we should be looking at this,' said Listen.

'Are they *spies* or something?' Cath said excitedly, opening another cabinet drawer and quickly closing it again. 'Listen, I haven't got my cell with me. Do you think you could get into the house and phone Redwood? To tell them that Cassie is here? In case they're worried.'

'OK,' said Listen, 'but I don't think we should look at this.'

'Hey,' called Cassie. 'I just found a whole lot of photos of that girl!'

Radcliffe yawned, stretched and said: 'I suppose I should fetch my toothbrush!'

He glinted at her, but Fancy said, 'All right then,' and they narrowed their eyes at one another for a moment.

Radcliffe walked down the hallway at the slow, steady pace of a bridesmaid.

'It's not a joke!' said Fancy, behind him.

'Of course not!' agreed Radcliffe, and grinned. 'It's a *holiday*!'

She watched as he packed his toiletries bag. He packed toothpaste, toothbrush, shaving cream and razors, and three cotton buds from the pack.

'I've been using this to paint the wart on the back of my heel,' said Radcliffe, picking up the nail-polish remover. 'Mind if I take it along?'

'A trial separation,' he repeated to himself, moving into the bedroom to find his overnight bag. 'I suppose you'll want me to finish that desktop publishing I'm doing at work?' he called from deep within the wardrobe.

Fancy stood at the bedroom door, and Radcliffe emerged and smiled at her. 'Because I don't know if I *should* be working on the Secret,' he said, raising an eyebrow, 'while we're on our *trial separation*. What do you think?'

At last Fancy understood. He was threatening her. He could not take this seriously because he had the trump card: he knew the Secret. He would go straight to the press. Of course he would. She could never leave him.

'Hm?' prompted Radcliffe, cocking his head to the side.

*

Cath was scrambling around the floor of the shed, surrounded by open drawers, spilling paper, books and cardboard. The photos Cassie had found were *all* of Cath. Now she opened and closed folders in a frenzy, grabbed at papers and dropped them. 'This is my *dog*,' she cried, 'my *school* report . . . my *string art*!' Cassie, sitting on the floor nearby, was turning the pages of another photo album, every now and then looking up at her teacher steadily and then looking back at the photos.

Radcliffe moved around the house again, carefully packing random items: a CD from the shelf; a kiwifruit from the fridge. He was bluffing. He knew that at any moment she would have to laugh, apologize, and tell him to stop.

Fancy felt a rising helplessness. The telephone rang and she jumped.

Climbing through the kitchen window into Grandma and Grandpa Zing's house, Listen thought she had better call a Zing, not Redwood Primary at all. There was something strange going on in that shed, and she was the one who had started it. She looked at the auto-dial buttons on the phone, each neatly labelled, and remembered that Fancy lived nearby. So she pressed the button labelled 'FANCY'.

'Listen! Hello, sweetheart, how are you?' Fancy sounded odd.

'Who is it?' That was Radcliffe's voice in the background.

'It's Listen! Listen's on the phone!'

'Fancy, I have to tell you something. I'm at Grandma and Grandpa Zing's place, and Cassie's here too.'

'Oh, honey! Well, they're not there. They've gone to look at some balloons! What did you say about Cass – how did *Cassie* get there? Why isn't she at school? Can you put her on the phone for me, honey?'

'I can't,' said Listen, bravely. 'She's in the garden shed out the back. She's OK though, because her teacher's there too. I think her name's Ms Murphy?'

Fancy was silent for a moment. There was the sound of breathing and then clicking fingernails on the receiver.

'Who did you say was there?' she said eventually.

'Ms Murphy. Cassie's teacher? She's in the garden shed with Cassie.'

'Listen? Can you get them out of there? I mean, right away?'

Now Listen was silent. 'Well,' she admitted, 'it's tricky. Ms Murphy is looking in the filing cabinets at the moment. I tried to stop her.'

Fancy took an immense breath of air and began to laugh: 'Ha ha ha!' It was a high-pitched laugh, and she repeated it: 'Ha ha ha!'

'What *is* it, Fancy?' Radcliffe's voice was in the background again.

'Oh well, Listen,' said Fancy in a fluting voice, 'the game's up now! Tell you what, I'll call my mother and get her back from the balloons. You sit tight and I'll be right over. Thanks for calling, sweetheart!'

Listen hung up and stared at the phone.

40

Radcliffe was standing on the porch, overnight bag on his shoulder, waiting for Fancy. She approached the front door and he grinned at her.

'I should go now?' he called. 'Check into a hotel?'

'That was Listen on the phone,' Fancy replied in her musical voice. 'And then I had to call my mother. Guess who's in the garden shed going through the cabinets?'

'Can't guess.'

'Try.'

'The *police*?'

'No, Radcliffe. Better! It's Cath Murphy! *She's in the garden shed!*'

Radcliffe turned pale grey. '*Cath?*'

'Yes!' cried Fancy, dim in the hallway. He tried to squint her into shape.

'Then the secret is out?'

'Yes! And, Radcliffe, I want a divorce!'

A gust of wind slammed the front door closed.

A gust of wind blew Marbie's hair all over her face, so that, for a moment, she was blinded. The same gust blew Nathaniel's eyes into narrow squints.

They had decided to walk to the park across from the Banana Bar so they could talk, and were standing on the median strip. Cars raced by in both directions, shaking their clothes with the speed.

'My phone's ringing!' called Marbie, hair in her eyes, taking one step forward, and looking down at her phone at the same time. 'It's Fancy!'

'Careful!' cried Nathaniel, pressing her back so abruptly that she did not stop on the median strip, but tripped into the lane behind, straight into the path of a sports car.

A gust of wind skidded across the yard and through the open door of the shed. It tossed papers in the air, extinguished three candles and knocked the fourth on to the WELCOME mat, where the flame took hold of a loose fibre.

Cath and Cassie, at the far end of the room, grabbed at the fluttering papers and photos and continued reading.

Among the papers and manila folders, Cath found: lists of every movie she had seen; charts showing her growth patterns from birth; an Excel spreadsheet of her favourite foods, colours, dance steps and magazines. Everything she touched was connected to her.

There were butterfly paintings she had done when she was six. There were dozens of close-up photographs of her face, aged eight or nine, hair in a high ponytail, leaning forward at her school desk. There were photos of her ankles. Photos of her walking home from school, swinging her school bag. Photos of her, aged twelve, talking to a horse named Buck and offering a secret carrot. There were lists of her favourite books, along with her own observations on these books. In one drawer, there was a collection of each of her favourite toys.

Although she continually gasped and murmured, 'Who *are* these people?' and 'What *is* this place?', she also murmured, 'That's *right*,' and 'I *loved* that doll!' She found herself feeling elated. Here it was! All of her! Here in this garden shed.

As she climbed back out of the kitchen window, Listen felt her eyes begin to sting. She looked up at the sky, which was a strange yellow-grey colour, as if someone had stretched a pair of nylons across it. Tendrils of black smoke were wafting through the open door of the shed.

She looked around for Ms Murphy and Cassie, but they were nowhere to be seen, so she ran across to the shed door. It was curtained in smoke and the heat thumped at her chest and threw her backwards. 'CASSIE!' she shouted, in terror. 'CASSIE, ARE YOU STILL IN THERE?'

She ran around the outside of the shed, pounding on the walls. 'GET OUT OF THERE! THE SHED'S ON FIRE!'

Cath was leaning over Cassie's shoulder as the child turned the pages of a photo album. 'That's me on a jet ski,' she said.

'OK,' agreed Cassie.

'. . . me riding a pony . . . me winning a medal at Brownies. That's me eating an ice cream . . . that's me behind that sunflower . . . that's me at a law class – who *took* that?'

Cassie quietly turned the pages, coughed and rubbed her eyes. Cath coughed, wiped sweat from her forehead and thought vaguely that she ought to open a window. She looked up to see where the windows were.

The front half of the shed seemed to have vanished.

'Help!'

Listen stopped thumping on the walls. A tinny voice was calling from somewhere deep inside.

'Help! Listen, can you hear us? We can't get to the door!' It was the Year 2 teacher, Ms Murphy.

'Call a fire engine!' That was Cassie's voice.

Listen backed away from the shed to look at it again: there were no windows and no back door.

She ran towards the front door again, but the smoke was gushing out now. An industrious rustle sounded, cut through by sudden pops of breaking glass.

Next she ran to the garden hose, which was neatly wound on a spool by the garden tap. She wrenched it out of its spool, turned the tap to full and pelted across the yard dragging the hose behind her. The hose reached its limit well before she had reached the shed and jolted her on to the grass. In any case, looking down at the slender plastic and feeling the weakish water dribble from the nozzle, she knew it would not have worked.

She stood again, squinting through the smoke at the burning shed. There must be another way out. Her eyes drifted up and caught a glint of sun on the skylight. It was too high for them to reach, but if she could somehow get on to the roof and lower a rope down to them, she could help them out. Where would she find a rope?

Her eyes swung to the gum tree and its old rope swing. She would climb the tree, untie the ropes and climb on to the roof of the shed.

But the shed had such slippery high walls, she knew she could never climb it.

She would have to jump from the tree to the roof of the shed.

The tree was smooth but the ropes of the swing were helpful. 'Use your feet,' the climbing instructor had always shouted. Her sneakers slipped on the bark.

Panting, she straddled a branch near the top of the tree, dragged the swing seat up to her level and began to untie the knots. They were tied in rethreaded figure eights, which was what they used at climbing. She wound the rope around the seat and looked over at the shed.

Black smoke billowed from the doorway and crept through cracks in the roof. Beyond the roof of the shed she could see the grounds of Bellbird High next door, where a small group of students was gathering. Now they were moving slowly across the yard, watching her.

There was no time to stop. She stood up on the branch and tucked the swing seat, wound in its own ropes, under her arm. The leaves above her tangled with her hair and twigs scratched at her neck, but she knew she had to start in the right position: one knee raised, the other bent, one arm forward, the other back.

There was only room on the branch for two and a half steps of the starting run, but she used them, bumping her head on the branch above. And then she leaped. She was rising into the air. There was a rush of wind in her face. Her legs were steady as a dancer's: for the briefest moment, she was flying.

She landed by the skylight with a self-conscious kick, which was the correct way to finish a flying side kick.

There was a small metal handle on the side of the skylight, which burned her hand when she touched it. She pulled an edge of her T-shirt to cover the handle and wrenched it open, so that the skylight lifted high into the air. Then she was on her hands and knees looking down into blackness.

Cath crouched against the far wall, pressing her arms, her T-shirt, her skirt against her face, but nothing would stop the smoke. She was clutching Cassie tightly to her body, the girl's face pressed hard into her stomach. *This is how my parents died,* she remembered. She looked around again for a way out. It was too high to climb to the skylight. Flames were hurtling around the room, excited by the scattering of papers and folders, melting into the plastic covers of photo albums. There was a shrieking wrench as timber crashed on to the floor. The heat felt tight, like a rubber glove.

There was a shout from above.

*

Listen lay flat on her stomach and lowered the swing seat through the open skylight and down into the shed. The ropes of the swing were looped around her wrists and gripped in her palms, but she had no idea if she was strong enough.

Cath saw the swing above her and reached for it, but then stopped to gather Cassie close again. With one hand, she caught the swing seat.

'Wrap your arms around the seat,' shouted Listen, 'and use your feet on the wall.' Cassie's eyes were tightly closed against the smoke, but she nodded and wound her arms around the seat. With Cath's help, she placed one foot high against the wall, and looked up towards Listen.

Listen slid back, pulling the swing ropes as she did so, and burning her knees on the shed roof, until the ropes were tight. Now she was dragging Cassie's weight: she started flat on her stomach, inching back along the roof, and then lifted herself on to her elbows and knees, until she was finally standing up, leaning backwards and pulling, arm over arm. Below, the shed was so dark with smoke that Cath was only a pale shape.

When she was high enough, Cassie reached a hand up and Listen helped her scramble out. They both fell back on to the roof for a moment and looked around. Smoke seeped out of the skylight.

Cassie crouched close to Listen while Listen lowered the swing again. Below, now pressed into a corner by flames, Cath grasped the swing and looked up doubtfully.

But this time, Listen felt the strangest surge of strength. She dragged at the rope with both hands, again sliding back from the skylight on her stomach, and within moments Cath's hands appeared at the edges.

Now all three huddled together, looking for a way to get down. They could hear the shriek of a fire engine; also, they could see that the Zings' back yard was crowded with students from next door, shouting and waving at them.

416

'JUMP! JUMP!'

Cassie straightened up, coughed once and jumped. A flurry of hands caught her.

Cath and Listen looked at each other and down at the school kids below, and then, feeling the heat burst around them, they both dived into the crowd.

Listen felt hands all over her stomach, arms and legs, and found herself carried in a tumbling rush to the front lawn, away from the heat. There was a bustle of shouting and excitement, and she was lowered on to the grass while students asked where it hurt and whether she was burning.

'Give her space!'

'Get some ice!'

'No, not ice!'

'Get the hose!'

The students backed away from her in a circle. They were quiet for a moment, watching, uncertain, as she lay coughing and staring up at them.

She tried to focus on the students, to stop them from shifting in her gaze. Just before she passed out, she saw three distinct faces: Carl Vandenberg, the black belt from Tae Kwon Do; Samalia Janz, the girl with the ponytail from rock-climbing; and Annie Webb, that new girl with the gold stud in her chin. All three wore Bellbird High uniforms.

The gold stud caught the light, and Listen thought she heard Annie murmur, 'Are you, by any chance, the sorcerer?'

Although she knew that this must be a dream, she felt the softest rush of gladness.

Part 21

Friday Afternoon

41

Fancy and Radcliffe arrived at the Zing house to a clamour of fire trucks, school children and smoke. Ambulances were parked at jaunty angles, and there seemed to be girls on stretchers everywhere they turned. Shortish men in uniforms leaned briskly over the stretchers.

'Cassie?' called Fancy, but no sound emerged. She watched vaguely as Radcliffe hurried into the jostle, throwing questions around him. After a moment, he returned and told her to get into the car.

They arrived at the hospital at the same time as Grandpa Zing, Grandma Zing, Marbie and Nathaniel, which caused some confusion in the revolving door. The confusion intensified when they found their way inside and were directed, variously, to Accidents & Emergencies, the children's ward, and the Burns Division.

In the lift, Grandpa Zing said to Radcliffe, 'We drove straight back to our place like Fancy said we should, and followed the ambulances here. What's going on?'

'I spoke to an ambulance officer,' Radcliffe told him, watching the lift buttons grimly. 'Apparently, Listen and Cath Murphy were climbing the tree in your back garden and it caught fire. Cassie had to rescue them. All that smoke, eh? From a single tree!'

In a corridor, Grandma Zing explained to Nathaniel, 'I don't think Listen was involved, Nathaniel. Cassie had an asthma attack, that's all, because of the smoke from a bonfire in the school yard next door. Now is this the right direction?'

On a stairway, Fancy said to Marbie, 'What have you done to your knees?'

'I fell into the path of a sports car,' Marbie replied. 'But it swerved.'

In a waiting room, a doctor said to Fancy and Radcliffe, 'We suspect that Cassie may have smoke inhalation poisoning.'

'What do you mean?' demanded Radcliffe.

'We understand she was trapped in the burning room – a shed, was it? Or a garage? In any case, she was trapped for some time. She's under ten. She's exhibiting difficulty breathing. And there is some slight discolouration of her skin. These factors add up and tell us smoke poisoning is likely. Now, she suffered only very slight burns, and we have already begun treatment – in these circumstances, the prognosis is good. But I must impress upon you that a condition like this can be extremely serious, and the major cause of . . . There *is* a chance . . . I must ask you to *prepare* . . .'

The doctor's voice seemed to fade in and out.

'She's asthmatic,' Fancy tried to say.

In a small office, a nurse said to Nathaniel, Marbie and Grandpa Zing, 'Now, it's *Listen*, did you say? Right, well, she has some bruising, cuts, some minor burns and grazes. She's exhausted and she's resting right now, but otherwise she's fine. We're keeping an eye on her for smoke inhalation, but am I right in thinking that she wasn't actually in the shed? She was the one who helped the others out?'

'The *shed* was on fire?' murmured Grandpa Zing. 'Has anybody told my wife?'

In a corridor, a doctor said to Grandma Zing, 'She's sleeping now, but we've treated her for second-degree burns on her arms – it looks like she was wrapping her arms around the little one, protecting her from the fire, like so . . . You need me to explain second-degree burns? No?'

For a while the family moved about between hospital rooms and sleeping girls in a state of agitated confusion, but eventually they settled down.

Radcliffe and Fancy sat by Cassie, watching her without a word. Once, Radcliffe cleared his throat and said, 'Fancy, the doctor mentioned that her asthma might be worse now, worse than ever.'

'Forever?' breathed Fancy.

'Than ever,' corrected Radcliffe.

Then they were silent again.

Nathaniel, Marbie and Grandpa Zing sat in a row by Listen's bed, occasionally chatting about the contents of the hospital menu, or the fact that Nathaniel's sneakers had a squeak. Mr Zing suggested he try beating them with a stick, or drowning them in a bucket of water for a day or two. He swore that these techniques were effective. A nurse noticed Marbie's bleeding knees and chastised her before washing and dressing them.

Grandma Zing, meanwhile, sat alone by the sleeping Cath, gazing at her steadily.

'Now, Cath,' she murmured eventually. 'If it's true that the shed burned down, I don't know what might be left of our garden there. Which is a shame, as I think you'd like that garden. We have so many flowers! Let me think. We've got sweet peas, begonia, pansies, petunias, snowdrops, cyclamen, daisies and orchids. No roses though, because of the thorns. We've got port wine magnolias, camellias, dahlias and azaleas. We've got a vegetable garden too, you know. Broccoli, carrots, beans and peas. Corn, cauliflower, lettuce, parsley, strawberries, tomatoes, mint and thyme. And there's David's little lemon tree, of course. You might have noticed that.'

*

Cassie dreamed of porridge. 'Never put porridge in your nose,' she told Lucinda, who only coughed in reply.

Listen dreamed of glimmers on the surface of the turtle pond.

'As a reward!' said the principal happily, 'for squeaking sneakers!'

'Bravo,' said a voice. It was Carl Vandenberg from Tae Kwon Do.

'It's silver,' Listen told him.

'Bravo,' Carl repeated, more quietly this time.

Cath Murphy dreamed that her cat, Violin, was evil, and she had to save him. It was too late: Violin was treading through dried brown grass towards nesting plovers which would pluck out his eyes.

'Violin!' she shrieked, but her cat gave a snort of contempt and ran his claws slowly down her forearms.

Cassie breathed a single, high-pitched wheeze, which surprised her. She turned her eyes towards her mother. 'I can run as fast as a bus,' she whispered. Her mother said, '*Can* you?' and burst into tears.

Listen opened her eyes and saw Marbie, her father and Grandpa Zing sitting by the side of her bed. 'Sorry,' she said. Grandpa Zing leaned forward and tapped her on the head with the hospital menu.

Cath woke up. A plump woman was sitting by her bed. 'Hello,' said the woman. 'Are you all right? The painkillers are working? I hear you've seen our garden shed!'

Part 22

Lunchtime on a Saturday

Two Weeks Later

42

Two weeks had passed since the fire, and Grandpa Zing had already built a gazebo on the site of the garden shed. It was here, for symbolic reasons, that the Zings held their 'explanation lunch' for Cath.

While in the hospital, she had been extremely confused by everything Mrs Zing said, so that, in the end, she spoke in her law-student voice to say, 'Why should I not call the police about your shed, please?'

Mrs Zing asked that she wait until she was home and felt better, and then they could hold an explanation lunch, and *then*, if she still wanted to, she could telephone the police. It was not clear what she could say to the police even if she did call them (the Zings could deny the contents of their burned-down garden shed), and what she really wanted was an explanation. So she had agreed to Mrs Zing's request.

Cath Murphy sat at one end of the table, and Mr and Mrs Zing sat at the other. The table was draped in a new white cloth and was surrounded by elegant garden chairs. Bellbirds chimed in the bush behind the Zings' back fence. A kooka-burra rested on the fence itself, silently watching the family as they in turn regarded their cucumber soup and reached for their serviettes and spoons.

Cath had been introduced to each of the Zings on the way out to the garden, and now she sat with her back straight and surveyed each Zing in turn. On her right sat the girl, Listen, who had rescued her from the fire, then Listen's father, Nathaniel, and Nathaniel's girlfriend, Marbie Zing. On her left sat Cassie Zing, then Cassie's mother, Fancy, and Fancy's husband, Radcliffe. Occasionally Cassie whispered an observation to Cath. She had already whispered that her parents were getting a divorce, but they were both going to come and watch her win races at the Redwood Sports Carnival the week after next. Now she was whispering something about the mint sauce.

'Well,' declared Mrs Zing, in a ringing voice, and people drew their hands back from their spoons.

'I thought I would begin with a general explanation,' she said. 'Then, if you have any questions, we can do our best to answer them.'

'Mmm,' said Cath faintly.

Mrs Zing breathed in deeply and began. Her narration was punctuated by clinking spoons, chiming bellbirds and the occasional chuckle of the kookaburra or whip of a distant whipbird.

'Several years ago,' Mrs Zing began, tilting her head slightly as if to remind herself of the details, 'my husband, David –' here, Mr Zing raised a hand to identify himself – 'yes, David here, went to Ireland to write a novel. While he was away, I got a job making pies on the set of *Pie in the Sky*. I had an affair with the star of that movie, Nikolai Valerio – yes, Nikolai Valerio. I had an affair and became pregnant with his child. I told nobody, not even Nikolai, until five months had passed. Then I told him. Mistake, I suppose! He promised to come to my house to figure things out, but I never saw him again. I got a note from the set decoration supervisor, pinned to an artificial rose, if I remember correctly, and it informed me that *Pie in the Sky* had been moved to a secret location. My pie-making was no longer required.'

She paused, and everyone looked at Cath, who was smiling gently.

'Nikolai's career relied, or so his people thought, on his loyalty to his wife, Rebekka. His image was that of perfection.

He was the romantic innocent. Now, there were already rumours surrounding Nikolai's friendship with me – people had noticed the way we caught each other's eyes, and, more to the point, a feisty young reporter was on our trail. Do you know, he had a photo of me and Nikolai, slipping into Nikolai's hotel?! This reporter had approached me, posing as some kind of a set electrician, and asked me all about myself. Me, being a chatterbox, mentioned that my husband was in Ireland and had been gone for almost a year. I think you'll see where this is going!'

Cath clenched her teeth and looked around the table. Apart from Listen and Cassie, who were staring at Mrs Zing in wonder, everybody was eating calmly, now and then glancing sideways at Cath. It seemed that nobody planned to stop this woman. Cath was going to have to participate in the humouring of somebody delusional and she was not sure that was very healthy.

'Anyway,' continued the delusional woman, 'the reporter had been asking questions. He didn't have much, of course – there could be all sorts of innocent reasons why I was with Nikolai outside his hotel. But if it emerged that I had become pregnant? While my husband was away? Well! You get the picture. So, Nikolai's people took steps. They flew Rebekka over to join Nikolai, and gave the reporter those famous photos of the two of them dancing barefoot in a meadow. They got my husband, David, to come home, to try to improve appearances. They rushed me, David, Fancy and Marbie –' Fancy and Marbie raised their hands, solemnly, to identify themselves – 'to a secret location by the sea. There, they offered me a deal.'

'A deal?' prompted Cath, still playing along, but growing increasingly irritable. She had not touched her soup spoon.

'Right. Valerio's people would arrange for you – you understand, of course, that *you* were the baby – yes, they would arrange for you to be adopted, and *I* could secretly keep an eye on you. They set up a company structure through which I would communicate with Nikolai, report on your progress and make requisitions for anything you needed. The corporation paid David and me a generous salary for our work. I'm sure you can never forgive me for giving you up, Cath, but let me assure you, I did it for your own sake. I wanted you to have a normal life. If I'd kept you, that reporter would have added things up, and it would have come out, and truly, if the world knew who your real father was –'

At last, Cath interrupted. 'My *biological* parents,' she said firmly, 'died in a house fire. I have a photograph of them at home, and I can assure you my father is not Nikolai Valerio. Nikolai Valerio! For heaven's sake. Of course,' she continued, her voice growing strident, 'I have adoptive parents who I consider to be my parents. They live in Perth and know nothing about what I found in your garden shed because I knew it would just upset and confuse them, but don't think for a moment that I won't tell them if I need to! I don't want to hear another word about Nikolai Valerio. I *know* who my parents are! I'll show you the photo if you like. But I want one sane person to tell me *right this moment* why you people had all that information about me. I mean, right now. Stop wasting my time or I'm calling the police.' She held up her cellphone impressively.

'Ah!' said Mrs Zing. 'The photographs of your *"parents"*! I'd almost forgotten. Yes, we arranged two photos. One, if I remember rightly, was of a young blondish couple, the other of a big firefighter who was supposed to have rescued you. All three were regular extras in Nikolai's movies. We made up the fire story so you'd never go looking for your biological parents.'

'Your adoptive parents seem like very nice people,' said Mr

Zing. 'It's probably a good thing that you haven't upset them with this.'

'About the shed,' Fancy put in helpfully. 'Well, we kept all our records about you there, as well as the photos. Medical, dental, educational . . .'

Cath choked on her gasp.

'Oh,' said Fancy sadly.

'It was like this,' tried Radcliffe, leaning his elbows on the table. 'Here's an example. You remember when you had that skiing accident when you were sixteen or so?'

'You needed reconstructive surgery for your knee,' Marbie reminded her.

'Oh yes!' said Mrs Zing. 'We all learned as much as we could about knees and knee operations! We became quite the experts! All the information is –'

Cath had stopped listening. 'How do you know about the photo of my biological parents?' she demanded, but her voice trembled. 'They *did* die in a fire. They're not *extras* in a film. How do you know about my photos?'

Mrs Zing suggested that they go inside and watch the DVD of *Turntable Troubles,* Nikolai Valerio's fifth movie. Radcliffe pointed out, as the movie began, that Cath had the same fine cheekbones and bump on the end of her nose as Nikolai. She ignored him. Mrs Zing paused at the spots in the movie when Cath's 'mother', 'father', and 'heroic firefighter' appeared as extras in the background.

It was confirmed that *Turntable Troubles* had been made five years after these people were supposed to have 'died'.

43

Extracts from the Zing Garden Shed

Comito R.B., 'Compression Pin Fixation of Articular Phalangeal Fractures', *Royal Bartholomew Orthopaedic Review*, Vol. XII, No. 2, February 1989.

Recurring Nightmare No. 4
A very scary rabbit stands in the centre of the road. It is ordinary-sized and ordinary to look at, but there is something very scary about it.
Number of Reported Recurrences: 3
Subject's Age: 11
Reporter: Newspaper delivery boy

SURVEILLANCE EQUIPMENT – CONSIGNMENT
Pencil sharpener with hidden camera, transmitter and receiver.
Retail Price: $250
Your Frequent Buyer Price: $225

44

Cath was staring at Cassie, who was spearing peas on to her fork. She had three peas on each prong of her fork and was trying for another.

'All right,' Cath said finally, looking up around the table. 'Just *assuming* that this story is true –'

'Oh, it *is*,' interrupted Radcliffe, buttering a slice of bread vigorously.

'Just assuming,' repeated Cath sternly, and Mrs Zing nodded her encouragement. 'How did you get all that information about me? You had photographs of me at my desk in primary school. You had photographs of me in my law classes! In my *dining room*! You had photos of my ankles! You had my *academic records*!'

'Well, good question,' said Mrs Zing. 'We had three main avenues of enquiry. First, and most importantly, we had spies. Second, we had gathering techniques. Third, we had one or two hidden cameras.' She raised her voice slightly, so she could pretend not to hear Cath blustering: '*Spies? Hidden cameras?*'

'In relation to spies, we chose people around the edges of your life. Your postman, the school secretary, the local florist, colleagues, acquaintances, bus drivers and so on. They had to engage you in conversation, ask routine questions, take secret photos of you and so on. And if we needed to get into your apartment for some reason we might send out an Urgent Request for a Distraction to all the spies. We recruited them by hinting that this was a top secret, yet slightly shady organization – you know, we appealed to their thirst for adventure. They didn't know anything about the Valerio connection, of course.

And they had to sign very strict confidentiality agreements. We paid them so well that it was hard for them to refuse. Also, easy for them to ignore any pangs of conscience . . .'

'Mum did most of the recruiting,' said Fancy. 'She always knew exactly the right people to approach. She never got a refusal.'

'In relation to gathering techniques, well, Fancy and Marbie developed all sorts of methods for getting access to school offices, dentists, doctors, physios and so on, and taking photos of your records. We were meticulous about maintaining up-to-date information. Cath, you really should eat. You need protein and carbohydrates to help recover from burns, I read that. Nathaniel, help Cath to the gravy, would you?'

'Of course,' said Nathaniel politely.

'And in relation to the hidden cameras?' Cath said coldly, ignoring the hovering gravy boat. Nathaniel set it down next to her plate.

'Well, don't worry yourself too much about that,' said Mrs Zing. 'They never had sound-recording devices, so we didn't hear what you said. We had several around your house when you were small.'

'We should let her know that her adoptive parents didn't have anything to do with this,' said Mr Zing.

'You're right,' agreed Mrs Zing. 'This had nothing to do with them. They never had a clue. That was a golden rule. But anyway, we cut back on the number of cameras as you got older to protect your privacy. From the age of twelve, we stayed out of your bedroom, for example – that's the age when I stopped going into Fancy and Marbie's bedroom, so it seemed about right.'

'You cut back on the number of cameras,' said Cath, 'to *protect my privacy*?'

Everyone looked down at their food, except Cassie and Listen, who both stared silently at Cath.

45

Extracts from the Zing Garden Shed

Interim Surveillance Report
Agent: Ella Hietzke (swimming coach, Olympic
Medal winner)
Subject: Cath Murphy
Subject's Age: 11
Oh! She is very sweet little girl but cannot swim to
save a life. I always think she is drowning but it's
just her breaststroke. Today I say again, 'You want
to be a lawyer? Why not be a lawyer? You make
lots of cash!', and she say she wants a horse. 'A
horse?' I say. 'What you want with a horse?' She
had a little cold, but not too se

Interim Surveillance Report
Agent: Leonie Marple-Hedgington (fellow student at teachers' college)
Subject: Cath Murphy
Subject's Age: 19

I have today engaged in further dialogic exchange with Subject in order to derive/arrive [at] conclusions/ suppositions in relation to her current (un)state of 'mind'. Subject applies discourses of 'fear' and 'anxiety' to [imp]ending end-of-year exams and her first practical teaching assignments. Subject [un]consciously accepts dictates of patriarchy (e.g. 'What are you supposed to *wear* when you teach second-graders?!') I invited

Interim Surveillance Report
Agent: Suzanne Barker (teacher, Year 1A)
Subject: Cath Murphy
Subject's Age: 22

As requested by you, I invited Cath and her new boyfriend to my place for dinner at the weekend. I gave them a nice roast but the potatoes came out floury, and, I don't know, maybe I overcooked the carrots? Cath seemed happy enough but I didn't take to the boyfriend. He is some kind of environmentalist and goes on about swamps and whatnot, and I thought: '*Well, hang on, is that interesting to the rest of us?*' My kids were pulling faces behind his back, which is a good sign – kids seem to have a sixth sense about things like this. He is just morbidly fascinated with his swamps and he'd leave Cath for one in a second. I saw Cath looking hopefully at the bread basket while he was talking, and he could have noticed and passed it over, but oh no, not him. Anyway, I just don't think she had the aura of someone truly loved and

Interim Surveillance Report
Agent: Professor David Carmichael
Subject: Cath Murphy
Subject's Age: 23
Subject appeared emotional and somewhat
unstable in my class today. Of course, she could
simply have been bored to tears, but I do try to
keep my lectures lively. Photographs of Subject at
her Desk (taken with Turban Cam) are attached
and, as you c

Interim Surveillance Report
Agent: Katie Toby (teacher, Kinder A)
Subject: Cath Murphy
Subject's Age: 23
This report is about something VERY
IMPORTANT which happened today!! I was in
the school car park and I saw CATH MURPHY
and the other Year 2 teacher, WARREN
WOODFORD, together. He is married, I should
add! Anyway, they were about to go to a movie
together, which I called in of course, but the thing
is, they seemed VERY nervous. Could something
be going on between them?!!! STAY TUNED and
I'll keep you post

Interim Surveillance Report
Agent: Debbie Harland (corner-store employee)
Subject: Cath Murphy
Subject's Age: 24

No more dreams to report *but* . . . (suspenseful drum roll) . . . I just wanted to tell you a brief event from last night. Cath and a *man* came into the store, around midnight, in the middle of the snowstorm. 'What have we here?' I said to myself, but it turned out he was a teacher from her school and they'd just come from a party. They bought crisps and salsa. He took a phone call while they were in my shop, and he said something like: 'Breda! Hi! Don't even worry yourself. No taxis, so I'm staying at Cath's. We're just on our way. You warm enough?'

Then he smiled happily, and told me fairly proudly that that was his wife.

In the circumstances – he was honest and loving with his wife; Cath seemed more keen on the snow than she did on him, etc., etc. – I didn't sense any romance, and I'd say things were all above board. And that's all, folks!

46

'Now,' said Mrs Zing, 'at least try a piece of Fancy's famous chocolate terrine!' She was slicing it up and passing dessert bowls down both sides of the table.

Cath was pale and silent, so Mrs Zing continued: 'The final thing we must explain is *why* we were gathering this information. There were two reasons, Cath, one minor and one major. The minor reason was this: you may find this hard to imagine, but your father, Nikolai, adored you. He was greedy for information about you – you are, after all, his eldest child, and his only daughter. So we compiled the information into regular reports, with photos affixed, along with the requisitions for certain funds – and this kept him happy.'

'And kept him happily sending us money to carry on,' Radcliffe pointed out.

At this, Listen accidentally interrupted by saying in a disbelieving voice: 'Nikolai Valerio?'

'But the *major* reason was that we wanted to make your life wonderful,' Mrs Zing continued. 'We wanted to give you gifts. We wanted you to have every opportunity to be happy and to develop your potential. So! Let's think of some examples, everyone!'

'Well,' said Fancy shyly, 'Marbie is a great swimmer but she never got swimming lessons when she was young. We thought you might have the same talent and we wanted to make sure it wasn't wasted. So we found a way to get rid of the mediocre swimming teacher you had – I remember us joking that we should trip her up so she'd break a bone! But we didn't do that, just got her another job offer – and replaced her with a former Olympic champion.'

'Any time you were sad,' said Marbie, 'we tried to think of a present that might cheer you up – like a trip to Disneyland or a puppy dog or a movie pass or a pair of designer sunglasses. And the same on your birthdays.'

'Nikolai gave you birthday presents too,' said Mrs Zing. 'But you probably never noticed them. He always got us to find out who your favourite singer was, and then he would write a song for you and get them to put it to music and release it on the date of your birthday. You remember Kylie Minogue's hit "Blue-Eyed Blonde Beauty" which came out on your twelfth birthday?'

'And there was that Eminem song on your twenty-first birthday,' said Marbie. 'I loved that song. About the student at teachers' college with the pet cat? Eminem added all the swearwords, though, which really annoyed Nikolai. I always wondered if you noticed the similarity to your life.'

'Not really,' whispered Cath. 'I didn't listen to the words.'

'Shame,' said Mr Zing.

'And we had *projects*,' added Radcliffe, 'for more major things. I remember when we decided that it would be good to broaden your horizons, so we tried to put you in the way of trips or jobs in exotic locations such as Mongolia and Nepal! That was Project 53, wasn't it?'

'Project 55,' corrected Mrs Zing.

'The funny thing about *that*,' continued Radcliffe, 'was that your friends kept swooping in and stealing the offers! It just goes to show, you can't –'

'The spies were supposed to find out what you were unhappy about,' Nathaniel cut in. 'Or what you really wanted. And then the family thought up ways to get those things to you.'

'Nikolai was also keen to steer you in certain directions,'

added Mrs Zing. 'It wasn't just us. Occasionally, he would send an edict – a special request for us to concentrate on some aspect of your life. For instance, he wanted you to be refined – a woman of resources. It was his idea to get you horse-riding lessons and that wine appreciation course, when you were older? Remember?'

'Ah yes!' said Radcliffe. 'And he was so keen that you become a lawyer! His dream was for you to eventually become the managing corporate lawyer for the Valerio empire! We tried *everything* to—'

'Anyway,' interrupted Marbie, 'the challenge was how to get these things to you without being obvious.'

'That was the fun part,' agreed Fancy.

'We used scholarships, prizes, raffles, free offers – things turning up on your doorstep – anything we could think of.'

'The magazines were the stroke of genius,' smiled Mrs Zing.

'Fancy wrote most of the content,' said Marbie, 'and Radcliffe did the desktop publishing at work – we all thought up the competitions.'

'We tried hiding things in taxis,' said Nathaniel.

'But you kept not noticing them!' cried Radcliffe.

'Or when you did,' said Mrs Zing, 'you gave them to the driver. You were so honest.'

Cath was breathing in, ready to unleash a stinging attack, when she realized they had stopped looking at her. They were chatting animatedly among themselves, reminiscing.

Extracts from the Zing Garden Shed

(From 'Minutes of ZFS Meeting', May 1994)
- F and M both adamant that C should be reading *Cosmo Girl* rather than *Dolly* if she wants to be 'cool'
- F has noticed that C's skin is breaking out and thinks she should try Clearasil Daily Face-wash
- R suggests a door-to-door make-up consultant offer free advice and free samples
- *Resolved* that sub-committee be formed, consisting of

(From 'Minutes of ZFS Meeting', January 2003)
- M thinks we should have project to make her wear more blue – thinks she looks great in blue and it brings out her eyes
- F proposes a project to get her to try Pilates, says she herself never has time to try it but

SURVEILLANCE EQUIPMENT – CONSIGNMENT
Sunglasses with hidden camera, transmitter and receiver.
Retail Price: $450
Your Frequent Buyer Price: $435

48

Cath was feeling pale.

She sat with her chair a little distant from the table, and her chin a little distant from her neck. The Zing family's words meandered along, while her forearms stung faintly and her vision blurred.

'Here,' said Fancy, quietly sliding the milk jug towards her. 'Coffee stays warmer if you add the milk straight away.'

'Does it?' said Cath, strangely calmed for a moment by this practical hint.

Fancy nodded: 'The milk is like a small, white blanket.'

'Oh!' cried Mrs Zing, from her end of the table. 'I've forgotten the chocolate strawberries! Hang on there while I get them.'

Everyone watched as she crossed the lawn and listened to the gentle thud of the back door closing.

The family set down their coffee cups and watched Cath.

'I still don't believe any of this,' said Cath. 'I wouldn't believe it at all if I hadn't seen that garden shed. But just pretending it's true, I have a question. OK, I can see that you might decide to keep an eye on a baby when you give it up for adoption, but why keep going? Why didn't one of you *stop* this? I'm grown-up now. I've got a job. Why did this go on for so long?'

'Well,' said Radcliffe, heartily, 'for one thing, there wasn't really anything *illegal* about it. And to be perfectly honest, it was a lot of fun! All the exciting subterfuge and espionage and so on!'

'Nothing *illegal* about it?' Cath turned an icy gaze on Radcliffe. 'You think there's nothing illegal about planting cameras in my apartment and stealing my medical records, do you?'

'We prefer not to think in terms of the legal/illegal paradigm,' murmured Fancy.

'You didn't know it was happening, so how could it hurt you?' Marbie cut in. 'Also, it was all for you. It was to protect you because, you know, if it had come out that you were Valerio's daughter, you'd never have had a normal life. The media would have watched you more than we ever did, *and* they'd have put it in the papers. We only put it in the garden shed.'

'Maybe that was my decision to make,' Cath said. But she said it half-heartedly: something Marbie had said seemed oddly familiar and was making her uncomfortable.

'We gave you a lot of presents,' Radcliffe pointed out.

'The thing is,' said Marbie, 'you became part of our life. You were the person we took care of on Friday nights.'

'Right,' agreed Radcliffe. 'Once you get your filing system up, it's hard to stop working on the files.'

'And we couldn't give you up,' said Fancy. 'We just couldn't. We loved you.'

Mr Zing cleared his throat. Everyone turned to him, a little surprised. He had hardly said a word for the entire meal. 'It's like this,' he said, holding out the palms of his hands. 'Some people like to change things by casting them in a different light – by telling the right stories about them. Let's say, for example, a man has a midlife crisis. He thinks he's destined for greater things than a family, and he runs away to a one-room apartment in West Ryde. Let's say his wife makes that event into something else. Let's say she calls it an *artistic mission*, a trip to Ireland to write novels. Now, take a look at that! He's not a selfish, depressed fool any more, he's a man with a dream.

See what I mean? Call a thing by a different name and you change it.'

Even the kookaburra was surprised into silence.

'You mean lie about it?' Cassie whispered.

'OK,' continued Mr Zing, pretending not to hear Cassie, and clearing his throat again. 'Now let's say this woman gives up her baby. Oh, she does it for all the right reasons – she thinks she's giving the baby a better life; she's struggling to feed the two kids she already has, what with her no-hoper husband, and she knows she can't afford another child. She thinks she's saving her family, but the fact remains, she gives away her baby. So, let's say she calls this event something else – a *Zing Family Secret*. A complicated secret with corporate structures, subterfuge and spies, a secret that is all about watching over the baby, *taking care* of the child. Let's say we ever put a stop to calling it that? We might have had to see what it was.'

Quietly, he pressed out his final words, 'It was a bribe, Cath. She gave up her baby and they paid her off. That's what it was.'

Somewhere, in the bush behind the fence, a whipbird commenced a long, suspenseful toooooo which ended in a sharp whip-crack. Then the back door slammed and Mrs Zing emerged with the strawberries.

Part 23

The Story of the Spell Book

49

Although Maude set out to be scrupulously honest in her narration of the Zing Family Secret, she did not tell Cath everything. For example, she did not tell her that, once Cath had been transferred to Valerio's people – after which the Zings returned home from the seaside – Maude lay in bed for several weeks. She only got up to do the ironing.

David slept on the living-room couch, made sausages and tomatoes for dinner each night, and did the girls' homework for them. In the bedroom, Maude lay still with her eyes open wide, exhausting her imagination by forcing it to hold, steady on her chest, the image, weight, fragrance and warmth of her baby girl. A soft little cat pressing itself ever closer.

When she did fall asleep, she dreamed that she was standing in the basket of a hot-air balloon. Behind her was her baby in a bassinet, and Maude, without pausing, gathered up the bassinet and tipped it over the side. A parachute opened as it fell, and Maude caught her breath: *the child is saved!*, but then she saw that the parachute was upside down. The bassinet crashed to the ground and was smashed to pieces.

Day after day, Maude lay in bed, snapping in and out of this nightmare: the balloon, the bassinet, the baby rushing to the ground. Each time she woke in horror at the sound of the crash and each time she sobbed: *I changed my mind, I changed my mind, I changed my mind.*

One night, waking from such a dream, she regarded the circle of the moon through her bedroom window.

I have given my child away, she thought, *but the dream means more than that.*

Why, she asked herself, did I do it? The answers rushed to her at once: You were on the verge of bankruptcy! You couldn't afford a third child! The child was born of scandal! You gave her the gift of a normal life! It was *all for the child*.

She stared at the moon and blinked. It was so sharp-edged, she realized with a start, it would sever the tendons in your hands if you reached up to hold it. The sharp edge cut into her soul and she thought: *It was for the money*.

That was the reason.

She had thought herself on the verge of a life of adventures and balloons. She had believed that the baby was her ticket into this life. Instead, the baby had frightened it away.

She remembered sitting on the couch in that house by the sea, her average husband beside her, profoundly depressed at her romantic loss, and resentful of her unborn child. Nikolai's men sat opposite and promised her astonishing wealth.

Well, at least I could be rich. That much I deserve. It had flickered across her mind. She remembered chuckling the thought away and gathering sensible reasons in its place.

What she saw now, however, was this: by accepting Nikolai's offer to conceal the birth of their child, she had agreed to live in a fictional world in which she herself was wealthy but her child did not exist.

I accepted a bribe to deny my child's existence.

It was like realizing she had murdered her own baby.

Maude wrote the entire Spell Book on her bedroom floor that night.

She typed with trembling fingers, knowing that her words were frenetic, infusing them with her own urgency. For she now saw clearly that this was a horror story – her affair with Nikolai, the birth of Cath – it was a story of betrayal, heartbreak and greed, a story of selfishness and denial. She needed to unravel it at once.

Her only hope was that stories, like all immense things, even horrifying things, are only collections of small fragments. Kneeling on the carpet with her typewriter, she took apart the fragments of the story. The small events that had taken place; the mean little thoughts that had fluttered through her mind.

The story began, she recalled, on the day that her husband telephoned a taxi and left her (*a Spell To Make Someone Decide To Take a Taxi*). Then she had discovered the pie-chef job in the *Trading Post* when looking for a new vacuum cleaner (*a Spell To Make a Vacuum Cleaner Break*). She had won the boat-scene role in the film when the leading lady fought with the director (*a Spell To Make Two Happy People Have a HUGE Fight Over Absolutely NOTHING*) and in such a way the affair had begun. The affair had ended, effectively, when Nikolai asked the set supervisor to send her an artificial rose (*a Spell To Make Someone Give Someone a Rose*).

At this, Maude had plunged into despair. She had yearned to be seen, to be acknowledged as Nikolai's true love, and had fantasized that the reporter might find more concrete evidence: a note in a jeans pocket; a sock in the hotel laundry. (*a Spell To Make Someone Find Something Unexpected In a Washing Machine*). She had been furious with Nikolai, and imagined him eating chocolate cake laced with walnuts, so that his lips would swell like balloons (*a Spell To Make Somebody Eat a Piece of Chocolate Cake*).

The filming moved to Lord Howe Island. Rebekka was flown in and those famous publicity shots were arranged. Nikolai and Rebekka, laughing together, bare-foot among the bees in a meadow. The tender shot of Nikolai carrying Rebekka in his arms, anxious eyes on her throbbing toe (*a Spell To Make a Person Get Stung By a Bee*).

She had received the first offer from Nikolai's agents while staring at those photos in a magazine. The offer seemed innocent enough. 'Get your husband home from Ireland,' the agent suggested, 'and we'll send your family on a holiday by the sea.' It was too late in her pregnancy for David to be plausible as the baby's father, but the agents wanted Maude's marriage resumed so the reporter would lose interest in her. (It never occurred to them to doubt that David *was* actually in Ireland.)

'Why not?' she thought despondently. 'If Nikolai is rescuing Rebekka from bees, I, at least, deserve a holiday.'

So she telephoned David at his apartment and asked him home. He only came, he admitted afterwards, because he was low with a fever and sore throat. Otherwise, his pride might have kept him there until his elusive invention was complete (*a Spell To Make Someone Catch a Cold*).

Once at the house by the sea, of course, the agents had arrived with their briefcases, and the final deal had been made.

Maude typed up a title page. She folded the pages between pieces of lime-green cardboard, stapled them together and printed the words 'SPELL BOOK' on the front.

Here, in her hands, was the series of events and thoughts that together told the story of Cath. On their own they seemed innocent and harmless. Childlike, even. But they could intersect in multiple ways to form multiple, different narratives. Now that she'd rewritten them as Spells, the horror story could be transformed into a fairy tale.

Cath could have the fairy tale.

These Spells would bring Cath back to life, Maude believed, and Cath's life would be perfect. Cath would have everything that Maude had never had, and Cath would never suffer as Maude did.

Just to be sure – that Cath, unlike Maude, would ride in balloons, that she would have the strength that Maude had lacked, that she would never be sad, and that, if ever a man left her behind, Cath would recover at once – just to be sure, Maude took a silver pen and wrote in tiny script on the back cover:

This Book will make you Fly, will make you
Strong, will make you Glad.
What's more, this Book will Mend your
Broken Heart.

Now she breathed again. She flicked through the Spells, feeling dazed by a new calm.

The paper she had folded round the other pages in order to create a title page at the front meant, she realized now, that at the end of the book, there was a single blank page.

There was room for one more Spell.

Something made her stop. She could write another Spell.

She could change the end of her *own* story. Her heart leaped ferociously.

What sort of Spell might change things? Nikolai would have to come back to her! The two of them could rescue Cath and set up a family of their own! *A Spell To Fly Nikolai Back Across the World!*

But even as she raised her fingers to the keyboard she knew she would not do it. If Nikolai came back, it would only mean more horror – his marriage splintered (and all the attendant scandal); her own family shattered (what of Fancy and Marbie?); even the new little Murphy family, Cath and her adoptive parents, even that torn to shreds.

No. If she was going to change things now, she would have to stop this fracturing of families. It was time to rebuild instead.

Her own family, for example, was as broken as the spring in the couch – she and David polite and cold with each other, Fancy floating around writing poetry (mistakenly believing that her father was a writer so she could keep him home by writing too), Marbie slipping out each night to swim in the pool next door (never knowing that Maude herself hid among the trees and watched).

But if she and David could find a way to be together again

– to be happy and in love as they once were – they could be a proper real family once again. They could be parents to Fancy and Marbie, and somehow, from a distance, they could be parents to Cath. They could carry out the terms of the agreement with Nikolai – keep a secret eye on Cath and send him regular reports. But they could do *more* than that. They could watch her constantly, find ways to solve her problems and guide her through life. She and David could be like fairy godparents; Fancy and Marbie, magical big sisters. They would not spend a single cent of their new wealth on themselves. All of it would be for Cath.

She turned back to the typewriter and wrote the final Spell. *A Spell To Make Two People Fall In Love Again.*

She climbed into bed and fell into a deep, dreamless sleep.

The next day, she set to work painting the garden shed and writing lists of potential recruits. She saw almost at once that the Spell Book had been the product of a feverish nightmare – at best, a sort of therapeutic exercise. What nonsense had she been thinking? Using 'magic' to transform the splinters of a horror story into a fairy tale? No, she was more sensible than that. The real point of her madness that night was that it had led her to the idea for the Secret. She would make Cath's life into a fairy tale with practical techniques – the Secret would be her new focus. It would become the foundation of her family.

Quickly, she forgot about the book, and it got lost somewhere, probably mixed up with Marbie's schoolbooks.

She also forgot the first revelation of that night. Within days she was convinced that she had given Cath away for the child's own benefit – in order to protect her from publicity and so that she and David could 'keep' her in their own remote way. If anyone had dared to suggest she had done it for the money she would have thrown a pot plant at his head.

Part 24

That Evening,
in Cath Murphy's Apartment

50

The evening following the Zings' 'explanation lunch' was a still and balmy one. Cath's apartment blinked, apprehensively, when she threw open its front door.

In her arms she held a Tupperware container filled with Mrs Zing's meringues and a brown paper bag of lemons from Mr Zing's tree. These she appeared to notice now, with startled exasperation, and she allowed them to tumble to her feet. She marched straight to the dining-room window and ran her fingers up and down the frame. It took only a moment to find the camera, although it was smaller than her smallest fingernail.

At the lunch she had calmed herself and set herself apart by finding the Zing family absurd. *I don't believe a word of this*, she had said to herself, comfortably, *but it's very amusing!*

But even as she reassured herself, the contents of the garden shed had rained like arrows through her memory.

And now, here was a camera in the palm of her right hand.

Was it all true? Had this tiny object been observing her all this time? Could something so slight as this have shaped her life? Had fat Mrs Zing watched her eat dinner, making notes about how much pepper she ground on to her food? Had those strange, smiling sisters slipped into her home and replaced or repaired the camera when she wasn't home? She brought her palms together hard, crushing the camera. When she opened her hands again she almost expected to see a drop of blood, as if she had killed a mosquito.

She began a frenzied search through the apartment, without knowing quite what she was looking for: more fingernail cameras, of course, but also anything electronic or odd, anything she might recognize from movies about spies or surveillance. The Zings had assured her that the only equipment in her apartment was the dining-room camera, but she thought she had also caught odd half-references to one additional camera which only ever photographed her ankles. So she ran a knife along the skirting boards, prised open electrical outlets and even turned her socks inside out. Her cat, Violin, watched.

Finally, she collapsed on to the living-room couch. She found that her head was shaking back and forth in disbelief and her hair was getting caught on the fabric.

She sat up and gazed around the room, from the low bookshelf to the standing lamp to the plasma TV on its chrome stand. At that moment her eyes caught the shape of a small green 'V'. It was the 'V' on her TV remote control. There was a similar 'V', she saw now, on the side of the leather-bound box by the DVD player. It was her collection of Valerio Classics.

Valerio! She had almost forgotten. The Valerio empire had been funding the whole thing!

Well, *that* part, she thought scornfully, was *certainly not true*.

Valerios connected to her mediocre life? It was ridiculous enough to think of the Zing family examining her ordinary days, but the Valerios! She had studied Nikolai's films in high school Social Studies! She owned a Valerio electric toothbrush and used Valerio conditioning treatments on her hair! She loved to eat Nikolai Gingerbread Men and had recently signed up for Young & Fit Valerio Health Plan. That small green 'V' filled her life!

She reached for the leather-bound collection of classics, opened it and took out the movie at the top of the pile. Nikolai Valerio smouldered up at her from the photo on the front cover. There was the trademark smudge of motor oil, and there were the elegant cheekbones.

'Dad?' she said, then laughed uncontrollably.

Unconsciously, however, she touched her own cheekbones.

I am the daughter, she thought doubtfully, *of Nikolai Valerio.* It was like thinking: *I am a princess.*

It's not true, she reminded herself, as Violin skirted her ankles. But just in case, she took the movie collection down the hall and hid it in the linen closet. Even as she pressed the cupboard door closed, she was distracted by the small green 'V' on the side of her coat rack. Her eyelid began to flicker.

Part 25

The Story of Monsieur Blanchard

51

The day after Maude wrote the Spell Book, she came out to breakfast. David pretended she was there every day and offered her the coffee pot. Fancy and Marbie, in their school uniforms, stared at their mother in amazement.

Maude and David scarcely knew each other. They had spent more than a year apart, and David had returned to the news of Maude's affair and pregnancy. Accepting that he was largely to blame because he had abandoned her, David had tried to be calm and understanding. He had suggested they raise the child as one of their own: change their names and run away, to escape the publicity. But Maude, oddly detached, had declared that there was no choice. 'We can't afford the two girls that we have,' she told him, coldly. 'And there's nowhere you can run from the Valerios.' Once, he had suggested timidly that they could keep the child and solve the financial problems by embracing the publicity: sell the story of Cath to a magazine. 'You think I would sell my *baby*?' she had shouted, throwing a pot plant at his head.

Then they had both been distracted: the house by the sea; visits from Valerio agents; legal documents and large sums of money; the terrible handover day.

Now that she was up again, they worked on the Secret together. They chose a colour for the garden shed and bought clipboards and maps. David was happy to oblige. At Maude's request, he figured out how to modify cameras and microphones, to conceal them in shirtsleeves and collars. He learned about zoom lenses and bugging devices. He cheered up enormously.

Together, he and Maude researched baby carriages, and their first major gift to Cath, presented as 'market research', was a state-of-the-art stroller. They were polite and friendly with each other, but David continued to sleep on the couch.

At last, after some months had passed, he knocked on the bedroom door and walked into the room. It was late and the girls were asleep. He pressed the door quietly closed behind him, his right hand still clenched from the knock.

There was no moon and the room was deep in darkness. He stopped still in perfect helplessness.

'I'll get the bedside light,' offered a voice from the bed. There was a click and a small glare of light, pooling itself on Maude's hair and the edge of her arm. She sat up against the headboard.

'I hope I didn't wake you,' David said. He sat on the far edge of the bed, in the shadows by the bumps of her feet. Their voices were bright but measured.

David edged his way along the bed until he was gazing at Maude's pale face. She studied his face also. They were silent, conscious that now they must speak. Their words would be soap operatic.

Maude would say: You left me for a year!

David would respond: That may be, but while I was away, you fell in love with someone else.

Maud would cry: But how could I know you would return?

David might be silent and torn.

Maude would whisper: My heart has been broken by another.

David would say bluntly: He's a movie star. Get over it.

Maude would say: I gave away my child.

The final truth would eclipse the other truths. In a soap opera, it would give way to an ad break.

Instead of speaking, they continued to stare at one another. David unclenched his fist, and there was a small, crackling sound. He revealed a folded square of glossy blue and handed it to Maude, who moved it into the light.

'That's next weekend,' said David, in a voice like a challenge.

The paper was a pamphlet, advertising a Festival of Balloons at Berowra. 'But you're not even interested in balloons,' said Maude, and then added pointedly: 'You're afraid of heights.' She caught his eye and they both acknowledged that this might be the only truth spoken.

'That's true,' he agreed. 'But that doesn't mean I wasn't interested in your balloons, Maude.'

'You didn't even listen to my stories.' Her tone was tear-filled, defiant and teasing.

'Oh, I didn't listen, did I?' He chose the teasing tone. 'Lie down,' he instructed. 'And close your eyes.'

She moved back under the sheets, so she was flat on her back, her head in the centre of the pillow, watching him. 'I'm not closing my eyes,' she said.

'But I've decided to tell you a story,' he said. 'And next weekend I'll take you to the festival. Look at this.' He took the pamphlet back from her. 'They've got balloons in every shape you can imagine. Rabbits, cats, cars and Pepsi cans. And they'll have arts and crafts for sale, those doily things you like, and they'll have steak-and-onion sandwiches, I bet, and fairy floss.'

Maude did not look at the pamphlet, but at his face. 'What story?' she said.

It had been years since Maude told David the story of Monsieur Blanchard, the first man to fly the English Channel. But that night, sitting on the edge of her bed, he repeated the story the way she liked to tell it, almost word for word:

'Now, Jean-Pierre Blanchard was determined to be the first

man to fly the English Channel,' he began. 'And he wanted to do it alone. Even the American physician who financed his trip was not to be allowed to come, although the doctor, in point of fact, loved the idea and, in second point of fact, insisted.

'Close your eyes,' said David, interrupting himself.

'Am I making you nervous?'

'I'm not nervous. It's supposed to be a bedtime story, that's all.'

He ran two fingers from her forehead over her eyelids, so that they closed, but she opened them at once.

'Jean-Pierre tried all sorts of tricks to stop the doctor from coming. One day, he wore a lead-lined belt in his trousers so that the balloon seemed to sink beneath their weight. "We're too heavy!" he exclaimed, sadly, to the doctor. "I'm afraid you'll have to get out!" But the doctor suspected a trick and made him turn down his pants.

'Look at this,' said David. 'The fitted sheet's come away. No wonder you can't sleep. Move over a moment.' Maude moved to the other side of the bed, and David dragged the bottom sheet back where it belonged, pulling it over the mattress corner. He straightened up the quilt, placing it carefully around her shoulders. Then he swung his legs on to the bed, and sat up in her place. She closed her eyes.

'Eventually, they sorted out their quarrel, and Jean-Pierre agreed that the doctor could come along. It was 7 January, 1785 when they set off from the Dover cliffs, carrying with them the following:

barometer
compass
thirty pounds of ballast
flags
anchors
cork jackets . . .

*

Here David paused, repeating the words to himself: '. . . flags, anchors, cork jackets . . .'

'A packet of pamphlets, a bottle of brandy,' prompted Maude.

'A packet of pamphlets, a bottle of brandy, some biscuits, some apples, a pair of silk-covered aerial oars . . .' He had taken her wrist, as if it helped him remember, and as he listed each item, he tapped her wrist bone once with his thumb.

'A rudder,' provided Maude.

'Hush,' said David, and tapped her wrist again. 'And a useless, hand-operated revolving fan.'

'Which *later* –' she began.

'Which *later*,' he reproved, raising a finger to silence her, 'which later would be useful as an aeroplane propeller.'

Maude nodded, satisfied. She turned on to her side, her head pressed into her pillow.

'The flight went very badly. The balloon zipped up and down like a yoyo, and they began, calmly at first, to throw bits and pieces overboard. Yes, they had to throw the brandy and the apples! By the time they reached the French coast, they were frantically hurtling more and more, and Jean-Pierre, most likely, eyed the doctor longingly! Instead, he took off his trousers and threw them overboard.'

David curled a strand of Maude's hair around his finger, let it slide away again, and said, 'I didn't listen to your stories, eh?' She smiled without opening her eyes. He had been sitting up on the bed, with his knees propped up before him. Now he lay down close to her and continued.

'The story has a happy ending.' He spoke the words into her hair and kissed her head once. 'They landed safe in the forest of Guines. They were entertained, as heroes, for weeks afterwards by the French.'

*

The Berowra Festival of Balloons was the first of several attended by Maude and David over the years. Later they took to bringing one or both of their daughters along, but this first they visited alone. Maude packed an overnight bag containing: four candles, flowers, a bottle of wine, bread, cheese, olives and chocolate brownies. She scarcely knew why she did this, but it did the trick.

Part 26

The Redwood Sports Carnival

52

Cath held an end of the finish-line ribbon and scanned the carnival crowd for Zings.

Aha. That was a Zing on a picnic blanket, trying out the ringtones on her cellphone.

Over there! A little Zing lining up to race.

That could be a Zing, that plump woman carrying the cranberry muffin –

No.

That was not a Zing.

That was Heather Waratah (teacher, Year 4C).

A year ago she hadn't even known the Zings. Now there was a spasm in her right eye when she saw one. (The letter 'V' had the same effect.)

So, that's it for me, she thought grimly as the finish-line ribbon fell from her wrist to the feet of a tumble of children.

Cath spent the morning of the Redwood Sports Carnival holding one end of the finish-line ribbon. She spent the afternoon supervising novelty events. The novelty events were anarchic: it was something to do with the pointlessness, Cath thought, of running with legs tied together, or with potato sacks strapped around your waist. She did not supervise closely, but allowed small episodes of chaos to erupt and subside while she considered her life.

Since the 'explanation lunch' at the Zings' house two weeks before, Warren and Breanna Woodford had resigned and Lenny D'Souza had returned as full-time counsellor. Lenny and Billson were together again, and everybody found them cloying. Cath, meanwhile, was not speaking to those who had been Zing family spies, such as Suzanne Barker or Katie Toby or the Friendly Bus Driver. But she also said little to anybody else.

What was there to say? She had no personality. She had watched the accumulated records of her life burn to cinders in a garden shed. In a gazebo, under the blackened bark of a scribbly gum, she had learned the explanation for practically every important event, surprise, or success in her life. She was nothing. An imaginary character. An elaborate Zing family fiction, *brought to your TV today* (she liked to add, with bitter humour) *by Valerio Soap-on-a-String*!

All that was real, thought Cath, *were these burn scars on her forearms and this incessant sensation of burning in her cheeks. The feeling of being watched.*

She had moved to a new apartment, choosing one through a reputable agent. She had discarded all her furniture and bought everything new from Ikea. She had washed down the walls and windows of the new apartment and padlocked the doors. She had also threatened the Zings with legal action if they so much as glanced her way. But still she narrowed her eyes if a sales assistant asked her how she'd been and flinched when she saw a camera.

She could tell the police, of course, or the media, but what was the point? Even if they believed her, her life would just be theatre once again.

She stepped backwards absent-mindedly and landed on an egg that had fallen from some child's spoon. Nearby children, seeing this, shrieked and jumped up and down.

The strangest thing was this: sometimes, in the darkest part of the night, she wished that the Secret continued. While her cheeks burned, angry and humiliated by their surveillance, somewhere in her heart was the cold recognition that now she was truly alone. It was almost as if, all her life, she had intuitively known they were watching and had basked in the limelight.

Children, she knew, imagined themselves to be performers. She remembered once when she was five or six, turning cartwheels on the sideline of a cricket game. She had believed that the cricketers were secretly watching her acrobatics, far more impressed by her skill than they were by their game. But children eventually realize they are part of a crowd. Had she herself ever learned that lesson?

Now she almost panicked when she woke in the night, alone and broken-hearted, and realized that no one was paying the slightest attention. She might never get over Warren. *She might never fall in love again.* And she had to face this alone: the yearning she would feel when she greeted next year's class on the Year 2 balcony; the starkness of the staffroom without him in it; her splintering memories of Warren: a glimpse of his shoulder through a moth-hole in his T-shirt; feet tapping, side by side, on the dark wooden floorboards of a jazz cafe.

Her broken heart, meanwhile, was complicated by guilt, self-loathing and hatred. She hated herself, she hated him, but she longed to have him back, and each night she begged: *Come back to me. Leave your wife. Find someone else, Breanna. Let me have him.*

At the time of the affair she had thought: *Breanna doesn't know that this is happening, so how can it hurt her?* Also: *I can't give him up, I just can't – I really love him.*

It was the morality of her seven-year-olds. If you don't get caught, it's not wrong. If you really, really want it, you can do it.

Also, it was the strange moral dimension of love: where love is concerned, the rules fall apart. You can hurt other people, other people can hurt you, and it makes no difference to say: *But he can't do this!*

Breanna, Cath thought, *please forgive me.*

*

As far as she could tell, the Zings had not known about her affair. But she wondered if eventually they would have found out. Would they have gathered in the garden shed, worried and arranged to send flowers and a 'Cheer up' note? (That had been them last year, and not the former boyfriend in New Orleans, after all.) Or would they have shaken disapproving heads, just as her own mother might have?

Then Cath remembered Marbie Zing at the explanation lunch. *You didn't know it was happening*, she had said, about the Secret, *so how could it hurt you?*

The final of the three-legged race collapsed into fits of giggles, and Cath caught a sudden glimpse of herself in a memory. It was the first week of her affair with Warren, and they were running through the streets of Bowral together in the rain. They ran with their arms held tight around one another's waists, towards the shelter of some shops in the distance, their legs keeping time like a dance.

The three-legged race was not pointless. You used these skills when you ran in the rain with your arm around your lover's waist.

The carnival, she realized, was closing down and thinning out. She caught the eye of Fancy Zing in the distance, opening a car door. Fancy smiled and waved, and then leaned to talk to her daughter.

We couldn't give you up, Fancy had said at the explanation lunch. *We just couldn't. We loved you.*

Their Secret was wrong, it was no excuse, but Cath began to wonder if, one day, she might understand.

She had not returned Fancy's wave. She had simply stared and turned away, but even from this distance, she thought, Fancy's smile was warm.

53

Heading towards her car at the end of the sports day, Fancy watched a flock of pigeons rise as she approached. She smiled to herself modestly.

It was strange how things worked out sometimes. Marbie had taken a day off work to bring Listen along to the carnival so they could watch Cassie win races. 'It turns out,' Marbie had confided, 'that Nathaniel doesn't need to have a revenge affair, because he already *got* his revenge.'

'How?' wondered Fancy.

'He pushed me in the path of a sports car!' Marbie's eyes shone.

It was even possible that their mother would win Cath around. She had been phoning her occasionally, and Cath had been hanging up. But now she had a plan: she would suggest that Cath *herself* carry on with the Secret. Nikolai would still be expecting reports, ready to authorize funds. Why not let Cath draft the reports?

'Would she really want to report on herself?' Fancy asked doubtfully.

'Who said she had to tell the truth?' replied her mother.

Fancy reached her car, opened the door and, coincidentally, there was Cath, way across the oval, staring at her. She waved and smiled, but then Cassie appeared, ribbons and trophies spilling everywhere.

Cassie's friend Lucinda was panting a few steps behind, trying to keep up.

*

'OK,' said Cassie from the back seat, polishing a trophy on her T-shirt as they drove home. 'OK, Lucinda. Never eat an apple and jump up and down.'

'Why not?' said Lucinda.

'The apple goes up your nose.'

'I'm going to try it as soon as I get to your place, Cass.'

'*Never*. Did you hear me, Lucinda? NEVER. What did I just say to you?'

'Take it easy, Cassie,' said Fancy, checking in the rear-view mirror.

'You could just get some apple and put it up your nose, if you wanted,' Lucinda commented. 'You wouldn't have to jump up and down.'

'*Lucinda*,' murmured Cassie, shaking her head.

Fancy turned into her driveway and pointed the remote control at the garage door. It rose.

While the girls ran into the house, she wandered down towards her mailbox. A mynah bird was pecking at her lawn, so she detoured slightly and approached the bird, watching with pleasure as it fluttered out of her way. This was Fancy's new regime. She *made things happen*.

She went to shopping malls as often as she could, so she could march towards automatic doors. She raised her right hand to make taxis stop. When she passed dog-walkers on the street she said, 'May I?' and then, holding a single finger in the air, she said, 'Sit!' Usually, the dog would.

Also, she had made her husband leave, simply by saying the words: 'I want a divorce.' Such small gestures led to such grand results!

Radcliffe had been surprisingly compliant once the Secret was burned to the ground. (At present, he was living in the camper van out the back of the Banana Bar, but she was thinking of making him move on from there. It was no place for Cassie to visit.)

All her life she had been so caught up with rules, she had hardly had space in which to live. She used to wear her blazer in her bedroom, because the school rules said the blazer must be worn whenever 'outside the school gates'. Once, at the gym, she felt a *frisson* of fear when a police car flashed by a window and she realized that her arms were not swinging. As if the police might arrest her for failure to achieve the optimum cardio workout.

The only freedom in her small, rule-bound life had been in her foolish fictions.

She glanced over at the Canadian's house, and *tched* at herself. She didn't even know his name! He was a figment, a fantasy, constructed of chocolate terrines and colourful lingerie!

Fondly, sadly, she recalled a particular fantasy she had developed around something he had said. He had come to her door to offer a cake, apologizing for something his brother had said. She herself had blathered that it didn't matter, that she wrote wilderness romance, that the only person she had ever slept with was her husband. At which moment, the door had squealed and the Canadian had said, 'I could fix that.'

Days later, she had begun to believe that this was a cryptic message. That he was referring not to the door, but to her desolate sex life! What a dreamer! What a fool she was!

She laughed softly and opened her mailbox. Its lid hung loose from its hinge and she wondered vaguely if she could replace it with a remote-control cover. Then she could *make* it open.

There was a metallic clang nearby. It was the Canadian. He was standing at his own letter box and had just let the lid drop closed.

'Nothing,' he called.

'Oh,' she replied.

At least, she admitted to herself, she had not imagined his

dark skin, nor the brightness of his eyes behind their spectacles.

'How about you?' Now he was walking towards her companionably. His feet were bare, and the edges of his jeans were frayed.

'Well,' she glanced down. 'This might be a copy of my latest book.'

'The wilderness romance?' he enquired politely. He was standing right by her shoulder, and she found herself beginning to chatter.

'Yes! It'll be my wilderness romance! I *know*, it's such a cliché! Me, a housewife in the suburbs, writing this sort of trash! This one's full of multiple orgasms, you know, and I've never even *had* a multiple or–' She dropped the letter box lid and it swung crookedly.

'I could fix that,' said the Canadian.

He was gesturing at her letter box, but when Fancy looked up, and into his eyes, she saw that they were dancing.

54

A flock of sulphur-crested cockatoos descended on a fig tree. Listen watched them for a moment and then turned back to the sea.

It was Friday night, and she and Marbie had driven from the Redwood Athletics Carnival to Balmoral Beach for fish and chips.

'So strange to be free on a Friday night,' Marbie murmured to herself on the drive over. She murmured this every day.

'She's in denial,' Listen's dad confided.

Listen herself was in denial. The last few weeks they had let her stay home from school, pretending she needed time to recover from the fire. She'd spent the days with her dad in the Banana Bar, or going to movies with Marbie (who took days off work whenever she felt inclined). The Zings, meanwhile, seemed not to have noticed that Listen was the one who had led Cath Murphy to the shed. Instead, they clapped their hands to their mouths or burst into tears of joy when they saw Listen coming. Fancy kept turning up with baskets loaded with peaches, chocolates, books, CDs and 'Thank you for saving my life' cards painted by Cassie. And the freezer was crowded with cherry pies baked by Grandma Zing. Each had the words, 'Listen Taylor – What A Hero!' piped in chocolate across the pastry lid.

But eventually, Listen knew, she would have to face the truth. Soon she had to go back to school.

She dug her toes into the sand. She would just have to find a new strategy for making friends.

It almost made her laugh now, thinking how she had seen

the Secret as a kind of 'strategy'. Even if she'd known what it was, nobody at school would have believed it.

She herself would not have believed it. It was so much crazier even than her own theories: that the Zings were spies, or 'Keepers of the Family', or hiding from the police. *Or maybe*, she thought suddenly, *you could say it was all three in one.*

She wondered how Cath Murphy must be feeling now. She must walk around tripping over different shocks all the time: that she was the daughter of Nikolai Valerio! That she'd never been as lucky as she thought! That people had been *watching her for her entire life!* That people had been *directing her life from a shed!*

Poor Cath Murphy. It had been interesting for Listen, watching her at the explanation lunch. Cath had been trying so hard to be cool and in control, and had even done this fake laughter thing while Grandma Zing was talking, trying to show she was the one sane person in the group. But then, as Cath realized the truth, she'd crumpled right up. (Strange, actually, to see a teacher seeming like a little girl.) And Listen had wanted to move closer to her then and comfort her. She'd wanted to say, 'By the way, I'm an outsider too, I'm not actually one of these Zings. You can talk to me if you like.' Even though, at the exact same time, she'd wanted to jump up and down with pride and shout, 'Cheer up, Cath Murphy! The Zings are my *family* and they're your family too, and they've got the maddest, most spectacular Secret in the world! Don't you agree?'

There was a scuffle of sand, and Marbie sat down beside her. She handed Listen a styrofoam box of fish and chips.

'Have I told you the story of the day a beach umbrella almost killed me?' Marbie said, tearing open a little packet of salt. 'See my scar?' She pointed to her forehead.

Listen had heard the story before, but she let Marbie tell it again, and this time it was different. 'I wasn't concentrating,' Marbie said. 'Everyone was shouting – *Look out for the umbrella!* And I was just sitting there staring out to sea. Why didn't I get out of the way? And that's the thing, Listen, most bad things can be avoided, if you just pay attention.'

'Hmm,' agreed Listen. 'What's your point, Marbie?'

'Well, I'm leading up to an apology,' Marbie said. 'I have to apologize to you because I did a stupid thing, and it caused me and your dad to break up.'

'What did you do?'

'I'll tell you one day,' Marbie said. 'But for now can we just say it was stupid? And there's no excuse. And I promise I'll watch out for sharp flying objects in the future. Am I making sense?'

'Kind of.'

'It's the sharp things, like bird beaks and thumbtacks, those are, kind of, *reality*, so we have to concentrate and . . . I'm not making sense, am I? I can see it in your eyes.'

Listen blinked. 'Did you say that the fight you had with Dad was because of something stupid you did?'

'Right. It was. And I'm so sorry, Listen, I can't –'

'So it wasn't a fight about absolutely nothing?'

'No.'

Then the fight was not her fault.

She had not done a spell which caused her dad and Marbie to break up. She poured a handful of sand through her fingers and smiled.

Actually, she realized, that meant that not a single one of the spells in that book had worked. No wonder it ended by telling her to hide it somewhere she would never see it again. It was trying to protect itself.

She hoped no one would find it hidden under that rock in the entranceway to Redwood Primary. It was a waste of time.

And then, swimming across her mind, came the silver italic words from the back cover: *This Book will make you Fly, will make you Strong, will make you Glad/What's more, this Book will Mend your Broken Heart.*

At least the Book had kept one of its promises. Her heart had been broken by Donna and the others. Now she thought it might be almost mended.

Although soon she'd be back at Clareville College and the heartbreak would start all over again.

'So, the thing is, you can think about *reasons*, which is a good thing to do, because it might help you not make the same mistakes, you know what I mean, but a reason is not an excuse.'

Listen realized that Marbie was still babbling. Who knew what she was babbling about?

'Exactly,' she agreed. She squeezed some lemon juice on to her fish.

'Like, let's say your friend, Donna, was ever unkind to you?' Marbie continued.

The lemon juice squirted sideways and hit Listen in the eye.

'I've met your friend, Donna, and she seems to me a very anxious person. So, let's say she ever decided to be unkind to you? That would be the reason: she's so anxious her judgement gets confused. And let's say the other girls went along with her? Well, that would be because it's easier to keep Donna happy than to have her fall apart. That would be their reason. Let's say Donna and those girls were ever mean to you.'

There was a long silence. They both watched a wave find its way along the sand towards them.

Eventually, Listen spoke. 'They sort of were mean to me,' she mumbled. Then she laughed and shrugged. 'It was no big deal, though. It was nothing.'

Marbie punched the sand and hissed, 'Those stupid girls were mean to you? Spoiled, moronic little brats!'

Listen looked over in surprise. 'But you just said they had reasons.'

'I changed my mind. There's no reason in the world. And even if there was, like I said, a reason is not an excuse.'

'Seriously, Marbie, you can't blame them. I'm a taker, not a giver. Because I don't really talk very much.'

'For a smart girl,' said Marbie, 'you're not very bright. You've got that the wrong way around. The takers are the people who talk all the time. The givers are the listeners like you.'

'Well, what if a person went to a school where nobody agreed with that? Where everybody thought that the person was a taker?'

Marbie scraped her heels slowly along the sand.

'I guess you know,' she said, 'that the person would have to go back to the school and try again. Somewhere at the school there would be friends for that person, if she just kept on trying.'

'Right,' agreed Listen quickly. 'OK. I know.'

'So that's what you know,' said Marbie, 'but here's what I think. I think Clareville College have had their chance with that person. I think that person is much too precious to go back to that school. I'm not letting that school anywhere near that person ever again.'

'You're not?'

'No way in hell. We're tracking down a different school. For that person.'

'Well,' said Listen, casually, 'Bellbird High seems like the kind of school a person could try.'

'So she could,' said Marbie.

And she did.

Part 27

The Story of the Confectioner

55

Once upon a time there was a confectioner who flew in a hydrogen balloon.

This was in 1810. He invited a friend from Bristol, and the flight began well enough: they drifted over the Bristol Channel towards Cardiff.

Four miles off Combe Martin, however, they crashed into the sea.

But they did not break their legs or drown; they did not catch alight and burn.

Instead, something extraordinary happened: the basket bobbed on top of the waves, the balloon billowed out behind them, and presto! *they were saved.* They spent an hour wafting along in this manner and were rescued by a boat from Lynmouth.

Maude has always preferred the confectioner's story to the tale of the watercolour painter whose parachute was upside down.

She likes to imagine how the balloon must have looked, floating on top of the sea. The tiny basket, the immense sphere of cloth, the hopeful little men, the great expanse of water and sky. So strange, so lovely, so mystical, as with all unlikely, dreamy things such as whales, flying fish, pavlovas and unexpected snowfalls.

But the confectioner's story was more. It was disaster transformed. A sailing ship conjured from a capsized balloon.

56

Extracts from the Zing Garden Shed

SURVEILLANCE EQUIPMENT – CONSIGNMENT

Covert collar camera: Just fit collar to cat/dog/mouse, *etc*. Collar houses Pinhole Camera with crystal-clear resolution & super sharp audio. Pinhole placement is a tiny half millimetre wide. Collar is plain design. Also available in COLOUR and with BELL.

57

Cath Murphy (teacher, Year 2B) stands at the carnival coffee table. Paper cups are set out in orderly rows, like a choir about to perform, and each has already been filled. How long has the coffee been sitting there, open to the breeze?

'Milk?' says Mrs Nestle (tuck-shop lady).

Too late, thinks Cath.

The oval is almost empty. The last children are climbing on to buses and into family cars. Mrs Nestle begins tipping coffee on to the lawn.

Cath heads to the staffroom, which is empty and still. She glances at the corner kitchenette: the sandwich maker that she and Warren bought; the coffee machine, where Warren teased Breanna for self-consciousness.

She collects her mail and handbag, locks the staff-room windows and imagines, for a moment, her evening: the new apartment with its bare linoleum and the fridge that beeps reproachfully when she opens the door for too long. She will rest her feet on her new coffee table and think about her broken heart; Violin, like a teasing scarf, will climb across her shoulders to sit on his side of the couch.

Outside again, in the school car park, Ms Waratah sings 'Farewell, Cath!' Mr Bel Castro straddles his motorbike and kicks aside the stand.

She drives towards the gate, but brakes slightly, as something in the rock garden catches her eye. It is the corner of a lime green school book, hidden underneath a rock. She puts her car in park, opens the door and pulls the book from under the rock. She waves it in the air and smiles self-consciously at

Mr Bel Castro, who is waiting patiently, revving his motorbike behind her.

She tosses the book on to the passenger seat and drives towards home.